W9-AHJ-691

BEFORE SHE IGNITES

A FALLEN ISLES NOVEL

BEFORE SHE IGNITES

A FALLEN ISLES NOVEL

JODI MEADOWS

KATHERINE TEGEN BOOKS
An Imprint of HarperCollins*Publishers*

Katherine Tegen Books is an imprint of HarperCollins Publishers.

Before She Ignites

For information address HarperCollins Children's Books, a division of HarperCollins Publishers, 195 Broadway, New York, NY 10007.
www.epicreads.com

Library of Congress Control Number: 2017943390
ISBN 978-0-06-246940-3
ISBN 978-0-06-279552-6 (special ed.)

Typography by Carla Weise
17 18 19 20 21 PC/LSCH 10 9 8 7 6 5 4 3 2 1
❖
First Edition

For the ones who refuse to be silenced

THE MIRA TREATY

the second day
of the month of Moracan
in the 2187th year
of the Fallen Gods

PREAMBLE

The following agreement, between the six island-nations of the Fallen Isles, who are our gods

Anahera, the Destroyer
Bopha, the Shadow
Damyan and Darina, the Lovers
Harta, the Daughter
Idris, the Silent
Khulan, the Warrior

represents peace and unity among all who follow the Fallen Gods, equality among the people, and a renewed devotion to the children of the gods.

On this day, as a collection of nations, we, the representatives of the people of the Fallen Isles, bow to the one true authority, the light of Noore, and acknowledge our devotion.

For we have too long permitted imbalance and suffering, the exploitation of our resources, and the folly of inaction. We have denied intrinsic freedoms and abused what should be protected. We have ignored the sacrosanct laws between mortal and divine, and have put ourselves at risk for abandonment by the gods we should most honor and protect.

This decree signifies our conviction to make the Fallen Isles into a good and holy place, with respect to the Upper Gods and the Fallen Gods. It signifies our acceptance of the peril of unforgivable conflict, should any party fail to uphold these tenets. It signifies our willingness to enforce the terms by actions deemed appropriate within the text of this covenant.

In the name of a child born this day, who shall be the bearer of our hopes, and with understanding that we sign this agreement for her and all the future of the Fallen Isles, we make this pledge.

PART 1: UNITY

Article 1: Trade among the islands

Article 2: Borders and neutral international waters

Article 3: Assurance of assistance

PART 2: DRAGONS

Article 4: Cease of ownership

Article 5: Drakon Warrior disbandment

Article 6: Relocation to sanctuaries

Article 7: Study, observation, and breeding

PART 3: EQUALITY

Article 8: Harta as an independently governed island

Article 9: Hartan exports and tariffs

Article 10: Economic stabilization

PART 4: MISCELLANEOUS ARTICLES

Article 11: Reparations

Article 12: Prohibited acts

Article 13: Failure to uphold the treaty

I shouldn't have told the truth.

But I did.

BEFORE

Sarai 15, 2204 FG

THE LAST DAY OF MY REAL LIFE BEGAN WITH DISASTER.

The ground gave a brief jerk, and everything shifted: a glass of water, the large family portrait, and my soul when I thought about all the lives affected by the abrupt movement of the world.

Less than an hour after the incident, I was placed before a crowd assembled outside the white-columned council house, a sheet of paper clutched in my hands. Councilors Elbena and Bilyana stood at my sides, two pillars of strength and authority, but every eye was trained on me.

"*There she is.*" A woman lifted a small girl to see. "*Hopebearer.*"

"*Mira Minkoba.* The *Mira.*"

"She looks beautiful."

I tried not to smile, though the compliment pleased me. Immediately after the tremor, Mother had sent me upstairs to don a coral-colored dress, with thin straps that left my shoulders bare to the summer sun; already, my skin prickled and warmed into a deeper shade of brown. My maid had unpinned my hair so that it fell in long, loose waves, then crowned me with a wreath of lala flowers that Mother said reminded everyone of my youth and innocence. The effort to straighten my hair was wasted, though; humidity was already bringing the curls back to life.

Then another girl said, *"I want to be her."*

My expression of detached pleasantness faltered and I dropped my eyes to the paper I'd been given. The words were there. All I had to do was use them.

I drew a steadying breath and counted. Twenty people in the front row. Twice that in the second. Twelve columns on this face of the council house. At last, my thoughts calmed.

"People of Crescent Prominence." I cleared my expression of everything but what was appropriate for the occasion of delivering distantly upsetting news. "The tremor you felt earlier is reported to have come from Idris. We felt it here; it must have been incredibly disrupting there."

Most people glanced westward, probably thinking of the immense space between our islands. Idris was on the far side of the Fallen Isles, shaped like a man bent over in prayer or anguish. The Silent Brothers ruled there, keeping the people almost completely isolated. They traded little. They traveled less. I couldn't imagine how they'd recover from an earthquake that big.

"Is there a landslide threat?" A woman held her palms against her chest as if to ease the pounding of her heart.

I glanced at the paper, even though I'd read it already. "It's the rainy season there, so a landslide is likely. There's a wave threat as well. All the western islands are under watch." That excluded us. Damina was the easternmost Fallen Isle.

"Is there anything we can do for them?" a man asked.

The Mira Treaty meant all islands were required to provide aid in times of crisis, but it was the way of our gods to offer help without being asked.

"That's uncertain." I consulted the paper again. The words written there fit easily into my mouth. "The Silent Brothers may decline assistance, as they have in the past."

I'd met a Silent Brother only once, and the interaction had been brief. He hadn't been *unfriendly*, but I'd gotten the impression that Brother Ilyas disapproved. Of me. Of the treaty my father had written. Of Damina and all the other islands. Of everything.

"What if their government doesn't accept our help?" someone asked. "We can't just let their people suffer."

"I'm afraid we won't have a choice." Because *The Book of Love* said that loving our neighbors meant staying out of their business when they didn't want us, we had to accept it. "The Mira Treaty does not permit unwanted assistance. That would be invasion, not aid."

The people shifted uncomfortably. No one liked to hear that their attempts to do good could actually be harmful.

A breeze lifted across the square, carrying the scents of fresh rice bread and spiced cloudfish. Palm trees rustled and swayed, and in the distance, waves crashed on the rocky cliffs. Goats bleated from farms and the nearby marketplace, and Water Street bustled with carriages and foot traffic. It was hard to reconcile the peace of Crescent Prominence with the devastation happening in another part of the world.

I closed my eyes and imagined children covered in dust and debris, tears making muddy tracks down their cheeks. I imagined men and women struggling to lift rubble off their neighbors. I imagined others searching for loved ones, only to find bodies whose spirits had already evacuated.

"We will offer assistance." I glanced at Councilor Elbena, who disguised a nod by tucking a tightly curled strand of hair behind her ear. The golden sunburst pendant on her throat shimmered in the midmorning light, bright against the umber of her skin. "As for whether the Silent Brothers accept—we can only pray they do."

My paper held the answers to a few more of their questions, and finally, I stepped aside while High Priest Valko said a prayer to Damyan and Darina, the god and goddess of love.

"Give us peace. Give us grace. Give us enough love in our hearts."

An incredible quiet surrounded his voice; only the sounds of breathing, seagulls calling, and clothes rustling in the wind touched the square. Distantly, human activity hummed along, and life proceeded as though this was the only moment that mattered.

That was an uncharitable thought. Life couldn't halt everywhere because of a tragedy in one place. But oh, my heart hurt for people I'd never know, in places I'd never see.

High Priest Valko finished with a blessing, echoed by everyone in attendance: "By the Upper Gods who stayed in the stars, and the Fallen Gods who came to Noore, we offer our thanks. Cela, cela."

With those words, my part in this disaster was finished. I returned to Elbena and Bilyana.

"Wonderful," Elbena said, hugging me. "The Luminary Council is so fortunate to have you ready to speak for us, Mira. Thank you for continuing to put the Mira Treaty first in your life."

I'd never been given a choice about it, but Elbena's approval was always welcome. She was such an admirable person, always willing to help and inspire. Only ten years older than me, she already held one of the highest positions in Damina. I liked her ambition.

When they finished complimenting my execution of duties, I approached my parents, who were waiting near the council house door. Anticipation simmered within me.

"Well done," Father said. "You'll make a fine politician one day."

I didn't want to be a politician, and it seemed there must be more to such a career than reading someone else's words off a paper, but I soaked in his praise because he so rarely noticed how hard I tried.

"You performed adequately." Mother tilted my chin upward and inspected my face for flaws. Satisfied, she gave a brief nod and stepped back. "And you looked stunning. That dress is perfect on you."

"Thank you, Mother." Adequately. I'd never live up to her expectations, but at least I performed adequately. "If there's nothing else, I'd like to visit the sanctuary." My hunting gear waited in the carriage.

She blew out an annoyed breath, but motioned at Hristo, who'd kept to the background during my speech. "Go on if you must. Don't get your clothes dirty."

Hristo rubbed his chin. It was a habit that betrayed his frustration with my parents, not that he would ever admit that out loud. He was my best friend, but he was also my personal guard, and he felt it was unprofessional to air such grievances to me; I'd heard said grievances from Ilina, the third member of our friendship trio. She was already at the sanctuary, and I couldn't wait to see her.

When we were alone, moving toward my blue and silver carriage, Hristo's quiet broke and he smiled at me. "Ready for dragons?"

My soul lightened. "I am always ready for dragons."

AFTER I CHANGED into my hunting gear, Hristo and I drove to the sanctuary.

An enormous wall protected it, closing in an immense space of land that stretched from the Skyfell Mountains to the sea. The wall was seventeen stories high—not high enough to prevent dragons from flying over, but most understood that it was for their safety. The dragons stayed by choice.

We passed through a huge stone gate, the words *Luminary Department of Drakontos Examination: North Entrance* carved into block letters above the arch. As always, my heart soared at the sight. I couldn't believe I was allowed here. With dragons. With LaLa.

As the carriage came to a stop, Ilina emerged from one of the blocky buildings that made up the department facilities.

"Did you feel the earthquake?" she asked as Hristo and I walked toward her. "The drakarium residents were shrieking for an hour this morning before it hit. They knew it was coming."

"Are they all right now?" I lifted the hem of my hunting dress off the ground as we headed toward the drakarium, where LaLa and Crystal waited.

"It's like they've already forgotten about it." Ilina wore the uniform of a sanctuary apprentice: a linen shirt and pants, dyed in gradients of browns and greens. Gold thread glittered on the high collar and cuffs, embroidered to look like dragons bellowing flame. She'd strapped a small pack over her shoulders, filled with all the necessary supplies an apprentice might need when making the rounds.

It was a nice uniform. Practical. One I'd be proud to wear. Unfortunately, Mira Minkoba did not wear practical clothes, though the hunting gear Seamstress Nadya had designed for me was at least somewhat better suited to the terrain of the dragon sanctuary. Rather than silk, I wore fine Idrisi cotton. Always a dress, but with matching leggings and calf-high boots. Different colors every day, of course; today was peach with green accents. And though it was hot and uncomfortable, a reinforced collar went high up my neck.

A roar of draconic voices sounded as we crested a small hill, and the drakarium came into view.

I'd always thought the drakarium had to be one of the most impressive structures ever created, its slender bones built from darkened noorestones. Seven different habitats grew along a spiral path, with a natural spring bubbling in the center. There were no walls, exactly; the building wasn't meant to keep dragons in, but to provide a safe place for smaller species to live and get the social interaction they needed.

Ten dragons soared above and around the drakarium,

squawking and calling as they played a complicated game of chase, made even more incredible by the fact that there were three different species in the game. *Drakontos quintus*, *mons*, and *aquis*, identifiable by the shapes of their wings, the size of their scales, and the width of their jaws.

Scales of every color flashed in the sunshine, a marvelous sight that only a few people would ever be able to see.

LaLa and Crystal were *Drakontos raptuses*, the smallest species, which lived on the rocky cliffs of eastern Damina. I knew the way to their nest in the drakarium, but Ilina's parents didn't like for humans to go in there often. It was rude, they said, to enter another creature's habitat without permission.

So as the three of us approached, Ilina and I both gave sharp whistles and clicks, and by the time we put on our protective gauntlets, the pair of *Drakontos raptuses* circled above us: one silver, one gold. Sisters, like the moons.

I lifted my gloved fingers. The golden dragon flipped and dived at me, spreading her bright wings wide at the last moment as she landed on my hand with a *thump*. Her talons dug in as I drew her toward me. "Good afternoon, little lizard." I kissed the top of her head.

She lifted her face, bumping her nose against mine.

I laughed and stroked the bony ridge down her head and neck, careful to move with the scales. Like cats, dragons didn't like to be petted the wrong way. And *Drakontos raptuses* had sharp-tipped scales that could slice open tender human skin. Mother had worried that I'd cut myself on her, or that she'd hurt me on purpose. But Mother didn't understand that LaLa wasn't a pet; she was a friend, and I was born for being with dragons.

"I love you, sweet dragon," I whispered.

Hristo strode toward us to greet LaLa, who immediately straightened her spine and gave a throaty purr. He rewarded her with a small bite of dried meat, which she devoured instantly.

Besides Ilina and me, Hristo was their favorite person. Probably because he said hello with food.

This moment. Right here. I had my two best friends and my two favorite dragons, and everything was perfect.

But I should have known better than to get comfortable. The next disaster was about to begin.

PART ONE

UNITY IN DARKNESS

CHAPTER ONE

Sarai 29, 2204 FG

FIVE WARRIORS LED ME INTO THE PIT, DOWN A NARrow, spiraling staircase. Deeper, deeper into the ground. Closer to Khulan.

Thirty-five. Thirty-six. Thirty-seven. I counted each step as I descended. Mother would be so disappointed.

Forty-three. Forty-four. Forty-five.

I kept my eyes down, deliberately placing my slippered toes on the stair below before committing my weight. With the endless spiral drilling deeper, and my wrists shackled tightly behind my back, it'd be too easy to lose my balance.

Fifty-seven. Fifty-eight. Fifty-nine.

Down, down we went. The air grew cooler and sharper with the scent of sweat and mildew and waste. Tears flooded my eyes.

Ninety-nine. One hundred. One hundred one.

My head spun with the slow descent, but even if I'd wanted to move faster, the guards' pace would have prevented me. They weren't in a hurry. Probably happy to keep me in this claustrophobic stairwell, surrounded by stone walls and enemies. Any excuse to torment a new prisoner was a good excuse.

"Aren't we lucky?" muttered one of the warriors. "The real Mira Minkoba. I wonder what she did."

My neck and cheeks burned with humiliation.

Another guard laughed. "I bet she threw a fit and tore all her clothes."

"Or defaced portraits of her enemies."

"Maybe she had a lover the Luminary Council didn't approve of."

They mused for another minute before the fifth warrior spoke up. Altan, another had called him. I called him my nemesis. "The Luminary Council wouldn't have sent their favorite puppet here without a truly serious crime, like putting the Fallen Isles at risk."

I tried to focus on walking, but my whole body trembled with fury and shame.

"Whatever the reason she's here," Altan went on, "we're under orders not to discuss it, or her, so forget her name and rank. She's just a prisoner, like all the others."

Just a prisoner. Anonymous.

At two hundred steps, the cool air gave way to warmth, growing over the next fifty-seven. (Two hundred and fifty-seven total.) Finally, we reached the bottom, where everything I'd thought I'd known about the Pit evaporated.

The stairwell opened into a magnificent hall, with over a dozen ornate pillars from floor to ceiling. It was so high that a *Drakontos titanus* would have been able to stretch its neck and wings.

Noorestones lit the chamber at regular intervals along the pillars and carved walls, and shone from immense chandeliers above. Hundreds of tiny stones glowed and glowed.

Altan prodded at my spine.

He was my least favorite guard already, because he kept *looking* at me. Studying. The others' jokes were uncomfortable, but his attention was more focused. More menacing.

His face told a story of recent fights, with healing cuts and fading bruises that covered his golden-brown skin. Eleven thin scars marked his right temple, like remnants of a childhood accident. He was handsome in a fearsome way; he had wide cheekbones, a strong jaw, and hard, brown eyes that stayed narrowed under a high brow. Like all the other warriors, his hair was close-cropped, and he wore a leather uniform. Only two iron chevrons were pinned under Khulan's crossed maces, which suggested he wasn't important, but there was another pin as well. Some sort of tooth or claw.

"Walk," he said.

Hot, damp air choked me as I started moving once more. Sweat trickled down my spine, making my silk dress stick to my skin. I couldn't recall ever feeling so subhuman in my life. What I wouldn't give for a bath. Steaming, clear water. Shea butter and honey soap. A citrus peel on my face. Orange blossom, jasmine, and shea cream in my hair. The sweet perfume of lala flowers wafting through the washroom.

I hadn't had a *real* bath in a decan. It felt like a year.

Huge panels of chiseled figures watched my shameful walk through the grand chamber. With every step, my mind tracked their size (ten paces wide, at least three times as tall).

The first panel showed the seven gods as they fell from the stars, streaks of fire shooting behind them. Darina and Damyan faced each other, toes touching toes as they plummeted toward the waves. Their eyes were bright with eternally locked gazes. Khulan had his great mace lifted, his body twisted toward Anahera, the Destroyer. We passed by too quickly for me to properly see the other three, though I knew their poses from tapestries and other depictions of the Fall: Bopha was always in shadow, even as she dropped toward the sea. Harta wrapped her arms protectively around her great, pregnant belly, loose clothes fluttering. And then there was Idris, bent over in contemplation as he ignored everyone and everything.

Seven gods. Seven islands. Six, if you counted Darina and Damyan as one, which most people did. That made

Damina twice as big as any of the other islands. The best. The most important.

At least, that was what I'd always believed.

Between the panels, statues of legendary warriors protruded from the stone, as if they were on the verge of stepping out. Their fists clutched the heavy chains used to lift and lower the chandeliers. They sent me loathsome glares.

Two of my escorts were discussing a card game, completely unimpressed by the surrounding magnificence. "I can't believe you lost that hand."

"I shouldn't have accepted the bet. Batbayar never loses when an extra shift is at stake."

There was a heavy pause. Here, Daminan men might have accused their friend of cheating, but for Khulani warriors, that sort of comment would mean truly questioning their friend's honor. Even if it had been meant as a joke, there would have to be a trial, a fight, and at least one demotion.

No card game—extra shift or otherwise—was worth it to these two, so they carried on, keeping any suspicions quiet.

The warriors opened a huge, creaking door and shoved me through it. I stumbled, nearly losing track of my steps, but my feet remembered the impacts—one, two, three, four.

Statues filled the tall alcoves along the new hall. These versions of the gods were marble and limestone and sandstone, beautifully carved and terrifying as they struck one another down, or crushed minuscule humans beneath their feet.

"Look." Humor edged Altan's tone. "She's scared."

"Probably worried about ruining her dress," said another.

"It's already ruined." Altan prodded my back. "Walk."

I wanted to shrink up and die, but I walked and kept my eyes on the statues.

Legend said that when our seven gods fell to Noore, humans all over the world perished in wind and fire. The devoted lived, and made their way across the ocean to settle on the Fallen Isles.

Of course, our ancestors weren't really the only survivors. The mainland held dozens of clans and kingdoms, all fighting for control of an enormous continent. For two thousand years, they'd been too busy warring with one another to notice us, but now the Algotti Empire ruled all along the coast. Some said the Mira Treaty was a direct response to the mainland falling under the empire's banner.

We passed monuments and chapels and mausoleums, and there it struck me: I'd always imagined the Pit was a deep hole in the ground, nothing but inmates wasting away, but this seemed more like a place of worship. This immense underground complex could only be one thing.

The Heart of the Great Warrior. The holiest temple of the Khulani people.

This was worse than I could have imagined. There was

no better-protected place on all of Khulan. And the Pit—the deepest prison in the Fallen Isles—was part of that.

Despairing, I counted my steps (twenty-seven in this hall) and the number of halls (five so far); I couldn't keep up with all the statues and doors and stairs.

Then, when I thought the hallways would never end and prison was this, walking and walking for the rest of my life, we came to a narrow, poorly lit corridor with grated doors every seven paces.

Here the warriors slowed, giving me time to peer into the cramped spaces as we passed.

The cells held prisoners, condemned to die here as punishment for some crime. There was a young man with white tattoos all over his arms and legs. He huddled on a bench, rocking and muttering to himself. A woman, perhaps my mother's age, scraped her palms over a wall, as though searching for a hidden door, but her efforts were focused on the wall shared with the next cell.

One was filled only with the remnants of previous inmates: empty shackles, a worn blanket, and smooth places in the stone. A dark stain splashed across the floor and walls. Dried blood, tinted deep purple in the dim blue glow of aging noorestones.

A small wooden cup sat in another shadow-filled space, though I couldn't see the occupant. If there was one. People probably didn't survive here very long.

"This one." Altan stopped me at the next cell, the eighth on the right side. There were more beyond, but I couldn't see them when the other guards blocked my way.

"You sure you want to transfer?" An older warrior glanced at Altan as he drew a huge ring of keys and stabbed one into a lock. "We're not short on prison guards."

Altan touched the chevrons and claw on his jacket. "I vowed to see this through."

"All right." The door slid open with a loud screech and rattle that echoed down the stone hallway. "I doubt you'll have trouble. It's always the fancy ones who break first."

I would not break.

I would *not* break.

But as much as I wanted to be strong, the weight of this place was pressing down. The warriors, the immense underground complex, and the shattered prisoners in other cells: I could feel myself beginning to crack, no matter how hard I resisted.

My heart pounded toward my throat as more keys clattered behind me. The shackles fell off my wrists. And at once, I was heaved into the cell.

"I'm not supposed to be here." The words came out before I could stop them. Sharp. Desperate. Pathetic, really. After everything else, reaching my cell shouldn't have been the thing that tipped me over the edge of hysteria. But it was. The cell was too *real*.

"Everyone says that." Altan accepted the key from the leader, a tall man with three chevrons and two claws under the crossed maces. "Thank you, sir. I'll take good care of her."

A shudder tore through me and I rushed for the door, but Altan drew it shut so fast the metal rang along the runners.

The other guards snickered. "This one will be fun."

What did that mean?

My fingers curled around the gritty, flat bars as a sob choked out of me. I wasn't supposed to be here. None of this was my fault.

"I'll see you soon, Fancy." Altan's smile made his eyes even narrower.

Dread knotted in my chest: a telltale collapsing of all my fears into a single writhing mass. Blackness fuzzed along my peripheral vision, crawling inward to blind me. It made me light-headed. Dizzy. I couldn't catch my breath as my whole body started to shake and sweat. The heat boiled up from my insides and buzzed in my ears. I couldn't see. I couldn't hear.

I had to stop this, but the panic was overwhelming. Too powerful.

A headache pulsed at my temples, echoing around my skull and down the back of my neck. Everything—absolutely everything—hurt, and the more I became aware of the various ailments, the worse it became.

In vain, I patted my clothes for calming pills, but the amber bottle had been taken from me on Damina. There was no way to stop this horrible foreboding.

One of the guards laughed as they walked away.

Focus. I had to focus.

I sucked in a deep breath. A second. Then a third. It cleared my vision, at least, though it didn't ease my racing heart or the smothering sense of doom.

I counted the number of bars across the door. Seven. Then the lumps in the stone floor between my cell and the opposite. Nineteen.

That helped.

Across from me, a girl with deep-brown skin and shorn hair sat cross-legged in the center of her cell, her eyes closed and her face serene. How could she be so calm?

I stared at her, hoping she'd notice my arrival. Maybe talk with me. Distract me. Tell me that none of this dread and doom was real. But she didn't look up. The other prisoners were mostly blocked from my view.

And this dread and doom *was* real, wasn't it? I was in the Pit. Trapped. Far from Ilina and Hristo. Far from the only people who knew the truth.

I pried my fingers from the iron grille. Ugly ruddy marks circled my wrists where the metal shackles had bitten into my skin. Mother would have been furious. What if it scarred?

The thought of Mother made me stagger back, deeper into my cell, as the crushing terror descended again, harder than before. My heart battered the inside of my chest, too hard, too fast, growing thunderous in my ears.

On Damina, prisoners were given time to wash and a change of sturdy clothes before they were locked away, but I'd received no such decency. My possessions had been taken from me upon my arrest. Hairpins, jewelry, and anything else that could be used as a weapon—everything was confiscated.

In the holding cell on Damina, I had nothing but what I was wearing—a once-beautiful wrap dress and matching slippers—and that was all I was permitted. I'd padded into the interrogation room in my wrinkled clothes, my hair wild, and a rank odor coming off me.

I knew why I'd been left there, though, sitting in my own stink for two days. It made me look deranged. Like a liar. Because of course filth and lies went hand in hand, and if I was a liar then I needed to look the part. Mother had surely protested, but when one's enemies included the entire Luminary Council, certain dignities were stripped away. Like bathing. Like looking human.

Like a trial, though I'd begged and insisted and demanded one.

Another sob exploded out, and I crumpled to the floor, palms flat on the stone, my forehead resting on my knuckles. The knot of horror grew until it filled every part of me. Fingers and toes and the tips of my hair. It swarmed around me. There was no escape. No respite. No calming pills. No hot bath with soothing oils.

Alone. Abandoned. Apart from everyone I loved. All because of one act of trust. One truth. One horrible mistake.

My head throbbed as the tears fell and fell.

Maybe they would drown me.

BEFORE

Nine Days Ago

After the sentencing, Ilina and Hristo were permitted to visit.

The room we'd been given had three noorestones and one window that took up most of one wall. Luminary Guards wearing off-white linen uniforms strode through the hall on the other side, not paying attention to us. At least, I didn't think they were. Masks covered the lower parts of their faces, while deep hoods shadowed their eyes.

I wished I had something to hide my eyes, too. They burned with hot tears, and my face felt puffy from hours spent crying in my cell.

"We don't have long." Ilina's voice was tight as she

placed her bag on the table and began removing combs and bands and moisturizers, but this hardly seemed like the time. "They said we could say good-bye, and I thought . . ." She lifted a comb.

"You're not my maid. That isn't your job."

"Let me," she said. "As a friend." She was trying not to cry, so obediently I sat and swallowed back my own sobs as she combed and pinned and spread passionflower-scented cream through my hair.

Hristo stood nearby, his arms crossed over his chest while he watched.

"I don't think I've ever done your hair before." She began twisting strands into flat ropes that would stay put for days—longer, if I was careful. "I wish I had. I just—I don't understand."

I couldn't bring myself to speak.

"How can the Luminary Council do this?" Ilina twisted and twisted my hair so tight it hurt. "I thought they would listen to you. How could they let—"

Hristo held up a hand and shook his head. "Someone could overhear."

Ilina kept working until my head had twenty-five tiny, flat twists and one of the Luminary Guards banged on the door to signal their time was up. "Can't we make some kind of appeal?"

"There wasn't even a trial." I stood to look at my friend and memorize her features: her warm brown skin, bronzed from so much time in the sun; her small nose, which she joked had been stunted from her parents poking it so much when she was a child; and her long black hair, usually in practical braids, but loose and straight today. My ache for her would be immeasurable. "An appeal is pointless. Besides, if you go to the council on my behalf, they'll wonder how much you know." And I'd worked too hard to keep Ilina and Hristo's names out of all this.

"I hate them," she whispered. "They're traitors. Every one of them."

I reached, and then she was hugging me tight enough that I couldn't breathe. But I didn't stop her or ask her to ease up, because this might be the last time we held each other.

"This isn't good-bye," she whispered by my ear. "You are my wingsister and I will come for you."

"How?" The word felt hollow. Hot.

"I will drain the seas and march there if I must."

The guard banged on the door again. *Thud thud.*

I wanted to sob with gratitude. "Bring LaLa and Crystal when you do."

Ilina pulled back, her hands resting softly on my shoulders. "Mira . . ."

"Now isn't the time." Hristo's face twisted with concern.

"Tell me."

Thud thud.

"They're gone," Ilina said. "They're not in the drakarium. They're gone."

My heart stopped. Gone like the others?

The door crashed open and two Luminary Guards thundered in. Just as Hristo and Ilina vanished from my view, I heard Ilina call out, "You are my wingsister!"

CHAPTER TWO

I WOULDN'T ALWAYS BE IN THE PIT.

Ilina's vow still echoed in my head. And my parents were surely doing everything in their power to secure my release. The Pit was a life sentence, but all my life I'd been an exception. I was Mira Minkoba. The Hopebearer. The Luminary Council needed me.

Didn't they?

Ghosts of anxiety still urged me to scream and cry, but I squashed them. There was nothing useful about letting the panic take over if I could push it back. The facts were these: I *was* here, on Khulan, and in the Pit. There was only one thing I could do now.

Survive.

All I had to do was wait until my parents got me out of

here. The Luminary Council would see reason.

If I wanted to survive, I needed to fit in.

The *Drakontos mimikus* was one of the more misunderstood species. Lots of people thought they mimicked other dragons to mock them, but the truth was that their scales changed color, their voices changed timbre, and their movements shifted to match the dragons' around them for protection. They weren't very strong on their own—as far as dragons went—but if they looked like another species, other dragons were less likely to pick on them.

I could be a *Drakontos mimikus.* Blending in with the tougher dragons.

Which meant I had to stop crying.

Too late for that. If Altan and the others had seen the panic attack—

"They didn't see it," I whispered to myself. "No one saw it." Even the girl across the hall was still in the same position. She hadn't seen it, either.

But surely others had heard.

They weren't guards. It didn't matter.

But . . .

"Stop." I scrubbed tears off my face. Grit from the floor scratched my skin, and my stomach turned at the patches of oil. And . . . a small, painful bump right on the tip of my chin. Oh, Damina. I was falling apart.

A small whimper escaped my throat. Yes, I had a pimple. Normal girls got them all the time. Once a month, Ilina complained about a blemish that grew just above her jaw. She always treated it, covered it, and no one ever noticed. It was hardly the worst thing that had happened to her, and it certainly wasn't the worst thing to happen to me.

With a deep and shuddering breath, I closed my eyes and listened.

To someone sniffing down the hall.

A cough.

A faint, tortured groan.

And someone crying in their sleep.

The three stone walls around me did nothing to muffle their voices. My own sobs must have been so loud and—

"Stop it," I muttered. The dregs of the first attack nipped at my mind. I couldn't let the spiral start again. I wasn't even sure how much time I'd lost to the first one. It felt like night, because of the stillness, and it was usually night by the time my attacks faded in a medicine-filled haze of relief, but maybe it was still the first day. Or the next day. Hours could have passed and I'd never have known, because the quality of light never changed. It stayed pale and dirty, slanting through the metal grille of my cell door.

"Do they ever cover the noorestones?" My voice was low and hoarse; it hurt to speak.

No one answered, but a sneeze echoed through the cavernous cellblock.

"I'm Mira—" I stopped short of adding my surname.

It wasn't wise to announce my identity. After all, I didn't know why anyone else was in prison. Even Altan thought it was best to keep my identity secret. I'd have to be more careful in what kind of information I released.

Trusting the wrong people was why I was here in the first place.

Pulling myself off the floor was difficult. Though the air was warm, my muscles felt cramped and stiff. My throat scratched with thirst, and my stomach hollowed with hunger, but who knew when they fed us here. If they ever did.

By the pale light of the hallway noorestones, I took stock of everything inside my cell.

1. *A low wooden bed that ran the length of the left wall.*

2. *A thin lump on the bed that turned out to be a blanket, or something that used to call itself a blanket. Filthy, but it was all dirt from the floor and not from . . . other things that could have been smeared on it.*

3. *A pillow. Most of the stuffing was gone.*

4. *A rusted iron lid over a sewage hole. It was better than a bucket, but not by much. Even though the hole was dark and empty and*

hopefully let out into a refuse area far away, the stink was overwhelming. I couldn't replace the lid fast enough.

I shuddered. During the journey here, I hadn't spent much time imagining prison; I'd been too busy being miserable about my immediate situation. But this . . . This was a hole in the ground. This was an insult. This was cruelty.

The noorestones went dark.

I jumped and screamed, then slammed my hands to my mouth to cut off any sound. It was just the dark. The light would come back. Surely.

It was *so* dark, though. Complete blackness. No matter how wide I opened my eyes, no light touched them. I couldn't see anything. Was this what it felt like to be blind? Complete blackness?

Noorestones didn't work like this. They didn't just go dark; they needed to be covered at night. This shouldn't be possible.

The absence of light was disorienting. Oppressive. Desperately, I squeezed my eyes shut until tiny stars burst behind my eyelids. It was something. Almost like I was in control. If I refused to acknowledge the darkness—

What if the warriors had done this to release some sort of slimy creature into the cells? The idea of a venomous snake slithering around my feet sent a spark of panic through me.

No. Not again. I wouldn't let the panic win again so soon.

I opened my eyes, desperate to see, but that just deepened the sensation of isolation. Like I was the only person alive. The only thing. This darkness was tangible—another medium to exist in, like water—and I just wanted to step out.

This was ridiculous. There was no creature loose. The darkness wasn't a force.

I breathed through the surging adrenaline, counting each exhale. One, two, three . . . Everything was fine.

Down the hall, someone else started to scream. A little relief trickled in, because I wasn't the only one who was terrified.

But his voice echoed off the walls, as strong as the blackness. And he wouldn't stop.

I tried to ignore the shrieks, but it was hard to keep track of how many breaths I was taking when his voice was overpowering. There was nothing to see. Not much to smell or taste or touch. Which left hearing as the sense I should have been able to count on, and it was like the darkness all over again. Instead of counting my own breaths, my mind switched to counting the number of seconds he screamed. Fifteen, sixteen, seventeen . . . How long could he possibly go on?

With my fingers stuffed in my ears, I imagined running to my door and shouting for him to stop. Begging. But I'd never been confrontational, and demanding someone to stop screaming when he was terrified—I couldn't. So I toed my way toward the bed, and when my knees bumped the edge, I shuffled around to sit. All I had to do was wait him out.

"You can wait, Mira." Not that I could hear myself.

Twenty-seven seconds.

Silence.

My ears rang, but the noise was gone. At last. Someone down the hall groaned in relief.

It was premature. Before I could relax, the screaming started again.

I whimpered and dropped my head between my knees, pressing on my ears so hard that my head ached. Someone else shouted, urging the screamer to be quiet, but the noise went on and on.

A small groan climbed up my throat as I grabbed for the pillow and blanket, and scrambled underneath the bed. Like that could protect me from his voice.

I wrapped the blanket around my head to muffle the noise, then squeezed as close as I could to the wall.

There, in the darkness, in the noise, I waited it out.

CHAPTER THREE

"MIRA."

I gasped awake.

For a moment, I imagined I was at home, and the thirteen days since confronting the Luminary Council were a dream. But then the voice came again—"Mira"—and my mind finally registered that this was a stranger's voice. The way it emphasized the syllables of my name was off. Meer-AH instead of MEER-ah.

The voice drew me into wakefulness, and at once, I remembered where I was.

In the Pit.

I startled and jumped, banging my head on the bottom of the bed. But before I scrambled out of the way, I remembered the darkness and the screaming. The latter had stopped, but the former was just as oppressive as before. I smothered a whimper and pressed myself deeper under the bed.

"Mira." Wood scraped the floor near my head.

I held my breath. There was someone under the bed with me.

Fear sparked deep in my stomach. A stranger so close. A dark and unfamiliar place. The complete lack of protection.

But that spark died as I registered three facts.

1. *The space under my bed was too narrow for anyone to have joined me.*

2. *The only heat came from the floor, not a body next to mine.*

3. *If that whisper had awakened me, the screech of my cell door sliding open surely would have jolted me conscious.*

No one else was under the bed.

"Where are you?" Even my whisper trembled.

"Wall."

In the wall? No, on the other side.

"Finish and give back." The voice was soft. So soft it almost seemed like it could have come from my own thoughts, but my thoughts were never that enunciated. That careful.

A slight pressure change near my face alerted me to the object placed there. "What's this?" I let my fingers crawl over the floor, cautious. I didn't want to knock it over by moving too swiftly.

"Cup." The voice was masculine, coming from close by. Coming from . . .

My fingers closed around the wooden cup. The weight indicated it was full, but I didn't drink from it yet. Instead, I marked its place in my mind, and walked my fingers toward the wall.

There was a hole in the crumbling stone.

It was the size of my hand, fingers splayed out. Just big enough to pass a small cup through. I could have reached into the adjoining cell, but a faint current of air brushed my knuckles as I mapped the shape of the opening. His breath. He was close.

I pulled away, back to the cup. "What's in it?"

"Water."

Such an unexpected kindness. Maybe he was from Damina.

I scooted out from under the bed, into the vast darkness of my cell. The blanket slipped off my head and crumpled to the floor as I tipped the cup toward my lips—and suddenly thought better of it. He could have been a murderer. He could have poisoned someone to end up in the Pit.

But the cup held only water, sharp with minerals, but water nonetheless. It felt wonderful on my aching, sob-racked throat. Part of me wanted to splash it on my face and rinse the grime off my skin, but there wasn't enough water to feel clean. And I was so, so thirsty.

The cup was empty too soon, and only as I crawled under the bed again did I realize I should have saved some for my neighbor. "Sorry," I whispered as I pressed the cup into the hole. "I drank it all."

He tapped on the floor in a quick pattern, and though a tap was just a tap, some gave the impression of length. Maybe he'd dragged his finger. One long, one short. A pause. One short, two long, one short. Then, like an afterthought, he said, "No problem."

"I should have saved some for you."

"Ceiling drips." He drew the cup toward him, and I tried not to think too hard about having just drunk ceiling water. That couldn't be sanitary. "Better?" he asked.

"Yes. Thank you." My neighbor wasn't much of a talker. "I don't think I've ever been that thirsty in my life. I keep fantasizing about a bath, too. Even if I could just wash my face, I'd feel so much better."

Three quick taps sounded through the little hole. "Sorry."

"Don't apologize. You're not the reason I ended up here."

Two taps: long, short. "No."

No, it wasn't his fault, or no, he was disagreeing with

me and he thought it was his fault? Daminan etiquette forced me to keep going—put him at ease by assuring him of his innocence.

"It was definitely my fault." A sigh shuddered out of me. "I just wanted to help."

On the other side of the wall, there was no sound but the faint rustle of fabric.

"I'm worried about my friends. Ilina and Hristo—" I shut my runaway mouth. Mother said one of my biggest flaws was that I didn't think about all the things people could do with information before I let it spout out of me.

"Well, never mind. It isn't particularly important." Yes, it was. It was possibly the most important thing I'd ever come across in my life. It had consumed me so much that when Ilina's mother asked me to leave Ilina out of my story, I hadn't considered what that might mean.

That turned out to be the only blessing in the whole mess. By the time I'd realized the Luminary Council wouldn't help, I'd known better than to say anything about my friends. If the council punished *me* for discovering their secrets, Ilina and Hristo would be in even worse trouble. Maybe killed.

I resisted the urge to touch the twists in my hair, no matter how close it made me feel to Ilina; too much fussing would ruin her work. "I trusted the wrong people."

He didn't respond, or acknowledge the invitation to tell me what he'd done.

Like I hadn't said anything at all.

Suddenly, I wondered if he wasn't real. Maybe he—and the drink of water—was just a sliver of my imagination and soon I wouldn't care that I was in prison because I'd start to hallucinate my way out. What if—

No. That wasn't what was happening. My neighbor was just very, very quiet.

Determined not to let the panic overtake me again, I reached into the darkness to pull my blanket under the bed with me.

"Do you have anything to cut with?" I hoped he was real, this person on the other side of the wall. Otherwise, everyone down the cellblock would hear me talking to myself.

"No." Two taps: one long, and one short.

Oh, right. Of course he didn't. Assuming he was real, he was a prisoner. Like me. No weapons. "It's just, I always wrap my hair at night. I thought I could cut off a piece of my dress."

Even as the words came out, I realized he didn't care. Everyone here had it just as bad as me, and my hair was definitely not a concern. Neither was my name or face or status. We were all trying to survive.

But everything was out of my control, and if I could just do *something* normal, I might feel human again.

"Sorry," he said. Another three fast taps. There was definitely a pattern, but I couldn't figure it out.

"How long will it stay dark like this?"

No reply.

"How do you think they got the noorestones to go out? I've never heard of that happening before." At home, we pulled curtains over wall-mounted noorestones and had thick cloths to place over the others. Well, the servants did it. Mother wouldn't allow Zara or me to perform what she described as a "menial task" except in the privacy of our own bedrooms when we were preparing for sleep.

These noorestones hadn't been covered, though. No one had come by; the light had just gone out.

What an alarming thought.

"Do you think they have some kind of device?" I asked. "Or special noorestones? I heard there are scholars who think—"

I bit off my words. I didn't want to start a discussion about noorestones.

Most people liked talking about themselves. They loved to brag, especially if they could make it sound like they weren't bragging. I had tons of practice encouraging these kinds of conversations. It kept people from noticing my shortcomings.

I started with something basic. "What's your name?"

Silence.

"Are you a real person?" Did those words really come out of my mouth? "I—Sorry. I just meant I didn't see you when I walked through." Which probably gave credit to the imaginary-person theory.

I sounded like a dolt, but if I was talking, I wasn't panicking.

"Real." There, that sounded like faint annoyance. "Hidden."

He was real, but he'd been hiding when I'd walked by his cell? That sounded like something a hallucination would say. "You're awfully quiet." Which meant he probably wasn't from Damina.

He grunted.

At least he agreed.

Well, I'd have to take his word that he was real. I was still thirsty, but I did feel like I'd had a drink of water. And I'd felt his breath on my knuckles when I'd inspected the hole in the wall. Those two things would have to be proof enough.

"What did you do to get here?" Ilina might have laughed at this one-sided conversation, but Mother would have died of mortification.

He sighed.

That was probably rude to ask. I was doing such a wonderful job of making a fool of myself.

This was getting uncomfortable, like a pressure building in the hollow of darkness between us. And yet, the questions kept falling out of my mouth. "How long have you been here? When do they feed us? Do we really just sit here for the rest of our lives and wait to die?"

That was a terrible thing to ask, probably, but I needed the distraction. From the panic. From the fear.

My heart thudded. Five times. Ten times. Twenty. I shifted around, trying to ease the tightness in my chest. Nothing helped. And I hated that he wasn't talking to me. *The Book of Love* told us to seek friends everywhere we went. It said we should form bonds, and that those bonds would strengthen us in our time of need.

I didn't want to be this stranger's friend, exactly, but I did want to learn about my neighbors. I wanted to be a *Drakontos mimikus.*

"What's your name?" I asked, one more time.

A loud *smack* hit the wall. I jumped and scrambled to all fours as the pounding shifted to the floor on his side. Longs. Shorts. But even as my shock subsided and I counted the beats, I couldn't make sense of the pattern.

I faced the hole in the wall, gripping the crumbling stone between us. "What does that mean?" A harsh note of fury edged the question. It was too much. I knew. I wanted to yank back the tone and smother it, but it was too late.

The words seemed to rip from him, louder than I'd expected. "Don't know. About dark. About food. About *doing* anything." He released a wordless cry, then dropped his voice and hissed, "You talk too much. Please stop."

I jerked back from the hole between our cells. "Sorry." Shock hit first, followed by shame. Mother always said I didn't talk enough. I wasn't charming enough. I wasn't *Daminan* enough.

"It's lucky you're so pretty," she always said. Not that

my beauty helped me here. My neighbor couldn't see me. And didn't that just prove that my face was all I had? *"It's almost enough to make up for your interest in that dragon."*

I missed LaLa, too. My golden dragon flower. I couldn't shake Ilina's words to me—that LaLa and Crystal were gone. Had they flown away? Had they been taken? If Ilina had known, she'd have said.

The uncertainty pierced me. I loved that dragon. As much as I loved any human. And Mother had never understood.

At home, I was too quiet. Too strange. My only friends were a *Drakontos raptus*, an apprentice dragon trainer, and my personal guard.

Now, in the Pit, I was too loud. Too chatty. Mother might have been proud, except for the prison part. And the panic attack. And all the near-attacks since then. And the rude questions I'd asked my neighbor.

He was probably most definitely real, and now I'd alienated him.

I shouldn't have told the truth.

Haltingly, I crawled out from under the bed and gathered my blanket around my shoulders. With my back against the edge of my bed and my knees pulled up, I lowered my face and prayed. Could Darina and Damyan even hear me from another island, though? I had to believe they could.

"Please," I whispered to them. "Please help me get out of here. Please help Ilina and Hristo. Please return LaLa and Crystal. Cela, cela."

When I prayed at home, sometimes I could feel warmth coming up from the ground. A radiating peace. A sense of love. But I wasn't on Damina. The Isle of Lovers was so far away.

Here, there was only the permeating sense of abandonment. Darkness. And the only person who'd made an attempt to be nice to me—well, he hated everything about me. *Everyone* doted on me at home. They said how pretty I was. How nice I looked in a new dress.

But this boy couldn't see me, only hear my ridiculous questions. I couldn't believe I'd asked if he was real.

My chest ached with pressure, but I wouldn't cry. Not again. I just let the hurt flake and float off me, shedding it with every exhale.

One.

Two.

Three.

Muffled noise signaled movement in the next cell. Wood scraped the floor, like he was putting the cup back in place. Then his voice came from the hole under my bed.

"My name is Aaru. From Idris. I wanted freedom."

CHAPTER FOUR

AARU.

Aaru from Idris.

I wanted to ignore him—to punish him for insulting me—but Aaru was from *Idris*, the Isle of Silence. That explained so much.

"Sorry." He spoke more gently, with a quick triple tap on the floor. "Shouldn't have yelled."

Yelled. He counted speaking sternly as yelling.

I released a long sigh and started to turn around. I should tell him about the tremor on his island; he deserved to know. But at that moment, blinding light flared from the hall.

With a shout, I slammed my palms over my face. All over the cellblock, similar cries echoed. The light leaked between my fingers, making my eyes burn and water. I groaned, trying to rub the stinging away in vain, but it was no use. After hours in the dark, my eyes had grown used to not seeing.

Footfalls slammed through the hall, followed by the rattle of metal on a cell door. My heart jumped. Was someone making an escape?

I scrambled to my feet and forced my eyes open. Through the film of tears, I saw a pair of Khulani warriors storming through the cellblock. They each carried small sacks in one hand, and a metal baton in the other.

The girl across the hall was on her feet, her back to the rear wall and her hands at her sides. She didn't look worried as one of the warriors opened a slot in her door and slung a sack inside.

When Altan appeared at my door, I followed the girl's example. My spine pressed against the cold wall, making the silk of my dress snag against the stone. I could feel the tugging and wanted to pull it free, but I didn't move. I made my face as cool and impassive as I could manage.

Altan dragged a baton along the iron grating of my door. *Clack, clack, clack.* In the opposite cell, the girl picked through her sack and removed a package of dried meat.

Food. The sack contained food.

I couldn't remember the last time I'd eaten, but it seemed like ages ago, and the only reason I hadn't fainted from hunger was because I'd been too scared. But now, my stomach felt achy and hollow. I wanted that bag.

Altan offered a sinister smile. "How was your first day?"

I didn't bother to answer, because the girl across the hall hadn't spoken to the man tossing food at her, either. And as he moved down, the other prisoners were quiet as well.

Altan hefted the bag of food. "This is yours for the next few hours. I suggest eating everything you can, because there's no hoarding allowed. Draws pests."

Hopefully there was a lot of food in there.

The warrior opened the slot in my door and tossed the bag at my feet. I didn't reach for it. I'd wait for him to go away, first.

"A few pieces of information for the new girl," Altan said, putting the baton in his belt. "Once a decan, you'll have the chance to clean your cell."

Once every ten days? That seemed . . . like not enough.

"A mop and bucket goes down the line. You're last, so it's going to be dirty by the time it gets to you. But clean your cell anyway. After a few decans, you'll thank me for the warning."

I'd always been a tidy person, but at home we had servants for the real work. Now I wished I'd paid more attention to what they'd been doing this whole time.

But if I was last in line for the mop, at least I could watch the girl across from me. See how she did it.

"After that, you go down to the baths. Wash yourself whether you want to or not. If the smell in here becomes too unbearable for us, you all get punished. So stay clean."

Damina, what I wouldn't give for a bath right now. I touched the spot on my chin. The blemish felt huge and inflamed, like it was ready to burst. Even the slightest pressure sent ripples of pain across my face.

My skin crawled with the oppressive, smothering sensation of dirt and oil. The thought of a bath . . .

Altan smirked. "You've probably never gone a day without a bath, hm?" He shook his head, like not bathing was a rite of passage of some kind—like everyone should try it at least once. "Well, you're lucky. It's mop day. And therefore bath day."

Today was Surday. Surday was bath day. I tried not to let my excitement show, but clearly I failed, because he just chuckled.

"The rest of the decan, you'll get breakfast, and we come in after three hours and collect your sacks. Don't vomit in there or you'll regret it." He leveled his glare on me. "But today everyone eats, gets their turn with the mop, and then they go off for baths. They get more food after that. It's a special day. Everyone's favorite."

Because we got fed twice?

I was dying to look inside the bag, but Altan's glare kept me pinned in place.

"You can earn freedoms," he went on. "Time out of that cell. You can take a job. More food. More water. More room to exercise. Maybe even move to a better cellblock, if you're good enough."

What kind of work did they need done in the Pit?

My question must have been obvious, because he added, "The Pit is a big place. We always need people to clean. There's usually blood on the floor. The prison kitchen needs more workers, too. If what I hear about the food in that bag is true, they need quality cooks."

He thought I knew how to cook?

"If you've done any kind of blacksmithing, we have places in the forge. Not, of course, for making weapons. The only time you'll touch a weapon is when you're on the wrong end of it." He shook his head. "Still, there are other duties a pretty thing like you might take on." His eyes dropped to my chest.

It took me a moment to understand what he was implying.

"No." The word came as a whisper, but he heard me.

His hand slid toward the baton on his belt. Fingers wrapped over the wooden handle. But he didn't draw. "Well, let me know if you change your mind. Working will get you out more. You'll stay healthier."

I did need to exercise. But working? And for *them*?

"One more thing, Fancy." Altan leaned closer to the door, his face suddenly in shadow. "One little piece of advice, because I'd hate to see something bad happen to my favorite prisoner."

He didn't make *favorite* sound like a good thing.

"Don't trust anyone. Everyone here is slime, including you." His shadow fell across the floor of my cell, ominous and oppressive. "Out there, you might have been better than them, with your special family and important friends. But in here, you're better than no one. You're all criminals. All equal, no matter what crime you committed."

I hadn't committed a crime.

"Even if that crime was simply knowing too much and refusing to shut up about it."

My stomach dropped down to my feet, through the floor, and deep into the center of the world. How much did Altan know?

A terrible smile split across his face, like my reaction had just confirmed everything he suspected. "This is the Pit, Fancy, and no one here helps anyone out of the goodness of their heart. Don't accept favors you can't return."

My gaze cut to the wall I shared with Aaru.

The guard laughed and shook his head. "That was fast. What did he offer? Something to help make your first day easier? Protection? An ear to listen to all your problems? No one really understands how difficult life can be when your dress is torn up."

Water. Aaru had offered me water. And I'd taken it without hesitation.

Did I owe him a favor now? What would he ask of me? When? I didn't have anything to give. I hadn't known. I hadn't realized.

Ignorance wasn't an excuse here. That was likely why he'd offered the cup of water immediately—before anyone had a chance to warn me that I shouldn't accept any sort of kindness. No favors were free.

"Well," Altan went on. "It could have been worse. At least you indebted yourself to an Idrisi boy who doesn't know what to do with a pretty girl like you."

Oh. Another shudder rippled through me. That again.

I wished I'd never accepted that cup of water.

"Down there"—he motioned out of my field of vision—"is a dragon poacher. He was caught selling to Bophan elite. They'd hobble the poor beasts and hunt them as sport, then celebrate their *victories* with a meal. Dragon meat is a delicacy to some people."

I wanted to be sick. My stomach rolled over and the taste of bile tickled the back of my throat. Down the hall, someone was giggling to herself.

"People like you don't do well in here," he went on. "They die in their first decan, but that poacher. He's a stubborn one. Just won't quit breathing."

This place was a nightmare.

"We also have a child-murderer, a thief who tried to steal from the wrong people, and one who attempted to defile every shrine to every god by defecating on them."

Defecating? Oh.

Ew.

"And that girl? Her name is Gerel." Altan motioned over his shoulder, where the girl was tearing through a small loaf of bread. "She used to be a warrior. You don't want to know what she did."

I shivered. Taking the mace was a great honor. Every

Khulani woman or man I'd met had boasted about the warriors in their family. Children. Cousins. And everyone could trace their lineage back to some famous warrior or another, often a Drakon Warrior: a dragon rider.

"But if you behave here, we might be able to help each other. Just think about it." Altan grinned and walked away to pass out the rest of the food.

After a few minutes, the cellblock was empty, save the prisoners. I swallowed back a sharp cry as I dropped toward the sack of food.

My hands shook as I reached inside. One packet of dried meat (three small strips). One leather container of liquid—water, I hoped. Half a loaf of hard bread with nuts and banana slices baked into it. And one apple; it had four bruises and two holes in the pale green skin. I'd never eaten an apple that might have had worms, but I was hungry. I took a bite.

And then I spit it onto the floor.

The fruit was bitter, sharp. The texture was off too, all soft and slippery. I gagged and spit until the taste was out of my mouth.

Across the hall, Gerel shot a disgusted look, like I ought to love rotten apples. Then she pressed herself onto her stomach and began a series of push-ups. The rhythm of her faint grunts ticked away in the back of my mind.

How could this be my life? I wished I were eating dinner at home, with Mother criticizing my performance in lessons, Father lost in his own work, and Zara complaining about all the things she complained about. I wished I were in the dragon sanctuary.

But wishing wouldn't help. I dropped my eyes to my food bag once more. The apple was inedible, but the bread might be all right. It was hard and dry, but I forced down a few chalky bites before a lump stuck to the back of my throat and I started to choke.

I dumped the apple and the bread down the sewage hole. A little hunger wouldn't hurt me; I'd fasted before, though never without a decan of preparation.

Gerel was still doing push-ups, fiercely ignoring me. Ninety-eight, ninety-nine . . .

How was I supposed to survive this?

Mother's voice echoed in my head: *"Everyone loves a beautiful girl. Use that."*

But Altan was my jailer. Aaru couldn't see me. And Gerel didn't care. My one advantage wasn't much of an advantage right now.

BEFORE

Ten Years Ago

A MAN TRIED TO KIDNAP ME ONCE.

My memory of the attempt itself faded rather quickly. Self-protection, perhaps. Rather, it was the moments after that stuck:

1. *Doctor Chilikoba, with sun-darkened skin and smile lines, as she explained my injuries to my parents. "The cuts won't scar."*

Cuts. Because I'd been shoved into my display case of tiny dragons. Mother was relieved. "It would be a shame to permanently damage that perfect face."

2. *My sister Zara, her pale pink dress glowing*

against her deep brown skin. "That boy." She motioned at the gardener's son. "He saved you."

"Isn't he Hartan?" I'd thought everyone from Harta was a pacifist. *Harta hates harm.*

The boy caught us looking and dropped his eyes.

3. *My parents, explaining that the attacker was a Bophan man who'd once owned a business on Harta. His business had done nothing but ship Hartan produce away from Hartan farms, and the newly established government had decided not to work with him. His company had folded and he lost everything. He blamed the Mira Treaty for granting Harta its independence.*

"To a lot of people, you *are* the Mira Treaty. If someone doesn't like it—"

They didn't like me. I'd always been told I should be proud of the Mira Treaty, though I had nothing to do with it. For me, the treaty had always existed: Harta was independent, the Fallen Isles were united, and dragons were protected.

"Life was different before," Father said. "Some people miss those days."

4. *The gardener's boy, who had dark eyes filled with cleverness.*

"What's your name?" Father asked.

"Hristo."

"Why did you help Mira? That man could have killed you."

"It was the right thing to do." Hristo glanced at me. "And she smiled at me once. Said she liked my lala flowers."

He'd planted a thick rainbow of them, white flowers in the middle forming the silhouette of a dragon. "They're my favorite," I whispered.

"Would you do it again?" Father asked. "Protect Mira?"

Hristo was only nine or ten, but he seemed older. Wiser. "Yes," he said. "I would."

5. *That night, I assessed the damage of the attack.*

All my glass dragons were broken. The metals were fine, but some of the stones had chipped.

Nine shattered. Fourteen disfigured.

Mother hadn't mentioned the cost, but she'd been thinking about it. Even though I wasn't smart enough to add all those lumes, I knew it was a lot.

She was upset about the injuries, too, especially the ones on my face. Father had decided to enroll me—and

Hristo—in self-defense classes, and Mother had mostly been worried I'd begin to look *rough*.

In the dressing room, I stood before the triple mirror. Seven small cuts marked my face. Forty-three marked my neck and shoulders. Five gashes had earned bandages.

For hours, I counted and recounted. When the sun peeked above the sea, I walked back to bed. One, two, three . . . Twenty-five steps from the mirrors to bed.

After that, the numbers lived in me.

CHAPTER FIVE

WHEN THE MOP CAME DOWN THE LINE, I WATCHED Gerel.

I watched the way she dunked the dirty mop, pressed the wringing mechanism, and then slid the wet end along the floor five times before repeating the process twice. She used a long, flat broom to sweep the water from her floor into the sewage hole.

That didn't look too hard.

Farther down the hall, I heard a guard tell a prisoner to come along, it was time for a bath. I could hardly wait my turn. When Altan moved the mop, bucket, and broom into my cell, I did exactly as Gerel had. Every gross plop of the mop fibers on the floor was one gross plop closer to a bath. To being clean. To feeling like myself again.

And while I worked, Gerel watched me, evaluating and judging my every move. It was a look I got from Mother all the time, usually followed by a lengthy criticism of my performance on tests, or how I didn't spend enough time with the Luminary Council.

I tried to ignore Gerel. She wasn't Mother. She definitely wasn't Ilina or Hristo. I shouldn't care what she thought of me.

When I finished cleaning my cell, I stepped to the back while Altan removed the tools.

"Make any important decisions, Fancy?" he asked, setting the empty bucket aside.

Cleaning had been easy enough. Swirl a rag around a dirty spot. Plus, as he'd said, there were benefits to taking a job.

1. *Exercise. (I needed to be strong.)*

2. *More—ideally edible—food. (I needed to avoid starvation.)*

3. *Pretense. (If Altan thought I'd cooperate with him, he might be nicer to me.)*

So I gave a short, serious nod.

A predatory grin spread across his face. "Tell me."

My heart sped up and I prayed I wasn't making a mistake. "I'll clean."

"Good. I'll inform Sarannai, your new supervisor." He strode away, too busy to keep taunting me. The rest of the hall was quiet with prisoners taking their turn in the bath. The other guard was gone for now, too, and a tense sense of waiting fell over the cellblock.

"Shouldn't have done that." Gerel had a low, melodic voice, not at all what I'd expected from a former warrior. She stood by her door, feeling at the top for something. Then, she lifted herself off the ground.

There wasn't much room to grab up there, at least from what I could tell on my door. Which meant she was pulling with just her fingertips.

"Why?" I added another item to my benefits-of-working list: I wouldn't have to spend every day watching Gerel exercise.

"You'll find out soon enough." She grunted faintly with effort. My fingers would have fallen off already. "Well," she said, letting go of the door. She hopped back and brushed her hands over her trousers. "It's not as though there's anything better to do here."

I frowned.

"None of the rest of us have been given the *opportunity* to work. Why do you think that is?"

How was *I* supposed to know? Maybe because they'd committed actual crimes?

"Altan wants something from you," she said. "Remember that."

A shudder ran through me. One of the jobs he'd suggested—

Gerel tilted her head. "No, not *that*. That, at least, is one thing you don't have to worry about here. Warriors won't take an unwilling partner. Khulan won't allow it. That offense would put a black mark on their honor for the rest of eternity and they wouldn't be permitted to fight in Khulan's Final Battle."

"I'm supposed to have faith in their unwillingness to besmirch their honor?"

She eyed me askance. "I don't know what it's like where you're from, but here, warriors take their vows seriously. Other people may not be watching, but Khulan is. Always." There was a pause, like she was thinking about her own dishonor. Her sentence to this prison. "Anyway, that's not something you have to worry about."

Thank Damina for that small measure of safety. There were plenty of other things the warriors could do to me here, but at least that wasn't one of them. Mother reminded me frequently about the importance of my virtue, and how I should protect it.

"But Altan wants something," Gerel said. "He was never a prison guard before. You must be important."

There was an implied question in that statement, but she didn't ask, and I certainly wasn't going to volunteer the information. "What do you think he wants?"

She shrugged. "How should I know? I can't read minds."

Well, neither could I.

"At any rate," Gerel said, "be careful. Sarannai is not an easy woman to please. Would-be warriors train under her when they come to the Heart." She stretched one arm across her chest, clenching and unclenching her fingers. "And she supervises Pit prisoners, when she's feeling testy."

I hadn't realized that warriors spent part of their training here, but it made sense, didn't it? I'd seen the statues and chapels. This was their temple.

"I came to the Heart for training when I was fifteen. Before that, I'd spent ten years preparing. Running. Fighting. Learning to use every weapon available. I was at the top of my class. None could best me."

Thank Damina humility wasn't one of the attributes of a good warrior.

"Then we came to the Heart. We'd heard about it all our lives, of course. No warrior completes training without time here." She rolled her shoulders as she spoke. "Our first night in the trainee barracks, everyone in the class ahead of us came rushing in, banging batons against the frames of our beds. It went on until the last one in our class—a boy who died a few days later—finished dressing and reported for cleaning duty. Under Sarannai."

A boy had died? Maybe he'd taken ill and the doctors hadn't been able to treat him.

"Sarannai said there were buckets with soap and rags stashed around the outer ward. Fourteen buckets. Fifteen of us. Everyone who got a bucket needed to have the outer ward spotless by dawn. If Sarannai found even a smudge of dirt, we'd all suffer."

I swallowed hard. "What about the trainee who didn't get a bucket?"

Her face went blank, completely free of emotion. "He's the one who died later. I don't think you'd like to hear how that happened."

Probably not. "Tell me."

Down the hall, a door slammed. She motioned for me to wait as footfalls hit the stone floor and four cell doors shuddered open. Prisoners put back in. Prisoners taken out. Lucky prisoners who got to take their baths *right now*.

Then it was quiet again, and Gerel continued with her story. "I didn't see all of it, because I got the first bucket. I was already scrubbing by the time it happened."

Of course. Top of her class. None could best her, or touch her bucket.

"Most of this is what I heard later." Her voice deepened, as though she was trying to hide some sort of emotion. Pain? Pride? "There was a fight for the final bucket. Sarannai had said that whoever didn't get one wouldn't be allowed to continue training, so everyone was inspired to do whatever they needed to ensure their stay. No one wants to leave as a dishonored trainee. Not even the most loving family would accept them back."

"That's very sad."

"That's Khulani life." She shrugged, but her voice was

tight, betraying some sort of emotion. "So that boy—"

"You don't even say his name."

"No one does," she said. "There's no honor in his name, because he didn't complete his training. He fought for the last bucket. Even after it was clear he'd lost and most were already cleaning, he tried to steal someone's bucket, rather than be dismissed to a life among the homeless dishonored. I can't say I would have done any differently. But he was interrupting everyone's work by then, and the outer ward wasn't going to get cleaned with him trying to steal. Plus, he was dripping blood everywhere, making more work."

Chills of dread rippled through my stomach. "What happened?"

"They beat him until he stayed down. The other trainees. Boys and girls he'd known for ten years. Been friends with. But they had to stop him. He was in the infirmary for three days before he died. Some said he'd been bleeding internally and the doctors hadn't been able to repair it, but others said he took too many painkillers."

"Because he hurt so much? He accidentally took too many?"

She shook her head. "No. Because he knew what it would do to him."

"Oh." And it was Sarannai who'd sentenced everyone to such an awful task. Who'd made everyone choose between their friend and their future. Where was the honor in that?

"Well, it's too late to change your mind." Gerel flashed a dark smile and moved to the back corner of her cell, where, in one swift movement, she stood upside down—her palms flat on the floor and holding up her entire body. Her heels dragged against the wall as she bent her elbows, then pushed up.

One. Two. Three. She went on and on.

At the end of the hall, a woman started singing—a generous description.

"Shut up, Kumas!" a man shouted. "If you can't sing in tune, don't sing at all!"

Gerel could have been lying about Sarannai. I had no reason to trust her, or anyone here. But the story had been so awful that it had to be true.

She had survived Sarannai because she was strong. Hristo would tell me to get strong, too.

I went to the corner of my cell and stared at the floor. Gerel had just sort of . . . dived into it. I tried for a tamer method of getting upside down: I bent over, placed my hands on the ground (internally shuddering at the filth I was willingly touching), and kicked one leg up.

The skirt of my dress fell around my head, blinding me, and my weight shifted to my arms for a half second—

I dropped to the ground in a mess of cloth and humiliation.

"*What* are you doing?" Gerel stood by her door again, fists on her hips. "Are you trying to kill yourself?"

"No." I climbed to my feet. "But I think I should have tied my dress in place."

"That would be a start." Her expression shifted somewhere between annoyed and amused. "A better start would involve beginning with something simpler."

"Like what?" I'd trained twice a decan with Instructor Boyan, so I wasn't a complete weakling. I didn't want to end up like that boy. I wanted to live. I wanted to get out of here. I wanted to see my friends and dragon again. I wanted to stand on Damina and feel that deep-rooted sense of belonging.

Gerel sneered as she looked over my form. My ragged dress. My dirt-streaked skin. "Maybe you have more muscle hidden in there somewhere, but I doubt it. One day of scrubbing floors is going to make you question whether you'll ever lift your arms again."

"You don't have to be so mean about it." I crossed my arms over my chest, but the posture came off as trying to hide, rather than competent and tough.

"You think I'm mean?" Gerel scoffed and pressed close to the metal grille of her door. "I am *kind*, Fancy. I'm your *best friend*."

No, *Ilina* was my best friend.

But I still wanted Gerel to like me. I wanted everyone to like me. It was one of the most basic Daminan tenets—that with love, anything could be endured—and though the Luminary Council had betrayed me, my beliefs had deep roots. I made my voice soft. "Does that mean you're going to help me?"

"No. It just means I hate you less than I hated the previous occupant of that cell. I was so glad when he died."

Maybe I didn't want to know this either, but . . . "What happened?"

"One day, his sores all burst open and he melted. It was one of the most disturbing things I've seen in a long time."

I eyed the cell warily. I'd *touched the floor* and now I desperately wanted to remove my hands.

"They cleaned after he died. Sort of." She waved away my concern, like it was dumb to worry about all the gross things that might be left over. "My point is that you never know who your neighbors will be. You're at least pretty."

I was visually more appealing than the man before me. Well, I supposed that was my face working in my favor again. Mother would be proud.

Gerel went back to her exercises. This time, though, she stood with her legs apart and slowly bent at the knees, then straightened.

I copied her. I wasn't as pathetic as she believed. I wasn't. But she didn't know I had the best self-defense trainer on Damina. Or that I hunted with a *Drakontos raptus*. Or . . . Well. That was probably it.

Gerel didn't say anything else to me, just glanced up every so often to see if I was still copying her. I couldn't tell if she approved or not. Probably not. Even so, it felt good to move around again, to force my muscles to flex and bend. If I wanted to survive, I needed to be strong.

I was a *Drakontos mimikus.* I was not like the others here, but I could blend in long enough for my family to secure my release.

After two hundred squats, seven stretches, and twenty push-ups, my face felt flushed and my muscles trembled. Gerel wasn't tired, though. She went back to lifting herself on the edge of the door. With her fingertips.

Well, of course she could do that. She was a warrior and she was on Khulan. She'd *just* told me that she'd been training harder than this her entire life. Top of her class, at least until she'd done something no one else liked.

But in the back of my head, I could hear Mother's disappointed sigh. Not smart enough. Not strong enough. *"Thank Damina you're beautiful."*

I touched the blemish on my chin and cringed.

Finally, it was Gerel's turn for the bath. And mine. But Altan approached my cell and didn't open it.

He tilted his head. "You just got here. What makes you think you earned a bath?"

Gerel caught my eye as she stepped out of her cell, but I couldn't decipher her look.

"As for this"—Altan hefted a sack of food—"you haven't earned it, either."

"But—" I pressed my mouth into a line. Everyone else got theirs—I assumed—so why shouldn't I get mine? And a bath? I'd cleaned my cell, same as the other prisoners.

Altan tossed the sack through the open door of Gerel's cell; it landed on her bed. "Get some rest, Fancy. You have a big day tomorrow."

My stomach growled and ached, and I thought bitterly of the rotten apple and stale bread I'd tossed down the sewage hole. Maybe I should have eaten it after all. I pressed my palms to my belly and curled over myself, but it didn't help. Maybe a distraction.

"Aaru?" I peered under my bed, toward the hole. "Are you there?"

Two taps answered. "No."

I sat on my bed, blanket pulled around my shoulders, and counted the cracks in the walls (three hundred and twelve) until Gerel returned. Then I watched her eat my food (three chews per bite, no matter what she ate, like she was afraid it might be taken from her).

She looked over. "Stop watching me. It's weird."

I dropped my gaze to my knees. She knew I hadn't been allowed to bathe, but she couldn't know I'd been denied dinner, too. For the moment, that made me both the hungriest and the dirtiest person in the cellblock.

Later, when the lights went out and the screaming started, I began to understand. This was day and night in the Pit. Faint light, and no light. No light meant whoever was so afraid of the dark screamed until he fell asleep.

This wasn't fair. I was being punished for trying to do the right thing. I should have been *rewarded*.

But life didn't always work like that.

• • •

I SPENT THE night under the bed. It seemed safer than on top.

I *tried* to sleep the normal way. When the screaming stopped, I peeled myself off the floor and felt through the black space until my fingers scraped the edge of the bed. But the moment I stood, this awful sensation of being lost—or somewhere else—came over me. Like if I took one wrong step, I'd fall off the edge of a mountain, or into another world.

By the time I made it into bed, my pillow and blanket in their proper places, I was trembling with the unknown. Like this thin wooden cot was a raft and I was drifting in the middle of the sea, no land in sight. All I could feel was the dark and the pressure and the lurking terror of something unnameable, like a beast lived in the blackness and if I moved wrongly, it would devour me.

So in a fit of bravery, I jumped off the bed and scrambled back under, protected on five sides. But it wasn't enough.

My head spun and my throat closed. I was choking on the darkness, and on fear that the dim crystals in the hall might never illuminate again.

I could be trapped in this darkness forever.

A high-pitched whine squeezed from my throat as I pressed my spine to the floor and my palms to the underside of the bed, like anchoring myself here. Like reminding myself there were physical things surrounding me. But every time I opened my eyes, there was only void. Darkness.

I needed my calming pills. I needed Doctor Chilikoba, who always assured me I wasn't dying when I felt like this.

"Breathe," she would say. *"Start with breathing."*

I gasped. Not a long breath, but enough that the muscles in my throat opened a fraction. Another inhale, this one more substantial. That could count as the first breath.

One. Two. Three. I breathed in, held the air in my lungs, and exhaled as long and slow as I could stand. Gradually, my racing heart eased.

As long as I didn't open my eyes. As long as I didn't move my hands from the underside of the bed.

And I listened to the whimper of someone in the throes of nightmares, to a whistling snore from a man down the hall, and to heavy silence. Like everyone was just waiting for something terrible to happen.

But what could be worse than this?

CHAPTER SIX

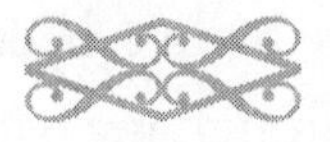

THE NEXT MORNING, ALTAN STOPPED IN FRONT OF my door, his eyes hooded and his mouth turned downward. A fresh cut ran the length of his cheek, not deep enough to need stitches or a bandage, but the brown skin around it had turned ruddy and ragged. It probably hurt. Good.

Damina's Law said one should never wish pain on someone else, but did that apply to one's jailer? Surely Damyan and Darina wouldn't begrudge me this one indulgence.

"Ready for your first day of work?" he asked.

I glanced at his empty hand, then beyond him to where the second guard was throwing a sack of food into Gerel's cell. First last night, and now today. I'd been under the impression that agreeing to work meant I'd get more food. Not zero food.

My nemesis grinned. "Not in here, Fancy. You get breakfast in the mess hall. And if the others want more food, they'll work for it, too."

Except the others hadn't been offered work. Why? Gerel's warning ran through my head again: Altan wanted something.

"I brought these." Altan motioned at a pair of shackles hanging from his belt. "You don't have to wear them if you promise to come without a struggle."

We both knew I wouldn't fight.

He opened the door.

I stepped through, and while Altan closed the door, I glanced toward Aaru's cell. Nothing was visible. Just the front corner, partially blocked by a guard hassling him about standing up and coming out from under the bed.

A twinge of guilt wrapped around me. He'd tried to apologize, and I'd forgotten about him once Altan offered work and Gerel started talking to me. It was rude to ignore people, Mother always said. And especially rude to ignore them after annoying them and accusing them of being hallucinations.

Then again, I'd tried to talk to him later, and *he'd* ignored *me*. Clearly he hated me.

Maybe I had made a mistake by accepting his water. Maybe I hadn't. After all, I couldn't trust Altan any more than I could trust the other prisoners. Ilina would tell me to find some way to win Aaru over. Not that I knew how to do that if I couldn't smile at him (the hole was too small) and giggle at his jokes (he didn't seem to know much about jokes). But Ilina would push me to find another way.

"Come on." Altan yanked the twisted ends of my hair so hard my eyes watered. "The Pit won't clean itself." With a smug look, he let go of my hair, but my head stung just the same. Gerel caught my eye; she looked . . . worried.

A hollow feeling stirred in my stomach. I was exhausted and hungry. How was I supposed to clean? I had no experience, save the few minutes with the mop yesterday.

My face and throat heated, like I was standing too close to an oven. Except this heat came from inside me. The burning spread through me as my heart pounded, harder and harder. My vision tunneled and I staggered, suddenly dizzy. Another attack.

I couldn't let the panic in this time. I had to stay calm.

But telling myself to stay calm made it worse.

But if I didn't overcome this, I'd never be able to work, and I'd never survive until Mother and Father saved me, and then—

"Remember your breathing," Doctor Chilikoba would say. *"Always start with your breathing. If you still feel panicked after ten deep breaths, take a pill."* Seven gods, what I wouldn't give for one of those pills now.

I had nothing, though. Just myself. So I started with breathing.

As I walked after Altan, opposite the way we'd come

in the other day, I sucked in the first deep breath, held it for five stumbling heartbeats, and released it through my mouth, like I was exhaling all the bad, anxious feelings.

On the way, I counted cells (twenty-four) and noorestones (eight), and times Altan scratched at the cut on his face (three). Holding the numbers in my head helped; they didn't leave much room for anything else.

I finished all ten breaths. My head felt clearer, but the danger lurked nonetheless. I had to be careful. Vigilant.

We walked up a set of stairs (thirty steps), and my nemesis watched me from the corner of his eyes. "You look gray, Fancy. Nervous?"

I shook my head. It was the truth. "Nervous" didn't begin to cover it. Terrified? Panicked?

"Try not to think about your anxiety," Doctor Chilikoba had suggested. *"That will make the cycle worse. Instead, focus on other things."*

That only made me count more.

Altan grunted. "I don't care if you *are* nervous. You probably should be. But don't vomit. You'll have to clean it up."

Nice to know.

I'd vomited exactly once in my life. Zara had teased that a meal I'd been enjoying was dragon meat, which had obviously been a lie (it was perch), but my stomach didn't see it that way. It had been one of my most disgusting experiences and Mother said it would ruin my teeth. I'd vowed never to do it again. Even my panic attacks tended to agree; while I often felt nauseated, I'd never again thrown up.

And I wouldn't give in to the queasy feeling in my stomach now, either.

We passed through the anteroom. (Five steps across, three narrow shelves with thin blankets and other bedding supplies, and three locked cabinets.) Next, we came to a long hall, with columns and metal sconces around noorestones, all with Khulan's crossed maces carved into them. The vaulted ceiling bore the same decorative touches, these painted blue and gold and red where Khulan's figure was twisted back as though preparing to strike down anyone in his path.

We passed thirteen doors (one hundred and five steps) before Altan motioned me down a side hall. "Prisoner meals last ten minutes. Breakfast is at daybreak—as soon as I come to fetch you. Lunch is an hour after noon, and dinner is a few hours before dark. Then you go back to your cell. We used to keep prisoners cleaning longer, but then they started dying from exhaustion."

"I appreciate the opportunity," I whispered, tilting my head in the way Mother said made hearts melt. It was a light touch. Without Damina's gifts, I'd had to learn on my own, just little ways of fooling everyone into believing I was deserving of my rank.

Altan gave me a look, like he couldn't tell if my

comment had been genuine or not.

Well, I *was* grateful for more food. And getting out of my cell.

We entered a small mess hall, already filled with seventeen people bent over plates of food. My stomach growled at the sight of cheese, fruit, and some kind of red meat that dripped grease. I'd never been allowed to eat that at home—I'd never wanted to—but now I couldn't wait.

"This way." Altan motioned me around the edge of the room, toward an ancient-looking woman standing over a pile of buckets, rags, and other unidentifiable items. She frowned as Altan and I approached, which just made her craggy, weathered face seem even older. Her skin looked as tough as the leather uniform she wore, which was decorated with gold and silver stitching along the flap that wrapped around her body. Knives and cuffs filled her belt, like she was just waiting for someone to give her an excuse to use them.

"Don't speak to her," Altan muttered.

I looked at him sharply. Was that a *warning*?

But his face was neutral. "Just nod or shake your head. Don't stand out."

Was he trying to *help* me? Gerel might be right about Altan's intentions. He wanted something from me.

I pulled myself straight, even though I could feel every crack in the floor through my thin slippers, and my dress was filthy and sagged to one side of my body.

"Mistress Sarannai." Altan bowed to the old woman,

who just eyed him like he was muck on her shoe. "I've brought you a new worker."

Before I could even register what was happening, Sarannai grabbed my right hand and turned it over, palm up. Her skin was rough and callused as she stretched out my fingers and wrinkled her face. "Pathetic." She spit on my hand and released me.

A pale whine gathered in my throat as her saliva dripped off my fingers. I suddenly didn't know what to do with my hand. Hold it there? Wipe it on my dress? Shake off her spit? None of those things seemed appropriate, especially wiping, because she was glaring at me with almost an amused tilt to her shriveled mouth.

I opted for not moving, but already I could feel my heart speeding and my chest aching and numbers fluttering through my head. Twenty buckets. Thirty seals or awards on Sarannai's jacket. Seventeen other prisoners gulping down their food. They looked stronger, healthier than the inmates I'd seen in my cellblock.

"This one doesn't know anything about cleaning," Sarannai said. "I don't want her."

Cold splintered through my stomach. What was I supposed to do if she didn't want me? How was I supposed to stay strong and fed?

"She doesn't know much about anything," Altan agreed.

My face burned.

"I thought you might consider her an empty vessel,"

Altan went on. "Fill her up with whatever you want."

It was only a miracle that prevented me from shuddering. My hand still hung between Sarannai and me, damp and cold. A thread of saliva dripped from my small finger.

Gerel had said I'd regret agreeing to take on a job. I hadn't realized she'd meant right away.

Sarannai narrowed her eyes at me. "This is the kind of criminal the other islands are sending us now? Soft little girls who've never worked a moment in their lives?"

A strange, almost angry sensation welled up inside of me. What right did she have to say any of those things? She didn't know me at all. She'd just looked at me, spit on my hand, and decided I wasn't worth the time it would take to tell me where to clean.

I stamped down those feelings. Mother would say—

Well, I didn't know what Mother would say. I shouldn't be cleaning, of course, but was that because I was too good for it? Or not good enough?

"This is what they gave us." Altan threw a dismissive look at me. "There are a few others in the first level, but they're not ready yet."

The first level. That was what my cellblock was called. The first stop for prisoners, the place to make us so miserable we broke and agreed to work for them in trade for better accommodations.

I wasn't broken, though. I wasn't.

Hristo would remind me to be strong. He'd come for me soon, once the Luminary Council realized they needed me. I just had to survive until then.

"We must work with what we have." Sarannai grabbed my wrist and yanked me toward her. The calluses on her hand scraped my skin. "Put on something more appropriate for cleaning. Then you can eat."

Fear and hunger rolled through me as she shoved and I stumbled toward a pile of clothes. Quickly, afraid of what she might do if I was too slow, I picked out trousers and a shirt that might fit me. Both were made of rough, cheap cotton that might have been blended with nettles or sea urchins before the weaving and sewing began. There weren't undergarments, but even if there had been, I wasn't sure I'd have been able to wear them. All these things looked secondhand. Maybe fifth.

At least I was able to wipe the spit off my hand without drawing notice. But what I wouldn't give for soap.

With my new clothes bundled under my arm, I scanned the mess hall for a place to change. Altan and Sarannai were still discussing my uselessness, offering no instructions as to where I should go, and the other prisoners were finishing their meals. A few were up, sliding wooden trays onto a rack at the kitchen window. Three of them leered at me—young men with ashy skin and ragged hair; they must have been here for a long time to look so washed-out.

There didn't seem to be anywhere private, and I was hesitant to leave the room, lest Sarannai think I was trying to escape.

After a moment, she glanced back at me. "Not dressed

yet? Don't you know how to do it?" She turned back to Altan. "Where'd you get this one?"

Oh. She expected me to change right here. In front of everyone.

I wanted to sink into the floor. I wasn't shy about my body. That was the one thing I knew was acceptable. But to strip in front of all these strangers? I'd never imagined such a degrading situation. I united crowds. I inspired them. I did not bare myself.

And while there'd been no direct threats against my person, there'd been mention of what a girl might be useful for here. I didn't want to encourage that line of thought. Gerel's assurance about the warriors was one thing, but she hadn't said anything about the prisoners. A few were still watching. Grinning.

Instead of stripping down, I turned my back to the room and pulled up the trousers underneath my dress. They didn't fit well, but I pressed all five buttons into their holes. The shirt was trickier, but I managed a complicated maneuver that involved putting clothes on top of clothes and then removing what had been deemed inappropriate.

Before they could take the ruined dress from me, I shoved it deep into the pile of clothes so I could get it back later. The dress was mine. It was one of the only things I owned in this whole place. They couldn't have it.

"Go eat." Altan jerked his head toward the nearest table. "You have two minutes left."

I wanted to argue that I'd been here on time and I was

only delayed because they'd made me change clothes, but that seemed like a good way to get in more trouble. So as the other prisoners made their way toward Sarannai to collect buckets, I pushed past until I found a window with a tray of food already prepared.

A girl my age peeked out from the kitchen beyond. Seven flat braids held her hair in place, the ends reaching past her shoulders. It was long, which meant she wasn't a warrior trainee. She might be a prisoner, too.

I risked a smile as I took my tray and headed to a table.

Two minutes. Less now. I'd never been a fast eater, so I went for the meat first, hoping it would fill me up. It was cool, greasy, and not very good, but I forced it down. No way was I throwing away food again, no matter how terrible it tasted.

The mess hall was almost empty, all the others heading out with their buckets.

I tore through the bread as fast as possible. It stuck to the roof of my mouth, but it was filled with raisins and bits of almonds.

"Soft girl!" Sarannai snapped, and pointed at the buckets. "Enough eating. Get to work."

Altan strode out of the room, sparing only a second to throw a smirk over his shoulder, as if to say he didn't expect me to last long.

I downed the mug of lukewarm tea as I stood, then hurried toward the buckets. "I'm ready," I said.

Sarannai slapped me. Red flared across my vision,

followed by a burst of sharp, hot pain in my cheek. I'd forgotten I wasn't supposed to speak.

But that was all it took: one mistake.

My fingers curled over my face. The skin felt hot already.

The old woman watched me, waiting to see if I'd make a sound. She ran her tongue over her teeth, sucking at something stuck in there.

I swallowed back a whimper and forced my hand back to my side. I wouldn't give her the satisfaction. In the back of my mind, I counted the tables (thirteen), chairs (fifty-one), columns (ten), and noorestones (thirty).

"Fine. A trial run, I suppose. Clean this mess hall. I'll come back before lunch and look it over. If you've done a good job, you can stay on. If not, you'll never leave first level." With that, she headed out of the room, straight backed and hands at her sides curled like claws.

I watched the door for a moment longer, wondering if I could rush out and get lost in the Pit.

But I *would* get lost. I didn't know the layout, or have access to food, or even have a plan. The other prisoners working throughout the Pit might give me away, too.

"You should get started." The voice came from the window where my food had appeared. It was husky for a girl's. She was really pretty: a lot like my sister, with her delicate, pointed features, smooth brown skin, and dark eyes. How she maintained herself on this . . . food . . . I could only guess. "She means what she says."

I didn't want to admit I wasn't sure how to get started, so I asked, "What's your name?"

"Tirta."

That was a Hartan name. How had *she* ended up in the Pit? *Harta hates harm.* It seemed impossible she could have done something that would warrant this kind of punishment. But Hristo had become my protector, and I was possibly the least charming person on Damina.

Being born somewhere didn't mean we were going to fit in.

So I didn't ask. Aaru had gotten angry with me. Gerel had never offered. I certainly didn't want anyone to know why I was here. So I just said, "I'm Mira."

"I know who you are." She smiled and motioned toward the buckets. "But even Mira Minkoba has to follow orders in the Pit."

Mira *Minkoba*. She knew my surname, not just that I was one of the thousands of girls in the Fallen Isles named Mira. The Luminary Council meant to keep my incarceration quiet, though I didn't know how they were explaining my absence.

Still, none of the prisoners should have even guessed I was the *Mira Treaty* Mira. A burst of fear fluttered through me. "How do you know?"

"Just rumors," Tirta said. "Don't worry. I won't tell anyone if you don't want."

That was a relief. "Thank you."

"When I heard you were here, I hoped I'd get to meet

you." She smiled.

Conversations that began like this usually required Hristo to loom a little extra. I proceeded with a neutral and noncommittal, "Oh?"

"I was born about six months after the treaty—in Sarai. I always felt sort of connected to you."

"Oh." How I wished for Hristo and his looming.

Tirta blushed furiously. "Sorry. I know I'm being awkward. It's just that without you—without the treaty—my life would have been very different. I wouldn't have belonged. I don't have much of a gift, you know. Working on one of the farms would have been a nightmare, but thanks to you and the treaty, I don't have to."

My heart twisted. Mother had always told me to just gracefully accept praise and thanks when people started talking like this, but I'd never felt right about it. "I didn't have anything to do with the treaty. I just happened to be born the same day, so my father named it after me."

"I know, but that doesn't mean you aren't the Hope-bearer." She smiled, relentlessly friendly. "Sorry. I can see it makes you uncomfortable. I just always liked you. That's all."

I didn't know whether to thank her or run away.

Ilina would tell me to make friends, and this girl clearly wanted to be my friend. I needed to let her. Besides, who was I to judge awkward attempts at closeness? Especially after what I'd done to Aaru. Maybe

Tirta was a little like me.

So I smiled. "Please don't tell anyone who I am."

"I won't. I promise."

I headed toward the buckets and rags.

"Do you know how to clean?" A note of amusement filled her tone.

"I managed cell-cleaning day." Barely.

Tirta stuck her head through the window. "I can't help you. I have a lot of food to cook. But I can give you instructions if you need. Start at the top. Use that pole to get the walls. And don't forget the underside of the tables. Sarannai will check there first."

This had seemed impossible before. But *under* the tables, too? And probably the legs and chairs and everything else, as well. How was I going to finish all of this by lunchtime?

Ilina would tell me to do what I must to survive. Zara would tell me to stop being a baby. Father would remind me that I was Mira Minkoba, and that I was a brilliant star. It was my duty to shine.

I grabbed a bucket. There was no time to waste.

BEFORE

One Year Ago

"IT'S TIME TO GIVE UP THE DRAGON, MIRA."

It was my sixteenth birthday and I was reasonably certain Mother was trying to ruin my life.

The upstairs parlor was usually a happy place, even in my family. Once a decan, my parents, Zara, and I met here an hour before dusk. We'd play cards, eat tiny pastries with honey drizzled on top, and watch the sun set over the mountains. I loved twilight, where sunlight glowed just behind the jagged peaks. I loved the glorious silhouettes. Those hints of majesty.

But tonight, Mother said the words I'd been dreading for eight years: give up the dragon.

I put down my cards, face up. The game didn't matter anymore. "Why?"

"People need to see you growing up, doing something good with your life."

I'd never been able to do anything with my life. That was the problem.

Mother glanced at Father; they were united in this decision and it was his turn to explain to their stupid child. He cleared his throat. "You represent the Mira Treaty. Use that power. When people hear *Mira* believes in better pay for Hartan servants, they will believe, too."

I glanced at Hristo, who was reading on the far side of the room. The sting of his rejection was four years old, dull now, but I'd never forgotten what he said—that we weren't equal. "Of course I think Hartans should be paid the same as anyone else on Damina—"

"Then it's settled." Mother plucked all the cards from the table to begin a new hand. "In the morning you'll thank Viktor and Tereza for the time with their dragon. Later we'll announce your intention to become more involved in civil policies."

My mouth dropped open. "But LaLa—"

"Oh, forget the dragon!" Zara sat back and crossed her arms. "You like that dragon more than you like anyone else."

That wasn't true. . . .

"The dragon was a sweet childhood hobby." Mother shuffled the cards. "Your responsibilities are different now. You can't always get what you want, but you do have everything you *need*."

Except the freedom to make my own choices.

"A dragon is not a need," Mother said.

"How will it look if I abandon LaLa? Keeping her will demonstrate that I take responsibility for those under my care—even dragons."

Father nodded faintly. "That's true, but I'm still not sure . . ."

"I'll use my influence." I rushed over the words, desperate. "I'll do what you want. Just don't make me give up LaLa."

Eighteen heavy heartbeats thumped by. "Fine," Mother said. "As long as you remember your responsibilities to Damina, you can keep the dragon."

That had been . . . easy.

And then it hit me. I hadn't won. The threat against LaLa had never been real. Mother just wanted a way to persuade me to do what she wanted.

I'd thought I'd been standing up for myself, but I hadn't.

I'd done exactly what Mother had expected.

CHAPTER SEVEN

I FINISHED CLEANING THE MESS HALL BY LUNCH.

Barely.

With Tirta's advice in mind, I started at the top and mopped the ceiling. It was possibly the most awkward, messy, and uncomfortable thing I'd ever done, but I went across all forty-five panels one at a time, wedging the mop into crevices to scrub off smoke stains. Dirty water dripped onto my outstretched arms and face and shoulders.

From there I scrubbed the walls, then moved on to the tables and chairs and lights. I worked as thoroughly as possible, especially when I got to the floor. The stains were too much for the mop alone, so I was forced to my hands and knees with a brush, scrubbing until the dirt loosened. The last thing I needed was to miss something and have to do it over again—or worse, for Sarannai to notice. How had maids at home managed such tasks?

My arms and legs trembled by the time Sarannai returned, a frown creasing her face. Her boots tapped the floor as she inspected my work, checking the undersides of the tables, just as Tirta had predicted.

"A fair job," Sarannai said at last. "Wash yourself and eat lunch when the others come in. Then I'll give you another room."

Another room. Great.

But when she went to the food window for her own lunch, I scrambled to the tap where I'd been filling and emptying my bucket all morning. When I'd realized there was running water here, it had taken every drop of my will not to throw my whole body under the stream.

Now, I indulged in a moment of spreading soap across my hands and arms, reveling in the simple pleasure of removing grime from my skin. Unlike the jasmine- and citrus-scented soaps from home, this one stank like animal fat, but it was so much better than nothing.

It was over too soon. Other prisoners began to come in, two and three at a time. No one spoke as they shoveled food into their mouths. The hall echoed with the sounds of chewing and grunting and burping. The ones who'd been leering earlier ignored me now, no longer interested or intrigued. For that, I was glad my anonymity was one of the few things I had here, and I wanted to keep it.

When lunch was finished, seventeen prisoners lined up to get orders from Sarannai. I carried my empty tray to the window and kept my voice low as Tirta acknowledged me with a nod. "I had a dress earlier," I said.

"I saw."

"I want to keep it." It was filthy, but it was mine.

Tirta glanced toward the pile of folded clothes I'd left on a table earlier. A sliver of silk peeked out. "I'll hide it back here. Get it after dinner."

I had to take the chance that she truly wanted to be my friend. "I want to wrap my hair," I whispered. The line for Sarannai was down to five; she barked more and more orders, sending others scurrying from the mess hall. I had to hurry. "Cut a square of silk for yourself if you want."

Tirta's eyes lit. "I will."

Just as the last person finished getting instructions from Sarannai, I rushed into line.

By DINNERTIME, MY whole body hurt and my hands burned from gripping the mop handle and soapy rags. But I finished my work and returned to the mess hall. Tirta offered a faint nod as I took my tray, and when I glanced toward the pile of clothes, the dress was gone. She'd kept her word. Or stolen my dress.

Just as I sat down to eat, Altan appeared in the doorway.

My chest tightened. I'd spent all day counting stones and brushstrokes and facets of noorestones, trying to distract myself from the swarm of fears circling my every thought. Not only did my muscles ache from the effort it took to clean a huge stone room, but they shook with the sort of exhaustion that always came when recovering from a panic attack. Even a not-quite attack.

And now, with Altan making his way across the mess hall toward me, every hard-won piece of calm threatened to unravel.

I measured my breathing and concentrated on my food. Slimy. Cold. Slightly spoiled. Either Tirta was a terrible cook, or everything she made went to warriors and trainees, and prisoners got leftovers. Still, it was better than what came in the sacks.

Then Altan took the chair across from me and leaned his elbows on the table. "Good first day, Fancy?"

The display drew sidelong glances from the nearby prisoners. They were probably wondering why a warrior would come over and talk to me.

Seven gods, *I* was wondering why a warrior would come over and talk to me.

I took a huge bite of rye bread and rinsed it with a swallow of weak tea.

"You've got a lot of days ahead of you, Fancy. They can be good or bad days."

Down the table, the prisoners who'd been pretending not to eavesdrop suddenly looked down. Away. Anywhere else. Whatever was going to happen, they didn't want to know about it.

"I have questions," Altan went on, like the uncomfortable

audience wasn't here at all. "I bet you can guess what I want to know about."

Why would he assume I knew anything?

One corner of Altan's mouth turned up. "I heard you enjoy hunting. I do, too. I like the truth. It's the most elusive quarry I've ever pursued, but always a rewarding catch."

Hunting. I didn't like hunting so much as I loved spending time with LaLa. The way she balanced on my hand, her wings fanned out to absorb the sunshine. The strange purr that rumbled in her throat when she was content. The way she pressed against my chest when she fell asleep.

My little dragon flower. Where was she now?

Then it hit me.

Dragons.

My heart pounded toward my throat, making it hard to swallow the lump of potato I'd been chewing.

This was why he'd switched to guard duty, and what he wanted from me, as Gerel had warned. He wanted to know what I knew about dragons and where they were. I would reveal nothing.

I went back to my meal, pushing food into my stomach even after I was full. If he got angry, this might be the last time I got to eat.

"Fine." Altan stood, his chair scraping the floor. A few nearby prisoners cringed, like he was about to beat them, but he just said, "Put your tray away. It's time to go."

Mealtime wasn't over, but I lurched to my feet and hurried to the window where Tirta waited, folds of silk clutched in her hands. "Is he looking?" I whispered as I put my tray on the rack.

She lowered the fabric. "Yes. Wait." She paused and peered around me. "He just started walking toward the door. No one is looking."

Quickly, I grabbed the folded cloth and shoved it down the front of my shirt. The silk was cool and smooth against my sweaty skin, a reminder of home.

"Let's *go*, Fancy," Altan called from his place by the door.

Tirta shot me a faint, worried look. "Be careful."

I adjusted the bundle under my baggy shirt. "See you tomorrow." Hopefully. After one more smile at my maybe-friend, I went to Altan at the door, and he guided me through the hall, almost companionable, as though we did this every day.

I supposed we would from now on, unless my silence changed his mind. But he didn't look angry or surprised. He probably thought he'd wear me down.

"You must be pretty sore." As if he was actually concerned.

I kept my face down like a good, humble prisoner. It wasn't hard to look pathetic and exhausted when every single muscle in my body trembled. I'd never been so sore in my life.

He scratched at the scab on his cheek. "If you need

something to help ease your pain, I can get it for you."

And have to reveal my secrets in trade? No.

As we came to the anteroom, I made my tone soft, adding notes of curiosity and concern. "What happened to your face?"

"I had a disagreement with someone." He deepened his voice and lifted his chin. Classic signs of boasting. "This was the least of the wounds inflicted."

Like I should be proud of him. If I were better at using Damina's gifts—if I'd received them at all—I'd have been able to say anything and it would have been the right thing. Instead, I had to search through all my potential responses to find something encouraging yet neutral. Something he'd believe. "It must have been quite the disagreement."

"Not everyone thinks it's worth having noorestones in the first level."

We descended the stairs (thirty, same as earlier) into my cellblock. The long hall was dim compared to the rest of the prison—only one noorestone to every three cells.

"I reminded them that those confined to darkness for extended periods of time will often go mad. Insanity makes for difficult workers when they move up to the second level."

How *kind* of him to look out for our sanity.

Then, we came to my cell, and he flipped through his keys to find the one for my door (fourth from the miniature mace). "Inside."

The cell felt smaller than it had this morning, but I

stepped inside and didn't flinch as the metal grille rang shut. The lock clicked. Trapped once more.

But this time, I held on to the last shreds of my dignity. I didn't cry out. I didn't rush toward the door.

Altan said, "Don't forget what we talked about at the table."

How could I?

"I don't like asking twice." His tone was a knife blade. "The next time we discuss this, there will be consequences if you refuse."

I wanted to ask what kind of consequences, but I didn't dare speak.

"Until tomorrow." And though Altan left, the knot in my chest did not. No matter how deeply I breathed, how many times I counted the metal bars across my cage, the knot squeezed.

"Why are you crying, Fancy?" Gerel frowned at me from across the hall. "Get a blister?"

"You were right," I whispered. "He wants something."

"I know I'm right. I usually am." She rolled her eyes and widened her stance for a series of squats. "Tell him or don't. Just stick with your decision."

Twenty times, she lowered and lifted herself. Gerel was smart. And strong. And she knew things about this place.

I needed to learn from her. I needed her to like me and help me survive.

But not right now. Right now, my whole body hurt. Maybe when I was stronger, I'd be able to work all day and then exercise with her, too. Not yet, though. After all, a *Drakontos mimikus* didn't imitate every part of another dragon all at once. They got the important, survival-pertinent parts first.

In the back of my cell, I pulled the dress from inside my shirt to inspect Tirta's work.

She'd folded the cloth. Not that folding meant much to silk; it slipped against itself with hardly a whisper, unspooling into a big square. Another length of no particular shape fell out and puddled onto the floor.

When I wrapped the square over my hair, it was the perfect size. And it might have been my imagination, but it seemed as though she'd tried to wash it. The remainder of my dress went inside my pillow, out of sight.

Across the hall, Gerel stretched her arm across her chest. "Your silent friend is trying to get your attention."

I crawled under my bed, muscles shivering with exertion. "What?" It came out colder than intended.

"Rude before. Sorry." He didn't *sound* sorry, just quiet. "You were kind."

"I'm trying to be, but you don't make it easy." Ugh. Even if it was the truth, I shouldn't say *that*. "It wasn't nice of me to accuse you of not being real."

Light under the bed was weak, but I could see pieces of his face through the hole: hollow cheeks, thick eyebrows, lidded eyes. In spite of the patchy stubble, he looked young, maybe my age, but it could have been the dim space. "I understand. I was rude too."

"Maybe we can start over?"

"Yes."

Idris was a serious, silent place. A place that valued politeness. I'd never been there, but Father had, and that was what he'd told me about the island. Very quiet. Very reserved. Very *secure*, when he'd stepped off the ship and had to be searched. He'd tried to joke with the inspectors that it must have been such a pain to search every single passenger from every ship, but he'd received only a glare. The entire exchange had been one-sided.

Even the Idrisi I'd met on Damina had always seemed uncomfortable, avoiding conversation. They thought the rest of us too free with our speech.

"There was a tremor," I said. "On Idris. Sixteen days ago."

"I know." His voice squeezed. So either someone had already told him, or he was a new prisoner, too. "People died."

"Were you there?"

"Yes." A great sadness filled that one word, shifting something inside of me. "Tried to help. Made it worse."

I knew how that felt. "When did you get here?"

"Day before you. Early morning. It was still dark."

He was just as new and uncertain as me. And maybe, like me, he hadn't done anything wrong. He'd said he'd tried to help. And the first thing he did for me was offer water.

What had I offered him?

Usually a smile made people like me, but here, I was dirty, tired, and Aaru couldn't even see me. Strip away the things that had made me special at home, and underneath I was just an awkward girl with panic attacks and a counting habit.

And reduced to this, I really needed my friends.

BEFORE

Ten Years Ago

It was dragons that brought Ilina and me together.

"Where should it go?" I lifted a new purple dragon, making the amethyst eyes sparkle. Its wings were delicate arcs, like it wanted to fly off.

Ilina considered my display case. "You could separate them by type. Glass here. Metal here. Stone back there. They could fight."

"We're building an army to battle Zara's unicorns. In-fighting is bad for morale."

She rearranged the ranks of figurines. "Put it there." She motioned to an empty spot near a blue, and there it was: a rainbow of dragons.

"Perfect." My collection was almost three dozen strong.

They were delicate, exquisitely made creatures. The stone took years to carve, or so I was told, and the metal came from the deepest mines on Bopha. It was an expensive collection, I was assured.

A hundred lumes for the pink sandstone, my first dragon; it was a birthday gift from my aunt, but Mother told me the price when she caught me flying it around my room.

Seventy-five lumes for the quartz, which I'd spotted in a shop window; the sandstone dragon needed a friend.

Two hundred eighty-seven lumes for the blown glass, this one translucent orange with a mesh of finely wrought gold scales across its body. Mother nearly swallowed her tongue when she saw the price, but Father bought it for me anyway.

After that, dragons began to arrive in small, silk-cushioned boxes, some from family, and others from the Luminary Council and important visitors. Zara had been jealous, so our parents started a collection of unicorns for her.

"There's a baby dragon in the sanctuary," Ilina said. "A yellow one."

"Really?" I hopped with excitement. "Can we see it? When did you get it? How big?"

"No visitors yet." We retreated to my bed, her sitting cross-legged, while I had to arrange my long, Idrisi cotton dress and sit with my feet to one side. Our parents had very different ideas about play clothes. "The adults either abandoned her or were killed. Someone heard her shrieking from her nest for three days before they sent for us."

"Poor baby!" I pressed my hands against my chest. "What species is she?"

"*Drakontos raptus*. She's as big as my palm."

"So cute." *Drakontos raptuses* weren't rare, as far as dragons went, but they were the smallest. "Imagine living five hundred years ago, when the big dragons all flew around the islands. *Drakontos rex*."

"Or *Drakontos titanus*!"

I let out a long sigh of wonder. "And Drakon Warriors rode them into battle. . . ."

Because of the Mira Treaty, it was illegal for *anyone* to ride dragons; the larger species were endangered and mostly lived in sanctuaries, and the smaller species were carefully monitored. All we had were dragons made of glass.

But Ilina was like me: we dreamed of something more.

CHAPTER EIGHT

A FAINT SENSE OF HESITATION PRESSED BETWEEN US before Aaru said, "Allies?"

"What?"

"Us. Allies."

Oh. He wanted us to be allies. That was better than enemies, but not as good as friends. Still, I wouldn't turn him down. "Allies have a shared goal. What is ours?"

He shifted closer to the hole, blocking all light from his side. The word puffed in like a cloud of wishes. "Freedom."

The word echoed around the small place beneath my bed. A promise. A hope. A dream. Just hearing the word aloud sent a pang of longing through me. I wanted freedom in the same way I wanted my next breath: an unspoken but constant desire.

"Mira." A note of annoyance skewed the way he said my name.

"Sorry," I muttered. "I was just thinking. About freedom."

He made a noise like he hadn't been aware I'd been capable of such an act. "Escape?" A series of taps on the floor accompanied the word. What *was* the tapping?

"You want to escape the Pit?"

"Yes."

"No one ever has." At least, as far as I knew. And I didn't need to escape. I just needed to survive long enough for the Luminary Council to realize their mistake and send for me.

Besides, he was an Idrisi boy who spent all his time under his bed. I was a Daminan girl with no practical survival knowledge whatsoever. What made him think we could get out of this place alive?

"Oh." Through the hole, I could just see him turning away, but not his expression or anything else useful. "Understand." He rolled onto his back and sighed. Then, like he wasn't quite aware of it, he beat a pattern onto his ribs. It didn't take long before he gained speed, the sounds coming so quick I could barely keep up.

There was almost a desperate quality to the rhythm, like he was trying to explain something but couldn't find the words.

"What is that?" I scooted toward the wall until I could

peer through the hole, catching only suggestions of a strong nose and prominent brow. He was still drumming on his chest, the same pattern over and over. He gave no indication whether he'd heard me. "Aaru?"

He stopped in the middle of a repeat, slamming his hands to his chest and holding so, so still. Like he was waiting to get caught.

I spoke gently. "What is that? The tapping, I mean."

A long breath heaved out of him. "Strength through silence."

"I see." But I didn't really. I knew that tense feeling of dreading trouble. I knew the compulsion that drove strange behavior. Counting. Thumping. But "strength through silence." I'd heard that phrase before. When?

During a (very short, curt) speech from a visiting Silent Brother. He'd been talking about the Mira Treaty and how it shouldn't just unite the islands against threats like the Algotti Empire, but encourage everyone to embrace their individual histories and cultures. On Idris, he'd said, the people found their strength through silence.

Aaru hadn't moved. "Idris's holy words."

"Oh." I hesitated.

"What?"

"I don't understand how silence can be strength." Mother always said our voices were power, and it was our duty to use them.

There was a pause where he might have muttered

about my confusion being so typical for a Daminan, but he didn't. "There is strength," he said slowly, "in knowing when to speak, and when to listen." His hands stayed on his chest, motionless. "And when to say nothing at all."

There was something in those words, some kind of pain, but it would be rude to keep digging. So I went back to his tapping. "You don't always do that pattern, though."

His fingers curled slightly, long arches over the fabric of his shirt. "You hear it?"

"Of course. These walls aren't soundproof." Everyone down the cellblock had probably heard.

"No—" He tapped twice, a long then short. "The patterns. You hear them."

"Of course," I said again.

His hand lifted just off his chest, like he was about to thump another pattern but then thought better of it.

"What is it? Why do you do it?"

"Quiet code." (Two slow, one fast, one slow. Pause. Slow, fast, slow, fast.)

"A code?" My sister had wanted us to share a secret code when we were younger, before she decided to hate me, but I'd never been good at remembering which letters exchanged for other letters.

"Idris language."

A language made of drumming different rhythms? That seemed complicated. "It's so you don't have to talk out loud?"

More tapping. (One slow, one fast, two slow.) "Yes."

How interesting. The benefit to using a tapped code on an island where silence was valued most of all—would be enormous. Maybe that was why Father had assumed no one spoke, not even to one another. They could have been communicating in a different way.

"I wish I could learn something like that."

"Not supposed to teach others."

That hadn't been what I'd meant.

"Already in prison." He turned his head—the tendons in his neck shifted, but that was all I could see—and sighed. His chest moved up and down. "What else can they do?"

Plenty, but suddenly I couldn't risk him changing his mind. It seemed ridiculous, wanting this code. It would take me ages to learn it. I wasn't smart. But I'd never gotten to have a secret language with my sister, and learning the quiet code would give me somewhere to put all my anxious energy.

"Allies need communication," he went on. It was the most I'd ever heard him speak, and it was definitely for my benefit. This was a negotiation. The quiet code in exchange for an alliance.

"That's true. And we *are* allies, right?"

He made a short, pleased noise. "We both escape?"

"We both escape." I didn't know what he'd done to get here, so maybe this was a huge mistake, but I needed help. I needed an ally. When my parents had me freed, I'd make sure they had Aaru released, too.

"Ready to learn?" he asked.

"Right now?"

"Have something better to do?"

I supposed not. "I'm a terrible student," I warned.

"I'm a good teacher."

Hopefully patient, too.

"Taught four little sisters, brother, and neighbor. Can teach you."

He seemed really sure of himself. "All right," I said.

"Get comfortable."

I grabbed my blanket and pillow and scooted toward the hole again. It wasn't remotely comfortable, but after a day of cleaning, nothing less than my own bed, with its feather mattress, silk sheets, and cloudlike pillow, was going to satisfy my aching body.

"It's very old. The code." As he spoke, he thumped his fingers against his chest, using both hands as though his ribs were a drum. But in spite of telling the story in two ways, he seemed to settle into it. Like he'd told it a hundred times. "Older than the Fallen Isles."

Then it was ancient. People had settled on the Fallen Isles over two thousand years ago—at least, that was what we'd learned in school. The mainland had a much longer history, but it was hard to fathom something so big.

"Two parts: long and short. Drag finger for tapping longs. Combinations make letters. Pause between letters. Long pause between words."

"One letter at a time?" It seemed like a lot to keep up

with, from the first letter to the last of a long sentence. I couldn't imagine keeping track of all that.

"Seems intimidating?" He almost sounded amused. "Toddlers learn quiet code and spoken words. You can, too."

"Idrisi toddlers can spell?"

He made a soft, almost chuckling noise, and quickly drummed his fingers against his ribs. Not in the code, but maybe like a laugh. "No. Little ones learn entire quiet code words with corresponding spoken words. When they're older, they learn to spell. Same as spoken words and reading."

That made sense, I supposed. Just, reading seemed a lot faster than listening to a series of sounds. But maybe it would be easier with practice. "Why do you use the quiet code?"

He hesitated.

"Do you have to? Is it a rule there?" Why did they even teach spoken language if they had a quiet code? Well, to communicate with the rest of the world, probably, but—*Idris is isolated.* That was the first thing we learned in school about the Isle of Silence. Most people there—with the exception of political figures and people who worked in shipping—never saw the outside world.

I added prisoners to that list of exceptions.

"Sometimes it's choice. Communicate without others knowing." He thumped the words against his chest. "Quiet code doesn't need sound. Flashes of light. Blinking.

Movement. Before my—" His voice caught. The thumping stopped.

I waited.

Nothing.

"Aaru?" If he'd been Ilina or Hristo, I'd have reached through the hole and touched his arm. But we were strangers, so I huddled by our shared wall and whispered, "It's all right. You can skip it, if you don't want to talk about it."

A shiver ran through him. "Sorry." (Three quick taps.) "Skip the bad parts."

He gave a jerky nod. "Parents held hands. Tapped on fingers. Wrists. They talked about my siblings and me. In front of us."

Had my parents ever held hands? I couldn't remember. But I imagined what it must be like to share that with someone. What an intimate mode of communication.

"That sounds nice," I said, not quite smothering the longing in my voice.

"Yes." (One long, one short, two long.)

"You said sometimes using the code isn't a choice."

"Rules. Many rules."

"Like what?"

"I love Idris. And hate it." His voice grew even softer. "Rather just teach."

"All right." If anyone understood loving and hating something, I did. "Sorry. I didn't mean to intrude."

"It's fine." He waited a few moments, as though gathering his thoughts. "Ready?"

"Yes."

"First letter." He tapped twice: short, long.

I repeated. That wasn't so bad.

But he quickly moved on to the next letter, and then the one after that, and through the entire alphabet. I struggled to mimic him, to make my letters just like his, but there were so many to remember.

Still, the one thing my counting habit had given me was a fair memory for numbers. Not adding or subtracting them, but I knew there'd been fifty fishing boats out the day my life changed, fifteen columns in Lex's cave, and fourteen total noorestones in this cellblock. I could remember what I counted.

"Now," Aaru said, once we'd been through every letter five times. "I say a letter, you tap it."

"Are you sure?" I frowned. This was moving awfully fast.

"Am sure." Without giving me a chance to ready myself, he began naming letters randomly.

I searched my mind for the appropriate combination of taps and drags. It was harder than just going through the alphabet, and he didn't bother to tell me whether I answered correctly, but at least he wasn't criticizing my every move.

Still, it was only a matter of time before he realized what a failure of a student I was.

"Moving on," he said.

"Already?" Didn't he believe in breaks?

"Common words and phrases," he said. "*Yes, no, I don't know*—those get shortened. First letters usually."

That actually made sense. "All right. But what if phrases have the same first letters?"

"Context." Like that had been obvious.

This was more complicated than I'd expected, though I should have known when he'd called it a language. Two years ago, Mother had enrolled me in an Ancient Isles language class, but had been forced to pull me out the first day when I'd shown no talent.

Just remembering her disappointment made the shame burn through me again. The last thing I wanted was to shatter this tentative alliance with Aaru because I wasn't smart enough. I had to get out of this. "I was wrong about being able to learn the quiet code. I'm just wasting your time."

"Prison, Mira. I have time." He turned onto his side, blocking most of the light as he faced me. Even in the near darkness, there was something gentle about the look in his eyes. "You can do this."

His encouragement made everything worse. "That's quite the declaration from someone who doesn't know me at all."

He drummed his fingers on the floor, just once. Like a faint chuckle. "Will prove it. Tap the letters."

"All of them?"

Four taps: one long, one short, two longs. ::**Yes.**::

Slowly, with long pauses between each letter, I tapped the alphabet onto the floor.

"Now Mira," he said.

"Now Mira what?"

"Tap your name."

My whole face felt like it was on fire as, even more slowly, I tapped out my name. ::**Mira**.::

"Yes," he whispered. "Want a challenge?"

As if this whole thing hadn't been a challenge. "All right."

He rolled onto his back again. There was just enough light that I caught the way his mouth lifted in the corner. "Islands."

"The islands? All of them?"

"All seven," he confirmed.

Which meant he wouldn't let me count Darina and Damyan as one. That was a lot of tapping.

When I didn't start right away, Aaru said, "And attributes."

I hadn't registered the knot of anxiety fading, but it slammed back into my chest like a punch. My hands twitched, and my face and neck burned, and my heart raced so, so fast. Aaru was trying to shame me. To show me how awful I was at his quiet code. This was my own fault. I should have known better than to think I might be able to learn something so complicated.

"Mira?"

I didn't remember pulling back and curling my whole body into a ball, but I must have at some point. My head pounded as I looked up.

Aaru peered through the hole, his fingers bent over the sides. He was so close to the wall, blocking the light. Only the whites of his eyes showed. "What's wrong?"

"I can't do this. I'm not smart enough."

He studied me while my heart pounded in my ears. Loud gongs only I could hear. This was humiliating. Here I was in prison, curled up on the floor under my bed, and making a fool of myself in front of some boy who'd taught his little sisters the quiet code but couldn't teach me.

"Islands, Mira."

"I—"

"Mira."

And now I was frustrating him. How wonderful.

A giant hole opened inside me. If only I could fold up and fall in.

"Mira." He didn't leave room for argument.

I could hardly breathe around the panic building. How was I supposed to focus enough to tap all those letters? But it would be dark soon. And the screaming man would scream. And Aaru wouldn't be able to hear if I finished the islands and their attributes or not.

I pressed my palm to the floor, imagining I could push all the small jerks and twitches of panic into the stone. Out of me. Away from me. One breath. Two breaths. Three.

"All right." My voice was ragged and hollow. "I'll try."

"When you are ready," he said, as though nothing embarrassing had just happened. As though he hadn't just witnessed a minor meltdown because of a secret code.

His kindness made me want to try harder—to get this right—so I cleared my thoughts as best I could and began.

The letters came slowly. Haltingly. I counted out each letter as I tapped the floor.

::Anahera asks answers.

Bopha bleeds blackness.

Darina and Damyan dance duo.

Harta hates harm.

Idris is isolated.

Khulan can kill.::

My heart thundered as I finished the final letter. I didn't really want to know, but still I asked, "How did I do?" He'd watched my face the whole time. I'd watched my hand.

His voice came warm. Kind. "Good, Mira."

That was hard to believe, but I caught a sliver of his expression as he pulled away from the hole. He was smiling. At me. "Really?"

"Very good," he whispered.

Just as I was registering those words—*very good*—again, and how strange they sounded when directed at me, the noorestones went dark.

Complete blackness flooded the cellblock, as ink-thick as the first night and the night before. I closed my eyes against it, my whole body tensing in anticipation.

Down the hall, the screaming man whimpered.

In the cell next to me, Aaru scrambled. For his blanket, maybe. Some way to cover his ears. That was a good idea. I wrapped my threadbare blanket around my head once more, over the thin layer of silk covering my hair.

Just as I tied the first knot in the blanket, the man began to scream into the darkness.

BEFORE

Sarai 15, 2204 FG

IT WAS TIME TO GET TO WORK.

Ilina already had horses waiting for us—stubborn mares who'd grown up around dragons and wouldn't shy at the sight of a *Drakontos maximus* on the horizon. Some people thought it was cruel to keep horses here, but the sanctuary was huge and we needed faster modes of transportation than our feet for even simple excursions. There were plenty of times Ilina and her family had camped overnight on their way to dragons' territories. (Mother had never allowed me to join them, of course.)

Crystal and LaLa took to the sky as we rode past the enormous collection of spindly, first-century ruins. The pair of dragons wove between the spires of pale stone, all broken arches and crumbling towers. Embedded noorestones glowed a faint blue, even after thousands of years. They should have darkened long ago, and while no one really knew why they still shone, the popular theory was that the ruins themselves formed some kind of conduit to the gods, which kept the crystals charged.

Quite unbecomingly, dragons liked to lick these noorestones.

The eight of us—three humans, three horses, and two dragons—moved west, uphill and toward the Skyfell Mountains. "We're checking on Lex today," Ilina said. "And we'll come back the long way to check on Tower, too."

Hristo was staring at the back of Ilina's head as she led the way. "You sound worried."

She glanced over her shoulder, and though she forced calm into her tone, I could hear the concern now, too. "It's nothing really. Probably just the earthquake."

"What is it?" I asked.

"Astrid." Ilina directed her mount around a creeping passionflower vine, heavy with pink and purple blooms. Butterflies danced through the sweet scent. "She wasn't home last night when I made my rounds near Red Cliff."

"You think she left her cave because of the quake?" I asked. "She knew it was coming?"

Ilina nodded. "Probably. As sensitive as the little dragons are to movement in the ground, the big dragons are even more. Astrid probably went somewhere more stable to wait it out. I'm sure she's back now."

"Maybe we should check," Hristo said. "Once we're finished visiting Lex and Tower."

I nodded, wishing I'd thought of it first. Hristo always knew the right thing to say. It was an annoying habit that had earned him a string of several short-term romances, which often ended because of his obligation as my bodyguard. That, and the girls assumed that he and I were romantically involved.

We most certainly were not.

Ilina flashed a smile over her shoulder, and Crystal gave a throaty chirrup. "That's a good idea, if we have time."

We made the rest of the trek up to the territory of a *Drakontos rex* named Lex. When Ilina and I were younger, we'd composed a song about her, which heavily relied on the rhyme of *rex* and *Lex*. Though we'd tried to persuade Hristo to sing it with us, he insisted professional guards didn't sing. We found out later that he was just self-conscious about his voice—not that we ever confronted him about it.

"There is a big dragon whose name is Lex," I whisper-sang.

Ilina snorted a laugh. "Surprise, surprise, she's a *Drakontos rex*."

"Her hot breath of fire's up with the best."

"Surprise, surprise, she's a *Drakontos rex*!"

Hristo groaned. "Not that again."

Ilina and I grinned at each other, the unease of earlier

momentarily forgotten. But then we reached a post with a horse carved into the wood. We dismounted, tethered the horses, and walked the rest of the way.

The scent of smoke billowed from the entrance, which rose in a graceful arc ten times Hristo's height. Like most of the bigger species, Lex had made the cave by blasting flame into a cliff face, hot enough to melt the very stone into hot rock.

It wasn't a fast process. Normal dragon fire didn't reliably liquefy rock, but they could eat dragonroot to manipulate their second lungs into producing a hotter fire. *Much* hotter. But it was an unhealthy diet to maintain, so they saved it for special occasions. Like creating living accommodations.

It had taken Lex three years to build this cave. She'd chosen a good spot, too, carving into a protrusion of rock that allowed a curved entrance so the wind wouldn't zip in and disturb her in the deeper caverns.

Ripples of obsidian and basalt flowed down the sides of the opening and down the hill, almost concealed now by the moss, vines, and ferns that had crept back over the years.

LaLa climbed up my arm and perched on my shoulder, making herself small against the curve of my neck. Crystal had taken a similar position on Ilina as my friend whistled for Lex to come out.

"It's all right." I petted the soft membrane of LaLa's golden wing. All the sanctuary dragons knew not to hunt the smaller species, but thousands of years of instinct didn't just vanish because they lived in the same place now. Dragons—big dragons—were very territorial.

We waited for the low rumble and scrape of scales on stone, but no sound came from the cave.

The three of us exchanged worried glances. Astrid going missing was one thing. She might have been out hunting, or avoiding a rockslide, or perhaps there wasn't enough prey in her territory anymore. She might have left the sanctuary, as unlikely as that seemed; the wall afforded them safety from poachers and thoughtless humans.

But Lex, too? They were on opposite sides of the sanctuary.

"Maybe she left because of the earthquake, too?" But even I didn't believe it.

Hristo didn't take his eyes off the cave opening. "Wouldn't she be back by now?"

"Probably."

We were all quiet for a few minutes, listening to the wind in the trees and the twitter of birds. This peace was an illusion. Something was very wrong here.

Ilina took a single, decisive step toward the opening. "All right. We're going in."

CHAPTER NINE

WHEN THE SCREAMING FADED INTO DESPERATE whimpers, Aaru leaned toward our tiny window again. "That one is Hurrok. From Bopha, I think."

"He's scared of the dark?"

"Must be. Aren't you afraid?"

"I don't like the dark." The disorientation. The uncertainty. The feeling of isolation. But Aaru's quiet voice felt like an anchor.

"Sisters are afraid of storms," he said. "Alya most of all."

I wished for a storm now, something to break up this darkness. I'd listen to the thunder, the rain, the wind hissing through the trees. We had wonderful storms in Crescent Prominence. Storms that set wind chimes clanging and palm trees whipping and my mind soaring with possibility. Dragons loved storms like that, because the crackle of electricity in the air ignited the spark gland at the roof of their mouths; they enjoyed it the same way cats enjoyed getting their ears scratched.

Here, we had only darkness.

"Do you help Alya when she's scared?"

Aaru gave a soft, affirming sound. "Of course. I tell her stories."

"What kind?" My voice trembled.

"Listen." He began to tap, but I couldn't keep up. Knowing what I wanted to say and understanding what he was saying—those were two different skills.

Still, I counted the beats, and the rhythm helped push back the penetrating night. Even though I couldn't understand what he was saying, I knew there were words in there. A story meant for me.

IT GREW INTO a routine.

My mind dutifully tracked every step I took, and I began to get a better idea of the Pit as I cleaned my way through hallways (footprints, sometimes blood), interrogation rooms (always blood, often vomit), and a space that might have been for recreation for the second- or third-level prisoners. There, I dusted tables, picked up tattered books, and scrubbed blood off a punching bag.

By cell-cleaning day, I was far better at using the mop and bucket when they made it to my space. I scrubbed as best I could, considering the dirty water, and emptied the bucket into my sewage hole to clear away some of the smell.

Then I waited, listening to the other prisoners leave and return, until a guard approached Gerel's cell. She slid off her bed and followed him—and no one came to get me.

Another decan without a bath? I'd been able to wash up here and there, thanks to working, but there was no substitution for a real bath. Not that I expected citrus and honey soap, or soft towels, or coconut milk for my hair. But I'd have liked the chance to wash more than my face and arms.

Gerel came back and took her second food for the day, not bothering to look at me as I sat on my bench, puddling into a filthy smear of despair. This wasn't fair. Not at all.

Then, Altan stepped in front of my cell. "Ready for a bath, Fancy?"

I jumped to my feet, pathetically excited.

"Bring your laundry."

I tucked my pillow and blanket under one arm and stepped out. But instead of turning right like we usually did—toward the mess hall—Altan motioned me left, which took me past the other prisoners.

At Aaru's cell, I glanced in, but he was perched on his bed with his knees up to his chest, his forehead rested on folded arms. Tall. Lanky. Not soft. The cup sat in the center of his space, catching the drip from his ceiling. After that first day, I hadn't let him give me any more water; I got enough, because I was cleaning.

Down the hall, I glanced through iron grilles to see the tattooed man lying on the floor and muttering prayers to his god: Hurrok, maybe. A woman petted the somewhat clean walls of her cell, and another man was shoving fistfuls of air into his mouth as though faced with an incredible—and invisible—banquet.

My dislike of them had thinned over my ten days here, and I suspected that at least two weren't (necessarily) criminals, just ill. They didn't belong here any more than I did. Mostly, I wished they'd shut up and let me sleep when the noorestones went dark.

Out of the cellblock, Altan took me past several familiar corridors. Numbers floated in the back of my head: steps, halls, intersections.

"You'll get half an hour," Altan said as we came to a large stone door. The arch above it bore the customary crossed maces, but these were made of inlaid gold, with gilt flames circling Khulan's holy symbol. "Everything you need is in there."

He wasn't coming in with me? That was a relief.

"This is the only door into this chamber," he said. "I'll be out here the whole time. Unless you want me to help you, of course."

My stomach turned and I pulled my belongings over my chest. Gerel's assurance that none of the warriors would take an unwilling partner rattled through my head again. I had to believe her.

I went inside. Alone.

It wasn't a large space—maybe ten steps deep and fifteen wide, and most of that was dominated by a steaming pool of sulfur-smelling water, lit by ten blue noorestones embedded in the walls. Four benches stood around the pool, with thin gray towels, baskets of muddy-looking soap, and piles of rags. There was even a comb, though the teeth were dull and three were missing.

One bench had clothes and a blanket drying over the back.

A figure pulled out of the shadows, a towel wrapped tight around her body, and her braids piled into a bun on top of her head. "Hot springs." Tirta loosened her death grip on the towel. "There's a whole series of them down here. This is the smallest and smelliest, so they sectioned it off for prisoners."

Actual hot water. I wanted to dive right in.

"I'm glad it's just you," she went on. "They try to keep it to a few prisoners at a time—so we don't conspire against them, you see—but you never know who you'll be stuck bathing with."

"So we're safe in here?" I asked.

"As safe as we are anywhere in the Pit." She draped her towel over the nearest bench and stepped into the water. "Do your laundry first, that way it can dry some before you have to put it back on."

I followed her advice, unloading my belongings. "How long have you been here?"

"Just a few minutes. I do my laundry fast."

Apparently. "I meant in the Pit. As a prisoner." Hopefully that wasn't too rude to ask.

"Oh. I'm not sure." She scrubbed water over her face, careful not to get her hair wet. "Time gets confusing down here. No sun. No proper calendar for prisoners."

She didn't *know*? It must have been a long time.

"Well, today is the tenth of Zabel. Just two decans until the Hallowed Restoration." Those were the five days at the end of every year. Six days every fourth year. The Hallowed Restoration was supposed to be for reflecting on the previous twelve months and looking forward to the new year.

"Oh, I love the Hallowed Restoration." She smiled dimly. "We don't get to celebrate here, of course, but my family lights remembrance candles every evening, praying for health and guidance. Sometimes we exchange gifts."

Lots of families had sweet traditions like that. I usually spent hours under the mistress of beauty's brushes, followed by thirty minutes of time alone in the parlor with my family, during which Mother would tell all of us how we'd disappointed her throughout the year and how we could improve over the next. Then we often accepted invitations from Elbena Krasteba; the Luminary Councilor was—by general agreement—the best hostess. Sometimes her gatherings went on until dawn.

Mother probably would have a *lot* to say about how I'd disappointed her this year.

I turned my attention back to Tirta. "Why are most

of the prisoners our age?" I'd seen a few adults in my cellblock and in the mess hall, but not as many as I'd have thought. "Do adults not get sentenced to the Pit?"

Her expression darkened. "Oh, adults are sent here too, but they *expect* things, you know? And then they die. We adapt better."

I didn't want to adapt. I wanted to go home.

But instead of saying so, I scrubbed my clothes and belongings clean, using the foul-smelling soap and a slanted area in the pool with several ridges carved into it. Not that I'd known how to wash my clothes until this very instant; I followed Tirta's instructions.

"You're going to do well here." Tirta wrapped herself in her towel again. "You work hard. You behave. I can't help but be curious how someone like *you* ended up in the Pit."

I wouldn't tell. Not even Tirta. Not yet, anyway. "I'm sure everyone wonders what a Hartan girl did to get here, too." I smiled as warmly as possible so she'd know I wasn't trying to be mean, just making a point. "We're both odd here, aren't we?"

With my laundry finished and hanging on a bench to dry—though how anything could dry in this steamy room was a mystery—I pulled up my twists and stepped into the water.

It was as I worked the soap down my arms and legs that I discovered the firmness in my muscles. Sarannai had said I was *soft* that first day of work, but after a decan, my fingers grazed the new ridge of muscle along my upper arm, a cord of strength down my forearms.

Yes, I'd done all the training exercises Instructor Boyan had given me. Yes, I'd regularly doubled as a perch for a small dragon. But I'd never been strong before. Hristo and Ilina would be proud.

"Gerel is in your cellblock, isn't she?" Tirta asked. "What do you think about her?"

"She's difficult to like," I said carefully. "But she knows about the Pit. She warned me about Sarannai." And about Altan.

He hadn't asked me about dragons again. Not since that day in the mess hall. Nevertheless, the threat of consequences haunted me. I couldn't begin to guess what he'd do if I continued to refuse. But how could I tell him something so important?

I just had to hold out until my parents saved me.

"Be careful of Gerel." Tirta picked a piece of dirt out from under her ragged nails. "Don't trust her."

"Why?" Gossip was the Daminan way. Everyone had real secrets—like my counting—and people worked very hard to keep those hidden, but most were merely illusionary secrets. So Tirta sitting there, wanting to tell me something about Gerel—I couldn't resist.

"I heard she tried to destroy the Heart of the Great Warrior and everyone inside it. Prisoners. Trainees. Warriors."

That seemed . . . impossible. The Heart was huge. And underground. And all stone. Not even a *Drakontos titanus* would be able to burn it down. "How?" I whispered. Not that I wanted to destroy the Heart. I just wanted to get away from it.

"I don't know." Tirta shook her head. "Sometimes I wish she'd succeeded. In my dark moments, you know? But you can make a life here if you work hard. It's not fun, but it's a life and it's better than nothing."

I hoped I never became so accepting of my incarceration.

After I climbed out of the water and dried off, she motioned to my hair. "Did you do your twists?"

I shook my head and pushed away the memory of my last visit with Ilina. Missing her would choke me.

"Do you know how?"

"No." At home, Krasimir had visited once a decan to wash and style my hair. My maid, Sylva, took care of it the rest of the time. "I mean, I know how to braid and twist, but I've never done my own."

"I can teach you. We might not always get paired and it's important to keep doing things here that make you feel human. Even if it's just your hair."

A bubble of warmth filled me. She understood.

"Some prisoners get their hair shorn like the warriors so they don't have to take care of it. But I always thought that was too much like giving up."

I nodded, then held still as she bent close to inspect Ilina's work.

"Whoever did this was smart. It'll last a long time." She

patted my shoulder and moved away. "Just don't soak your hair, don't undo the twists, and try not to touch any of it."

"Ever?" I couldn't stop the horror in my voice.

She laughed a little. "When you can't stand it anymore, or the twists start coming unraveled, I'll help you do it again. Until then, just scrub your scalp a little."

Before I was ready, Altan and another guard strode into the room. "Time's up, Fancy."

Grudgingly, I shoved my damp belongings into my pillow once more and looked to Tirta just as she thrust a small pile of rags into my hands. "For . . . you know. Bleeding."

I hadn't even thought about that yet, but now I couldn't stop wondering what I'd do with the dirty rags and how I'd get more—or if I was expected to wash them in the bath area, too. That could *not* be sanitary.

Tirta and I left the bathing room, and behind us, the guards carried on a discussion about unrest . . . somewhere.

"It's bad," the other guard said. "And it'll probably get worse before they ask any of us to go help."

"People setting other people on fire is pretty bad," Altan said.

People *burning others*? I wanted to ask what was happening, but didn't dare speak.

"Certainly not the worst thing people have ever done, though." The second guard reached forward and shoved Tirta. She stumbled, but caught herself and resumed walking without so much as a whimper. "Think we'll get any of the burners here?"

"Probably a few. Those the Twilight Senate want punished the most. They'll probably just put the rest to death."

The Twilight Senate—that was the governing body on Bopha, the Isle of Shadow. I hadn't heard of anything happening there, but I'd been rather focused on my own problems.

"What about the Idrisi?" asked the other guard. "Think we'll get more?"

"I doubt it." Altan sounded smug. Like he knew everything. "The Silent Brothers deal with their own. I hear they're putting the rioters to death. Public execution. The boy is an exception."

Riots. On Idris? Was it because of the tremor?

Altan made it sound like Aaru had been involved with the riots, but I couldn't imagine how. He was so gentle.

Then, Tirta's guard pulled her down another hall, but before she disappeared, she shot a pale smile and trailed her fingers down her braids—like a reminder to keep any shreds of humanity I could.

A thread of warmth bloomed in my heart. *The Book of Love* declared the importance of close friends no fewer than seventy times. Those passages detailed how we should treat our friends, how we should appreciate them, how we should put their needs above our own.

In the first level, Gerel still treated me like a disobedient child. Aaru, though we talked and tapped every night, maintained that we were allies; our conversations revolved around the quiet code, the layout of the Pit, what kind of supplies we'd need for our escape. (I hadn't told him that my family would get me out soon. Any day now.)

But Tirta was different. With her, I could feel Darina and Damyan's blessing. She wanted to be my friend as much as I wanted to be hers.

The warm feeling cooled as Altan shifted his attention to me. "I hope the last several days have given you enough time to think about what I asked about before."

I glanced around the hall; we were completely alone.

"I can be a good friend to you, Mira. Or I can be your most ruthless enemy."

"And you'll leave it up to me to decide which you become?"

A heavy frown darkened his face. "This is not the time for imprudence. I know you have information. Be a good girl and tell me what you wouldn't shut up about before."

He made it sound like I'd gone around telling everyone what I'd discovered. If only I had. Instead, I'd confronted the Luminary Council about their traitorous actions and they'd responded by sending me here.

"I know it has to do with dragons." His voice deepened. "And why there are so many missing."

My jaw ached from clenching, but I wouldn't tell him anything about the Crescent Prominence sanctuary. I wouldn't.

"You know where they are."

Blood pulsed through my ears, rushing, roaring, overwhelming. "I won't tell you anything." My own voice sounded far away, and in the back of my mind, I remembered again that we were alone in this hall. He could do anything. He could beat me and there would be no one to witness or help.

"All right." The tangle of my anxiety muted his words, but he didn't sound angry. His face—those hooded eyes, that scar-touched brown skin—seemed eerily calm, considering I'd refused him twice now. "Let's go. Just remember, I offered you a chance."

He hauled open the door to the first-level cellblock and ushered me inside.

Something had changed.

I paused, earning a shove forward, and stumbled farther inside as I realized the problem. Silence.

The first level was usually quiet, most people focused inward, but there was always some kind of audible evidence of their presence: sighing, scuffling, coughing. *Something*. But now it was so silent I might have wondered if I'd suddenly gone deaf—but I could hear *my* footfalls just fine. And Altan's.

I glanced at him, questioning.

He acted like nothing was wrong.

As I approached the first cell (seven steps), I half expected the man inside to be dead. Just one body on the floor. But there was no one.

No one in the next cell, either. All nine cells that had previously been occupied were empty. No Aaru, no Gerel.

Forty cells. Zero people.

Altan opened my cell. The ring of iron was horribly loud.

"Where is everyone?" My question sounded too loud, too.

"Gone."

"When are they coming back?"

"Get inside the cell."

My heart pounded. I didn't want to confine myself to that small space again, especially after the taste of freedom in the bath, but the baton hung from his hip, and the crossed maces on his uniform were a constant reminder that he was stronger and faster. Even the best fighter from another island couldn't defeat a warrior while on Khulan.

So I went inside my cell and dropped my bundle onto my bed.

"Mira Minkoba." My full name sounded strange.

I wanted to say something smart, but I couldn't shake the sensation of something awful creeping up around me, so I just looked at him.

His face was hard. Lean. Predatory. His narrowed eyes met mine as he said, "I hope you use this time to reconsider your refusal." Then, he tossed a small sack at my feet and shut the door—a second too-loud ringing.

His boots thumped down the hall, and he was gone.

I was alone.

Off-balance at this sudden isolation, I picked up the bag and took it to my bed. There was food inside, and a container of water.

I couldn't believe he'd moved everyone away.

At least, I hoped he'd only moved them.

What if he'd killed them?

This was because of me. Because I'd refused to give him the locations of the missing dragons.

My mind boiled over with visions of Gerel fighting for her life, Aaru being slaughtered, and Tirta being led from her bath to her death. And what about the others? I could almost hear Hurrok's howling, crying, begging for mercy. . . .

A *slam* echoed down the hall. I jumped, spilling my food across the floor.

Just as I bent to gather everything, the noorestones went out.

Darkness.

Complete darkness.

And silence.

No whimpering. No screaming. No tapping from the next cell over.

The panic rushed in, overwhelming; I waited and waited, counting seconds and minutes and hours.

The lights did not come on again.

PART TWO

AFFINITY FOR DRAGONS

CHAPTER TEN

THE DARKNESS WENT ON AND ON.

Long after the first wave of panic passed and a constant, low-grade terror settled in, the darkness persisted. It became a force, a pressure that squeezed me in on myself, until I awakened huddled under the bed, praying for the light to return.

But even the hole between my cell and Aaru's became a threat in the dark. I could *feel* the emptiness of his space leaking through to mine, swallowing my existence.

Soon, I would not be real.

MY FOOD WENT quickly.

I gathered everything as soon as I regained my sense of self. Before-the-Pit Mira wouldn't have thought to do that.

She'd have stayed perfectly still, wondering if the noore-stones were broken, assuming the lights would return. But In-the-Pit Mira knew better.

The Pit had made me hungry. Sharp. Aware of how quickly a vague sense of wanting to eat could turn into hollowed-out agony.

My food had scattered everywhere, so each expedition into the cell was slow and careful, because if I crushed anything, I might render it inedible. And I needed every bite. I would never again waste food, as I'd done my first day.

Using the bed as an anchor, I reached out, patted the floor, and found an apple. I stuffed it into my bag. Then I repeated the process, shuffling forward until I'd checked as far as the opposite wall. I retreated to the bed to begin again.

In the end, I had four apples, two small loaves of bread, a big wedge of cheese, seven pieces of dried meat, and a single container of water.

This was more food than usually came in the bag. And that meant . . . What? How long was I supposed to make it last?

I took my bag and hid under my bed, as if the darkness couldn't reach me there.

OUTSIDE, ON THE surface, the moons and stars kept the true darkness at bay. Even on the rare nights both moons were new, stars still littered the black sky with silver and gold. On those nights, the faint pink shapes of faraway darkdust glowed a little brighter.

Underground, the moons and stars blocked from view by layers and layers of earth, there was no ambient light. The noorestones were out, and the darkness was complete.

Five things I learned about the dark:

1. *There was something physical about complete blackness, like the absence of light granted extra substance to the air around me.*

2. *The inability to see made even a formerly known room suddenly unknown. It challenged the dimensions of the space, obscured everything, so that even without moving, I was lost.*

3. *Without the light to show me where my body ended and the rest of the world began, sometimes I felt as though I'd expanded to take up the entire cell. Other times, I felt as though the darkness shrank me and I became smaller and smaller, ready to collapse in on myself. Most of the time, it seemed as though there might not be a firm boundary between where I ended and the darkness began; we'd melted together.*

4. *Darkness had a sinister way about it. Any noise, even my own breath, became a threat. Every time I faded into sleep, I lurched awake once more, startled by the sensation of the darkness devouring me.*

5. *I hated it.*

I spent as much time as possible cataloging my thoughts on darkness, organizing them in my mind to hold the terror at bay. But as time crept by—at a pace I couldn't discern without light—the pages of my mental lists began to scatter apart. Thirst and hunger made it hard to think.

I tried to be frugal, nibbling here and there, taking tiny sips of water only when thirst threatened to overtake me.

Now, I reached inside my bag and found only a sliver of cheese and one apple core. I ate the cheese. I sucked the remaining fruit off the core.

And that was it. The food was gone. The water was gone.

My mind scrambled for lists and numbers, but a fog drifted through my thoughts, preventing movement. Connection.

I tried to sleep, and I must have lost consciousness for a while, because when I awakened, my body screamed with thirst. I could feel my skin cracking and crumbling. I could feel my tongue scraping the back of my throat. I could feel my eyelids fall like sand over my eyes.

In the unwavering silence, I heard the drops of water falling from Aaru's ceiling and landing with a faint *plop* into his cup. Eventually the sound of the water drops changed, deepening as the cup grew fuller, and then the hiss of a small splash followed.

The cup was full. Overflowing. I shoved my hand through the hole like I'd really be able to grab the water. I shoved my arm, even my shoulder, as far through the hole as I could reach, but my own body blocked me. If my arms were longer. If I were tiny. If I were able to change into smoke and float through the hole and dive into the water . . .

A hysterical giggle fell out of me. If I could change into smoke, I'd be able to escape the Pit, guards none the wiser.

As quickly as the laugh happened, I stopped it. I buried it. My heart thrummed in my ears, but that was an inside-me sound. It wouldn't break the silence. Not the way a laugh would. Besides, who laughed in prison?

A headache raged behind my eyes, and deep, aching thirst festered inside me. Hunger, too, but mostly that desperate thirst for the water in the next cell. It was there. So close. With only a wall between that cup and me.

Why hadn't my parents freed me yet? They should have been working night and day to secure my release, and how hard could it be to convince the Luminary Council of my importance?

What if Mother and Father weren't even trying?

What if I really was meant to stay here forever?

Give me peace, I prayed. *Give me grace.* And then: *Save me, Darina. Save me, Damyan. Cela, cela.*

But the only answer was the smothering dark.

I CLAWED AT the wall, desperate for the water on the other side.

I passed out, exhausted from my struggles.

I counted my own raspy breaths until even my numbers failed me because they, too, needed to be fed. Sometimes, I dreamed of rushing rivers. Wide rivers. With giant green plants growing on the banks and thousands of fish swimming along the current. And a chef to . . . do whatever it was that people did to prepare fish for eating.

Distantly, I was bored. Of not moving. Of not seeing. Of not hearing. Even if I'd had food or water left, I'd have devoured it all just for something to do. Sometimes, I felt like I was floating.

A day or a million years after Altan locked me in the dark, I finally heard a noise. A sharp *clang* of metal smacking metal.

Alertness flooded my body. I tensed, cocked my head, and listened around the thud of my own heartbeat, but the sound didn't return.

Perhaps I'd imagined it. Mother always said what an imagination I had.

Wait. No, she didn't say that about me. She said that about Zara, her favorite daughter. Zara with the imagination. Zara with the perfect grades. Zara who got to stay out late and could spend entire days in her nightgown if she didn't have anything better to do.

Zara who didn't interfere where she didn't belong. Zara who hadn't ended up in the Pit. Zara who was probably eating an enormous meal right now, of big, flaky cloudfish seasoned with a thousand different spices, sitting on a bed of quinoa and cheese and spinach.

She'd probably complain about it. She hated spinach. And cheese. And good things.

Right now, I hated imaginary Zara.

I'd give anything to see her again.

The *clang* came again. It had definitely been real.

As quietly as possible, I pushed myself onto my elbows and leaned out from under the bed. I listened *hard*, holding my breath so the noise of air rushing through my nose wouldn't deafen me. But that made my heart beat louder, heavier, and my chest ached with a different kind of starvation. I dropped my mouth open and pulled a breath through a wide-open throat, but air scraped my raw and parched flesh.

Only silence waited in the darkness. Even when I squinted and tried to see through the sticky blackness, there was nothing.

A swarm of dizzying winds fluttered through my head. My throat ached from the air, and I had to drop back to the floor and breathe regularly. I closed my scratchy eyes, praying for relief. Praying for tears. Maybe if I could cry . . .

My body was too dry to cry. My body was a desert. I touched my rough, swollen tongue to my lips. Cracked. Split. Blood crusted in the creases. And when I ran my fingers across my forearm, skin hissed against skin. Skin flaked off. Muscle flaked off. My fingers dragged against bone. I was falling apart.

Clang.

My eyes flew open and in the darkness I saw a huge draconic face glaring down at me. *Drakontos maior*, probably, if the jaw horns were any indication. But it was hard to tell when the fourth-largest species of dragon was right above me. How did it even fit inside the cell? Or under the bed? I should have heard it coming in, but this was the quietest dragon I'd ever met.

The great golden scales burned across my vision, searing my eyes just enough to elicit a single teardrop in my right eye.

The head reared back—how it did that without bashing its skull against my bed, I couldn't say—and inhaled with its secondary lungs.

I tried to scramble away, but I was too weak, too slow, so I saw everything:

The flare of its nostrils.

The chasm of its mouth.

The spark glands igniting at the moment it exhaled.

Blue fire unspooled from the back of the creature's throat, turning white and red as it surged toward me. I squeezed my eyes shut and lifted my hands like I could protect my face. My knuckles scraped wood—the underside of my bed, not a dragon. There was no fire.

There was no dragon.

Just the darkness.

A faint whine escaped my parched throat as a distant part of me realized what was happening: I was hallucinating. And of course I was seeing a dragon. Dragons were the reason I was in here in the first place. Because I'd failed them.

I gathered the scattered threads of my thoughts and focused on breathing. Somewhere around fourteen or seventy, I lost count and had to start over, but even that was better than imagining dragons trying to kill me. I tried again and again, but the counting failed me every time, sometimes with sleep, sometimes with mind fog, sometimes with spikes of terror that came from the impenetrable darkness.

Then came the footsteps, a faint *tap tap tap* down the hall.

Finally.

Someone was coming to get me.

I tried to move—scoot out, sit up—but my limbs were too heavy and held me down. Even if I'd been able to move them, would I have been able to tell? The darkness made me question everything.

"Hello?" At least, I tried to ask. What really emerged was a faint, desperate croak.

The footsteps continued on like they hadn't heard me.

Because they were hallucinations. Of course. Anyway, footsteps couldn't hear. Only people. And hallucinatory footsteps couldn't belong to people.

Laughter threatened again, and I didn't have the energy to stamp it down. But it didn't matter, because my aching throat closed and refused to do any more. My entire body was breaking down. I could almost feel my organs slouching from hunger, becoming brittle and scattering apart from lack of water.

I was *so* thirsty. Even hunger fell behind the aching thirst.

For a while, the footsteps continued. Slowly. Maddeningly. I tried to count them, but as before, the numbers fell beneath the agony of starvation.

Tap, tap, tap. Like the quiet code.

Tap, tap, tap. Like my father's fingers against his desk.

Tap, tap, tap. Like the weak motion of my heart.

Everything grew sluggish. Thoughts. Movements. Awareness.

Then the footsteps vanished.

I was alone.

Again.

In the dark.

As consciousness fluttered in and out—mostly out—the darkness crept toward me. Between the metal grille. Through Aaru's hole. Across the floor.

The darkness went on and on, until it devoured me.

CHAPTER ELEVEN

A LIST WITHOUT NUMBERS:

Drops of water in Aaru's cup.

Too far away to reach.

How did anyone make noorestones go dark?

That wasn't supposed to be possible.

I wished I were a dragon.

I'd burn everything.

• • •

"MIRA?"

It sounded like Aaru was here with me, but his voice came from a million leagues away.

"Mira." It was Gerel this time. Even farther. Why were they all so far away? Didn't they know I couldn't reach them, or move, or speak? Didn't they know I'd give anything to answer except . . .

I wished I were a dragon. I'd . . .

The scrape of wood on stone caught my attention, like silk snagging on a nail. The sound was familiar. I'd been here before.

"Mira." That was definitely Aaru, or at least a convincing hallucination. Like the clanging. Like the dragon face. Like the footsteps. He wasn't real.

I wasn't real.

"Must drink." A note of urgency filled Aaru's voice. "Mira. *Drink*."

Drink. Oh, Damyan and Darina. I was so, so thirsty. But when I opened my mouth to say so, only a low groan emerged. My tongue was dry. Swollen. Scratchy. It hurt to move. I couldn't even open my eyes because of the dryness. Like a desert. Some parts of Anahera were desert. I had visited the island three times, but never the desert part. Only one species of dragon lived in the sandy wasteland: the *Drakontos sol*, which was small and sand colored, and covered in scales that absorbed the sun's light and converted it to fire energy. Most dragons couldn't do that.

"Cup," Aaru whispered. "Take."

A cup? Of water?

Through the smoke filling my mind, I recalled the cup in Aaru's cell—how I'd been listening to it fill and straining to reach it, desperately thirsty. But the cup was still on the other side of the wall, wasn't it? Sitting in the middle of Aaru's cell, collecting water, taunting me.

Or had it moved? I'd heard Aaru's voice, but I'd heard footsteps before, too. It seemed unlikely he was truly here, but maybe. Maybe he'd come back and moved the cup for me. I needed only to pick it up and tip the water into my mouth.

I had to try.

My hand was too heavy to lift off my stomach, which felt too low, too hollow. I opened my mouth again, jaw popping in protest, and sucked in a shallow breath. Like maybe I could breathe in the water.

Frustrated tapping sounded from beyond the hole. I just wanted to go to sleep again. If I couldn't reach the water, sleep would help.

"What's happening over there?" Gerel almost sounded worried. This was definitely a hallucination. "Is she drinking yet?"

Two taps: long and short. I knew that one. ::**No**.:: Then his voice came, too: "No."

"It's been four days. Even if she rationed her water,

she's dehydrated. You'll have to help her."

The cup hissed over the stone floor, so close to my face. Oh how I wanted that water.

And then.

Then cool skin brushed my jaw. Knuckles braced against my chin. "Open," he whispered, and I did, and water trickled onto my face.

I sputtered as liquid found its way up my nose and dribbled down my cheeks, but after a moment, a stream of water poured between my lips, filling my mouth. Wonderful, mineral-sharp ceiling water I could *feel* soaking into my parched skin.

He stopped pouring too quickly, but that was for the best.

I couldn't swallow.

My tongue was a dead weight in my mouth. Water flooded through my sinuses and suddenly I couldn't breathe. Terror spiked. Abruptly, I was *awake*. Alert. And acutely aware that I was about to die.

I gagged and coughed, struggling for air. It seemed so unfair that my first sip of water in four aeons would drown me.

But then, my head was lifted up and gravity did its work. The water found its way toward my throat, soothing the raw places inside me: tongue and cheeks and through my chest. The cold traveled all the way into my stomach, spreading around. A strange, uncomfortable sensation. But water. *Water.* Glorious water. I opened my mouth for more.

Aaru lowered my head and took up the cup once more. Of course. He could fit only one arm through the hole, and his range of movement was limited.

He poured another mouthful of water into me, helped me swallow, and then withdrew. "Wait for more."

I didn't want to wait. I was so, so thirsty. More thirsty than I'd been in my life. But he'd taken the cup and I could hardly move, so I didn't have a choice but to do as he said.

And if he wasn't real, this was the best, most vivid hallucination I'd ever had. Water. Little streams of mineral-bitter water. Did *Drakontos sols* crave water this much?

"Did she drink?" Gerel hissed from across the hall. "How is she? Tell me what's happening."

"Yes," he said. "Ill, but alive." How strange. Suddenly, the silent boy was my voice.

"Good." Gerel almost sounded relieved, which was odd. I'd have thought she would classify almost dying of dehydration as a personal failing of mine. I should have had the good sense to draw water from the air.

A few minutes later, Aaru gave me another sip, again pressing his arm through the hole to tip the cup, then to lift my head so I could swallow. It got easier every time, and with the water came renewed energy. I couldn't talk yet—my tongue was still too swollen—but while Aaru was replacing the cup under the drip, I managed to move my hand toward the hole.

Even that small movement was difficult, leaving me

panting, but it was more than I'd been able to do an hour ago.

When Aaru squeezed back under his bed, I forced my eyes open, groaning at the grit and sting and brightness. It was day—or what passed for day in the Pit—and the noorestones were lit. They'd always seemed so dim before, but after days in the darkness, even the distant light was too much. It felt as though my eyes would burn away.

Some of the water Aaru had accidentally poured on my face had fallen into the corners of my eyes, though, which helped ease the pain. My time in the darkness had sucked away all my tears, too.

"Don't rush," Aaru said.

He was right. The harder I tried to push, the more damage I risked doing to myself. I let my eyes fall shut again, but pressed my hand toward the hole. Toward him.

Raggedly, I tapped a message onto the floor: one long, a pause, a long, a short, and two more longs. ::**Thank you.**::

Cool fingers pressed over the back of my hand. A short message fell on my knuckles, but I was asleep before he finished.

THE NOORESTONES STILL glowed when I awakened.

Maybe they glowed again, from a day passing, but it didn't feel like an entire day had gone. I could taste the bite of ceiling water on my tongue. Aaru's hand covered mine. On the far side of the cellblock, low voices discussed how much food they'd eat if they had an infinite amount.

Everything was as it had been before, so I must have slept for less than an hour.

I hated the steady light. Like the unchanging darkness, it offered no indication of how long I'd been out. But . . . light. I was grateful for the light. I wanted to bathe in it.

My breathing must have changed, or my fingers twitched, because Aaru patted my knuckles—in comfort, not in code—and withdrew to fetch the cup.

A moment later, more water fell inside me. I swallowed easily this time, drinking until there was nothing left. When Aaru replaced the cup beneath the leak, the drops of water made short, flat *plops*.

I wanted to thank him again, but I couldn't force my mouth to make the words, and I couldn't force myself to tap loudly enough for him to hear.

But then his hand moved toward mine, his rough fingers floating across sensitive skin. From my fingertips to my knuckles to the back of my wrist. He settled there—over, not on—and tapped a quick message:

::You're welcome.::

Because I'd missed it before.

I could hardly believe I remembered the code. Granted, he'd used the basic abbreviations he'd taught me, and he used my same crawling pace so that I could keep up, but I remembered. I understood. That was incredible.

::Where?:: I asked. I hoped he could fill in the missing words I didn't have the energy to spell out.

::They came while you were in the bath.::

Oh, the bath. I remembered that. Water. Feeling clean. Tirta inspecting my twists. That was a good memory: human touch.

At home, few people touched me. Not Mother and Father. Nor Zara. Why should they? Strangers certainly were not allowed. Hristo, as my personal guard, felt it unprofessional unless he was saving my life. Ilina could, but rarely did, now that we were older. Krasimir did, because it was her job. She was always efficient and careful as she worked. And kind, too, of course.

But Tirta hadn't checked my hair because it was her job. She'd done it because she wanted to help. Otherwise, in the Pit, there'd been Altan and Sarannai and other guards. I didn't want to think about those.

And now there was Aaru. Efficient, like Krasimir. Thoughtful, like Tirta. It must have been horribly dull for him to tap the code so slowly, but I hadn't been up to his speed even before the lights went out. Now, half-dead from dehydration . . . definitely not.

But then, I recalled my skin: paper dry and falling apart. I couldn't be sure how much of that had been real, but days without water must have had some effect. And he was touching me. Feeling my awful skin. He must have been so disgusted. What I wouldn't give for a handful of coconut oil or shea butter. My skin thirsted just as much as my throat.

At home, Mother had jars and jars of lotions of every

scent. Jasmine, lavender, orange blossom, apple, rose, ginger . . . others, too. I wished I had them now. With a little more effort, I could imagine spreading the smooth cream on my arms and legs and face. Glorious, sweet-scented moisture.

Aaru gave no indication that he minded my rough skin, though. He continued with his tapped message like he didn't notice. Still, this was the first time he'd ever touched me. I wished I could have been soft.

I hated Altan a little more for destroying the only things anyone liked about me.

::**Some didn't want to go,**:: Aaru said, oblivious to my whirlpool of distress. ::**They've been here so long. But no one had a choice. Those who resisted were dragged out in chains.**::

Who had resisted? Aaru? Gerel? Hurrok or Kumas?

::**We were taken to a different cellblock. Brighter. Better. Guards said it was to encourage us to behave and take jobs.**::

Given the questions Altan had asked me before darkening the noorestones, I doubted simple encouragement was the real reason for their removal.

No, I was being punished, but I didn't have the energy to explain. Already, my thoughts were sluggish. I wanted to sleep, but even more, I wanted to keep this connection as long as possible. Just because he hadn't let go of me before didn't mean he wouldn't if I drifted off again. I'd been alone for days. I never wanted to repeat that.

::**Did it work?**:: I asked.

His forefinger was motionless on my knuckles for five heartbeats. Ten. Twelve.

Then he said, ::**Two meals a day. More water. Bigger cells with real beds. It was better there. Three stayed.**::

::**But you did not.**::

He closed his hand over mine and squeezed. "I did not," he whispered.

Chills swept through my heart, carrying a fantasy that he'd returned to the first level because of me. Because he wouldn't leave me behind. But that was foolish, of course. This strange and fluttery feeling was simply a result of his kindness and I was starving for human contact.

::**They all lie.**:: Aaru tapped my knuckles again. ::**I will not give them what they want. I will not abandon my ally.**::

When he pulled away, deeper into his cell, my hand was cold and empty. My fingertips fell still and silent on the floor, my code-voice removed as simply as his withdrawal. As for my throat-voice, it was useless right now, but I tried, anyway, to bring him back.

"Ah—" The pathetic sound ground upward from my throat, across my tongue, and died on the floor beside me.

Aaru reappeared at the hole. "Checked cup."

Oh. Relief trickled through me.

He squeezed his hand through the hole and rested it over mine. His skin smelled sour, like the prison, but somewhere under the filth, I caught notes of open fields and rainstorms and lightning-shot skies. "Still empty," he whispered.

Of course. Since I'd just drunk all the water. All of *Aaru's* water. Again. Same as the day of my arrival.

He had so little. He gave so much.

Before I could respond, heavy footfalls slammed through the hall, and I recognized the cadence of Altan's stride. Six, seven, eight . . . He was coming closer, from the direction of the mess hall, not the bath. And there was someone with him—someone larger, who took two steps for every three of Altan's.

The panic spiked. My hand shook, knocking Aaru's away. He released a sharp, quiet cry as his knuckles bashed against the edge of the wall hole.

Adrenaline flooded my whole body, making my face and throat and chest heat.

No, no, no. I couldn't have an attack now. Not when I was already so weak. But I couldn't stop it. All the breathing exercises and calming thoughts Doctor Chilikoba had ever taught me were burning up in the fire of terror. Useless.

Breath huffed out of me in jagged gasps and all my thoughts jumbled into a giant nothing. I was falling apart. Falling to pieces. Floating away.

My cell door screeched and Altan and his companion came inside. The panic overtook me, a storm I could not outrun.

As unconsciousness seized me, the last thing my mind registered was the numbers. Always numbers.

::**Strength through silence,**:: Aaru was banging on the wall of his cell. ::**Strength through silence.**::

When Altan and his friend dragged me from under the bed, those words became my last thought:

Strength through silence.

BEFORE

Sarai 15, 2204 FG

"LEX COULD BE HURT." ILINA STARED INTO THE mouth of the cave.

My heart jumped. I'd never been in a dragon cave before. Mother had forbidden it, because it was too dangerous. And, as with the drakarium, it was generally considered rude to go tromping into a dragon's home. But I didn't want to tell Ilina no; not when I desperately wanted to go in myself. To help. And because I'd always wanted to see the inside.

Ilina fished the calm-whistle from her pocket, then motioned at her backpack. "Get a noorestone, will you?"

Hristo felt around the bag until he found an elongated noorestone, shining bright white-blue. Crystal, momentarily distracted from the scent of a larger dragon, stretched her neck as long as it would go and gave the noorestone a small trill of approval.

"Ready?" Ilina's voice trembled.

"This is a terrible idea," Hristo said, but not in a tone that discouraged.

He wasn't wrong. If Lex was hurt, she could lash out. We could be cooked inside the dragon cave. Even the sweet tone of the calm-whistle wouldn't do much to save us from a frightened *Drakontos rex*.

A tendril of dread wove through our group. No one expected to actually find Lex.

Hristo held the noorestone high as we stepped inside the cave. The walls were dark, more melted stone, but some of the faces were polished enough to reflect the noorestone light.

It was another world in here. Five steps. Ten. Stone crunched under our boots, and I was grateful for the thick soles. People without the proper protective gear usually ended up with shredded feet when they came into the sanctuary, or any place where big dragons lived.

Fifty paces in, we came to a huge central chamber, with fifteen delicate columns to brace the ceiling, and molted scales scattered across the floor like red coins. Evidence of an absent dragon. Three other tunnels branched off into darkness.

Piles of noorestones shimmered along the walls, illuminating the vast space like clusters of fallen stars.

This felt intrusive, coming into Lex's home. This was her private space, and these were her possessions. She hadn't invited us here.

"Look." Hristo's mutter echoed off the walls as he jabbed his noorestone toward the center. "Do you see it?"

Now that he pointed it out, I saw a pair of long depressions in the rock and dirt littering the floor, and—

"Are those wheel tracks?" The words felt heavy and unreal.

Hristo crept closer to the wide gashes in the debris. "Yes." His deep voice echoed across the cavern. "Someone was here."

With a cart. And a load that carved deep tracks into the dirt.

They hadn't left anything, or taken anything . . . except.

"Someone took Lex," I breathed. How could someone just *take* an enormous dragon?

Tears shimmered down Ilina's cheeks. "Who?" The word seemed to choke out of her.

I reached for her hand, but I didn't have a good answer. Poachers, maybe? That was a horrible thought.

"We'll have to tell someone," I said. "Your parents, first." But we'd take it all the way to the Luminary Council if necessary. Dragons were protected. This was an insult to the Mira Treaty, and worse—an insult to the Fallen Gods themselves.

"Did you see tracks in Astrid's cave last night?" Hristo

searched farther into the room, pausing at the first slender column of black rock. He picked up a shed scale, which glittered ruby in the light of his noorestone.

"I don't—I didn't look." Ilina's voice was hoarse.

"Let's go." I tugged her toward the tunnel again. "We should check on Tower."

"Right." We headed outside again, squinting at the bright sunlight, and aimed our horses toward Tower's cave. We had to know.

None of us really expected her to be there. And she wasn't.

"We'll find them," I said later. "We'll do whatever it takes to get them back."

CHAPTER TWELVE

THIRST GNAWED AT ME, BUT THE HOLLOW AND ACHE weren't nearly as acute as before. I was on my back, lying on something not exactly soft, but far more luxurious than the stone floor of my cell. A thin bed, maybe.

"Four days?" The feminine voice was distant, distorted by my own muggy mind. "You left her in there for four days and thought she wouldn't die?"

"She's still alive." That was Altan's voice. Of course I knew his voice. I'd been waiting to hear it every moment since he closed the cell doors after my bath—dreading to hear it.

If he'd offered just a sip of water, I'd have told him everything he wanted to know. I wouldn't have been able to stop myself. I'd have done anything for drink, especially once the hallucinations started.

He moved closer, still talking. "That's what matters to you, isn't it? Keeping her alive?"

"We need her healthy, too. In case the Luminary Council sends for her. You've heard the rumors from the Shadowed City." The voice was feminine, definitely, but too far away for me to know immediately. More likely I didn't know her at all. There were a *lot* of people in the Heart of the Great Warrior, I had to keep reminding myself. "It's a miracle that she's alive," she said.

"I left her with enough water to survive, as long as she rationed. And she did." Altan stood so, so close to me. Too close. "She's not as stupid as you think. She knew to save her supplies."

"You're *lucky*," the woman said. "That's all." They were both quiet for a moment. Papers rattled. Metal clanged. Then: "What did she do, anyway?"

"I caught her stealing food to give to her neighbors. You know those Daminans. They just can't help themselves when it comes to charity."

My heart sped up. I *hadn't* been stealing food for Aaru and Gerel. What was he talking about?

"She'll recover in a few days," Altan went on. "She's already improved. Look. She's responding well to the treatment."

Treatment?

Vaguely, I became aware of a faint pressure against my inner elbow, and strength flowing in. I could breathe easier. My heart beat at an even pace. Drowsiness made my thoughts float away, but the panic had subsided.

I must have moved or made a sound, because Altan said, "Good morning, Fancy." Fingertips grazed my forehead, like he was brushing aside a loose strand of hair. Disgust rolled through me, but I couldn't find it in myself to move away. His presence was paralyzing. "Certain people thought we'd lost you, but I knew better."

A shudder ran the length of me. That wasn't true. Altan didn't know *anything* about me.

My mouth still felt too dry to speak, but even if I could have, I wouldn't have known how to respond. At least I could open my eyes now.

Two people stood over me. Altan, of course, wearing his customary smirk. A middle-aged woman I didn't know, and didn't want to; a scowl looked permanently etched onto her face. A tall wooden stand held a canvas bag aloft, and a thin tube ran from the bag and met its end at a needle, which pressed into my arm.

"Coconut water." Altan watched my gaze. "Inserted directly into your veins. Commonly used to revive warriors and trainees who collapse from heat and dehydration."

I'd heard about that, actually. Doctor Chilikoba had been called to Khulan to consult on whether the Khulani doctors should be allowed to continue this practice, though I'd never been told the decision reached. When she'd returned, she'd spent our entire visit telling me why she liked the theory behind this, but not the technique used. *"It's a quick way to rehydrate someone, but there's not enough prevention of air bubbles from being introduced into the blood. Even a small bubble could kill someone. It's a brilliant idea, but Khulani doctors need to perfect the treatment before continuing to use it on patients. They risk killing as many as they save."*

Her lecture had been distantly interesting, but I'd never thought it might apply to me one day. I'd always assumed Doctor Chilikoba would be the *only* doctor looking after me.

But the Pit changed everything. What if the liquid ran out and they had to add more? What if they hadn't been careful filling the bag in the first place? Anything could add a bubble of air that moved directly into my veins.

Considering how concerned they were about my life and health, this seemed like an unnecessary risk. With my free hand, I reached for the needle.

The frowning woman slapped my fingers. "Don't touch."

A whimper crawled out of my throat. I did *not* want that thing inside me. Yes, it was saving me right now, but every second it stayed there risked a surprise death.

Altan gestured toward the scowling lady. "This is Rosa. Yes, she's Daminan. No, she won't help you escape. She works for the Pit infirmary." He offered a cup. "Drink."

The coconut water cloyed on my tongue. I'd never liked it, even as a child. Too sweet. But now, I emptied the cup in seven long gulps. The cool liquid flowed down my throat and stomach, repairing the damage done by days without a drink. As I lowered the cup, I finally got a look around the room.

I was in an infirmary. One I'd cleaned before. Four stone walls, five empty beds, two observation windows, and one open door with a retreating figure. The woman Altan had been talking with before he noticed I was awake? It hadn't been Rosa; her voice was too rough.

Two more cups of coconut water went down before my throat no longer felt like a desert.

I wished I didn't know about the missing dragons. I wished for ignorance. For the freedom to continue life as before, with my mother and father and sister who didn't understand me, with my guard and friend who *knew* me, and with my tiny dragon who meant everything in the world to me. I wished for that innocence again.

If I hadn't snooped in places I didn't belong, I wouldn't be here now. Starved. Dehydrated. Dirty. Miserable. Trapped. The unnatural sensation of liquid dripping into my arm, a small bubble of death ready to strike any second.

Altan stood over me, tall and imposing. "What did you think of being alone?" A muscle ticked by his jaw. Two, three, four times. His eyes were narrowed, all humor pressed out of them.

Strength through silence, like Aaru had said. If I refused to respond, nothing I said could be used against me. Of course, it was my silence that had gotten me locked in my cell. Alone. And starving.

Four days. It had seemed like so much longer.

"How did you like the dark?" Altan's voice deepened as he leaned toward me, more dangerous than ever. "Were you lonely? Afraid? Hungry?"

A low groan built in my throat. I didn't want to think about the nightmare of that isolation. My body didn't obey, though. My hands shook and my heart sped, warning of an attack. I fought to steady my breathing, in through my nose and out through my mouth. One. Two.

Three. Four.

Five. Six.

Seven.

Eight.

Please, Damina.

Nine.

Please.

Ten.

But my head buzzed and my vision tunneled, like the anxiety didn't care that I had no energy for another attack right now. The anxiety never cared.

"Maybe we don't have such different goals." Altan stood straight and shook the danger from his tone, confident I wouldn't forget the threat. He gestured to Rosa. "Will our guest live if you remove the needle now?"

The woman nodded.

"Then do it." He curled his lips at me. "Here's what's going to happen if we can't get along: I'll have a private cell prepared for you, apart from the rest of the first level."

My heart leaped, making my whole body jerk as Rosa pulled the needle from my arm. Coconut water dribbled from the tip of the needle before she pinched the tube and moved to put away the lifesaving death trap. Then she left the room.

"What do you think?" A smile slithered across Altan's face. "Will some more alone time help you?"

Alone again. In a strange cell, not my own. Not even the faint familiarity of the first level, with my sewage hole and space beneath my bed. Just a vast darkness and maddening silence.

No, I didn't want that.

But I couldn't tell Altan anything. He was not trustworthy.

But if I insisted on keeping the dragon secret, he'd lock me away.

But the dragons.

But the darkness.

The awful choice only encouraged the headache pulsing behind my eyes and back through my temples. No matter what I did or didn't do, there would be consequences. "What do you want with dragons?" My voice came harsh. Raspy.

"I want to save them," he said. "Of course."

I couldn't believe Altan wanted to save anyone or anything. As a warrior, part of his duty was to protect all of the Fallen Isles, but how could that be true when he delighted in cruelty?

If I said nothing, it was into a new and terrible cell for me. And I couldn't . . .

I couldn't do that again. I couldn't handle that terror. I'd lose my mind to the darkness. The strange woman had sounded like she wanted me kept alive, but Altan had already demonstrated that my life was inconsequential to him.

I *should* have died. It wasn't as if I'd ever been forced to ration food like that. Damina was a wealthy island, and my family wealthier than most, thanks to Father's ties with the Luminary Council. I'd always had enough food, carefully prepared by one of the best chefs in all the Fallen Isles. Even three years ago—the year there'd been a drought and tables all across the Isles of Lovers were leaner than usual—I'd had enough to eat.

I didn't know how to be hungry.

The fact that I was still alive truly revealed Darina and Damyan's love, because I could not have survived that on my own.

"You know what's coming for you, Mira." Altan loomed over me, full of barely contained fury.

I had no doubt that he would follow through with the threat to lock me in a more isolated cell. Alone. In the dark. Starving.

The thought of another day like that—let alone four more—made me want to curl up and die. I wasn't strong enough to bear it.

"All right." My heart thundered in my ears so loudly

that I could barely hear my own whisper. "I'll tell you what I know."

I hated myself for the words, but they worked magic. Immediately, Tirta appeared in the doorway bearing a tray laden with food. One plain ceramic bowl with a dark liquid inside. One plate, piled high with fish and beans and rice. One fork, one spoon, one napkin.

At home, it would have been a very uninteresting meal, but here—right now—it was a feast. For a second, I didn't even care about the utensils. I wanted to dig my hands straight into the rice and shove it in my mouth. I couldn't even imagine taking the time to chew. Such was the hollow pain of hunger.

But Tirta's gaze darted toward Altan and she placed the tray on the bed next to mine, just out of my reach. "Sorry," she mouthed. Her seven braids swung down the back of her neck as she turned away, keeping her face down like a proper prisoner.

Oh. Of course. He'd make me wait to eat until after I told him what he wanted to know. Showing me the food before—that was just another way of taunting me.

My stomach gave a pathetic growl. I wanted that food, but I was still so weak I could barely lift my head, let alone launch myself onto the tray.

Altan glanced at Tirta. "Out."

Her mouth dropped open, as though she wanted to protest, but instead, she nodded and exited the room, shutting the door firmly after her. Altan and I were alone.

"Now, tell me what you know." Altan crossed his arms over his chest. Muscles strained beneath the leather jacket, like I needed the reminder of his ability to overpower me. Like I needed the reminder of my own frailty.

Ilina would say I was trading the dragons for a few bites of food and company in my cellblock.

Hristo would say I needed to do anything I could to stay alive.

And Mother would say I should not tell the truth.

"Dragons have vanished from the Crescent Prominence sanctuary," Altan said. "I know that much. And I know that *you* have information on their whereabouts."

How did Altan know about vanishing dragons? I hadn't even known until a month ago—the day of the earthquake on Idris.

"What makes you think I know anything?" I clamped my mouth shut, praying he wouldn't lock me in the isolation cell on principle.

A knifelike smile split his frown. "I have friends everywhere. I wasn't always a prison guard." He touched the clawed pin on his jacket. "And I won't stay a prison guard once I have everything I want from you."

My whole body shuddered. Altan had spies—or access to spies—in the Luminary Council. Or someone who worked for them, more likely, or else he wouldn't need me.

"Well?" He glanced pointedly at the tray of food Tirta had left behind. "You know your options. Do you really want to spend more time alone in the dark?"

No.

I couldn't.

I'd die.

There was no telling when Mother and Father would get me out, and I wouldn't survive until then if I kept clutching this secret. Tirta had said so many adults died in the Pit because they *expected* things. Maybe I was like that—expecting food and water and decent treatment.

Now I knew better.

Tirta had said that prisoners who adapted survived longer.

I had to adapt. I had to be a *Drakontos mimikus* and change myself for protection.

Give up my secret or die. There were no good options.

"Very well." I closed my eyes and sucked in a deep, dread-filled breath. "I don't know much. I—" I swallowed a knot in my throat. "I found shipping orders. Instructions to move fourteen large dragons to the mainland. Someone is sending our dragons to the Algotti Empire."

BEFORE

Sarai 15, 2204 FG

AFTER WE FOUND THE WHEEL TRACKS IN THE EMPTY caves, Ilina, Hristo, and I went to Ilina's parents' office with the news: someone was stealing our dragons.

But when we arrived, the room was empty, just a pair of desks and a mountain range of scattered papers.

"The sanctuary keeps logs of everyone who visits." Ilina began digging through the papers. "Whoever took the dragons will be listed on one of these."

There were *so many* papers, though. It was hard to believe there was any kind of order to all this chaos. Nevertheless, Hristo and I began searching for the entry logs, too.

That was when we found it.

Shipping orders.

Sitting on her father's desk. Evidence that someone had betrayed the Fallen Isles.

ILINA'S PARENTS ARRIVED a short time later, bursting into the office and asking what in Damina's name was going on. We told them about the caves, showed them the papers, but they insisted it was fake.

"I'll take it to the Luminary Council if I have to," I said. No one made *fake* shipping orders like that. Especially about dragons. They were the children of the gods.

"Please don't," Ilina's mother said. "Please just leave it alone."

"I don't see how I can." I glanced at Ilina, who nodded. "If we let injustice go unchallenged, how are we any better than those committing the crimes?"

Ilina's parents looked at each other with tears in their eyes, and her father said, "We can't stop you, Mira, but please, whatever you do, leave Ilina out of it."

IT WAS LATE by the time Hristo took me home, and Mother scolded me for missing dinner. I didn't care. The shipping order was a fire in my pocket that kept me burning with rage all through the night. How could anyone steal dragons? How could Ilina's parents ignore something so terrible? They ran a sanctuary for dragons; they should have been outraged.

I kept thinking, too, about who might take these

dragons. Poachers? Another sanctuary? Someone else? The Crescent Prominence sanctuary wasn't perfect, but the keepers had always put the dragons first. None of this made sense.

That rage grew and grew throughout the night, though I took two pills from Doctor Chilikoba's amber bottle. They did nothing to break through the most intense panic attack of my life; the anticipation of what I was about to do was so overwhelming.

I spent the whole night moving between praying for strength and calm, and reading the shipping orders.

At breakfast, I insisted that I visit the Luminary Council. Mother and Father didn't even ask why; they were just happy I was finally showing an interest in politics. Zara merely glared as though I'd committed some grievous and irreparable wrong.

Noorestone light gleamed off marble columns and gold-inlaid walls as I entered the council chamber. The space was so full of light and warmth, and filled with twenty-seven elected officials charged with protecting our islands—and our dragons.

Elbena Krasteba was one of the younger councilors, and often my self-appointed companion when I traveled. I'd always considered her something of a friend. After I presented my findings, she left her seat and glided toward me.

"Thank you, Mira, for bringing this to our attention." She took the shipping order from my hands. "It means so much to all of us that you came straight here. But don't worry. The dragons were removed for health reasons. There's a breeding program on the mainland. We are doing our best, as caretakers of the children of the gods, to ensure their continued survival. This is just one way."

She was lying.

If that had been true, Ilina's parents would have said so right away. They'd have told Ilina before we ever found the empty caves. And we would have believed them, because we believed in the sanctuary's goodness. We believed in the Luminary Council's goodness.

Not anymore.

"I know you're lying." My whole body shook with rage. "I know it. We're not finished."

I left before they could say anything else.

TWO DAYS LATER, I returned to the council house with an apology.

Morning light streamed gold through the windows as I stood before my government once more, but instead of arguing their claims, I offered deception.

Of understanding.

Of asking forgiveness.

Of accepting their lies.

Twenty-seven councilors listened to my words, and because I was the Hopebearer and I'd always done as they asked before, they believed me now.

Or so I'd thought.

• • •

I TOOK A copy of the shipping order to High Priest Valko in the Temple of Damyan and Darina.

The temple had always been a strange mix of safety and expectation, with its soaring arches, elaborate friezes, and delicate limestone columns. Embedded noorestones gleamed from around the windows, and from silver chandeliers, and from the base of the immense statues of Darina and Damyan at the front of the room.

The Lovers' sandstone embrace would draw the eye even without the mirror-focused noorestone light to highlight the exquisite details. Sheer clothing rippled across skin, strands of tightly curled hair played in the wind, and even eyelashes fanned against full cheeks. This statue, carved by one of the First Masters, was one of our island's greatest treasures.

"Mira." High Priest Valko met me in the center aisle.

"Can we speak in your office?" I glanced over my shoulder, toward the daylight pouring through the thrown-open doors. No one had followed me—they had no reason to doubt my apology was anything but sincere—but this was not the sort of thing I could discuss in front of the dozen people who'd come here to pray or enjoy the art.

"Of course." The high priest motioned for me to join him, but we made it only three steps before Luminary Guards strode into the temple, with Elbena leading the way.

With one look, I could tell she knew that I'd meant

to share the shipping order with High Priest Valko. That I'd meant to destroy the Luminary Council by pitting the gods' voice against them. That I'd meant to tell the world that the Luminary Council didn't care that our dragons were being shipped to the Algotti Empire.

She knew my apology had been a lie.

"Don't make a scene, Mira. Just come with me."

And until the Luminary Guards deposited me in a holding cell, I hadn't even realized that was the moment of my arrest.

CHAPTER THIRTEEN

"WHO IS SENDING THE DRAGONS?" ALTAN ASKED.

"I'm not sure." It was the truth, and I prayed he could hear it in my trembling voice. Guilt worked its way through me. I shouldn't have said anything. I should have been braver. Stronger. But I was a coward who didn't want to be alone for a few days.

Altan blew out a long breath. "You saw shipping orders."

I nodded. "I saw shipping orders."

"And the Luminary Council was so upset that they sent you—their precious Mira Minkoba—here. To the Pit. The most notorious prison in the Fallen Isles." He cocked his head. "That doesn't make sense. Why didn't they just lie to you about the shipping orders? A girl like you would have believed them."

"They tried," I whispered.

"What then?" An amused turn of his mouth suggested he thought I was a fool.

He wasn't wrong.

Altan's smile grew wider. "Tell me everything the shipping orders said."

"I can't."

"You didn't just happen upon shipping orders and not bother to read them carefully. Someone who's been given special permission to train a *Drakontos raptus* at the Crescent Prominence sanctuary would have read that a hundred times."

"I don't remember what it said."

Altan planted one hand on the side of my bed and leaned, blocking the light of the noorestone next to me. He was huge. Overbearing. His dark eyes drilled into mine, searching for the truth. "You might think I can't tell when you're lying, but I can tell when anyone is lying. And you're not very good at it to begin with."

My breath turned shallow, frantic, desperate. "I don't remember."

His smirk fell and he leaned farther toward me, keeping his voice low but razor sharp. "Do not play the fool with me, or there will be very real consequences."

Numbness pushed through me. Gone was his joking

manner, and the gleam in his eyes like we shared a secret. This was real. As real as the minutes before he took me inside the empty cellblock and locked me away.

The danger was far from over.

"I need a map," I said as a dull throb began in my temples.

He sent for one immediately. Several minutes later, two trainees arrived with an enormous map of the Fallen Isles framed in mahogany. They propped it up on the end of my bed, barely giving me time to move my feet out of the way.

"Tell me what I want to know," Altan said when they were gone.

I tried not to glance at the waiting tray of food, but the hunger was overpowering.

"Where are the dragons?" Altan deepened his voice. "You can eat after we're done."

My stomach knotted. As much as I wanted to eat, and to *not* be put in a dark cell somewhere isolated, this was wrong. I knew it.

But I scooted toward the map and pressed my mouth into a line.

The six—or seven, depending how you thought of Damyan and Darina—islands were drawn in faded black ink on the age-darkened paper. It was soft, like cloth, and bordered with tiny drawings of dragons of every kind. *Drakontos rex, Drakontos titanus* . . . I wanted to look at them all, but Altan cleared his throat.

"Today."

"I'm thinking." The words hissed out of me. "It's been a long time since I saw the shipping order." Twenty-eight days, to be exact.

"Think faster. The longer you take, the more danger we're in." He angled toward me and peered at the map, as though he could divine the locations from the ink.

Connections snapped in my mind.

Altan was a believer. Altan was on a *quest*.

"The more danger we're in . . ." I tilted my shoulders, adjusted my tone, and made myself look as encouraging as possible. "You mean, from the gods abandoning us?" It was a risk, questioning him. Altan was unpredictable: this might pacify him, or swing him farther into anger.

"I took an oath to Khulan and all the other Fallen Gods that I would protect the Isles from every threat. Including the Great Abandonment."

The Great Abandonment was one of the few shared stories in every holy book. *The Book of Love* described it as the end of our relationship with the Fallen Gods, while *The Book of Warriors* said it was the beginning of our war against them. Other books described it in different ways, but one threat remained the same: the gods would leave us if we didn't care for the dragons.

I touched the lines of the map, the islands shaped like gods. Darina and Damyan, so close their toes and chests touched. Khulan, his mace raised in warning. Idris, far from the others and stumped over in contemplation.

"Some people think it's a myth."

He let out a low rumble. "It's no myth. The Great Abandonment is a very real threat. Khulan's holy texts tell what the unbinding would be like: earthquakes, violent storms, unrest among the people. Does that sound familiar?" He didn't wait for an answer. "Our survival depends on dragons living here, entreating the gods on our behalf."

"I think it's true, too. If we lose the dragons, we lose the gods."

"And our very homes will unbind themselves from the sea and abandon us, because we could not take care of their children." He turned and studied me, more thoughtful now. "I'm glad you believe it."

"Even those who don't should understand that we are the caretakers of these islands and the creatures on them. Including—and maybe especially—the dragons."

"Tell me where the dragons are right now. Khulani warriors will rescue the dragons and slaughter those who'd take them from their rightful place. I swear it."

That stilled me.

We both wanted the dragons returned to the islands.

I didn't know how I felt about the warriors slaughtering everyone—besides negatively—but I did like the idea of keeping the dragons from being taken to the Algotti Empire. That was why I'd confronted the Luminary Council, wasn't it?

"Well?" Altan's voice came at a low growl.

I turned to my numbers, counting the days and decans

since the sanctuary dragons had been taken, and I'd seen the shipping orders, and the number of days it took to sail from Khulan to the various points that were listed on the shipping orders.

"Mira." Altan's mouth thinned into a line.

If I told Altan where he could find the dragons, the warriors could go rescue them.

But then the warriors would have the dragons.

But the Algotti Empire wouldn't.

Wanting the same thing as Altan didn't make him my ally.

I couldn't trust Altan.

But if I didn't, I'd go back in the dark. And then what? What about the dragons?

I took one long breath in, and pushed one long breath out. And pointed. "Here," I whispered. "They'll be at Crestshade from Zabel the twentieth to the twenty-ninth, and then they'll be moved again. There." I pointed to Thornfell. "They'll reach it on the first day of the Hallowed Restoration and stay there for a decan. That is where they'll begin the voyage across the sea."

"And they'll be unreachable."

I looked sharply at him.

"By our ships," he explained. "I can think of perhaps two vessels capable of crossing the open sea. The rest were built for moving between the islands. They're smaller and faster, but they wouldn't make it even halfway to the mainland. Not without the crew starving to death."

"Do you have access to the ships that could cross?"

He shook his head. "The Khulani vessel is on patrol around the islands. The other belongs to the Daminan and Anaheran governments."

The *Star-Touched* was a magnificent vessel. I'd seen her from my window a few times: she had seven masts, with every sail colored to represent a different island, and she required three of the largest noorestones in existence to power her. She patrolled the eastern reaches of the Isles, and was the first line of defense against an attack from the Algotti Empire.

"There's a small chance we could commandeer the ship transporting the dragons and turn it back toward the islands, but if we reached them more than halfway to the mainland, we'd risk some of the dragons starving. Not to mention the human casualties."

That thought was sobering. "How long does it take to reach the mainland?"

"From Thornfell, it takes seventeen days."

Fourteen immense creatures, meant to soar in the sky—not be chained down in a cargo hold. Fourteen huge predators, meant to hunt their prey and eat it whole, not be fed whatever livestock the crew shoved in. If the crew fed the dragons at all.

It was a massive undertaking, provisioning for the crew, the livestock, the dragons, and potential emergencies. All to steal dragons from Crescent Prominence and take them to our enemies. But *why*?

"You're angry," Altan observed. "Good. You should be."

I wasn't angry. I was *furious*. At the smugglers. At the Luminary Council. At Altan.

At myself.

"What I don't understand," he said, "is why it's taking so long to leave the Fallen Isles. Why move the dragons around for decans before sending them away?"

"To weaken them." That had been one of my first questions, too, but Ilina had provided a theory. "Most dragons don't eat every day."

"I know that." A note of annoyance colored Altan's tone.

I flinched away, but he didn't make any threatening moves.

"Go on," he said.

"Unless they're unusually active, big dragons usually eat once or twice a decan, and snack between. But they can go two decans and stay healthy, as long as they conserve energy."

"So they're starving the dragons to weaken them." Altan sounded disgusted. "To make them more complacent on the journey."

I bowed my head, too easily imagining the starving dragons just waiting for food.

I knew the pain of hunger because Altan had nearly killed me.

Hate was a strong word—an emotion I'd never truly felt before. But now, I thought I understood it. A fire ran through me, different from the fire of panic.

Hate burned hotter. It seared my veins, up my chest and throat and face, and made a faint red glow surround the object of my ire. I indulged in a moment of imagining I was a dragon and I was setting him aflame.

The effect vanished as he stepped away from my bed and strode toward the door. "I assume you know to keep this talk a secret."

"Wait," I called, heart thundering in my chest. "Why do you care so much? Is it just because of the Warriors' Oath?"

"It isn't *just* an oath, Fancy." He softened for an instant. "I thought of everyone here, you would understand. You were taken from your sanctuary. Mine was taken from me."

With that, he opened the door and left.

Rushing filled my head so loudly that I could hardly hear. Everything felt weak. From my legs to my lungs. I was so stupid.

Horribly.

Ridiculously.

Stupid.

Altan was so interested in what I knew about dragons because *he* was a Drakon Warrior. Or he wanted to be.

According to the Mira Treaty, the Drakon Warriors should have disbanded, and the dragons all been sent to a local sanctuary where they could grow even more ancient in peace. There'd been rumors that the Drakon Warriors had remained, although it was said they were simply an elite division, not actually dragon riders anymore.

But his sanctuary had been taken from him. That seemed like . . . there had been dragons here. In the Pit. Recently. Khulan's warriors had ignored the Mira Treaty.

Then, whoever was behind the exportation of dragons—the Luminary Council, or someone else?—had come and taken the dragons from the Pit.

Even worse, it meant that the removal of dragons from the Crescent Prominence sanctuary wasn't an isolated event. This was so much bigger than I'd realized if the Drakon Warriors' dragons were victims as well.

The burden of this knowledge shouldn't have fallen to me. Who was I but a pretty face and mouthpiece for the Luminary Council? They should have been the ones to fix this. Protecting Damina was the reason they'd been elected and appointed.

And *that* was the question Altan hadn't asked: why—instead of finding who was responsible for smuggling the dragons, and then making every effort to prevent the Algotti Empire from obtaining the power to destroy the Fallen Isles—had the Luminary Council instead tossed me in the Pit?

I'd told Altan what he'd wanted to know, and I hated myself for that. But at least . . . at least I'd only told him part of it.

The rest concerned a weapon: the most dangerous weapon the Fallen Isles had ever seen. Maybe the most dangerous Noore had ever seen. And no one—especially not Drakon Warriors like Altan—could be trusted with that kind of power.

I would never tell.

Not even to save my own life.

BEFORE

Seven Months Ago

I MADE A MISTAKE.

I'd made lots of mistakes in my life, yes, but this one was different. It happened in the sanctuary. And we almost died.

SWEET JASMINE PERFUMED the foothills of the Skyfell Mountains as Ilina, Hristo, and I made our way up the path toward Siff's lair. She was the final visit for today, and all the hiking showed in our heavy steps and sweat-dampened clothes. Even LaLa and Crystal seemed tired, though they'd been riding on our shoulders for the last hour, and now Crystal had one of Ilina's braids hanging from her jaws like she was about to bite it off.

"I dare you," Hristo told Crystal.

Ilina glanced over her shoulder, gently tugging the braid from her dragon's teeth. "Don't encourage her bad behavior. She's rotten enough."

"I thought you looked good with short hair," I teased.

"Short hair. Not *singed* hair." Ilina paused while Crystal flapped and readjusted herself, but I blazed ahead.

That was my mistake.

Heavy foliage sheltered a clearing in front of Siff's lair, a tangle of passionflower and ferns, and immense trees that reached for the blue sky. While Ilina and Hristo lagged behind, still joking about dragonish haircuts, I rounded a wall of buttress roots and tripped.

Five things happened at once:

1. *LaLa abandoned my shoulder.*

2. *My knees slammed into something broken and wet: a partially eaten lamb.*

3. *Ilina shouted, "Watch out!" and scrambled for her calm-whistle.*

4. *Hristo grabbed for me, but I'd fallen too quickly.*

5. *From across the clearing, Siff barreled toward us. Fire poured from her jaws.*

She was incredible: a *Drakontos ignitus,* with wicked facial horns, a large wingspan, and—at least in adults—the ability to cause the very *air* to burn.

Ilina brought the calm-whistle to her lips, and a sweet tone played over the chaos, but it was too late. Already, the air shimmered as Siff's scales heated, and her great wings fanned, becoming red-gold.

Safety instructions flittered through my head, but instead of playing dead or hiding behind Hristo, I reached for the raging dragon and . . . she stopped.

The noise. The heat. The wild look in her golden eyes. One moment, Siff was ready to kill me for falling into her leftovers. The next, she was tugging the lamb carcass out from under me, not minding that Hristo was pulling me to my feet. Relief flooded me so thoroughly I could barely stand.

Ilina's whistle must have worked after all.

"Mira, what did you *do*?" Ilina whispered as Siff disappeared into her cave, dragging the lamb.

"I messed up." My throat went tight with residual terror and misery. If Mother ever found out, she'd never let me return to the sanctuary. I'd never see dragons again. "I wasn't paying attention and I tripped."

"No, I mean you—"

Hristo touched Ilina's hand and gave a slight shake of his head. "Don't worry her about it now."

Ilina frowned, but she nodded. "All right."

"You can't tell anyone," I whispered. "Especially my family."

"All right," Ilina said again. "No one will ever know what happened here. Not from us, anyway."

We never spoke of that afternoon again.

CHAPTER FOURTEEN

AFTER BREAKFAST THE NEXT MORNING, ALTAN CAME into the infirmary, a set of cuffs hanging from his belt.

The iron clattered with every step, striking two, three, four times as he assumed a position halfway between my bed and the door. He was still too close. "It's time to go back to your cell, Fancy."

With great effort, I swung my shaking legs off the edge of the bed and tested my weight. The stone floor was warm, even through my slippers; we were *so* close to Khulan that his heat seeped through the rock. It was a strange sensation, being this near another god, and I missed Darina and Damyan even more.

"Come on." Altan grabbed my elbow and jerked me from the room. "We don't have time for this."

Maybe he should have thought of that *before* he'd left me to starve.

Numbers skittered in the back of my head as Altan returned me to the first-level cellblock. We came to the anteroom (five paces across, three paces wide), the stairs (thirty), and the empty cells on the way to mine (twenty-four). The numbers had not changed. That was one of the things I liked about the counting. It was reliable.

My cell waited for me. Empty, save the bed, pillow, blanket, and sewage hole (still covered). I stood at the entrance, staring into the dimness. I couldn't bear the thought of stepping inside, trapping myself between those walls where the light of the nearest noorestone barely reached.

Maybe Altan would move the stone if I asked. Since I'd told him what he wanted to know.

But before I could find my voice, he shoved me into the cell and slid the door shut. Iron sang against iron, and through the grille of metal, I saw his eyes even more narrowed, his mouth pulled into a smirk, and the ring of keys on his belt. His fingers brushed across the handle of his baton, not menacingly, but more like a habit.

I'd seen men and women like him before—during my visits to the Luminary Council chamber, or at events with foreign dignitaries, though no weapons were permitted at such secure functions. They'd touch their belts, hips, or even their sleeves, where they sometimes concealed knives in special wrist sheaths (or so I'd heard). Mostly those men and women were Khulani, accustomed to having weapons on their person, though it always seemed like their bodies counted as weapons, too. Even away from the Isle of Warriors, the Khulani people were strong; they were trained for combat in ways the rest of us could only imagine.

Unconscious movement or not, every time Altan touched his baton, I received a clear message: I would pay if I were lying.

"I hope you took advantage of the infirmary and got lots of rest, Fancy." He glared at me and dropped his voice low. "I was the only one who believed you'd live. I know you're stronger than you appear."

I didn't want compliments from him.

He smirked a little. "I also know you're smarter than you appear."

Clearly he hadn't had a good conversation with my mother in which she detailed every one of my failings.

"And I know," he went on, "you're too smart to tell me everything at once. You want to keep something to bargain with. You need that advantage. I understand. But *you* should know that I will be back for more. It would be better for you if you just told me what it is."

He knew. He *knew*.

And worse punishment was coming.

I reached for an expression of calm, but that was impossible with my heart racing and sweat gathering on my hands. Numbers flooded my head: seven bars across the door, two chevrons on his jacket, eleven scars on his face.

He just shook his head. "I thought there was only one useful thing you could possibly tell me. What luck that your skinny face gives away everything. Until tomorrow, Fancy." He turned on his heels and left me standing there, reeling.

Gerel watched from her door, unmoving while we listened to Altan's footfalls down the hall. Her eyes were thinned with suspicion as she studied me. When the door slammed, she muttered, "What makes you so special?"

Nothing. Not anymore. "He hates me."

"I told you he wanted something." She leaned her weight on one hip.

"I'm not strong like you, Gerel." I lowered my eyes, humiliated. "I don't mean just physical strength, but emotional. Resolve. Endurance. You've been here for a year, right?"

She shrugged, like time meant nothing to her. "Where did you hear that?"

Oh. Gossip was probably frowned upon here. I kept talking, like I hadn't heard the question. "But you haven't broken. You haven't given up. You're resilient and that's so"—I fumbled for the right word—"admirable."

And that was the truth. I ached to be strong like Gerel. She'd tried to destroy the Pit, knowing what her punishment would be if she failed. She'd made her attempt anyway, not cowed by fear of the first level, or of knowing the guards would treat her even worse than if she'd been a regular prisoner, because she had been a Khulani Warrior and she'd put a black mark on her honor.

Gerel was strong in unnameable ways, and I would give anything to be like her.

Of course, she scowled at me. "I'm glad you're not dead."

She didn't *sound* glad.

"But." Of course there was a *but*. "You're dangerous. I've stayed alive so long because I don't get involved with people who attract the guards' attention. You should have died. Altan tried to *kill* you."

He hadn't. He needed me alive.

Gerel's expression hardened, like suddenly she was carved from iron. "You've gotten a second chance here. No one else has. Ever." With that, she turned away and began a series of push-ups. I couldn't tell if she was truly happy I was alive or just sort of stunned.

Apparently dismissed, I retreated to my bed and sat on the edge, elbows on my knees, head in my hands.

The mystery woman from the infirmary had been clear: the Luminary Council still needed me. That was why I'd been given a job early, so I'd be fed and moving around. I'd thought a job was just another way for Altan to hurt me. But truly, it was preferential treatment.

Another artifact of my status before.

Tap, tap. Two long beats sounded on the wall behind me. The first letter in my name. ::Mira?::

My heart lurched as memory came flooding back to me: Aaru, pouring his small supply of water into my mouth; Aaru, reaching through the hole to lift up my head so I wouldn't drown; Aaru, reading my vague quiet code when I couldn't speak.

He'd saved me, I was sure of it.

::Thank you. For before.:: I beat the pattern onto my knees, loud enough for him to hear in the quiet cellblock. When I leaned against the wall and closed my eyes, I imagined I could feel the long hallway, the forty cells, the fourteen noorestones.

::Of course. I'm glad you're all right. Gerel is, too, even though she doesn't show it.::

I glanced across the hall. Gerel was still exercising; her faint grunts every time she lifted herself caught in the back of my head, adding up one by one. (Fifty-three push-ups so far. Fifty-four, fifty-five . . .) She didn't like me, that was obvious. Even Aaru's interest in me was because of my fascination with the quiet code, and our alliance.

He wasn't Daminan; he didn't *need* friendship like he needed air. At least, to my knowledge, *The Book of Silence* didn't have dozens of long passages about the joys of loving neighbors.

Complaining wouldn't win him. But I didn't understand how one went about making friends in the first place. Hristo befriended me because I liked the way he'd planted the lala flowers. Ilina and I were forced together, but our shared love of dragons bound us for life.

We'd been young then, but maybe the same ideas applied.

::What do you like?:: I asked.

::What do you mean?::

Was that a hard question? I tried again. ::What do you enjoy?::

::Eating,:: he said. ::Telling stories to my sisters and brother. Silence.::

Before coming to the Pit, I'd never realized how much I enjoyed eating, too, but maybe food wasn't a safe topic. Not when Altan and the guards kept us all on the edge of starvation. As for silence, well, after four days in the dark, silence was terrifying.

That left stories. ::What stories do you tell on Idris?::

::We tell about the Great Fall,:: he said. ::And the journey of our people from the mainland to Idris. Often we tell about Hadil, the first prophet of Idris, and the commandments Idris put in his heart after a decan spent in silent prayer. And, of course, we tell the story of Ramla, who committed the sin of sound. She was Hadil's wife, and when she would not repent, he was forced to silence her.::

Ominous. ::How did he do that?::

::He took her life.::

A chill swept through me. I wanted to ask about the sin of sound—what exactly that meant and why it was punishable by death—but my hands were rooted to my knees and my throat closed against my voice, like it had heard about Ramla's sentence and didn't want to take the risk.

::Sometimes, we tell how the god of silence pulled

away from the others even before the Great Fall, or the eternal struggle against Damyan and Darina, or the trouble of Harta.::

My tutors liked to remind me that all the holy books were written two thousand years ago, when our ancestors came here from the mainland. They were from the perspective of each god, written by the men and women of those times, but sometimes it seemed like nothing had changed.

It was true that Idris and Damina sometimes clashed. Still, that was two thousand years ago. Or centuries and centuries before that, even, if you took into account that many stories took place *before* the Great Fall.

::**I'm from Damina,**:: I said. ::**Are you and I at odds?**::

That was a bold question, out before I realized. Which meant my quiet code was improving, but also that I could run away with that as quickly as I could with my mouth. I'd have to be careful.

::**You and I are not at odds.**:: There was a faint shuffling around on his side of the wall. ::**Because of the treaty, we're not supposed to tell those stories as much, but of course they're passed down. They're part of the texts.**::

I wanted to ask if he believed Damina and Idris were in constant struggle. *The Book of Love* said very little on the subject. Mostly, Darina and Damyan seemed baffled by the continued snubbing they received from Idris, no matter how they tried to befriend him.

But of course the god of silence didn't want to be

friends with the charismatic and earnest god and goddess of love.

And what about their trouble with Harta? I couldn't imagine anyone disliking the Daughter's people. Gifted Hartans brought life to the land. That was the (entirely cruel) reason other islands had occupied Harta for so long: they wanted ownership of the bounty Harta and her people provided.

I didn't ask. We were treading too close to uncomfortable territory.

::**The Mira Treaty,**:: he said. ::**Were you named after it?**::

::**Mira is a common name on Damina.**:: It was the truth, just not an answer to his question. ::**What about plays? Music? Do you have those on Idris?**::

::**No.**:: He was quiet a moment. ::**Not like you do, I think.**::

"Will you show me sometime? I miss music." The off-key singing that came from the end of the cellblock notwithstanding.

"Will try." His voice came soft. Rough. It was a nice voice. A kind voice.

He started to tap something else, but Gerel groaned and rolled onto her back. "Stop the percussion. You're making me lose track of my repetitions."

On the other side of the wall, Aaru fell silent. I imagined him slumped, head hanging down, hands motionless on his knees. But that image was probably wrong. That was what *I'd* do, and I didn't know Aaru well enough to guess how he'd move in the face of such admonishment.

"You're on three hundred and five." I wanted to scold her for being mean to him, but I couldn't make the words come. That would have been confrontational and I was nothing if not a coward, as Altan's threats earlier had proven.

"How do you know?" she asked. "Were you counting?"

"Yes." Had she guessed about my numbers? Or had the question been sarcastic? I didn't know how to tell the difference when it came to her, so I took my cowardly ways and scrambled under the bed. I'd talk with Aaru through the hole.

"Fine." Her body thumped on the floor as she rolled over again.

I turned toward the hole and pulled my pillow under my head, eager to muffle the noise of Gerel exercising, but still glad to have her back.

Aaru was waiting for me. He was pressed close to the hole, his long fingers stretched through to my side. His hand blocked his face and muffled his whisper: "You count."

"What?"

He switched to quiet code. ::All the time. You count everything.::

My heart stumbled. He knew, and he wasn't being sarcastic about it. He *knew*. "How could you tell?"

He made a deep, pleased noise in the back of his throat. ::You learned the quiet code fast. That is unusual.::

My chest and throat and cheeks flamed. That was it? The quiet code? I wasn't even good at it, but it had given me away. My traitorous need to have a secret language with someone had revealed my deepest shame.

Mother would never have let me get to this point, if she'd been here. She'd have warned me about trying to make friends with a boy from Idris. She'd have warned me about trying too hard to use the Daminan gifts when I clearly had no talent for them. Some people had strong gifts while others had weak ones, but Darina and Damyan had skipped over me completely.

::**You count in your sleep,**:: Aaru went on. ::**I hear you most nights.**::

And I kept my silent neighbor awake, on top of everything else. I was rude. Inconsiderate. Noisy. Lacking in all charm and manners.

A sob choked out of me. "Sorry." The word sounded thick and forced. "I didn't mean to." What could I do to muffle not the noise of everyone else, but my own blasted mind?

Humiliation burned in me, a fire that roared through my ears and thoughts. No one was supposed to know about the counting. It was embarrassing, not just for me, but for my entire family. How could anyone possibly respect us if they knew *Mira Minkoba*—the *Hopebearer*—couldn't control her own thoughts? That she counted because of the anxiety attacks?

Oh, Darina and Damyan, how I wished for Doctor

Chilikoba and her amber bottle of pills. Without it, I was at the mercy of my own tempestuous mind.

::You don't like it.:: He peered at me through the hole.

"Of course not." My voice cracked. On top of everything, my *voice cracked.*

Speaking of cracks, maybe one would open in the floor and I'd fall in.

::Then I will not ask about it again.::

Gratitude warred with the humiliation. Of course, he was just being nice because we were trapped here together, but I wouldn't turn down that courtesy. **::Thank you,::** I tapped.

He was so kind. Thoughtful. For a moment, I closed my eyes and recalled how he'd given me water, and the gentle way he'd held his hand above mine. Close enough to touch, but light enough not to crush. Maybe it had been nothing for him—he seemed like the kind of person who'd have saved anyone—but I wanted to replay those memories over and over, polishing them like a pretty stone, until they became a safe place to go when the panic loomed around me.

::What do you like?:: he asked.

That was a question you asked someone you wanted to be friends with, not what you asked the girl you were stuck with. So why had he asked *me*?

Mother would warn me it wasn't because he wanted my friendship as badly as I wanted his. He was from Idris—therefore not from Damina and not to be trusted.

(Hristo wasn't technically from Damina, either, but she trusted him because he'd lived most of his life on Damina and had already nearly died for me.)

Hristo would tell me to be cautious, but Ilina would suggest Aaru's interest could be genuine.

Krasimir was always telling me to be bold—to be myself, counting and all. I wasn't bold, though, and I didn't want to count. Or, rather, I wanted to be able to make it stop.

I searched my mind for another absent person's advice, but I couldn't guess what Father would say. He was never around to say much. And Zara? She'd stopped voluntarily speaking to me three years ago.

That was it. For one of the most famous people in Damina—maybe in the Fallen Isles—I was really, pathetically, alone. At least when it came to people I took advice from.

I came back to myself. Back to the gloomy space beneath the bed. Back to the boy waiting on the other side of the hole.

Aaru hadn't moved. He didn't ask again, or make impatient motions, or fall asleep. He just . . . waited, giving me time and space to consider my answer. What did I like?

::**Why do you ask?**:: My throat would have closed against that question and made my voice sound pitiful. But with the quiet code . . . He couldn't tell how much I dreaded the inevitable answer: that he'd asked simply to be polite, because we were allies and if I ever escaped, so would he.

Our hands were close together. I hadn't realized it before, but now, he reached out and, with a breath-light touch, stroked down my smallest finger. It was a tiny thing, but it sent warm thrills through me. And then he whispered, "I want to know you."

Five words. They destroyed me. They destroyed everything I thought I'd understood about why he was nice to me. He *wanted to know me*.

In the same way I wanted to know him?

But why? He couldn't see my face. All he'd witnessed of me were my fumbling attempts to befriend him, and crying, and near death.

He was so unlike all the boys on Damina. The outgoing boys who could charm a rock. The polished boys with perfect manners and practiced smiles. The boys who always knew exactly the right thing to say.

No, Aaru wasn't like them. He was quiet. Mysterious. Patient. Achingly generous. Without ulterior motive. I liked the way he spoke—with careful deliberation, as though every word mattered as much as the last. I liked the way he touched my hand, and the flutter of yearning it ignited deep inside me.

Why would he want to know me? I was nothing.

No, his wanting had to be different. His wanting was yet another effort of his Idrisi upbringing. He was kind.

He was considerate. He'd have saved anyone's life. We were allies.

There. That was better. Safer.

That left two choices: give him the truth, or give him one of the manufactured answers Mother and Father had designed for me, because the truth was not appropriate for parties and important social functions. The truth drew curiosity, making people ask me questions when it was my duty to encourage them to talk. After all, they were much smarter and more interesting.

But we weren't at a party now. Or an important social function. Here, I wasn't the Hopebearer who needed to dazzle. No. We were in a deep-underground nightmare, and Aaru already knew my most secret shame. He promised not to speak of it again, and I believed him; he was filled with such *ardent* silence and mystery. Maybe, with him, I didn't have to hide the parts of me that had always been deemed unacceptable.

Here I was just an anonymous girl who liked the same thing a thousand other girls liked.

::**Dragons,**:: I said at last. ::**I like dragons.**::

BEFORE

Nine Years Ago

MY EIGHTH BIRTHDAY WAS THE BEST DAY OF MY LIFE.

Mother told Sylva to put me in a silk dress as gold as the sun, and put my hair into an elaborate braided bun. Then Father gave me a wrapped box to hold the whole carriage ride out of Crescent Prominence. Hristo sat across from me, already my constant shadow.

It didn't take long before I realized where we were going: the Luminary Department of Drakontos Examination.

The carriage stopped in front of the department facilities. I stepped out, peering around, but I didn't see even one dragon flying. How disappointing.

Inside the building was another matter. We tromped into a recovery ward, where Ilina and her parents waited.

A tiny gold dragon slept in Ilina's arms. *Drakontos raptus.* The baby dragon she'd told me about.

"Open your box," Mother said.

Inside I found one large leather glove with flowering designs along the cuff. It was pretty, but wouldn't look right with any of my dresses.

"It's for hunting," Father said. "There's more equipment, of course. And you'll have to train every day."

Before I could ask how a glove would help me hunt, Ilina slipped the baby dragon into my arms. "For your birthday."

The dragon was lighter than I'd expected. Hollow bones, like a bird. Her scales were warm and slick, sharp at the tips, and she matched the color of my dress perfectly. "She's mine?" I could hardly breathe for the joy building in my chest.

"Yours," Ilina's mother confirmed. "Yours to train, that is. And you'll have to do it here."

Of course. Because the Mira Treaty not only limited the public's contact with dragons, but prevented ownership. It was too hazardous for regular people to spend much time with dragons, since they were endangered. Ilina's parents must have trusted me a *lot*. And coming here to train the little gold dragon? That meant I'd get to visit every day.

"She has a sister," Ilina said. She hadn't told me that before. "A silver. And now *we're* sisters—wingsisters, like dragons—because the silver is mine. I named her Crystal."

I wanted to explode with all the good feelings, but just then, my dragon opened her golden eyes, like a beautiful lala flower blooming. "LaLa," I whispered. "That's her name."

She must have liked it, because she rubbed her face against my knuckles and made a throaty sound, almost like a purr. And for the first time in my life, I knew what true, unconditional love felt like.

CHAPTER FIFTEEN

JUST AS PRISON LIFE WAS RETURNING TO NORMAL, A new inmate joined us in the first level.

It was evening, only an hour or so before the noorestones went dark. Gerel was exercising, and I was mirroring everything she did whether she liked it or not. (I honestly couldn't tell.) Already, my muscles ached. I'd been sent back to work this morning, made to scrub the same infirmary where I'd been treated. My lower back kept pinching and Gerel wasn't speaking to me enough to make me risk asking if there was a stretch to fix it.

So I worked through the pain, holding back every whimper that threatened to emerge, because aside from still being in the Pit, it had been a relatively good day: the noorestones had illuminated in the morning, I'd been fed three times, and I'd sneaked several long drinks of water when Sarannai wasn't looking. Or, I supposed, equally possible was that she'd been instructed to let me drink all the water I wanted, but I had trouble imagining she wouldn't have at least slapped me for slacking off.

No one in the cleaning group had said anything about my absence. Not that they'd ever said anything to me anyway. Ever since the first day when Altan began talking to me at the dinner table, they all ignored me, like proximity to someone he was interested in could hurt them by extension.

Gerel stopped hopping from side to side and lifted both of her arms high in the air, seeming to reach and reach and strain to touch the ceiling. Like she could, if she just tried hard enough.

I copied her stance and stretched my fingers toward the top of my cell, holding the position until she began to bend forward at the hips, and lower her arms until her hands brushed the floor. I mimicked her, and while I hung there, blood rushing to my face for five, six, seven deep breaths, a knot of tension in my back released. I groaned with relief.

When Gerel drew herself upright, she wore a knowing smirk. I wanted to say something smart to her, but that would have involved having something smart to say, and I was too relieved that whatever had been pinched in my back was no longer a problem.

Then we heard it, both of us at the same time: the

door at the bath end of the hall screeched open, and a warrior barked for someone to move forward.

My heart jumped. What if it was Altan, coming back for the rest of my secrets?

Gerel frantically scooted to the back of her cell, spine pressed against stone. Though I wanted to rush to the bars and peer out, I did the same. She was practically an expert at being a prisoner and I was a *Drakontos mimikus.* My heart pounded as I listened to the cadence of steps and the ragged breathing of the new person.

They came across the front of my cell so quickly I barely had time to study them. Three warriors, all strangers, created a triangle around the new prisoner.

She was tall—taller than Gerel even—and held her chin high as she strode past. Black braids—too many for me to count—hung to her waist, bound together with a copper band. She liked that color, apparently, because her clothes matched: she wore a loose, long-sleeved shirt, and trousers with so much fabric they might be mistaken for a skirt. Aside from her fingertips and face, every part of her skin was covered.

It was only when she glanced my way that I noticed the tattoos.

Copper-colored tattoos swirled around her left eye and down her cheek, bright against her shadow skin. Her eyes, too, were the same brilliant shade as her tattoos, and when her gaze passed over me, I had the unsettling sense that she saw more than most people.

I saw something, too, though. A face I recognized. I knew this girl. And she knew me.

Then she was gone, past my cell.

The door next to Gerel's opened. The copper woman stepped inside. One of her guards explained the food and bathing schedule to her, and then the warriors left.

When the door shut behind them, a hum filled the cellblock. Down the hall, older prisoners murmured about the new. Snatches of conversation reached my end:

"She looks important."

"Who is she?"

"The Dawn Lady. She's the Lady of Eternal Dawn."

I met Gerel's eyes, but couldn't think of a way to talk about the new prisoner without the new prisoner overhearing. Not the quiet code. Last night, I'd asked Aaru if he would teach Gerel his secret language. He'd said no; she was too far to learn it without the other prisoners overhearing.

Instead, I moved to the front left of my cell and peered through the metal grille toward the Dawn Lady.

She stood at her door, too, with her head high and copper eyes trained on me. Her skin was flawless: smooth and dark and unmarked, save the tattoo on her left side, which curled from her hair down her temple and cheek and chin. The copper swirls disappeared beneath her clothes.

Envy burned through me. She looked perfect, even in prison, and though I hadn't seen my own face in a month, I knew I was a mess. My skin felt dry in some places, oily in others. All I had to do was look at my hands—cracked knuckles, ragged fingernails, callused fingers—to know that I had changed. After nineteen days in the Pit, I was no longer the beauty my mother had loved to brag about.

So it was possible Chenda didn't recognize me—not without the dresses and cosmetics. I couldn't be sure, though. We didn't have much history.

I'd first seen her four years ago. She'd been sixteen. I'd been thirteen. Some of the Twilight Senate had come to present the newly selected Lady of Eternal Dawn to the Luminary Council and other important figures on Damina. She'd been making her way through all the islands' capitals, and we were the first stop.

I'd been invited to stand with the Luminary Council, of course.

"If the Twilight Senate is going to show off their special teenage girl," Ilina had joked, *"of course the Luminary Council will, too. They have to be the best."*

Ilina had a higher opinion of me than was really warranted, but she was my best friend so I forgave her.

The presentation ceremony had been unbearably long. We'd spent three hours in the Theater of True Light; it was the only building in Crescent Prominence that could hold so many people. I'd had to stand beside the Luminary Council and various others they'd deemed worthy enough, while Ilina and her family (and most other people lucky enough to get an invitation) sat on the main floor and in balconies.

Chenda had been just as beautiful then as she stood at the center of the stage, brilliant noorestone light focused on her; she didn't have the tattoos yet. There had been speeches, a short demonstration of shadow skill, and finally, generous gifts of jewelry and trinkets exchanged between both governments.

Elbena Krasteba, my minder from the Luminary Council, had chosen an elaborate hairpin for me to give to Chenda. It almost looked like the sun rising over the horizon. In turn, Chenda had given me a small copper dragon.

With the addition of a formal dinner, during which neither of us had time to speak with the other, that was the extent of our meeting.

And now, Chenda M'rizz, the Lady of Eternal Dawn, was here in the Pit.

Like me.

Curiosity burned, but I didn't ask.

"Hello," I said. "I'm Mira." Like we didn't know each other at all. Like I didn't have a surname. Hopefully she would realize I was anonymous here, and play along.

Here we were: two girls with famous pasts, both of us wrongly imprisoned (I assumed). Neither of us were meant for this place. I wondered if she'd be offered a job, too, as an excuse to keep feeding her. I wondered if she was just as scared and confused as I had been, even if she was doing a better job hiding it. And I wondered if she felt this faint connection between us, formed four years ago when we hadn't been given time to talk, and reignited now with both of us trapped in the most terrible part of the Fallen Isles.

I could warn her about Altan and the horrible methods the guards used to extract information. I could warn her about Sarannai, should she decide to take a cleaning job.

We could be best prison friends.

"Leave me alone." She took a measured step backward and vanished from the doorway. "Don't talk to me again."

Oh, yes. Best prison friends for sure.

I MADE A few more attempts over the rest of the evening. Every time, Gerel gave me a look that said I was stupid for trying.

She was probably right.

"Maybe it was murder," one man said. Kason. That was his name. Gerel had told me who was who the night before, but I'd had so many other things on my mind. "Maybe the Dawn Lady killed someone with her glorious light."

Varissa snorted. "I heard it was her shadow. It withered away and they couldn't keep her any longer."

"And *how*," Kumas asked, "would you hear that? You haven't heard anything the rest of us haven't."

"Oh." Varissa sighed loudly. "I thought that's what my daughter said. But she's still on Bopha, isn't she?"

Kason groaned. "You're not Bophan. You're Daminan. And furthermore, you don't have a daughter. At least, you didn't when you got here and introduced yourself to us seven times."

"Oh." Varissa began to sob. "I'm not Bophan?"

"No."

"I wanted the Dawn Lady to bless my daughter."

"You don't—"

The conversation on that end of the cellblock grew jumbled and even more confused. Someone shouted about the Dawn Lady's shadow again. Hurrok insisted that she'd *eaten* someone else's shadow. And finally, Chenda stepped toward the door of her cell and cleared her throat.

Everyone stopped speaking.

Even when they couldn't see her, they felt the power of her presence.

"Yes." Chenda lifted her voice. "I am Chenda M'rizz, the Lady of Eternal Dawn. And now I am caught in the great maw of the Pit, like the rest of you."

One of the other prisoners whimpered. Hurrok, perhaps.

"I was not imprisoned for murder or a withering shadow or *eating* anyone else's shadow. I'll tell you the truth of the matter, but only once. So pay attention."

Even Gerel leaned toward Chenda's cell to listen.

"The Twilight Senate discussed a problem, which I found important and dear to my heart. There are many who believe Hartans should be deported, and have begun protesting their continued presence by setting them ablaze."

Bophans were setting Hartans on *fire*? My stomach turned over and I wanted to be sick, but I couldn't stop listening.

"It is a great insult to my people, dying like that, your shadow snuffed out." She shook her head, braids sliding across her clothes. "After riots across Bopha, the Twilight Senate met to discuss a course of action. It was proposed that Hartans should return to Harta for their own safety and the well-being of Bopha. For a year now, Hartans have been accused of destroying the land." She paused and frowned. "For centuries, wealthy Bophans have hired Hartans to come tend fields and farms. Even after the Mira Treaty, many Hartans chose to remain."

Like Hristo's father. My parents had hired him as a gardener when Hristo was just an infant, and he'd stayed with us after the treaty. He always said he liked working on the prominence, and he was so, so good at it.

"But recently, fields have gone fallow, and not even the most gifted Hartan can make them fertile again. Or, as many Bophans believe, they *won't* make those fields fertile. All across Bopha, my people have accused Hartans of poisoning the land."

That was outrageous. Hartans would never harm the land.

"During the discussion," Chenda went on, "I stood for Hartans. Many have lived on the Isle of Shadow since childhood. They have nothing in Harta. No promise of work, no place to live. My opponents insisted that Hartans are loving people: they will gladly take in their fellow Daughter-born. But I said that we cannot count on that. For centuries, the Twilight Senate blocked Hartan independence, and as people who committed such a grievous wrong, we must do everything in our power to make it right."

I nodded. Her words rang true.

"The Twilight Senate said the people of Bopha could not bear the burden of their ancestors' guilt. They said Harta had been independent for seventeen years—most of my life—and I could not begin to understand how different the world is now."

I'd often heard the same words from the Luminary Council.

"In the High Tower, in the center of the Shadowed City, we argued the matter for days. Meanwhile, protests and riots broke out all across the island. Suddenly, before the fifth day's meeting, I was arrested and taken from my home. They said I had been feeding information to a Hartan rebellion on Bopha—through my Hartan lover."

I gasped.

"They claimed he had started a riot that killed fourteen Bophans, including three members of the Twilight Senate. They claimed he had burned them alive, slaughtering their shadows. They claimed I had told him the time and location to do this. I knew this could not be true. Nevertheless, he was ripped from his home and beaten to death during the arrest. No proof could be found of my involvement, but my association and defense of the Hartan people was enough to earn a sentence to the Pit."

My heart was pounding and my knuckles pale around the metal grille.

Chenda met my eyes, and for a moment, I thought I saw a spark of recognition. Like she knew me. Like she remembered me. But I had no distinctive markings, and I was so changed from the Hopebearer version of me. Maybe she *didn't* know me.

She said, "I am here because I stood up for what was right."

She was so brave. I wouldn't have had the courage to stand up like that.

As the evening crawled toward lights-out, I sat in the center of my cell, trying to imagine myself saying the things she'd said, defending the people she'd defended, losing someone I loved like she had. I tried to imagine myself retaining my composure and strength after such heartbreak.

And mostly, I sank beneath the crush of understanding: we'd both defied our governments and tried to do what was right. The Luminary Council's betrayal was one thing, but the Twilight Senate as well?

I'd been naïve to think my parents would be able to persuade the Luminary Council to free me, or that the Pit would take prisoners just temporarily. The Pit was for life.

No one was coming to get me.

I WAS ON my own.

If I didn't want to stay in the Pit the rest of my life, this dark threat of Altan's hanging over me, I needed to do something about it. I needed to escape before he could pry out more secrets.

But not right now. It was almost dark, and I didn't want to be caught in it.

First, I found my silk square and fastened it over my hair. Second, I checked to make sure my pillow and blanket were under the bed, where they belonged.

"Are you all right?" Gerel sat on her bed already, arms looped around her knees. Showing off, clearly. The normal sleeping location held no terror for *her*, after all.

"It doesn't really matter, does it? I can't change anything." The words came out colder than intended.

"You spent all last night crying and kept me awake. So yes, it matters. You need to learn to overcome your fear, that way the rest of us can get some sleep."

My chest stung from her comment. I hadn't spent *all* last night crying. Just . . . some of it. "Sorry to inconvenience you. Try sleeping during the day while I'm working."

Before she could respond, I spun around like I had somewhere else to be. At that moment, the lights went out.

Panic stole my breath. The darkness disoriented, but I kept my numbers: I took the two steps to my bed, knelt, and scurried to the safety of that small space.

Down the hall, Hurrok opened his lungs and released his terror into the hall. The sound echoed, filling the cellblock like liquid. As much as I hated his screaming, it was a reminder: this was normal darkness, filled with other people. This was not alone darkness. Isolated darkness.

Still, I found myself counting, gathering my numbers until there was nothing else.

I made it to five hundred and eight before I registered the heat of Aaru's hand on mine. He was tapping, telling a story.

::**Wait,**:: I said. ::**Will you start over?**::

The screaming man stopped at last, leaving behind an aching silence.

::**Very well.**:: From Aaru's quiet code, I couldn't tell whether he was annoyed or not.

"Sorry." Mother would have had a fit if she knew how often I ended up apologizing to an Idrisi boy; she'd have said it was beneath me. Unless, of course, I was being *the* Mira, and I needed to be gracious to everyone. But then I'd have been in trouble for not paying attention.

::**Why?**::

"I was rude. I wasn't being attentive."

::**You were scared.**:: He petted my fingers, as though brushing the fears away. It was such a simple motion, but it made my heart pound with a painful yearning. ::**I would have stayed if I could have.**::

"You saved me," I whispered. "When you came back, you saved me."

Before he could reply, I scooted toward the hole, forcing him to pull his arm back to his side. It was most comfortable for me if I let him be the one to reach through the hole, but after my days in the dark, pressing my arm through for his cup of water, I knew how uncomfortable that was.

So I moved closer to the hole and slipped my hand through in offering. A breath played across my upturned palm. His mouth was so close; if I stretched my fingers, I could touch his face.

I didn't move.

He did.

It was just a rearrangement of limbs, adjusting his position, but for an instant, his face brushed across my fingertips. Mouth? Cheek? Nose? It was too brief to tell. But still, my heart raced.

Then, warm, rough skin slid the length of my fingers. Our hands curled together for a moment before he turned mine over and drew me in a fraction farther. His mouth grazed my knuckles before he released me.

My hand stayed there, suspended in the air. I wanted to act, to map his features with my fingertips, but what if this wasn't an invitation? What if I ruined everything?

"Mira." His voice came soft, and in little puffs across my knuckles. He'd kept his strange pronunciation: Meer-AH.

I moved. And I found his eyebrow, his temple, and a sharp line of his cheekbone. I traveled downward and met the curve of his top lip, and there I could feel the rapidness of his breathing.

Though I wanted to continue this exploration, I withdrew. I couldn't tell if he was nervous or upset, excited or panicked, so I pulled my hand back to the neutral territory of the hole.

He didn't say anything, aloud or otherwise, but when his hand pressed into the hole with mine, some of my worry melted away. Maybe he hadn't minded.

"I've decided," I whispered.

He waited.

"I don't want the story."

He drew back just a breath.

Oh. He thought I was rejecting him. This. Whatever this was. "I mean . . ." I cursed my lack of Daminan gifts. I didn't have the right words. The right tone. "I want you to tell me about *you*, not just any story."

Two, three, four heartbeats. And then: "Me?"

I echoed his words from before. "I want to know you."

More heartbeats raced between us. Eight, nine, ten. "Really?"

I cupped his hand in both of mine. ::**I want to know everything about you.**:: My face heated. I hadn't meant to be so obvious, so pathetically fascinated by this strange and silent boy.

But if he noticed, he chose not to embarrass me. ::**What do you want to know?**::

::**Everything. Anything you'll tell me.**:: Oh, by the seven Fallen Gods. And all the Upper Gods, too. I couldn't trust my mouth not to speak without my mind's direction, and it seemed I couldn't trust my hands, either.

Aaru chuckled, both aloud and by drumming his fingers in a quiet-code laugh. ::**Narrow it down, curious fr—**::

He didn't finish the last word, and suddenly *that* was

what I most wanted to know about. But he'd stopped his sentence for a reason, so I chose another question. ::**Are you close with your family?**:: It seemed like he must be, and I'd always wondered what that was like.

::**They are everything to me. When we escape, I will return to them.**::

And leave me. It shouldn't have surprised me, or stung, because we'd known each other only eighteen days. He had to help the people he loved, and I had to rescue the dragons before the Algotti Empire got hold of them.

Still, the thought of losing him opened a deep loneliness inside of me. I'd been wrong earlier, when I'd thought I was on my own, because at this moment, I had Aaru. He'd wanted to escape all along, while I'd been content with mere survival while waiting to be rescued. I'd thought my release was imminent and there was no reason to act.

But I could not wait for change. I had to *make* change.

Aaru opened my hand, trailing his fingers from the hollow of my wrist to my palm. ::**What are you thinking?**::

::**I'm going to help you see your family again.**::

His breathing hitched, and the way his fingers grazed mine felt like a smile. ::**How do we begin?**::

CHAPTER SIXTEEN

THE NEXT DAY, I STOPPED EATING DINNER.

Well, mostly. I ate just enough to convince the guards and other prisoners that I wasn't doing anything wrong, but then I pulled out strips of silk I'd torn from the remnants of my dress, and wrapped bread and fruit and slabs of fried meat. Everything went into my pockets and down my shirt.

"What are you doing?" Tirta hissed as I took my tray to her window. "You're going to get in trouble again."

"*The Book of Love* says to ensure our neighbors have enough to eat, and my neighbors are in need. If I can help, I should."

"Is it Gerel?" Her frown said she disapproved.

"If I try hard enough, she will like me." Surely Tirta

could understand. This was a basic Daminan need: without friends, without love, we could not be whole. I might not have had the divine gifts that made people want to like me, but that didn't mean the desire wasn't there. "But also for the boy in the cell next to mine."

Tirta's eyes widened. "Do they mean that much to you?"

If I told her how much I wanted to escape, and about my alliance with Aaru, she'd protest. Instead, I whispered, "Please don't tell anyone."

"I won't." And, because she was Tirta and she was kind, she slipped a small container of water through the window. It wasn't much—a few swallows at best—but I could give it to Gerel; Aaru had his cup.

"Fancy!" Altan roared from the far side of the mess hall, and I sucked in my stomach as far as I could, as though I stood a chance at hiding all the food stashed inside my shirt.

His eyes narrowed, but if he noticed the bulge, he didn't mention it. Instead, he escorted me back to the first level without speaking. Or, rather, with the sort of expectant quiet that hinted he was waiting for me to speak first.

In the anteroom, he paused before opening the cellblock door. We stood alone in a small room, me with a bundle of contraband food stuffed into my shirt, and him with his arms crossed over his chest. "This is your chance to tell me what else you know."

My heart thrummed in my chest. Last time he'd

confronted me outside the cellblock, he'd left me in the dark.

"I don't know anything." The words came breathy. Scared.

He sighed and opened the door. Voices threaded through the hall, bringing a slight measure of relief. "All right," Altan said. "Have it your way." Finally, I was deposited in my cell, along with the dark sense that he had something terrible in mind.

As soon as he was gone, I divided the food into three even parcels, then took the first one under the bed. "Aaru."

He was already there. ::**Mira,**:: he tapped, and then switched to speech. "I have questions."

"About?" A thread of worry spun through me. Had he figured out my identity?

"How dragons make fire."

Oh. Now *that* I was happy to answer. "Take this. Then I'll tell you more than you ever wanted to know." I pressed the package of food through the hole.

A moment later, he peeled open the layers of silk. "Mira."

I waited.

"This is too much."

"It's not nearly enough." When I slipped my hand through the hole to his side, flashes of last night played through my mind. The way his skin had heated under my fingers, the quickness of his breath, but mostly the in-between moments, when we'd finished discussing a topic and hadn't yet found a new one. I should have pulled my hand away. Or he should have. But neither of us did.

And now, his hand breezed over mine again. ::**You need to eat too.**::

::**I should have been bringing food for you all along. I get plenty, and allies share resources.**:: I scooted out from under the bed before he could protest further. "Gerel, I hope you're good at catching."

"Keep it." She crossed her arms. "After we were moved out, Aaru told me about your alliance, but alliances with you are too dangerous. It's not worth the risk."

"Don't you want to"—I dropped my voice—"escape?"

"I want to *live*."

"This isn't living."

She glared, and I almost backed down, but warriors admired strength. She hadn't said anything about the way I mimicked her exercises, but there was a sense of approval sometimes. She didn't talk with me the way Aaru did, but she liked me better than the previous occupant of my cell and she was glad I wasn't dead. That was something.

"Fine. I'm not really hungry, but toss it over."

I did. First the bundle of food, the ends of the silk tucked into a fold so it wouldn't come undone, and then the small water pouch Tirta had given me.

The food was gone before I realized she'd even opened the bundle.

"I have another," I said. "For Chenda."

In the cell next to Gerel's, Chenda looked up at the sound of her name. But she didn't move or reach out for her food.

"Pass it to her." I tossed Gerel the third package, and though she tried to hand it around the bars, she was resolutely ignored.

"I don't think she wants it." Gerel eyed the bundle like she'd gladly dispose of its contents.

"We should share it," I said at last. I wouldn't accept defeat, though. This would not be my last overture of friendship. "If Chenda won't eat it, then we should share it with the others."

"You have food?" asked the singing girl down the line. Kumas. "I love food."

Gerel frowned, but she said, "Yes, Mira brought food for you all. Make sure you share it evenly."

There wasn't much food to split between four people, and it would be a challenge to toss the parcel from cell to cell without spilling, especially since most of the cells weren't currently occupied.

Gerel barked dire warnings about what would happen if they dropped food, or if the guards caught them, or if they even whispered about what I'd done. Miraculously, everyone swore to keep silent as they took some of the food and passed the rest on.

After several minutes went by, filled only with quiet moans of food-induced pleasure, the silk square came back to me. I pulled out a knot, and a smooth brown pebble fell to the floor: a weight, so the cloth could be tossed.

"Good job," Gerel said. "They're yours now."

That hadn't been the point of bringing food, but I hoped she was right.

AARU AND I made a short list of ways to prepare for our escape:

1. *Help allies by feeding them.*

2. *Get stronger by exercising with Gerel.*

3. *Learn about the layout of the Pit, and especially its exits.*

4. *Behave for the guards so they wouldn't suspect anything.*

5. *Look for opportunities to escape.*

It wasn't much, but given our limited movement within the Pit, the sharp knife of constant hunger, and our general lack of experience in great escapes, it was what we had. As if it were a dream that might slip away if we didn't discuss it, we spent the next decan polishing our plan until it felt real.

And in the pure blackness after the noorestones went

dark, I found Aaru's hand, and we talked until we fell asleep.

"I ACCEPTED THE job." Aaru's whisper slithered through the dim space as I passed him a bundle of food through our hole. "Start tomorrow."

A bright spark of hope shot through me. "Good. That gets us one step closer."

He made a faint noise of affirmation.

"We've been here a month and a day now."

Again, another noise—a barely audible *hmph*.

"Three decans and a day," I said. "Thirty-one days." Thirty-two for him, if we wanted to be accurate. Which my brain did.

Another *hmph*. Now he sounded a little annoyed. Of course he knew. Idris had the same calendar as the rest of the Fallen Isles.

I pulled back to the actual conversation, forcing my numbers to the background. "This is going to make a difference."

"We will escape."

Progress was slow, but we'd agreed from the start that we needed to be careful. Deliberate. We'd get only one chance, and we needed to make it work.

Fortunately, we had Gerel. She didn't really believe we'd accomplish anything, but she played along. She knew the Heart better—she said—than any other trainee in her group, so she was able to give us a full list.

There were three exits:

1. *The one I'd been brought through (it opened into a small grove of trees outside the city).*

2. *The exit for dragons (which I'd suspected, but now I had confirmation).*

3. *An exit into Warrior's Circle (very public, not ideal for escape).*

I'd have preferred to map the routes in my head myself, counting steps and intersections, but my movements were carefully monitored. Gerel's instructions would have to do.

And now Aaru was going to work, too.

That meant he would be allowed out of his cell every day. He'd get to move around. Exercise. *Eat.* It wasn't cleaning, like me, though. He'd been selected to work in the forge, where prisoners helped build the great chain links of the God Shackle.

Neither Aaru nor I had even half a clue about what the God Shackle was, so Gerel had rolled her eyes and explained that it was part of the Khulani solution to the Great Abandonment. Decades ago, when it was first noticed that there were fewer dragons than ever, the Khulani people had begun work on the immense chain—to literally bind their god to the seabed.

It seemed horrible to me, but the Warrior and the Lovers had such different views. It was probably a comfort to them.

::**We will escape,**:: Aaru repeated in quiet code, as I shimmied out from under the bed to distribute the rest of the food.

I glanced at Chenda, but her back was turned toward me, as usual. Even so, her changes were evident. Her braids looked ragged. Her copper clothes gathered snags and rips. Her perfect skin turned blotchy and blemished.

It was more difficult to see into her cell than Gerel's, but sometimes as I walked by to and from work, I caught Chenda running her fingers across a tattered sleeve or down a long braid, like she could smooth the hairs back into position. She mourned her beauty. I understood. And that was why I kept trying to befriend her, no matter her rebukes.

Again tonight, she didn't accept any of my food, but when the package went down the line, a few cheers went up. "Mira!" shouted Varissa. "My daughter the food bringer!"

Shortly after I'd started bringing food, Varissa—the woman who thought she had a daughter but didn't, and thought she was from Bopha but wasn't—decided to claim *me* as her daughter. I didn't particularly want to be caught up in the fantasies of troubled minds, but resistance posed just as many problems.

I'd learned to give Aaru-like grunts when Varissa

talked about our lives. She blamed our incarceration on a theft of mercy; apparently, we'd stolen bread for a homeless child with a magical singing voice and a box full of kittens. For that small crime, we'd been sentenced to the most horrible place on the Fallen Isles. At least, that was usually the story. The other story she liked involved a palm tree, a duck, and twenty-seven officer jackets "borrowed" from the town militia.

Then there was Hurrok, who screamed at night, and Kumas, who sang all the time though she had no talent for it, and Kason, who seemed to hate everyone but me. Probably because of the food.

When the food was all gone and the strips of silk returned to me, I hid them inside my pillow and copied Gerel's stance. Aaru and I were both exercising with her now, though when I'd told her it was for our alliance, she'd made me promise to never try standing on my hands again.

"I wanted to be a Drakon Warrior," she said during a series of squats. "That's why I joined. I was small for my age, so no one thought I could do it. I endured the other trainees' taunting for the first year—and then I broke every nose in my group within a few minutes."

My gasp made her smile.

"Were you punished?" Aaru asked. Idris had very strict rules, he'd told me before, and even stricter punishments. Mostly, they seemed to involve locking people in basements.

Gerel shrugged. "I was reprimanded and made to

apologize, but immediately given the top position in my class. On account of my fierceness and clear fighting skills." She glanced at me and . . . didn't quite smile, but almost. "Besides, noses look ridiculous. I improved the situation."

I giggled in spite of myself. "They do, don't they? But can you imagine our faces without them?"

"Oh, seven gods. No." She gave a shiver of disgust.

"Did you become a Drakon Warrior?" Aaru spoke carefully, quietly, like waiting for someone to catch him. One did not speak aloud to their superiors on Idris—not without invitation—and he, like most of us, considered Gerel an expert here.

"No." A frown tugged on her mouth. "The Mira Treaty went into effect when I was three years old, but I always believed the part outlawing the practice of dragon riding would be repealed."

"Right. Forgot that part. Sorry."

Gerel shook her head. "I don't know how you could forget the worst part of it. I hate the Mira Treaty."

"Barely affects me." Aaru said it like a shrug.

"What do you think of it?" Gerel looked at me. "After all, you have the unfortunate distinction of sharing a name with it. I bet you have an opinion."

I was of the opinion that the Mira Treaty did more good than harm. It *helped* the dragons. It *freed* Harta. It *united* the islands. Sure, dragons were illegal to own now, and if anyone understood the desire for dragons, I did. But we did what was necessary to care for the children of the gods.

I weighed the idea of asking Gerel whether she knew the Drakon Warriors had not truly disbanded. Altan had all but admitted his involvement, but he didn't say *when* he'd joined them. Gerel might know, but there was equal chance she didn't, and it wasn't my place to tell her when I didn't have more information.

"Well?" Annoyance edged Gerel's tone. "You probably got teased in school. You must have thought about it."

I pulled myself back into the present. Gerel had been nice to me for the last few days, and I wanted to keep her that way.

"I have." I just hadn't thought of a way to talk about it while hiding that I was *the* Mira. And since Gerel hated the treaty, it seemed best not to give her another reason to despise me. "It seems to me that the Mira Treaty—"

"I tried to kill Mira once," Hurrok said from down the hall.

Gerel stopped in the middle of stretching her arm across her chest. Her eyes cut to me.

Then his words registered.

"What did you say?" Gerel's voice was deep. Angry. She'd always seemed powerful to me, but when she gripped the bar of her door and peered out the side—not that she could see much—she was terrifying. Her knuckles stood sharp. Her eyes narrowed. In the dim, shadowy light, every muscle went taut with readiness. She looked *fierce.*

Hurrok spoke slowly, like he was attempting to communicate with someone very stupid. "I said I tried to kill Mira Minkoba once. That's how I ended up here."

"Why?" The question fell out of my mouth, but maybe I didn't want to know.

"She ruined my life!"

I couldn't see him from my position, but still I pressed my face to the bars of my cell and peered down the hall. "How?" Five heartbeats raced in my ears, loud. Painful.

"You don't have to humor this waste of breath." Gerel looked as though she might crush the cell bars with her bare hands.

::Gerel is right,:: Aaru added. ::He doesn't mean you. He means the Hopebearer.::

"I wanted her dead!"

A faint cry of hysteria escaped, and I shuddered, but Gerel didn't notice. She was too busy attempting to break down the door, though I couldn't imagine why. She didn't like the Mira Treaty me *or* the me she thought she knew.

"I hate her," said the screaming man. He sucked in a noisy breath. "I tried to sneak into her house a year ago. It's up there in Crescent Prominence, where the Luminary Council lives. She lives there, too, like she's someone important. She was getting ready for a party. I could see her through her window. Through the open door of her dressing room, where that woman was helping her."

As he described it, I could envision myself sitting at the dressing table with Krasimir brushing cosmetics across my face. The screaming man was right. He could have seen me through the window if the dressing room door was open.

Another shudder rippled through me.

"I had an arrow dipped in poison. I was ready to do it."

My heart hammered against my chest. A hundred times. A thousand times. It ached. I didn't want to hear how he'd almost killed me, but I couldn't lift my voice to tell him to be quiet. I couldn't gather enough breath.

"Just as I'd nocked the arrow, her Hartan guard dog came into the bedroom. He slammed the dressing room door shut and he came at me. I tried to shoot him instead, but he threw something at me and knocked me off the window ledge. Next thing I knew, I was on trial and sent here."

I remembered that day. I'd been preparing for a charity ball at Councilor Elbena's mansion. The money was going to benefit research into the ancient ruins across the islands. My dress had been long, layered, golden, and trimmed in topaz. Krasimir had done my hair in a series of loops and braids, adding strings of crystal so that I sparkled. I'd never felt more beautiful.

Then the door had shut with a *bang*. Krasimir had been so surprised she smeared the line across my eye. She'd muttered about having to start over. But thirteen minutes later, the door opened again and Father stood there, impeccably dressed and brooding. The ball was off. Crescent Prominence was on lockdown for the rest of the night. Half the regular guards had been fired from their positions.

My questions about *why* had been ignored, and though I'd mourned the loss of that charity ball, others had followed and I had mostly forgotten about it.

Until now.

Until Hurrok described how he'd tried to assassinate me in my bedroom. Just like that man when I was little. And how many others had there been? How many times had Hristo saved my life and not told me?

I was on the floor, shaking. My whole body trembled against the memory and I knew I was making a scene, but I couldn't stop imagining person after person sneaking into my bedroom, wanting to kill me. Hristo always acted like he wasn't really necessary, but secretly . . .

Maybe Mother had forbidden him from saying anything. That was something she would do, but why had Hristo obeyed? He was supposed to be my friend, the person I trusted above all others, and surely I deserved the truth.

"Are you all right?" Gerel snapped her fingers at me. "Get up."

Still trembling, I forced myself to my feet. "I'm fine. I just hadn't realized—"

"What?" She scowled like I was a worm in her salad.

"Didn't you realize what kind of monsters you're trapped in here with?"

"We're all monsters," added the screaming man. "Every one of us."

I closed my eyes and took three steps back from the door. My heel bumped the sewage hole lid. "I'd like to go to bed now."

"Someone is testy tonight," Gerel muttered.

"Someone gets that way when other people casually talk about trying to commit murder." A strange venom laced my tone.

Gerel stared at me.

The screaming man was quiet.

Chenda watched me from her cell.

And Aaru? Who could tell with him. As always, he was the very absence of sound.

Then, footfalls stormed into the cellblock. Three guards. Maybe four. Noorestones flared bright, blinding, making me squint. Through the cacophony of boots pounding on the stone, a voice rose above the others.

"Mira!" Altan's voice. "It's time to answer more questions."

Cold terror touched my heart, and I couldn't forget the truth: no matter how terrible the prisoners were, the guards were worse.

CHAPTER SEVENTEEN

ALTAN HAD QUESTIONS.

More questions.

Hope died inside me as he halted at my cell, twisted his key in the lock, and threw open the door. "Let's go."

Two more guards flanked him, both in leather uniforms with chevrons pinned around Khulan's crossed maces. And there was the claw, too, which had mystified me before, but now I knew it must be the insignia for Drakon Warriors.

Did all the Drakon Warriors know about me, then? And Altan was tasked—or had tasked himself—with squeezing any information out of me?

So quickly that my head spun, Altan yanked me from my cell and practically flung me into the hall. I tried to root myself to the floor while he shut my door and prodded me forward.

The other two guards didn't speak, or even touch me. If they were worried about the possibility of me running, they didn't show it.

Altan had probably told them I wasn't brave enough for that.

After four steps, Altan motioned for me to halt. I obeyed, too afraid to do anything but.

At once, I realized that I stood even with Aaru's door, and I risked a look inside, expecting him to be sitting on the bed with his knees up, or hidden beneath the bed. But everything was different today.

Even Aaru.

He stood at his door, regarding me with fearful curiosity.

I shouldn't have been able to read his expression, not when I'd never really seen him before. Only in dim pieces through the hole.

But now he was an arm's length away, his stubble-covered face obscured only by the grille of metal. His skin was dark—a few shades browner than mine—and he was almost a head taller, with a lanky build made gaunt by a month of constant hunger. A mess of too-long hair framed nighttime-black eyes. He was . . . not handsome. Not beautiful. But compelling, even under the grime and starvation. I wanted to look more.

Suddenly, I realized he was studying me in the same

way: noting my half-unraveled twists, my trembling hands, my face, which had been pretty three decans ago but now must be changed by my time in the Pit.

"I'm sorry," I mouthed. For this moment. For staring. For being less beautiful than I'd wanted him to see. For being the one who was taken from her cell and . . . I didn't know what I was apologizing for.

But then Altan flung open Aaru's door and took him by the arm. "You too."

Aaru's black eyes widened as he staggered forward. Questions rushed between us, but there was no time to give them voice. Altan and the other two dragged us from the cellblock, through the anteroom, and down the hallway. Numbers flitted through my head as we moved—steps, stairs, intersections.

My mind cataloged the heavy footfalls of the three warriors, and the lighter stride of Aaru. I wanted to look over my shoulder at him. He was there. I could feel him. But I didn't know *why* he was here, and that was what scared me.

::**What's happening?**:: His quiet code was quick, but not quick enough that it wasn't noticed. A guard shoved him, and he stumbled. One, two, three: his bare feet slapped the ground before he caught himself.

I didn't dare answer his question. Even if I knew the answer, Altan was too observant. He'd notice the tapped exchange and have questions.

Then we stopped in front of a door and Altan's grip on

my arm grew tighter. "Here's your chance. You can tell me what I want to know—right now—or we can go inside."

When I turned to Altan, my voice trembled. "What do you want to know?"

"Your secret, of course." He smirked. "Your *second* secret."

The chill that ran through my body felt like ripples from a punch.

He rested a hand on the doorknob. "I told you I would come back for it. Did you think I'd forgotten?"

I couldn't bring myself to speak. He'd known I'd held something back, and I'd been waiting for him to ask. Of course. But what could I say to him? I couldn't tell him the truth; that was too dangerous. And I couldn't lie, because he'd know.

"Very well." He pulled open the door and frightening familiarity stole me.

I knew this place. I'd cleaned this interrogation room four times, scrubbing blood and urine off the floor until my hands grew raw. I knew each stone on the floor, wall, and ceiling. I knew the crystals lighting the grim space. I knew the echoes of terrible things that had happened here.

On the far side of the room, a strange chair loomed. Leather straps hung from it like stranglemoss—harmless by itself, but deadly to creatures caught in its embrace.

Aaru stood next to me, surveying the room in absolute

silence. He didn't move, like LaLa's prey hoping she wouldn't notice it if it stayed completely still. Only his gaze darted around, eyes wide with alarm.

The back of my hand brushed his. A bad idea, I realized too late.

"Take him."

At Altan's command, the other two guards dragged Aaru toward the chair. He struggled, but he was whip-thin and hungry. The larger men easily overpowered him and shoved him into the chair.

"No!" The word was out before I could stop it.

"I warned you about making friends," Altan said. "But now I wonder if I should have warned *him* about *you*."

Quickly, the guards bound Aaru's limbs to the chair. One leather strap around each wrist. One around each ankle. Two more went around his forehead and his chest.

Aaru didn't have shoes, and even from here I could see dark scars crisscrossing his feet and forearms and the bottoms of his calves. His torn clothes weren't quite long enough.

"You seem attached to this one." Altan dragged his knuckles against mine, a mockery of the way I'd reached for Aaru's hand. My stomach turned over. "That's good for me."

I couldn't read Aaru's expression anymore. His throat remained silent against his voice; so was his face against his feelings.

"Why don't you sit?" Altan didn't make it sound like an invitation as he motioned me toward a small table and chairs near the wall.

My hands shook too badly for me to move my chair out. Altan laughed and did it for me, a knowing smirk on his face. Then, he pulled off his jacket, as though settling in, and draped it over the back of the other chair. I didn't like this helpful, casual Altan. I didn't trust him.

"Here's what's going to happen," he said. "You're going to think about why you kept a secret from me, and what that secret is actually worth. While you consider, we're both going to test that Idrisi boy. What does it take to make him sing?"

The thought of Aaru singing would have made me laugh if I didn't know Altan meant something else. "Why?" I whispered.

"Do you really need me to tell you?" Altan looked disappointed. "I thought you were cleverer than that."

"I'm being punished."

He nodded.

"Because I kept secrets from you."

Again, he nodded.

I looked up at Aaru, now fully strapped to the chair. After the isolation incident, when Altan had been scolded for nearly killing me, his leaders must have forbidden him from physically hurting me again. That left one option: hurt me by hurting others.

And they'd chosen Aaru. The two guards with him stepped aside as three new figures came into the room: one was Rosa, the Daminan doctor who'd given me the coconut water treatment, and the other two were warrior trainees, each carrying a large iron basin. They positioned them in front of Aaru, scraping the stone floor.

Inside each basin rested a noorestone the size of a fist.

If Aaru was worried, he didn't show it.

"I'm sure you've heard," Altan said, "that we are moving toward new uses for noorestones."

A terrible sinking feeling overwhelmed me.

Across the room, Rosa muttered to her assistants, too low for me to hear. One of them dripped a dark concoction onto each of the noorestones, making the room stink of sulfur and . . . something else. Something familiar, but too distant to identify.

"It's taken some effort to find the best type of noorestones for this treatment," Altan went on. "We lost over twenty prisoners during the testing phase, but eventually we found that small, old crystals are the most effective."

Anxiety wrenched inside my chest.

"Noorestones aren't normally hot to the touch," Altan said, as if I needed reminding. "But these—well, I wouldn't risk it."

As the trainees slid one of the basins under Aaru's left foot, my silent neighbor gasped and jerked his leg, but it was too tightly bound.

"What's happening?"

"A heat transfer." Altan cocked his head. "Have you ever had a fever, Fancy?"

I could only nod. Once, I'd been truly ill. I didn't remember much from the days I'd lain in bed, just sweat and chills and Doctor Chilikoba ordering me to drink more and more water when I only wanted to sleep. The days felt long and the nights felt longer. Strange how fever could manipulate time.

"Think of this the same way," Altan said. "Heat from the noorestone is moving through his skin and spreading throughout his body. It won't cause burn marks, but if we leave him like this long enough, his blood could boil. Isn't that fascinating?"

Aaru bore it with grim determination, but already sweat trickled down his temple, cutting a path through the dirt. Then, without ceremony, Rosa signaled the assistants again, who moved the second basin under his right foot. Suddenly, his hands clenched and he strained against the bindings.

I surged to my feet; my chair screeched against the floor behind me. "Stop this."

Altan grabbed my forearm—hard—and dragged me back to my chair. "I'm making a point to you. Your silent friend will endure this until you've learned your lesson."

"Why?" The word scraped out of me.

"I want you to see the consequences for defiance."

I cut my gaze toward Aaru. He was breathing heavily.

Gasping. Shaking. Under the bright noorestones, the whites of his eyes shone all around his irises. His face gleamed with sweat.

"Make it stop." I turned back to Altan. "I promise I'll be good. You know I will. I'm a good prisoner."

He produced a stack of papers and a pencil and placed them in front of me. "There's only one way to make it stop."

"Write it down?" Why? Why not just ask for the information out loud, like before?

The room's other occupants?

Aaru closed his eyes, and he clenched his jaw against the agony of fire. Tendons stood sharp on his neck. Rosa spoke to the trainees, though her words were too low for me to hear. And the other two guards stood at the doorway, hands on their batons.

He didn't want them to know.

He couldn't be sure what the information was, but he knew he wanted it and he knew he would do anything to get it.

"Every moment you delay is another moment he suffers." Altan leaned onto the table, casting a wide shadow. "Just write what you know and this can stop."

Anxiety rushed in without warning. It came like thunder as my heart raced louder in my ears. It came like the sea over my head as my lungs struggled to expand. It came like a swarm of gnats crawling over my skin, itching, burning, complete in their distraction.

This was a nightmare. Aaru was only ten paces away,

fire running through his body, and Altan expected me to reproduce information I hadn't seen in four decans.

"I assume it's related to the dragons." Altan drummed his fingers on the table. "Since you care about it so much."

"It's nothing. I promise, it's nothing you're interested in."

Altan glanced at Aaru appraisingly and lifted his voice. "He's taking this quite well. I wonder if these noorestones have already been depleted. Rosa?"

"They're the proper age and size." She glanced at one of the trainees. "Find another."

The girl bowed and left the room.

A third noorestone? How could anyone bear such heat?

After I'd told Altan about the dragons, I'd declared I'd never tell him about the rest—not even to save my own life. But what about Aaru's life? I couldn't let him die, not if I could save him.

My trembling fingers crept toward the pencil. I could hardly take the wooden barrel, but somehow I fit my hand around it and brought the charcoal tip to paper.

But then.

My fingers jerked.

A slash of charcoal marred the page before the tip snapped off and black dust scattered everywhere.

"Gods!" Altan pounded a fist on the table, making everything jump. The broken pencil rolled off, and he strode around to retrieve it.

From the death chair, Aaru stared at me, a delirious sheen in his gaze. Sweat drenched his clothes, and his whole body shuddered against the fever.

I glanced at his hands, at his feet—everywhere—looking for the quiet code, but even if he wanted to communicate with me now, he was too weak.

::I'm sorry,:: I tapped on the table: **::Forgive me.::**

Aaru groaned in agony.

The sound tore through me. One second. Two. Three. Four. On and on and on. He breathed at thirty-three seconds, just a faint gasp before letting the sound rip from him again. Never before had I heard such torment in a single voice.

"Please," I begged. My voice sounded hollow. "I can't think while he's in pain."

Altan took a small knife and carved a new point for the pencil. "If you want this to end, you know what to do."

At that moment, the trainee returned with a third noorestone. Rosa gave it a quick inspection, then nodded. The crystal tumbled into the basin under Aaru's right foot with a racket. The strange sludge was poured over it.

Aaru's head rolled back. The whites of his eyes were bright against his sweat-drenched skin. And then, he began to sob—huge, racking gulps that filled the room. "Stop," he gasped. "Make it stop."

I couldn't let him suffer. I had to end this.

I had to steady my breathing. One long breath. Two. Three. When my hand no longer trembled, I pressed the pencil point to the paper.

Noorestones, I wrote.

Then, a long, low howl fell from Aaru's throat. The sweat had dried and his skin was flushed dark with burning. When one of the trainees prodded at the noorestones in the basins, the howl became a scream.

More than anything, I wished I were the kind of person who knew how to fight. Who could leap over the table and rip the bindings from him. I wished I could escape this awful place, Aaru and Gerel and Tirta with me.

I wished I were someone in possession of any measure of courage.

On the shipping order. My writing was jagged, almost impossible to read, but under the bombardment of Aaru's screams, I kept going. *Trading with our enemies.*

Soft pounding sounded from the far side of the room. Aaru's fists struck the chair arms with a familiar pattern: **::Strength through silence.::**

He repeated the phrase. Two times. Three times. Four.

Altan breathed over my shoulder, reading my note. "Why?"

"I don't know." My words were a sob. "I don't know. Please let him go."

"I wish I could believe you."

::Strength through silence.::

"I'm not part of the Luminary Council." I could barely think around the buzzing anxiety in my head. "They don't tell me why they do things."

::Strength through silence.::

Altan studied me for a long moment, then shook his head. "No, you know why they're shipping these, too."

::Strength through silence.::

"I told you what I know." But he could see my lie. Hear it.

::Strength through silence.::

"The longer you resist me, the longer he stays like that."

Aaru strained against the bindings. His eyes were squeezed shut, like he couldn't bear to acknowledge anything because the fire was too intense.

"Let him go!" Without thinking, I grabbed the pencil, twisted, and jabbed at Altan's face. He was fast; he dodged without a problem, and my momentum carried me to the floor behind him. I crumpled against the wall.

Prison guards stormed toward me, and Altan drew back his hand to slap my face.

But then.

Aaru's screams stopped. A sharp keening sliced through the room for a half second before three things happened at once:

A noorestone exploded.

All twenty-three crystals went dark.

And complete and smothering silence flooded the room.

BEFORE

Sarai 15, 2204 FG

THE DAY ILINA, HRISTO, AND I DISCOVERED THAT dragons had gone missing, we waited in Ilina's parents' office and riffled through papers and reports. There, we found the shipping order that changed everything. Dragons weren't the only things being shipped.

"They're sending ten noorestones as well." I stared at the paper, numbers filling my head: dimensions, weights, power. . . . These noorestones were as big as Hristo. "We don't trade with our enemies," I whispered.

"What does it matter?" An angry sob choked her words. "The *dragons—*"

"We especially don't give them the ten biggest noorestones in the Fallen Isles," I said.

"What?" Hristo took the paper from me and frowned at it.

Most people cared about one thing when it came to noorestones:

1. *They glowed.*

Most people never really thought about these five things:

1. *The best noorestones came from Bopha, though all the islands had deep mines.*

2. *Noorestones possessed an inner fire that burned for centuries, but the stones themselves were cool to the touch.*

3. *Most of the ruins found on the islands had embedded noorestones, which still glowed after thousands of years—long after regular noorestones would have gone dark.*

4. *Dragons really liked noorestones.*

5. *Ships used noorestones to traverse the islands quickly, though the stones needed to be fresh (most potent) and giant (larger capacity).*

"Most of our ships travel exclusively between the islands," I said. "Partly because we have nowhere else we'd want to go, but also because of noorestone limits. Only two of our ships have the ability to go beyond, because the noorestones that power them are immense."

"The *Star-Touched* and *Great Mace*." Hristo's eyebrows knit together.

Panic fluttered in my chest, and I wished I'd thought to bring my calming pills with me today. But I'd never needed them in the sanctuary before. This had always been the one place panic was never triggered. "And four years ago, the *Infinity*."

"The *Infinity* sank," Hristo said.

I closed my eyes and breathed. Once. Twice. Three times. "She didn't just sink. There was an accident. A dragon—a *Drakontos milos* named Ives—was on board and got loose."

"All right." Ilina frowned. "What then?"

"We don't know much," I said, "because the only person to get away didn't see everything. But the *Infinity*"—I forced the word out—"exploded."

"What?" Ilina's jaw dropped.

"Why doesn't everyone know this?" Hristo asked.

"The Luminary Council didn't want to alarm anyone. They said the people might lose faith in the navy if they knew the truth, and it was such an isolated incident. But something terrible happened between the dragon and the giant noorestones—"

"Dragons hoard noorestones." Ilina gripped the back of a chair so hard her knuckles stood sharp. "They *lick* noorestones. A dragon wouldn't use noorestones to hurt anyone."

Hristo placed his hand on her shoulder. "I don't think that's what Mira is saying."

I shook my head. "Those were the arguments made. I heard the survivor's whole story when she came before the council. She saw the dragon on one of the noorestones. A lot of councilors thought the explosion was because of the noorestones' size. The crystals required to power a vessel like the *Infinity* or *Star-Touched* are enormous. And rare. They're not as stable as the smaller stones."

Ilina stared at me.

I nodded. "After an investigation, it was determined the incident was unlikely to happen again. Still, new regulations were put in place for safety."

"So what does this mean?" Hristo handed the shipping order back to me. "Both dragons and giant noorestones are going to the Algotti Empire?"

I touched the descriptions of noorestones, my fingernail scraping across the paper. "Look at this. These stones are huge. Ten stones could power three ships like the *Star-Touched*. Why aren't those stones going to new ships of that class for the Fallen Isles?"

Color drained from their faces as they both realized what I had:

Someone was sending our dragons to our enemies, along with objects that would give the empire the ability to travel to us more quickly—or to attack us.

CHAPTER EIGHTEEN

IT WAS AN OPPRESSIVE SORT OF DARKNESS, THE KIND of darkness that smothered even sound.

I couldn't see. I couldn't hear. I'd suddenly stopped existing.

But when I moved my arm, my fingers hit the wall. No *thump*, though. No auditory evidence of the wall's existence and no sign the nine other people in the room were still here, either. I couldn't even hear the pounding of my own heartbeat, though it thrummed against my chest, painful and violent. (Five, six, seven . . .)

I'd never realized how many noises my own body made: the sound of swallowing, the hiss of air through my nose, the crack in my knees when I crouched and scrambled away from where the warriors had last seen me. Only with the absence of those sounds did I realize how I'd used them to give me a sense of orientation.

Now I didn't know where the others were, if they were even alive. The warriors had been after me. Altan had been about to slap me. But now? Nothing.

I crawled under the table.

Complete darkness.

Complete silence.

The days of being trapped alone in my cell crashed down on me again, making me sway through the inky space. I would crumble like this. If the lights ever came back, if sound ever returned, Altan and his friends would find me huddled beneath the table, wondering if I was trapped somewhere between life and death.

And what about Aaru? He'd been . . . tortured. While I'd done nothing to stop it.

The table was in the same place as Before Darkness; I had to assume everything else was as well. Including Aaru.

With a murmured prayer for bravery—which, of course, I couldn't even hear echoed in my head—I scooted out from under the table (not the way I'd come, where the guards and Altan would be) and risked the two steps to where Altan had left his jacket on the other chair.

It was still there, the leather soft and worn in my fingers. My sense of touch, at least, remained. As I mapped the room in my head, a part of me wondered who else was risking movement. Could they see or hear? Maybe I was the only one trapped in this void of sight and sound.

My stomach twisted at the thought. If I was the only one, everyone might be watching me. I could be grabbed at any moment.

But nothing had happened yet. And I had to move if I wanted to help Aaru. It was my fault he was here. It was my responsibility to help him.

I draped the jacket over my shoulders and let my numbers do the work. One, two, three . . . I stepped in Aaru's direction, both of my hands slightly in front of me, in case I miscalculated.

My foot slid over a sharp, slick object that cut through my slipper and grazed the sole of my foot, but didn't break the skin. Still. I had to be more careful. The object had made no scrape on the stone, offered no indication of what it might be. There could be more debris from . . . whatever had happened.

It took extra time, and I had no idea how long this darkness and silence would last, but I had to know what I'd stepped on. I knelt and felt around the floor until my fingers brushed the offending object. It was slightly warm, smooth sided, and sharp along the edges. Crystalline.

A noorestone shard.

One—or maybe more—of the noorestones had exploded. I remembered now.

I forced myself three more steps, even more cautious as I crept toward Aaru. Seven more shards rolled under my feet, and countless—even to me—tiny fragments slipped beneath me, like the floor was covered in a thin layer of sand.

Here. I should be standing right in front of Aaru. But this vast and unending silence locked away any shout for help, any whisper of reassurance, any gasp of pain.

"Please, Damina." The silence swallowed my voice.

I lifted my hand ahead of me until my fingertips grazed hot skin. Aaru, I hoped. His head, most likely.

He didn't move. Didn't flinch. Maybe he was dead.

That was a horrible thought. I wanted to crush it as soon as it formed. But it was a possibility, wasn't it?

"Shut up." Like the anxiety ever listened. Like I even had a voice now.

My fingers crept upward along a smooth plane of skin. His cheek, it felt like. I let my fingers travel up his temple until they reached the strap on his forehead. I searched for the buckle, unclipped it, and slid the leather off.

As fast as possible, I found the other five straps and unclipped them, then lifted his feet out of the basins. Away from the hot noorestones.

With Aaru free of the bindings, I threw the jacket over him. He was burning up, but I recalled chills during my fever; he'd need the warmth. If he was alive. I couldn't tell if he was, or how I was supposed to get him out of here, or if there was any sort of hope at all.

I took Aaru by the shoulders and shook him. "Wake up." But, of course, I had no voice here. There was only silence.

::**Wake up,**:: I tapped against his shoulder.

Nothing. He didn't move.

I let one hand slide down to his chest, and the other up to his throat. Slowly, distantly, I found what I'd been seeking: his pulse fluttered under my fingertips, and his chest lifted with breath. He had a heartbeat.

Just as I was ready to try throwing Aaru over my shoulder, a haze of blue light flashed through the room. Noorestone light.

It vanished quickly, leaving me no time to inspect Aaru or look for the other occupants of the room. Its only gift was light spots that danced in front of my eyes, and heavy tears squeezing from between my eyelids. I blinked them away. Now, I knew four things:

1. *I was not blind.*

2. *The lights were not gone forever.*

3. *Altan and his friends would be furious.*

4. *I had to move.*

In the dark again, I grabbed for Aaru's arm and pulled him forward. His whole body shuddered as he slumped toward me. I angled my right shoulder under him and tried to lift, but in spite of being so thin, he was *heavy*. Or I just wasn't very strong.

Light tore through the darkness again, and this time, I caught hints of movement from the guards. Or maybe that had been Rosa; the light was gone too soon for me to tell.

"Come on," I hissed. I could hear my own voice, though it was muffled inside my head. In addition to not being blind, it seemed I wasn't deaf, either. Likely, I still existed as well, which was distantly comforting.

I heaved Aaru up, but he was too heavy, too tall. I fell backward with a sharp cry, the weight of an unconscious boy on top of me. My breath whooshed out in a faint *oof*, and pain sliced through my back and shoulders and legs. The shattered noorestone. I'd forgotten about it and now shards cut through my skin.

Tears dripped down the sides of my face, both from the stabbing pain in my back and for the horrible realization that I wasn't going to get out of here. Not with Aaru unconscious. Not with the fire of hot noorestones slicing through me.

While I struggled to breathe through the pain, I stayed absolutely motionless, in spite of the body on top of mine. He grew heavier and heavier, it seemed like, defying all the natural laws I'd once thought I'd understood. Or maybe it was just that my back *hurt*.

Sound returned more steadily than light, but it wasn't very useful. Fragmented noises came from everywhere and nowhere, and it was too hard to tell what was in my head and what was real. But I needed to place the others. I needed to know what I was up against and if maybe there was a chance of getting out of here—

Dim illumination pulsed through the room in time with Aaru's heartbeat.

No, that couldn't be right. But when I slid my hand down his chest again, the *thump* of his heart came at the same moment as the light flared.

Then I understood.

Aaru had done this. Aaru had caused this darkness, this soundlessness. My sad, silent neighbor.

For seven of his heartbeats, I waited, hoping the light and beat would fall out of synchronization, but even as Aaru's heart rate increased to a normal speed, so did the pulses of light. It was Aaru. There was no question.

Far away, I heard magic-muffled shouts. Crunches. Orders: "Secure the girl" and "Fetch more doctors."

With all my strength, I shoved Aaru until he rolled off me. His body hit the floor with faint thumps. Once his weight was gone, the noorestone shards gouging my back eased. Hopefully Aaru hadn't fallen onto a particularly sharp fragment, too. Maybe since he'd just rolled, he wouldn't get stabbed the same way I had. It seemed especially awful for him to get stabbed just after enduring torture and then . . .

Magic.

My body screamed as I forced my way up to my knees, but I did it.

The light was steady now, released from Aaru's hold,

and it grew brighter. It came from the twenty noorestones shining in their sconces, but also from shards and dust spread across the floor. Beneath me, the debris was wet and dark with my blood.

Altan appeared in the fractured light. Five guards followed him, all with their weapons drawn.

"Stay down!" The warrior's order sounded faraway on the first word, and then leaped into normal volume for the second word. "Stay down!" he shouted again as he stopped just three paces away. Two pairs of boots crunched over the ground behind me and halted.

At least six people surrounded Aaru and me. There was no escape.

Altan stormed toward us with fire in his eyes. His baton was drawn, and as he thundered through the room so loudly that I began to regret the return of sound, a wild growl tore out of him. He rushed beyond me.

The other guards were no longer advancing. With agony slicing through my back, I glanced over my shoulder.

Bodies. Three of them.

Two were the trainees who'd been assisting. The other was Rosa.

She was facedown in a pool of blood, illuminated by noorestone shards. Fourteen pierced her motionless body, brightening the puncture wounds with their eerie blue glow. Blood almost looked purple as it flooded around her.

All three were dead.

"How did this happen?" Altan asked.

"Three noorestones exploded." The guard's tone was deadly calm, like a dagger dripping with poison. "The ones in the basins."

"How?"

"I'm not sure, sir."

But I knew.

Aaru stirred under my hands. I bent toward him, keeping my voice soft and under the rumble of discussion. "Can you hear me?"

He looked at me, but his eyes were unfocused, like he was dizzy, or not quite awake, or still in shock. Dark circles hung down to his cheekbones, and even his blinking was erratic. "Oh, Aaru," I breathed.

When he opened his mouth and made the shape of my name, nothing came out. He frowned, swallowed, and tried again. Still, nothing.

He'd lost his voice screaming. Even through our small hole in the wall, I so rarely heard him speak. The screaming was probably a year's worth of voice for him. Maybe more. "Are you—" Not all right, because he wasn't.

In the background, Altan said, "Maybe someone tampered with the noorestones."

Aaru blinked five more times, still trying to focus. Again, his mouth shaped my name, but only silence emerged.

Shame burned through my veins, igniting the edges of panic. He was hurt because of me. My ally. My . . . friend, maybe.

He struggled to push himself into a sitting position. My shaking hands slid off his sweat-slicked skin as I tried to help. But in spite of our disoriented fumbling, he made it up and tugged the jacket tighter around his shoulders. Shivers racked through him. The sudden absence of the noorestones' fire seemed to leech all the warmth from his skin.

Before I could think better of it, I drew him toward me and wrapped my arms around him, like I could take some of the cold from him. Pain rippled through me as the noorestone shards in my back shifted, but I dismissed it. This was only a fraction of what Aaru had endured.

He leaned against me, shuddering as his cheek rested on my shoulder.

"Is it possible to sabotage noorestones?" someone asked.

"Anything can be sabotaged." Altan's voice was like gravel. "Find whoever did it. Notify the trainees' commanding officers. I want this taken care of immediately."

Altan could never know the truth. It was impossible to say much about his relationship with Rosa, or whether he'd even known the trainees' names, but surely his honor demanded harsh retribution.

I pulled Aaru closer to me. After so long with a wall between us, I'd wanted to see more of him than just fragments in the dark. I'd wanted to do more than just hold his hand. But not like this. If I'd known that Altan would use Aaru against me . . .

"I'm sorry," I whispered. "I'm so sorry, Aaru."

He started to tap something in the quiet code, but his hand trembled too badly. I seized his icy fingers and pulled them to the hollow of my throat.

"Don't try to speak yet." The chill in his skin made my own feel hotter. "Can you get up? Run?" The words were just for him, barely perceptible even to my own ears.

He shook his head.

No. Of course not. He'd just been tortured. And with crystals still digging into my back, I wasn't in the best condition to run, either. Where did I think I'd go? With what food? With what knowledge of the Pit?

Tirta had access to food. To the rest of the Pit. She was third level, with more leniency.

My gaze cut to the warrior blocking the only exit.

I'd never be able to get both of us past him.

"Could it have been the girl?" one of the warriors asked. "Maybe she used her Daminan powers on the noorestone."

"You think she charmed it into exploding?" Altan gave a sharp laugh as he stood, the bodies of Rosa and the trainees at his feet. In the eerie blue light, the bodies were like paintings: lifelike, but clearly lifeless. "No, it was someone else, so stop speculating and find them. And get these prisoners out of here."

I pulled Aaru closer to me, like I could protect him, but it was futile. From behind, a warrior grabbed me under the arms and hauled me to my feet.

Aaru collapsed to the floor, and for the first time I noticed the bloody shreds of his feet. It had been the noorestones in the basins that had exploded, killing three people.

A dark part of me celebrated. They'd deserved it.

PART THREE

EQUALITY IN SHADOWS

CHAPTER NINETEEN

I AWAKENED IN THE DIM INFIRMARY, ALL BUT ONE nooorestone covered for the night. A deep stillness filled the room.

Fragmented memories surfaced: medicine that numbed my pain and my thoughts, doctors removing crystal shards from my back, and scattered conversation about what they'd do with the boy's feet.

Which meant—though Aaru had been *tortured*—they'd treated me first. Why? Because I was Mira Minkoba? That name shouldn't make a difference, especially not here. Aaru had barely been alive when I'd dragged him off the chair; he should have been given priority.

Gerel had once told me that warriors weren't allowed to murder prisoners; it was against their code of honor.

But sometimes there were "accidents," which accounted for the suspiciously low population of the Fallen Isles' most infamous prison.

My back ached as I pushed myself into a sitting position and surveyed the infirmary. It was the same one as before—the only one in the Heart of the Great Warrior that accepted inmates—and I knew from experience there would be several uninterrupted hours of peace.

In the deep-blue gloom, I found one other bed occupied.

With a strangled groan, I slid off my bed and tiptoed to his. Aaru was asleep, a gray sheet pulled across his body. He looked better, at least. Not what I'd call healthy, but his skin had been scrubbed clean and the cadence of his breath was long and even. Bandages covered his feet and ankles, so at least a day had gone by; it would have taken several hours to remove all the crystal shards from both my back and Aaru's feet, clean the wounds, and stitch them shut. Plus, the medication they'd used to numb me was mere dregs now, and I'd *felt* like I'd been sleeping awhile.

"It's my fault," I whispered. The night made my words seem insubstantial. I started to take his hand, like I might convey my regret through physical contact, but hesitated. After what happened, he probably didn't want me to touch him. So I knelt next to his bed and bent my head in repentance. "What happened to you is my fault."

His breathing didn't alter, but his presence shifted from asleep to awake; I'd felt that change often enough as we lay together at night, a wall in between our bodies. But now nothing separated us except a bubble of propriety and uncertainty.

"I thought Altan would do something else to me. Before, when I refused him, he threatened to isolate me again. Worse, though. And I thought . . ." My ragged fingernails dug into my palms. "It never occurred to me that he might hurt you."

Aaru's fingers twitched, then slowly moved into the quiet code. **::You're a kind person. Cruelty does not occur to you.::**

My jaw trembled. "How can you forgive so easily?"

Slowly, he turned his head to look at me. Noorestone light limned the curve of his cheek and jaw with pale blue, and the urge to touch that space where illumination met skin overwhelmed me. I pressed my fingers against the mattress instead, feeling the soft vibrations of his tapping. **::Forgiveness is easy when there's nothing to forgive. He did this. Not you.::**

I couldn't imagine being so clearheaded and merciful if our positions had been reversed.

::The Book of Silence says unwarranted blame is an affront to Idris's ears. We must take care not to place it at the wrong person's feet.::

I pressed my mouth into a line. **::The Book of Love says something similar.::**

::We are not so different.:: Pain racked his features as he shifted onto his side, but when I offered to help, he shook his head. So I stayed put, my knees digging into the floor, and watched the way he moved. In our darkened little space beneath our beds, I'd never gotten a sense of his size, but now I couldn't help but notice how *much* of him there was. Long and lanky, yes, but corded with lean muscle from years of hard work.

"We aren't the same, Aaru."

He lifted an eyebrow in question.

"Where do I begin? Our upbringings, stations, and families—those are just a few examples of things that separate us."

::**But not the thing you want to discuss.**::

I added his perceptiveness to the list.

::**Will answer your question.**::

Now I was embarrassed to ask, but he'd offered. "You did something incredible," I said. "Do you remember? At the end, you made the noorestones stop glowing and smothered all the sound."

::**I didn't know I could.**:: His teeth flashed bright white where he bit his lower lip. ::**Idris grants powerful gifts to the worthy, but I am not. I am of the least of his people, not like the Silent Brothers.**::

Damyan and Darina gave charm to their people, but there were spectrums of power. Elected officials, theater actors, and people in the public eye had all the charm in the world, while others (like me) made do with the barest scrapes.

::**The gift is silence,**:: he went on. ::**Noorestones make a**

sound that most cannot hear, but it illuminates the stones. I silenced it.::

"And everything else."

He nodded.

Most gifts were muted away from our home islands, which meant Aaru was *powerful*. If he could silence noorestones here, what could he do on Idris? "What about in our cellblock?"

::Not me. Another. Better and stronger. More precise. They silence light without silencing sound.::

And for Aaru, it was all or nothing, but perhaps with more practice, he could be more precise as well. "It's amazing," I whispered. I'd always believed the Idrisi divine gift was passive—the ability to move silently or *be* silent. But *making* other things silent? That was incredible. Dangerous.

::Please tell no one.::

"I won't tell anyone. I promise."

He rolled onto his back again, mouth dropped open with a soundless groan.

"Aaru . . ." My knees ached as I stood to help him, but I was too slow. He'd finished rearranging himself and was panting with the effort. "I'm sorry." I sat on the bed next to him, not quite touching his hip, and hung my head. "I'm so sorry he did this to you, and for my part in it. I should have known better."

His fingers breezed against a lock of my hair, loose from its twist. The barest heat from his skin touched my cheek.

At once, his face darkened and he withdrew.

I wished he'd do it again, but I wasn't about to suggest it. Not when I was the cause for his pain. He shouldn't feel like he had to comfort me.

::**Why does Altan hate you?**:: Aaru asked. ::**Why did he hurt you before? And now me?**::

Of all people, Aaru deserved answers. But what could I say without giving away my identity? "I have information." My voice trembled. "I know things I shouldn't. That's why I was sent here."

::**And he wants to know what you know.**:: Aaru nodded to himself. ::**He won't stop.**::

"Not until he's satisfied I've given him everything."

::**What will you do?**::

"What would you do?"

His gaze was steady, not judging, but appraising, and I couldn't help but wonder what he saw. A scared girl from Damina? Someone who'd never known true fear or hunger until now? Maybe a thoughtless person who caused others pain?

::**I would ask Idris for guidance.**:: He turned his face to cover a yawn. ::**Sorry. Tired.**::

"Then go to sleep." I studied him a moment longer: the sharp lines and full lips and heavy brow. He had a kind face, and eyes filled with deep thoughts and emotion; I wished I could read them.

::**Will you do something for me?**::

"Of course." A flurry of impossible requests came to

mind as soon as the words were out. He might ask me to get him out of the Pit right now, or give Altan the rest of my information, or even fly. I could do none of those things.

But this was Aaru. He said, **::Tell me about your life before this.::** He lifted his hands toward me like an offering, melting away all lingering doubts about his forgiveness.

He still wanted whatever it was that we'd been growing this last month. Our alliance, or . . . maybe friendship? Our injuries set back our plan at least a decan—neither Aaru nor I could work while we were recovering—but we'd begin again as soon as we were released from the infirmary. We'd keep feeding Gerel and Chenda and all the others (I tried not to think of Hurrok), and we'd find a way out of here. Together.

Heart pounding, I let my fingertips play across the backs of his hands, finding the ridges of bones and tendons and knuckles. His breath caught; he closed his eyes; my name fell soundless from his lips.

This was forward, at least on Idris. On Damina, this might be just the beginning, but Idris was so reserved in the giving and receiving of physical affection.

Still, we'd held hands before.

There'd been a wall between us.

But he'd placed his hands into mine.

An invitation to hold his hands was not an invitation to indulge the fluttery feeling deep in my stomach. I squashed it, and ordered myself to do as he'd asked: tell him about my life.

But as I began to describe Crescent Prominence in stumbling quiet code, Aaru opened his eyes and cocked his head—listening.

Footsteps in the hall.

Before I could scramble away, back to my bed, the door slammed open and bright noorestone light shone in from the hall.

"Mira Minkoba." Altan stood in the doorway, obscured by my light-induced tears. "I'm happy to see you're awake." His tone contradicted his words, though, and as he strode into the room, a pair of white-uniformed men at his sides, he frowned at the sight of me next to Aaru.

Behind me, Aaru's curiosity at my surname burned, and my mind dutifully counted the letters of my name tapped against the back of my hand, but it was the pair of newcomers who held my attention.

Their clothing was off-white linen that glowed against their brown skin, with seven gold stars embroidered around the deep hoods. Seven buttons down the left side of the jackets gave the illusion of the wrap style that was fashionable in Damina, while medals were pinned right in the middle. They wore matching trousers, boots, and gloves, and both had long daggers at their hips. From one side of the hoods to the other, an off-white mask stretched. It concealed their noses and mouths, leaving only dark eyes to watch me.

I knew those uniforms. I'd seen them all of my life and never truly paid attention—not until the day they'd come to arrest me.

Altan's glance darted from me to Aaru and back, and a spear-sharp smile grew on his mouth.

"What's happening?" I spoke the words, but I could hardly hear them under the rush of my pulse through my ears.

Behind me, Aaru pushed himself up and tapped questioningly at my arm, but I couldn't bear to look at him.

"Your wish has come true," Altan said as the white-clad guards marched forward. "The Luminary Council has sent for you, Hopebearer."

CHAPTER TWENTY

::**Hopebearer.**:: AARU'S HAND SLID OFF MY ARM.

And oh, the mountains of hurt he conveyed in that one motion. My identity revealed. My betrayal complete. I'd had every opportunity to give him my whole name, but I'd kept that secret and now he heard it from the man who tortured him. My nemesis; his nemesis.

Cast adrift, I slipped off the edge of Aaru's bed. The stone floor chilled my feet through my shredded slippers. "The Luminary Council has sent for me," I repeated, numb.

Why, though? Perhaps they'd finally realized their mistake, but why did it have to be *now*, when I'd already resigned myself to the necessity of escape? What about my friends and my plans?

Altan strode through the infirmary, his mouth pulled back in a smile. By now, I knew him well enough to understand this particular smile was one not of triumph, but of concealment.

My release was a surprise to him as well.

Of course, if he'd known my summons was imminent, he wouldn't have made me watch Aaru's torture. He knew the risk of upsetting me right before I returned to the Luminary Council.

Because what if I told them he was a Drakon Warrior? What if I revealed his plans to them? With a word, I could ruin him. Within days, the Fallen Isles could know that Khulan's holiest warriors had not obeyed the Mira Treaty.

The utter stillness at my back put a stop to that line of thought.

I could not move against Altan while Aaru remained in his custody. And Tirta. And Gerel. And Chenda. He could kill them faster than I could have them freed.

"When do I leave?" A million questions knotted inside that one: what did they want from me, who'd come for me, where were we going? And mostly: was this forever, or a mere furlough? But I kept curiosity buried tight so that Altan wouldn't see all the weakness in me. Only the Hopebearer.

"Immediately." He stopped directly in front of me, a dark tower of hatred. "Are you planning to resist?"

"Why would I resist?"

"Occasionally you manage to surprise me, Fancy."

He motioned toward the Luminary Guards, who'd stationed themselves in the center aisle. Now that my eyes were used to the brighter lights of the hall, the pair looked like white shadows in the dim infirmary. Out of place. Ghostly. "That girl will take you to the bathing chamber before you leave. You smell like sewage, and I don't want anyone saying I don't take care of my prisoners."

I took a step toward the Luminary Guards, but paused and risked a glance over my shoulder to where Aaru sat, his feet wrapped in layers of gauze and linen.

Just minutes ago, I'd thought he was so much bigger than I'd realized before, but among the large warriors and Luminary Guards, and suddenly silent in presence as well as voice, he seemed to be shrinking.

He lifted his eyes to mine, his hurt evident for all to see.

I searched for something to say, something to make this better. But how could I reassure my ally—former ally now, probably—when I'd omitted important information, and now I was *leaving*? Without him. What could I say to someone I was abandoning to Altan and the Pit and the merciless darkness?

::I'm sorry.:: I tapped the words against my thigh, but if he noticed, he gave no response.

"Don't worry about your friend," said Altan. "I'll take care of him."

Foreboding dripped through me like slime. **::I will not abandon you.::**

Before I could wait for another nonresponse, the Luminary Guards moved to corral me toward the door, where Tirta waited, her head down.

I chanced one last look at Aaru as I stepped out of the infirmary, only to catch the deliberate way he turned away from me.

"This way." Tirta's voice was soft as she guided me through the halls, the Luminary Guards at our backs. She didn't ask questions, or try to reassure me. As Altan had promised, she simply took me to a bathing chamber, though not the usual one.

This room was bigger and smelled less like sulfur. Besides the bricked, kidney-shaped pool of steaming water, there were seven stone benches with crossed maces carved into the backs. Three noorestones were embedded into each bench—one above the maces and one on the end of each arm (twenty-one bench noorestones total), and twenty noorestones were planted in sconces around the room.

Noorestones had been so innocuous. Once.

Alone—we'd left the Luminary Guards in the hall—Tirta took my hands and squeezed. Her eyes were wide with confusion. "What's going on?"

My voice caught in my throat. Too many emotions bombarded me at once. Shock. Joy. Relief. Hope. Anticipation.

Guilt.

How could one person bear the guilt of leaving while her friends could not?

Tears weighed down my eyes. I couldn't forget Aaru's immense pain caused by my betrayal. What would Tirta think if she knew how deeply I'd hurt him? And Gerel? Gerel would be furious when she found out. All her worst thoughts about me were coming true.

"All right," Tirta said when I couldn't find my voice. "Let's do this quickly, before they come in to get us."

I glanced over the new bathing chamber again. The table in the back held a pitcher of water, condensation gathering on the glass, and a pair of cups. There was even a plate with grapes, orange wedges, and strawberries arranged in three neat rows. Baskets on the benches held soaps, cloths, and hairbrushes.

Tirta followed my gaze. "Sometimes they use this room to reward prisoners for good behavior. Not usually first-level prisoners, though."

This definitely wasn't a reward.

Careful of the bandages on my back, I shed my grimy clothes and tossed them in a corner. The Luminary Council had sent a simple dress for me, along with all the other comforts from home.

"Which soap do you want?" Tirta asked. "There are several scents." She said it like it mattered. Like we were girls living in Crescent Prominence with nothing better to do. But she rattled off the various fragrances and I chose one that Krasimir had always said worked nicely with my natural scent.

She handed me a basket filled with the wonders of

my past. Shea butter and honey soap. Orange blossom and jasmine hair cream. Three soft linen cloths. A wide-handled comb with *all* the tines. Even a peel for my face. When Tirta poured a glass of water, I drank the whole thing down in long gulps. The fruit followed shortly.

Carefully, I let out what remained of Ilina's twists. The ends of my hair were ragged and needed a trim, but that wasn't the worst: brittle pieces broke off and scattered in the water. A strained whimper squeaked out of me.

"It's just stress," Tirta said. "It's living in this place. Not being able to take care of yourself properly."

"But—"

"No one will notice." She went to the table and picked up two jars. "Look, we can make it nice again. You tell me what's going on, and I'll help with your hair."

I gave her the comb and closed my eyes as I forced out a short summary of the last two days.

She lowered her voice as she smoothed creams into the mistreated strands of my hair. "Mira, do exactly as they say. Don't be brave. Just be smart."

If only I knew what being smart in this situation entailed.

"You're getting out, though. That's good." She smiled, but if she thought I couldn't tell how strained it was, she was wrong. "I knew they couldn't keep you here forever. You're too important."

"No one has said how long this will be. They might send me back."

She shook her head. "You're Mira Minkoba. The Hope-bearer." She always said that with such sincerity; it ached. "I bet this was all a cruel lesson and your life will go back to the way it was before."

My life could never go back. I knew too much. I'd lived through too much. "What about you?" I asked. "And all the others?"

She lowered her eyes. "There's no hope for the rest of us. All we can do is try to make the most of what we have here."

Finally, I was clean. With my hair pulled into a loose bun, and a soft red dress covering my aching body, I hugged Tirta—"I won't forget you," I whispered—and left the room.

The Luminary Guards took me through the Pit, into an immense hallway I'd never seen before.

Bright noorestones illuminated heavy banners all bearing Khulan's crossed maces, gold on red. Columns loomed on either side, with statues and glass-encased weapons in between. It reminded me of the grand hall, where I'd first seen the true glory of the Heart of the Great Warrior, but this, if anything, was bigger. Even more impressive.

And there was a warm yellow light at the far end. For one second, wind gusted through the hall.

Outside.

Sunlight.

Anticipation made my heart thrum in my ears. When I walked faster, the Luminary Guards kept up.

Fifty steps.

Seventy-three.

One hundred and four.

That was how many steps I'd taken from seeing the exit to reaching it. I stopped moving right in front of the huge, thrown-open doors.

The guards stopped, too.

Great, golden light poured across me. I lifted my face to the outside and breathed in the scents of sun and sky and a wide-open world. Tears poured down my cheeks. Fresh air curled around me.

For one moment, everything else was forgotten: the Pit, the torture, all the reasons for this nightmare. A sense of triumph stirred inside me; all I had to do was lift my hand into the brilliant light of freedom.

A silhouette formed against the shine, resolving into a familiar shape.

"Congratulations, Fancy." Altan strode toward me wearing a dark smirk.

Suddenly, the trance brought on by this unexpected look at the open world snapped and vanished, replaced by yawning despair. This wasn't freedom. Nor was it triumph. Whatever waited for me out there was worse than all I left behind.

"Do as you're bidden, but don't tell our secret." Warning entered his tone as he paused and asked, "Do I have to explain what happens if you betray me?"

In my mind, all I could see was Aaru strapped to the

chair, noorestones pressing at his feet. All I could hear were the desperate cries.

"No," I whispered. "You don't have to explain."

"Very good." Then he brushed past me and was gone, only the echo of his threat settling in me like a phantom. I could not unhear the words. And I could not ignore them.

I took three steadying breaths.

And one step outside.

BEFORE

Seven Years Ago

KRASIMIR WAS THE MOST BEAUTIFUL PERSON I'D EVER seen.

She was ageless, with luminous brown skin, high cheekbones, and deep-set eyes that reminded me of a cat. She had this confident way of moving and speaking that I envied.

The first time we met, I waited until my mother was out of the dressing room before I told Krasimir what I thought. She laughed and took a cloth from her kit, splashed a citrus-smelling solution onto it, and wiped it over her face.

The cosmetics came off. Beneath the powders and creams, there was just a woman. Same strong features, but less pronounced. Her eyes were not cat eyes. She was mortal after all.

And there, on her right cheek, a drop of white marked her polished-amber skin. Only one spot, but I shuddered.

Krasimir's expression remained blank. "Do you think it's ugly?"

"No," I whispered. "It looks like a rose about to bloom."

She smiled and the tip of the rose expanded across the apple of her cheek. "I've always thought so, too."

"But you hide it."

"Yes." She pulled a few items from her kit. "What would your mother say about it?"

Mother would say it was ugly. A mark of shame. That no mistress of beauty should have something that imperfect.

"Now you're one of the few people who've seen my real face," Krasimir said as she applied a tinted cream to her skin. The white rose vanished. Then the rest of her face became a flawless jewel, like before. "The only other person who's seen the mark is my wife. Besides my parents, but they died years ago."

"Why show me?"

As she pressed dark powder onto her eyelids, I began to understand. She drew attention to her best features: the shape of her eyes, the lines of her jaw, and the fullness of her mouth. "I showed you," she said, "because you're hiding something too."

"You told Mother my face is perfect."

"It is." She glanced at me in the mirror. "But you're not hiding something on your face."

The counting. She knew about the counting. "I'm trying to stop."

Krasimir smiled. "Only stop if that's what *you* want. Personally, I think the counting is one of the things that makes you beautiful."

"Your rose is beautiful."

She finished lining her eyes, a cat once more, and looked at me. "Imperfections reveal true beauty."

I wanted to be grateful for permission to count, but I banished those thoughts. Mother would never accept it.

Still, I was always happy to see Krasimir, not only because she brought new soaps and creams and combs, but because she gave me hope that I, too, could hide the thing that made me different.

CHAPTER TWENTY-ONE

SUNLIGHT BLINDED ME AS I STEPPED OUT OF THE Heart of the Great Warrior.

And the *sounds.* I could hardly sort through the cacophony of life up here. It was overwhelming, disorienting.

I blinked, resisting the urge to duck my face; I wouldn't show even more weakness in front of the guards.

When my vision finally adjusted and the burning daylight eased, I could finally see the world that had been denied to me for more than a month.

Thirty-three days of darkness. Thirty-three days of ceiling water. Thirty-three days of slowly being smothered underground.

But now, I stood under a sweeping blue sky, rich with

orange and pink and purple clouds that huddled on the horizon. It was just after dawn and daylight had been reborn.

A huge red-and-gold carriage waited four paces from the door, blocking most of my view, but I caught the impression of a busy street that curled into a circular drive. Four enormous columns stood on either side of the door, with crossed maces carved into the marble.

"Let's go." A Luminary Guard prodded me to the carriage. Seven horses were harnessed to the front, their ears flicking and hooves stamping while they waited.

Then there were the guards. Seven, at least that I could see. Two with me. Three at the carriage. Two more near the warriors standing at attention by the entryway.

Once, I'd believed anyone with Luminary anything in their title was an ally. Now I knew better. Anyone could be an enemy.

The carriage door swung open to reveal another enemy.

Elbena Krasteba sat on a padded bench.

"Get in," she said.

"Where are my parents?"

"Not here."

Hadn't they orchestrated my release, though? Maybe that had been nothing more than a wild, unfounded assumption. A hope that my removal from the Pit meant something good.

There was nothing good about this.

A wild urge to *run* overtook me, but the Luminary Guards would be fast. The warriors would be faster. I couldn't see much beyond the carriage and columns—just the suggestion of a crowded street and tall buildings—but even if I could run past all the guards, I'd soon become lost in a tangle of streets.

This was Khul-tah, the City of the Warrior, and I would not survive here on my own. I was not capable of such heroics.

I took the four steps from one prison and climbed into another.

Two benches facing each other, a small mahogany table (bearing two covered plates, two glasses, and one covered pitcher), and curtains pulled tight against the view: these were the contents of the carriage.

The door closed after me, choking off all the light but that of three noorestones.

I rocked back in my seat, disoriented. For a moment, I was in the interrogation room again, cradling Aaru's feverish body, whispering apology after apology, wishing I could strip away all his pain.

Elbena motioned to the pitcher. "Water?"

"No." A desperate thirst stirred inside me, but I wanted nothing from her.

"Very well." She smoothed back stray hairs that had escaped her long braid. "I'm here as your friend, you know."

Doubtful.

Some people said Elbena had won the position because

of her youth and beauty. And it was true that she was both young and beautiful, with smooth skin the shade of umber, wide brown eyes, and a smile that dazzled. But I'd voted for her because she'd always seemed to care so much for the Daminan people. I'd liked the way she encouraged everyone to think of more than just themselves, to always look out for their neighbors.

Hristo had never liked her; he'd noted that she never mentioned Harta in all her speeches. He hadn't been permitted a vote, though, because he wasn't a natural-born citizen of Damina. Now, I wished he had been allowed; he could have negated my (clearly wrong) vote.

"How was your time in the Pit?" she asked.

"You don't want to hear about that," I said. "Unless you've been longing for stories about bathing in filth, relieving oneself over a hole in the ground, and never getting a good night's sleep because someone down the hall is afraid of the dark."

She folded her hands on her lap. "That sounds positively miserable."

Thumps sounded on the carriage, but Elbena didn't react. It was probably the guards climbing onto their riding platforms. Though there was enough space for four more people to fit comfortably in here, it seemed the councilor wanted privacy.

In case I started talking about dragons, perhaps.

"I'm sorry we had to do that to you," Elbena said. "I didn't think you'd be there for quite so long."

"The Pit is a life sentence."

"Not for girls like you."

"Does that mean I'm not going back?" Hope and guilt crashed inside me.

"I didn't say that." Her smile was dazzling. It was the sort that won elections because people wanted to trust her. She could appear so genuine—but that was Damina's charm at work.

"What do you want from me?"

"I want to give you an opportunity."

"What sort?" I asked.

As the carriage started to move, Elbena leaned across the table and pried open the curtains, though the tops and bottoms were pinned together, so she revealed only a small sliver of the outside.

Still, even this glimpse drew me.

This was Warrior's Circle, one of the oldest sections of Khul-tah. In the center of the drive stood an immense golden statue of Khulan with his maces lifted in victory; he had to be three times my height, though I couldn't see all of him right now.

Paintings always showed the Khulan statue from one of two angles: from the great doorway, to show the height of the city that had grown around the warrior god; or facing the doors (sometimes open, sometimes closed), to show him guarding his temple, the most sacred place of all his island.

"The Fallen Isles are experiencing some . . . difficulties.

Therefore, the council wants to show the world that you're still present. Reassuring the people is a very important duty. It's what keeps the peace." Elbena gazed out the sliver between the curtains as she spoke, as though she could possibly need to see the outside world nearly as much as I did.

"Maybe the council should have considered that before dumping me in the Pit."

"Watch your tongue." She snapped the curtains shut and leaned back in her seat, one leg thrown over the other, and crossed her arms.

"You didn't answer my question before. What *sort* of opportunity?" I said, this time with Mother's I-don't-like-to-ask-twice tone.

"You used to be such a nice girl," Elbena muttered. "But if you don't want to be nice, we can turn around. I said the council *wants* to show that you're still present. But we don't *need* to."

I clenched my jaw and said nothing. *Strength through silence.*

After a moment, Elbena went on, pleased with my apparent docility. "I have a speech for you," she said. "All you have to do is read it."

"What does it say?"

"Nothing unusual," she assured me. "The same kind of speech you've given a thousand times."

Over my years of reading their words, the Luminary Council had always made sure I was in agreement. But now that I knew better, I was sure they'd done some persuading. I couldn't remember anymore. Every interaction was tainted with deep suspicion. What had they made me think I believed?

"Do exactly as they say," Tirta had warned.

"If you do your job well, you will be rewarded."

If I didn't, I would no doubt be punished. "What's the reward?"

Elbena offered a warm smile as she leaned forward and took my hands. "Mira," she breathed. "You could come home."

I DIDN'T WANT to be tempted, but the idea of going home consumed me.

Seeing my parents again, Zara, Ilina and Hristo . . . *LaLa*, because I had to believe she'd come back to the drakarium. Here I was. Out of the Pit. Carrying a promise of freedom. All I had to do was speak a few words.

I didn't *trust* the Luminary Council. They didn't care about *me*, clearly, but they cared about my title. They wanted to go back to the way things were before, when I did their bidding without a second thought.

Yet, Elbena hadn't given me the speech I was to recite, which was entirely irregular. I could only guess what she expected me to say. Maybe she'd force me to announce the council's innocence in the dragon matter, if that was public yet. Or support her reelection. Or . . . it could be anything, I supposed. The mystery woman in the infirmary had suggested the Luminary Council might want me for something; I wished she'd been more specific.

We traveled for five days by carriage, and when we reached Lorn-tah, we boarded the *Chance Encounter*, the same ship I'd taken from Damina on my way to the Pit. By now, it was easily my least favorite of all sailing vessels.

It was impressive, though: a four-masted barc with red-and-gold sails, three lower decks, and one of the largest noorestones I'd ever seen. This ship was *fast*. Travel to . . . wherever we were going (Elbena still hadn't told me) wouldn't take more than a decan. Unless we were leaving the Fallen Isles.

That thought made me shudder. I'd been to lots of places, but never beyond the Fallen Isles.

THE VOYAGE LASTED only three days, which I spent in a small cabin with Elbena chattering like we were still friends. Whenever she left, I passed my time by exercising until every muscle trembled. Arms, legs, and stomach: I had to be strong. And because my back had mostly healed, I *could* be strong.

Sometimes, I looked out my porthole and thought about my maybe-friends in the Pit, my family that abandoned me, my best friends somewhere unknown, and my tiny dragon.

Why had she left? And where had she gone?

I missed LaLa constantly, but *thinking* about her ripped open a chasm in my heart and let loose a tide of grief, and I had to keep those emotions at bay; I couldn't let Elbena see me weak.

Finally, the *Chance Encounter* docked. "Where are we?" I asked.

"You'll find out soon enough." Elbena flashed a smile, as though we shared a secret. "You're going to love this surprise. It's all going to be so grand."

This felt familiar. Not the uncertainty, but the looming grandeur. Elbena's delight. The way they'd sneak me off the ship into an inn. This part wasn't so different from being *the* Mira Minkoba. I was always being protected, watched, secreted from place to place when I traveled, even before now.

It was for my own good, Elbena had always said. It was so people didn't see me fresh off the ship, smelling like the sea and in need of a long bath. It was so I remained a pure, untouched-by-nature symbol to the whole world.

Now I wondered if it had been to keep me isolated.

"Stop tapping." Elbena shot an irritated glance at my hands beating on my knees. I'd been tapping the islands in quiet code, like Aaru had taught me; I hadn't even realized it. "Try not to be so fidgety during your speech tomorrow night."

"What *is* the speech? When will I get to see it?" What was so important that Elbena had come for me herself?

"This evening."

Finally, a knock sounded on the door: just two raps of knuckles against wood. A masked Luminary Guard opened the door and motioned us outward. "We're ready."

Elbena pushed herself off her hammock and pulled in a deep breath, steadying herself before she smiled brightly at me. "Ready to get off this boat?"

The captain and crewmen would probably protest calling the *Chance Encounter* a boat, but I just nodded and followed her out the door, into the noorestone-lit passageway. My footfalls thumped on the old wood: eight, nine, ten . . .

Slowly, with the ship rolling on the sea, we made our way up a narrow set of stairs and onto the upper deck.

At first, sunlight overwhelmed me. I'd been underground for so long, then trapped in a carriage and ship, that my eyes refused to adjust to the brilliant light. I hid my face behind my elbow and blinked, listening to the sound of ropes creaking, seabirds cawing, and crewmen calling out to one another.

Cool, salty air fluttered across my body, tangled through my hair, and made the red cotton of my dress flap.

"Come along," Elbena said. "We don't have all day."

I peeled my face from the safety of my elbow and squinted at my surroundings. Sun-darkened crewmen watched me with raised eyebrows. Only one met my eyes.

Then, not quite casually, she placed three fingers against her lips.

What was *that* supposed to mean?

I risked a faint smile before smoothing my expression.

I glanced around, praying no one had noticed her. There was no telling what my keepers would think if they'd seen what she'd done.

Maybe she hadn't done anything and I was just imagining things.

As I followed after Elbena, I finally lifted my eyes to see where we'd berthed. Above, the sky was mostly clear, though a mass of clouds boiled on the western horizon. And to the north, I saw the Shadowed City, capital of Bopha.

For a place devoted to shadows, the city sang its love to the sun.

The buildings were tall, graceful spires made of white marble, threaded with copper in intricate, spiraling patterns. Twenty-five of these stood in the exact middle of the city, one for every phase of shadow—or so Father had told me when we'd come here years ago.

The central tower stood the tallest, and brightest. In the highest floor, surrounded by floor-to-ceiling windows that sparkled in the late-afternoon sun, the Twilight Senate met.

Without Chenda. *"I am here because I stood up for what was right,"* she'd said. She was like me: betrayed by the people she had once trusted to do the right thing.

Elbena nudged me down the gangplank. "Don't dally." Her tone was pleasant, but held an edge of ice.

I hastened to follow her orders. "Sorry."

Smaller buildings surrounded the Shadow Spires, but

low hills and broad-leafed trees blocked most of the view from the docks. On the western horizon, the mass of clouds darkened.

Before we'd finished walking off the docks, the rest of the Luminary Guard had joined us (or, at least, ten of them). A white-and-copper carriage waited ahead, standing out against the crowd of carts and wagons on the road. It had the air of importance and authority. Trunks already sat on the stowage areas on top and bottom.

All around us, dockworkers carried crates to and from ships. Sweat poured down their faces and backs; their clothes clung to their lean frames. They had to move around a group of people holding signs that said things like *This is our land* and *They destroy shadows.* Were they talking about Hartans? Briefly, I thought of Chenda and the way she'd fought to help Hartans. And how she'd been punished.

And how people were being burned alive here.

For all the beauty of the Shadowed City, it was not without ugliness.

A busker played an unidentifiable tune on a tattered fiddle, not quite keeping a beat to keep the workers moving. People from the ships hollered orders. And a pair of police officers strolled down the boardwalk, batons swinging at their sides. But if they were worried about trouble, they didn't show it; their faces were bent together in deep discussion.

As for our procession—most people ignored us at first.

Then, a few workers looked up, met my eyes, and seemed to recognize me, even as changed as I was. Suddenly my name rode on a small ripple of voices.

"*Hopebearer,*" they whispered, and the enormity of that duty weighed my steps.

We approached the carriage, and the door swung open for me to enter.

Just as I was about to climb into the cavernous space—black velvet cushions trimmed in copper—an explosion sounded toward the west.

Everyone stopped. Turned. Gasped.

Wooden debris fell onto the docks and ship and into the sea. Calamity reigned as people hurried out of the way, but that wasn't what held my attention.

From the ruins of a huge galleon, an enormous red dragon erupted.

And screamed fire.

CHAPTER TWENTY-TWO

A DRAGON.

Here.

In the Shadowed City.

But this wasn't just any dragon. I knew the shape of this one, the flash of brilliant red scales, and even the pitch of her scream as she clawed her way toward the sky.

"Lex!"

Her name tore from my throat, and before I could think better of it, I was running toward the raging dragon. Slippered feet pounded on the dirt, then the docks, and then the thuds vanished under the cacophony of shouts and cries and chaos.

Everyone was running. Dockworkers, buskers, vendors—most fled the spray of fire and rush of smoke.

Others stared in wonder and terror, because there was a *dragon* on the docks.

But I ran toward the flames as they caught on barges and pillars. "Lex!"

Someone screamed my name, but I felt as though I were flying. My whole body was hot with fury, and my thoughts an inferno of anger. Some foreign instinct took over, guiding me through the crush of people trying to escape the fiery wrath, and once they were behind me, I saw her fully.

Lex was coiled around the mainmast of the galleon from which she'd erupted, her talons gouging into the wooden flesh, wings pumping. She hadn't finished her climb into the air, and now that I could see her more clearly, it was obvious why: jagged rips left the bottom of her left wing in shreds like a decorative fringe. No matter how she flapped, the wing prevented her from scooping enough air to escape. Maybe in time she'd be able to compensate, but not now. Not half-crazed with hunger.

Hot wind made fires jump around her, and the whole ship groaned and shuddered under the violence of an angry *Drakontos rex*. It was going to sink, and she would fall with it.

Heat gusted, pushing me backward, but I pushed forward. This was dangerous, I knew. Unwise. But there was still some part of me that believed I could help this dragon.

I reached out my hand through the heavy, dry air

which tasted of ashes. I reached as though I could touch her. "Lex!"

Still, she thrashed her head and roared at the sky, spitting out flames that sputtered deep red. Her fire was dying, and so was she.

"Lex!" I took another step forward, my arms open toward her.

This time, she heard me. Or she saw me. I couldn't be sure. But either way, she released her grip on the mainmast and abandoned the sinking galleon. With one heavy pump of her good wing, she leaped to the docks.

Wood cracked and crumbled beneath her, falling into the churning sea. Lex clawed toward me, her gaze locked with mine.

And behind me, screams began anew. Everyone thought the dragon was coming to eat them; they didn't know Lex would never harm a human.

Well, not before all this. Now? I couldn't be sure.

My heart pounded as the great *Drakontos rex* prowled forward, head low and wings arched. Her talons gouged into the docks, and bloodred fire burned deep in the back of her mouth, behind a hundred knifed teeth.

"Lex," I said, as gently as I could. How many times had I actually met her? Ilina had far more contact with the big dragons than I, but Lex *had* seen me before. With Ilina. Multiple times.

I kept my hands lifted toward the great dragon. From

here, I could see that her scales were duller than they'd been, and her eyes sunken inward. She was ill. Starved. Abused. If she'd been LaLa, I could have taken her in my arms and kissed her nose, but Lex was as big as my bedroom. She was a wild creature, not one who obeyed my commands.

And yet, as she reached me, Lex rested her chin on the docks at my feet, her golden eyes turned upward to me. Her wings pulled in, and the rest of her body lowered as well.

"Hello, my sweet." Slowly, I began to kneel. Heat rose off her scales in waves, cooling as the shock and anger wore off. A soft groan worked through her throat. "Poor Lexy," I murmured.

"Now!" a man shouted.

Bowstrings *twanged* and a volley of arrows flew in from the north, dragging a heavy net behind them.

Latticed ropes crashed onto Lex, and at once, I realized my mistake. All of my focus had been on her, and none on my surroundings. While I'd been distracted—while I'd kept Lex distracted—police and soldiers and guards had staged themselves at a distance, just out of my peripheral vision.

"No!" The scream ripped from me, but I was too late.

So was Lex. She reared back, but the arrows plunged into the water, drawing the net tightly over her, and pinned her great wings to her sides. Flame curled from the back of her throat, but there wasn't enough to save her. The fire died at the tip of her tongue.

And then, her golden eyes shifted back to me, and she surrendered. Breaking free of the ship had taken all her effort, and now she was resigned to captivity once more.

"Go," I rasped, reaching for the net. "Try one more time." But before I could even touch the net, everyone swarmed in: soldiers and police to Lex, Elbena and Luminary Guards to me.

I was surrounded. The white-uniformed men took my hands and arms, drawing me away from the fray of everyone struggling to contain Lex. I thrashed, feeling as wild as the dragon, but it was no use. The Luminary Guards were bigger. Stronger. And there were ten of them. "Stay still!" one shouted.

"Let me go!" All I wanted was to get back to Lex, but I couldn't even *see* her through the wall of bodies. "Let me go!" I jerked my arm free, only to find another's hands clasped around it.

"Release her!" Elbena shouted.

All ten Luminary Guards stepped away, and I started to run toward Lex again, but Elbena stood in my way. It was over. Lex was lost to me.

I crumpled to the ground with a desperate sob.

"Oh, Mira." Elbena pressed her hands to her heart. "What a *brave* thing you did. Are you all right?"

Adrenaline rushed through my veins and my chest

squeezed. I was not all right. But what could I do but nod? The movement was jerky, and I was certain that nothing I did right now looked natural.

Elbena extended a hand to me, her smooth brown fingers in a delicate arc. "Let me help you up, dear."

We were in full view of everyone who could bear to take their eyes off the dragon.

I counted the masked guards ringing us. Still ten. Twenty-five Shadow Spires in the city. Fifty people gathering nearby, gawking at us, and at the display on the docks behind us.

Innumerable cries from Lex.

"Mira." Elbena's voice was firm. She still held her hand toward me.

Hating myself, I placed my work-callused hand in hers and allowed her to pull me into a brief hug. "Don't do anything to jeopardize your freedom," she murmured.

I gave a jolting nod, but couldn't bring myself to give voice to assurances of my behavior. It was all I could do to keep my trembling at a minimum, and my tears caged inside me.

"Good." Quickly, she smoothed my hair, straightened my dress, and pulled me around to survey the activity on the docks.

The burning galleon was half-drowned by now, and a terrible shrieking came from within. Not a shrieking of the ship, but something else. Something real. Something terrible.

I staggered forward, but a Luminary Guard held me back.

"Stay," said Elbena. "It's too late for them."

"For them," I repeated, like a question, though it wasn't one. I already knew what she meant, and it made my voice tight and high. "How many dragons?"

"There were three aboard the *Whitesell*. I suppose the other two are lost now." Disappointment filled her tone—the kind of upset that came from a bad investment or a burned meal. Like the loss of two dragons was simply an inconvenience that she'd have to deal with later.

Seven gods. What if the other two were LaLa and Crystal?

My knees gave out and I would have fallen to the ground again, but one of the Luminary Guards stepped forward to hold me up, and a spark of clarity hit. They weren't LaLa and Crystal. The voices were too big, too loud to belong to anything other than a large species.

It was a cold comfort. Two dragons were dead. One was captured and on the verge of death.

I didn't understand it. I didn't understand *her*. She felt none of this devastation for lives lost, but it was the only thing I could feel. All I could *hear* were the shrieks of the dragons burning and drowning within the ship.

The Great Abandonment threatened a catastrophe of tremors and landslides. Why didn't the ground open now and swallow everything?

Right before my eyes, the *Whitesell* was sinking into

the sea. A brigade had already put out fires on the neighboring ships and on the docks, while police and guards coordinated to secure Lex and push back the growing crowd of onlookers. Because of course people wanted to gawk at her suffering.

All the while, a Luminary Guard held me upright, and Elbena muttered under her breath. Already preparing how to deal with the *inconvenience.*

When Lex was sedated and the guards had the crowd under control, Elbena took my hand and strode forward.

"Here she is!" She lifted our fists into the air and let her voice ring out over the din of shocked cries and groaning wood. "The girl who stopped the beast from destroying the Shadowed City: Mira Minkoba!"

As one, the crowd turned to us and began to cheer. *"It's Mira!"*

"The Hopebearer!"

"Look at her!"

"She charmed the dragon and saved us!"

Elbena looked at me askance. "Smile, Mira. You're a hero now." And then, when my expression didn't change—couldn't change—she gave me a little shake. "*Smile*, Mira. Or there will be consequences."

I forced my mouth into the correct shape, but I couldn't imagine anyone would mistake it for something real. Still, as long as I did what she ordered, maybe it didn't matter.

"Why is Mira here?"

"Where is her family?"

"How did she know what to do with the dragon?"

"Why were there dragons on that ship?"

Distantly, I registered that those were good questions, and at least I wasn't the *only* one who didn't know all the answers.

"How did the dragon get out of the ship?"

Elbena held up her other hand to quiet the crowd. "We don't have time for questions. All we can say right now is that these dragons were on their way to your local sanctuary as part of an interisland breeding program. Unfortunately, one mistook our intentions and escaped."

People nodded.

How easily they accepted her lies. Elbena had long ago mastered that talent.

"Thank the Fallen Gods and the Upper Gods, too: Mira has extensive experience with dragons, and she was perfectly aware of what she was doing. As soon as Mira and I heard the crash, I sent her to calm the dragon, because I knew she was the only one here who could possibly accomplish such a feat."

"She knows their hearts," someone said. "Mira the Dragonhearted."

"Yes!" Elbena shouted. "Mira the Hopebearer, and Mira the Dragonhearted!"

A dark chill ran through me as Lex drew my gaze once more. Rope bound her wings tightly to her sides. A steel muzzle caged her jaws—something that would never have been possible even a decan ago. But now that she was weakened by starvation, the metal held her teeth shut together—not that she tried to open her mouth and shoot fire anymore. She knew it was pointless. Her golden eyes had dulled into dim acceptance of my betrayal.

Like when Aaru discovered my identity.

I hurt everyone I cared about.

I wanted to scream that I hadn't done this on purpose. That Elbena hadn't wanted me to run toward Lex, and this was her effort to make the situation work in her favor. But Elbena squeezed my hand so tightly my bones rubbed together, and I forced my grimace into another smile.

"She saved the city! Mira the Dragonhearted saved the Shadowed City."

The cries of joy went on and on, rising in fervor as the *Whitesell* sank deeper into the sea. As salt water quenched dragon fire. And as the voices of two dragons were silenced forever.

THE STORM ARRIVED and loosed its fury across the Isle of Shadow.

It was to the drum of rain and roar of thunder that we drove to a grand inn, which loomed over the water-shrouded street. Wind made palm trees dance and bow, and cold air seeped into the carriage through the windows, but when we pulled into the drive, Elbena held up a hand.

"Wait." She nodded at the Luminary Guard who'd been sitting next to me. "Make sure everything is secure."

The Luminary Guard unfolded himself and opened

the door, admitting a gust of stinging rain into the carriage. And then, the rush was cut off, leaving Elbena and me alone in the dim space.

"This is going to change things," Elbena muttered, almost inaudible under the storm.

I could hardly breathe for the numbness creeping through my body. From the cold rain. From the sight of the ship sinking. From the memory of Lex in chains.

I'd done that. Maybe I hadn't physically put the muzzle on her, or captured her in the net, but without my interference she might have gone away from the city—toward freedom, rather than toward me.

"Is this why you brought me here?" My voice sounded scraped away. Hollow. "Did you bring me here to name me a savior of the people while I watched dragons die?"

A smile twisted up her face. "I brought you here to give a speech. Do you recall giving a speech while you watched dragons die?"

Strength through silence. I desperately wanted the kind of strength Aaru displayed, but he had a lifetime of practice and I had a lifetime of doing as I was told.

"But I suppose," she went on, "anything is possible. You think I'm some sort of monster now, and perhaps a monster would arrange for a dragon to escape its confines just at the moment of your arrival."

The shipping order I'd seen had given the Shadowed City as one of the locations where dragons would be, but the transport ship should have left over two decans ago.

So why were they still here? Or rather, why were only *some* of them here?

Elbena wore a faint smirk as she watched me struggle to decipher her intentions.

I dropped my eyes to my hands and forced my expression neutral, though even *thinking* the word *dragon* made hot tears swell in my eyes.

"Tomorrow is a big day." Elbena leaned back in her seat. "Your speech will be given at a state dinner in the evening, so you'll spend the day preparing. Hair, face, clothes—everything. It will be just like before, though your mistress of beauty won't be here. The inn has a wonderful staff that will assist you in her absence. I'm sure you don't mind."

My heart squeezed at the thought of Krasimir, but of course she wasn't here. She was too sympathetic to me. "When will you give me the speech?"

"It will be waiting for you in your room. Councilor Bilyana will have brought it when she arrived in Bopha on last night's tide. Your speechwriter sent it with her so that she could have a couple extra days to finalize it." She leaned forward. "It's a delicate thing, you understand. We needed to make sure every word was perfect. And if you have any questions, we can talk about it tomorrow."

"What will the speech say?"

She shook her head. "We'll discuss that tomorrow."

Dimly, I knew that denying me answers was another method of controlling me. Maybe she *had* arranged for

Lex's escape, and the deaths of the two on the ship. I wouldn't put it past her. Not since learning of the council's involvement with the disappearance of dragons. Or, if not involvement, concealment for sure.

"You said if I give the speech tomorrow, then I'll be set free from the Pit."

"Yes, although I suppose I shouldn't have assumed that you knew your good behavior was also a factor." She gave me an annoyed look. "You aren't as necessary to the council as you think. We could easily elevate another pretty face to replace you." Her lips curled up. "Unfortunately, prison time doesn't seem to agree with your pretty face."

Her blow to my vanity stung.

Before I could devote any more thought to it, someone pounded on the carriage, and a Luminary Guard opened the door. Quickly, I was shuffled into the inn. The space was dim and quiet, save the inconsistent number of Luminary Guards prowling through the parlor as though searching for threats.

Without stopping to greet the owners, Elbena took me to a room upstairs. Before we could enter, yet another Luminary Guard emerged.

Above the white mask, his eyes darted first to me, then to Elbena. "It's clear."

My heart stopped. I knew that voice.

"Thank you," Elbena said.

The Luminary Guard bowed and started toward the stairs. He didn't look back.

Elbena nudged me toward the open door. "In you go."

"Where are you staying?" My words sounded breathless. I could barely form them around the pounding of my heart.

She smiled sweetly. "Down the hall. You're on your own tonight, but there will be guards outside your door and window. Everything is locked and I'm the only one with the keys. I hope you'll behave."

I gave her a look that just oozed obedience, and when I stepped inside the room and shut the door, I barely paid attention when the lock turned behind me with a heavy *clunk*.

Instead, I was thinking of the miracle that had just occurred. The barest eye contact. The timbre of his voice. The mask pulled tight against his dark skin.

Hristo.

BEFORE

Five Years Ago

WHEN I WAS TWELVE, I PROPOSED MARRIAGE TO HRISTO.

It was a dragon day. Ilina and I were hunting small game in the sanctuary, near the ruins. LaLa perched on my glove, her wings pulled open to catch the sunshine, while Ilina and Crystal took their turn. LaLa and I had already finished for the day.

Ahead, Crystal had just caught a rabbit, and Ilina was rewarding her with a treat—in trade for the dragon giving up the rabbit. Sometimes this worked. Other times, they realized this wasn't a fair trade and set their kills on fire instead.

"It makes sense, right?" I kept my smile bright, even as the number of my steps ticked away in the back of my head.

"I'm not sure what you mean." His lowered his voice. "Why would we get married?"

"When we're older," I clarified.

"But *why*?"

I couldn't believe I had to explain this. "I have two best friends. You and Ilina. When it comes to potential marriage partners, I'm reasonably certain I like boys, and you're my favorite boy." Plus, he'd saved my life when I was seven, and he always carried LaLa's kills for me. If that didn't qualify him to be a great husband, I couldn't imagine what would. (At twelve, I hadn't considered that being *in love* with someone might also factor into my decision.)

He scanned the ruins for danger that was never there. "Why are you thinking about this now?"

"Mother received five inquiries regarding my matrimonial future." Just thinking about it made my chest tight with worry.

"Any she's taking seriously?"

"I don't want to risk finding out."

Hristo scratched his chin. "Why do you think she'll marry you off if you don't get there first? Everyone on Damina gets to choose. This isn't Idris."

Because I never chose anything. Not my clothes, my hair, my food. Nothing small. Nothing big. Nothing important. Everyone on Damina got to choose—except for me.

"Besides," Hristo went on, "I'm a servant. What would the Luminary Council say if you married a Hartan boy?"

"We're past that now. The Mira Treaty—"

"Harta may be independent. The treaty might *say* we're equal. But that doesn't make it true." He stopped walking and gazed down at me, almost sadly. "You're better than me. Your mother says so all the time."

"She says I'm better than everyone, but she can't mean it. I'm not smart. I don't rescue people. I don't do anything but dress up and stand where she tells me. That doesn't make me better."

"Your status makes you better." His jaw clenched. "Your upbringing. Your ancestors. The place where you were born. Your parents. The treaty named after you. The title of Hopebearer. All of that makes you better."

But none of it was anything I'd done. I didn't understand. Which just made me feel more stupid and unworthy.

"I'll protect you," he said. "I'll be your friend. But I won't marry you. Ever."

CHAPTER TWENTY-THREE

HRISTO WAS HERE IN BOPHA.

My heart swelled as I recalled the way he'd glanced at me, like warning, like assurance, like—

Like my protector was finally here, and everything was going to be all right. Oh, Damina, I couldn't wait to see him again. Even the smallest glimpse would be enough to sustain me for a month.

I leaned against the door, basking in the knowledge that Hristo had been right here. And deeper in the room—likely checking under the tall bed, inside the mahogany wardrobe, behind the floor-length curtains made of brocade silk. The room was the colors of the moons, white with gold highlights, and definitely expensive.

Twelve noorestones stood in gilt sconces on the walls

(three on each wall), all with black velvet covers draped along the backs.

So this would not be like the Pit, where noorestones were silenced by some mysterious Idrisi. Here, I was the master of light. I could cover the stones or not. I could cover all but one.

The relief drained out of me when I saw the sheet of paper resting on one of the embroidered pillows.

The speech.

The *opportunity* to leave the Pit forever, abandoning Aaru, Gerel, Chenda, Tirta, and the rest of them.

The way people had named me Dragonhearted for my betrayal of Lex.

Curiosity drew my eyes toward the page again, but I couldn't go to it yet. I needed to steady my thoughts.

A lidded tray sat on a three-legged table made of carved mahogany wood. I pushed myself off the door and took five paces toward it. Under the silver dome, I found a huge, hot meal. Slices of roast boar, with onions and garlic and honey tucked over and around them. Steamed carrots. Tiny potatoes. Set away from the hot food, there was a small bowl of chocolate-dipped strawberries, a pitcher of chilled water, and a glass of red wine.

I hadn't seen so much food since I was arrested. This would be a feast for the first level. Aaru would—

My chest tightened and I started to count the noorestones again, but shifted to the wooden panels on the wall instead; for all the light they gave, there was a dark side to nooresstones that I could never forget.

Numb, I sat at the table and ate. I forced myself to chew slowly, twenty times for every mouthful.

Only when I finished eating did I take the sheet of paper from my pillow.

This part used to be so comforting. It had always seemed that my speechwriter—a brilliant woman named Kahina—never struggled to find the right words. She'd kept me from vomiting whatever inane thought passed through my head. She'd saved me from humiliating social gaffes.

But now, as I read her delicate hand, a chill crept through me. These were not words I wanted to speak. To think. To know.

It was late, and the storm raged across the Shadowed City, but restlessness clawed at me. So I roamed the space, counting my footsteps, hoping Hristo would come. Maybe he had a plan, some kind of news about anything that mattered. Maybe my parents had sent him, since they couldn't come themselves. Maybe he had a way to spirit me away from this awful place.

He was in disguise. Regardless of his motive and method for being here, he'd hidden his identity and needed me to play along. I'd learn the truth as soon as he was able to tell me; I just had to be patient.

Voices carried from the hall. They were too low for me to understand, but loud enough that I knew Hristo would not be able to come.

Again, a prisoner. This time with a nicer cell.

Had I ever *not* been a prisoner? The Luminary Council had always kept me like this, under close watch, under careful guard. I used to think it was because I was precious to them. Now I realized the cell had always been there, just invisible.

I hated the grim acceptance that settled inside me, but I was no heroine in a story. I was not the kind of girl who could leap from her window, dash through the stormy city, and disappear into the wilds. I couldn't commandeer a ship and sail . . . somewhere. I couldn't do anything but obey commands.

A pendulum clock *tick-tocked* on the wall; it was late. I moved around the room covering the noorestones with the squares of black velvet, blocking their cool blue light. Nine, ten, eleven.

I left the twelfth uncovered. The room stood as dim as my cell in the Pit, but when I closed my eyes, I couldn't imagine myself back there. The Pit seemed far away, almost like a false memory. And the *sounds*: muted voices, thumping footsteps, the roar of thunder, and the crash of rain. It was all offensively loud.

Nor could I imagine what Aaru was doing right now. Had they moved him back to his cell yet? Were his feet healed enough to send him to the forge to work on the God Shackle? It was night, but the position of the sun meant nothing underground; perhaps he was awake right now, too, wondering about me.

Probably hating me.

I pulled back the heavy curtains and peered through the rain-drenched darkness. Below, I could just make out the glow of noorestones as the Luminary Guards patrolled the inn. Was Hristo down there? And what about Ilina? Was she here somewhere, too?

On impulse, I tested the window, but it was nailed shut. *Someone* had clearly believed I was brave enough to slip out and try to navigate down the steep roof.

The curtains fell closed as I backed away. Grimly, I returned to the speech and read it five more times.

If I spoke these words, like Elbena wanted, there would be consequences for thousands of strangers. If I refused, there would be consequences for my family, my friends, and four people I *wanted* to call friends.

With shaking hands, I covered the final noorestone over the headboard. Darkness washed across the room, but it wasn't absolute.

The faint glow from the window.

The hints of light beneath the noorestone covers.

The dull illumination from beneath the door.

I closed my eyes against the not-darkness, feeling like I was melting into the bed. The speech swirled through my mind with its awfulness:

> *Seventeen years ago, the Mira Treaty took a stance against discrimination, against occupation, and against the pillaging of our islands. The treaty states that to truly honor the Fallen Gods, all islands must be equal*

and independent. Anything less is immoral. Unethical.

This truth is indisputable.

Since then, many strides have been taken toward making reparations, ensuring the success of Harta and her First Matriarch, and offering the freedom of choice for those who want to work and reside all across the Fallen Isles.

But in doing so, we have inadvertently disrespected the gods, and the standards of our individual islands. We must protect our cultures and societies as fiercely as we protect our people. Our history, values and ethics, accomplishments and triumphs, and divine gifts must be preserved.

Remember, our gods grant gifts to the people born of their islands—of their bodies. Those gifts become muted when we leave, and to leave forever is to forsake their gifts and graces. That is no way to give thanks. We must show our gratitude by staying loyal to our gods, and to our islands.

To that end, it is my belief that Bophans belong on Bopha, Hartans belong on Harta, and approving this decree will be the first step in restoring the balance the gods wanted for us from the beginning. We are united, and we are equal, but it is by our gods' will that we remain separated.

There were so many problems in that speech, glossed over and hedged with pretty, reassuring statements, that even *I* could not count them all. I hated that someone could wrap so many lies in layers of truth.

This was how Chenda had ended up in the Pit: refusing to say something like this. And now the same choice fell on me, only I *knew* the terror of the Pit.

And I didn't want to go back.

ELBENA SPENT THE next day reminding me what it was like to be *the* Mira Minkoba.

She came to my room two hours after dawn, leading a troupe of five maids. The women kept their eyes downcast as they laid out a breakfast of salmon and cheese quiche, fresh berries drowned in yogurt and honey, and a strong, black tea that Mother never would have let me drink for fear of staining my teeth.

"This is a traditional Bophan breakfast," Elbena said, scooping a spoonful of yogurt. Behind her, the maids glanced at one another, exchanging looks I couldn't fully decipher—but I knew they weren't positive.

As the maids moved around my room, drawing a bath and laying out my cosmetics, I thought about the speech and how it would affect life on Bopha. I wished I could ask, but with Elbena here, I didn't dare.

Throughout breakfast, Elbena went through the latest fashions and gossip from the different Isles, as though I'd been away a year, not a month.

"What about Chenda M'rizz?" I asked. "Will I see her tonight?"

Elbena cocked her head. "Chenda? It's possible, I suppose. I didn't realize you were close."

So either Elbena didn't know that Chenda was in the Pit, or she didn't want me to know. It was hard to say which.

"We aren't close," I confirmed. "But I've always wanted to be." No need to mention I'd spent thirteen nights across the hall from her. It wasn't as if we'd actually talked.

"Well." Elbena leaned forward. "I heard that the Dawn Lady had quite the scandalous affair. People say she and her paramour were going to run away together, but he was killed during one of the riots."

She spoke so casually about someone dying. Had she always been so callous? Maybe I'd simply never noticed.

"From what I understand, she's been taking some time to herself for the last couple of decans. I'd be surprised if she joined us tonight."

Time to herself. Was that the excuse the Luminary Council had given to explain my absence? Had I been *taking some time to myself* with hard labor, starvation, and torture?

When breakfast was finished, it was time to prepare for my visit to the central Shadow Spire. We began with the bath. While I soaked in blissfully hot water, scented with lavender and chamomile, the maids began the process of restoring me. Two started on my callused hands and cracked nails, while the others took to washing and combing my hair. Quietly, they mused about what to do with it, because the once-soft strands had turned brittle and broken during my time in the Pit. Several pieces (too many to count) fell out, and every time, the maids tensed as though expecting a reprimand.

But when I said nothing about it—what *could* I say?—they moisturized with coconut oil and shea cream and strong, gentle hands. They weren't Krasimir, but they were good, and for a few minutes, I forgot.

About the dragons.

About the speech.

About the Pit.

About the people who . . .

The day went by swiftly after that, with a pause only for a light lunch of tiny crab-cake sandwiches, soup, and honey-drizzled strawberries. Then, my hair went into a single, sweeping braid, with three gold wires in each strand to distract from all the broken ends.

"That looks *wonderful.*" Elbena's hands floated around the back of my head. "Just wonderful. It's simple, but elegant. Bophans value simple elegance. You know that, right?" She cast me a sidelong glance, urging me to join in the praise.

"Thank you," I murmured, unable to give Elbena what she wanted, and unable to give these women what they deserved. In only a few hours, I was supposed to put my support behind a decree that would send all Hartans to another island, whether they wanted to go or not. And Elbena expected me to pretend like nothing was wrong.

How could someone who'd been raised in the light of the Lovers be so cold?

"We're happy to do our part for the Hopebearer," said one of the women.

My face heated. They knew who I was, but I didn't even know their names. And with Elbena looming over me like a vulture, I didn't dare ask.

Instead, I forced my hand steady as I applied the cosmetics, all carefully arranged just how I'd kept them at home. I erased my sleepless night, and with warm shades of powder, I softened the sharp lines of my cheekbones and darkened my eyes to appear deep and knowing.

If only I could look the part, perhaps I could persuade people to the truth. But what was the truth? I used to believe I knew all there was to understand about the world, but if the last two months had taught me anything, it was this: for the rest of my life, I would question everything.

Then, I could delay no longer. The sun edged westward and it was a good drive from my inn to the central spire, with checkpoints along the way.

"They can't be too careful these days," Elbena said as she and a squad of seven Luminary Guards escorted me downstairs and out of the inn, where the white-and-copper carriage waited for us.

The front garden was huge and green, with trimmed hedges and climbing vines that flowered on the fence of gorgeously wrought iron. The gate stood closed, as if the owners expected attack at any moment. As if they had anything to fear from the restaurants and shops nearby. The people strolling along the cobblestone street wore fine white silks and tall boots as they stepped around puddles from last night's storm.

The carriage door swung open, and Dara Soun, the lady president of the Twilight Senate, unfolded herself from the interior.

Elbena leaned toward me and murmured, "Remember to watch what you say."

"I'll be good." It wasn't as though Dara was going to help me escape. She'd been the lady president since before I was born and if she'd bothered to help Chenda, it clearly hadn't worked. Dara Soun was no ally of mine.

"Elbena! Mira! Welcome." Dara's voice was huskier than I remembered, and her face bore more lines around her eyes and mouth; even the copper tattoos that crawled up her neck had started to sag and wrinkle. She smiled, but it looked forced and uncomfortable.

"Thank you for welcoming us to your island." Elbena bowed deeply. I followed a moment later.

"Always a pleasure. It's not every year we have such esteemed company to welcome the Twilight Senate back after the Hallowed Restoration." Dara returned the gesture and ushered us into the carriage. "If you're ready to go . . ."

I waited while a Luminary Guard made a show of not appearing as though he was searching the carriage for danger as he offered a hand to help me step inside.

That was something I'd always hated: we acted as

though we trusted our neighbors, even as we expected them to betray us.

The Luminary Guard was Hristo, though, so when I took his hand to climb into the carriage, I never wanted to let go.

But I did let go.

Right away.

Because if I'd held on even a moment too long, Elbena would have noticed. The thought of her realizing Hristo wasn't really a Luminary Guard and punishing him—that was more than I could stand.

I slid to the far side of the carriage and straightened my gown. The long skirt and train had been bleached into a silvery white, but the bust was all gold brocade, filled with tiny draconic details. A matching sash circled my ribs, creating a high waist that disguised my gaunt form. I'd worn this to a charity ball just six months ago and received twenty-seven compliments on it. When I'd seen my seamstress again, I had repeated every kind thing people had said about her creation, word for word. She'd been so happy she cried.

The gown was loose now, though my muscles beneath the silk were harder. Still, it felt amazing to wear something so luxurious. Even after everything had been stripped away in the Pit and I'd learned to live with less, I still wanted this: my personal guard, meals cooked by renowned chefs, and things that made me feel pretty.

Maybe that was silly.

"Will Councilor Bilyana be joining us tonight?" I asked as Elbena slid into the seat next to me.

"Of course. You can see her later, if you want."

"Of course," I said, mimicking Elbena's tone. "I can't wait."

She shot a warning look at me.

Soon, Dara, Hristo (in disguise), and one of Dara's men joined us in the carriage. It was a close fit. As we eased into motion, only to stop and wait for the gate to open, and then start again down the street, Elbena kept patting my hand where it rested on my knee. But rather than glare at her as she intruded on my space, I turned my attention to the bright city outside.

People walked down the road as though nothing horrible was happening anywhere. As though dragons weren't being seized and neglected and killed. As though earthquakes weren't destroying families. As though—somewhere on another island, hidden beneath the ground—people weren't kept in small cages with their own filth, rewarded with rancid food for good behavior.

I tried not to imagine going back to that. To chapped hands, to pitch-black nights, to the weeping of my neighbors. To Altan.

I shook away those thoughts and focused on the Shadowed City. I needed to be alert.

Streetlights stood sentinel every five paces: noorestones placed in high steel cages, the crystals arranged so that the ground beneath them would never be dark.

"What are you looking at?" Dara watched me as I peered at the outside world.

"You have so many streetlights here." I'd counted twenty-one already, and we hadn't left the block where my inn was located.

"Bophans don't like the dark," she said. "You might have noticed."

"That's always seemed odd to me. You worship the Shadow Goddess." I wanted to suck the words back in—Elbena was frowning—but Dara just waved away my gaffe, as though it had never happened.

"There are no shadows without light, Mira. And where there is light, there are always shadows." She spoke the words as though imparting some great knowledge or understanding of the universe upon me. "In Bopha, our worship is twofold: the shadow, and the light that makes the shadow possible. To expect one without the other is"—she paused, as though trying to figure out how to explain this to an outsider—"the same as expecting a shout to have no sound."

I thought I understood. "It wouldn't be right to worship only shadows without also loving the thing that makes shadows possible?"

Dara smiled warmly. "That's correct."

"You said the worship was twofold, though. Light and shadow, but something has to block the light to make the shadow. Do you worship that, too? What makes shadows?"

The lady president leaned forward, her neck tattoos twitching as she drew a breath. "We do, Mira. We block the light to make shadows. That is human nature."

The carriage turned a sharp corner, and when we straightened, the Shadow Spires rose ahead, filling the sky with their enormity.

"You can see," Dara said, "why these recent arson attacks have been so horrific."

"Lighting people on fire is always horrific."

"Of course." She said it like she was agreeing so we didn't argue. Like lighting people on fire was somehow *worse* here. "It destroys a person's shadow. A terrible fate anywhere."

I searched my mind for their afterlife beliefs. Daminan people were united with their soul mates for eternity. Khulani warriors were taken to fight in a great battle. Hartans were given endless, loving families. Bophans . . .

"Only our shadows move on," Dara said. "I could see you trying to remember."

I blushed. "Forgive me. It's been some time since my studies covered other beliefs."

"Worry not." She leaned back in her seat. "Bopha takes our shadows and adds them to her own. But without, we cannot join her in eternity. That's why the fire killings are even more abhorrent to us. A person cannot cast a shadow when the light is coming from them."

"What happens if they die without a shadow?"

Dara bowed her head. "Nothing happens, dear Mira. Nothing at all. They simply end."

I shuddered. The thought of nothing happening after death was enough to haunt me for days. I changed the subject. "What do you think will be served at dinner tonight?"

That was an easy question. Dara had chosen the menu. While she described all seven courses, I divided my attention between that and the window. But mostly, I wished I were sitting next to Hristo. If I could even meet his eyes, that would be something, but he sat on the other side of Elbena, and everyone would know something was wrong if I leaned forward to look around her.

If Hristo had known the quiet code, I could tap a message. I could say hello. I could say I missed him.

The carriage stopped at three points on the drive, and every time a police officer opened the door, peered around the interior, and asked to see Dara's papers. "Thank you, Lady President Soun."

"They know who you are," I said the last time, as we drew closer to the spires. "Why do they need to see the papers?"

"I may be the leader of the Bophan people, but I am still a person like anyone else. If I insist on checkpoints to ensure the safety of tonight's dinner, I must submit to the inspections as well."

If only she felt so passionately about the equality of Hartans.

A wide band of park ground ringed the Shadow Spires. Broad-leafed trees grew at regular intervals. Benches (I counted five) and tables (two within sight) had been sprinkled across the grass. All were painted bright white, and already glowed under the streetlights.

The spires themselves were something else entirely.

From the docks, I'd thought the buildings were marble and copper, but that had been under the afternoon light. Now, as we passed between two of the towers, I noticed the noorestones embedded right into the walls. They'd been placed next to the veins of copper that swirled over the exteriors, like the tattoos that covered Dara's throat, or Chenda's face.

When the carriage stopped and we were released, I dropped back my head to find that the bright noorestones climbed up the towers all the way to the top of every spire.

Three footsteps thumped behind me. I held my breath, hoping it was Hristo, but the sound was too noisy to be him; Hristo moved like a ghost when he wanted. And he wouldn't risk his cover.

"It's beautiful, isn't it?" Elbena stood next to me and lowered her voice. "Doesn't it make you wish you could see beautiful things like this all the time?"

I kept my voice equally soft, under the gentle cacophony of a stream of people on their way to the wide-mouthed doors of the central spire. "Of course."

"Don't forget." She touched my arm so I'd go with her. The party waited. "All you have to do is deliver the speech."

CHAPTER TWENTY-FOUR

DELIVER THE SPEECH.

That was all.

That was always the Luminary Council's wish of me. Say the words. Look the part. Inspire confidence.

My long gown gleamed in the noorestone light, bright against my skin. I missed this—feeling beautiful—but how could I embrace this life now that I knew the cost?

Conflicted, I followed Elbena and Dara to the enormous open doors of the High Tower, where eight armed guards waited. They searched our bags and waved us into the grand lobby. The five of us strode through the huge space, with ceilings that stretched far higher than normal, making Dara's voice carry as she pointed out pieces of art and architecture, and educated us on their historical importance.

A bubbling fountain with a map of the Fallen Isles on the bottom, and dozens of small fish meant to signify the Upper Gods, who'd chosen not to descend to Noore.

A lightless chandelier constructed after the North Mine collapse, when thirty miners were killed in a cave-in.

And a statue of Bopha herself, her arms and hands and fingers stretching toward a window so narrow that it would admit the morning light only twice a year.

Finally, we reached a marble staircase in the center of the room. The steps spiraled up and up, with noorestones embedded in copper all along the inner handrail. Our shadows moved against the white walls, silent reminders of Bopha's power here.

Music drifted through the building—the gentle *one-two-three* beat of a waltz caught and tangled on my counting. The only music in the Pit had been what I'd brought in my mind, Kumas's sad attempts, and the horrible noise of Hurrok's screaming every night.

This music—real music—drew me upstairs. My soul was starving for it.

On the landing, we turned one corner into a huge ballroom where a dozen musicians played on a tall stage that sat under a great, circular window in the back. I identified a flute, violin, and some kind of bass stringed instrument before Elbena's gasp drew my attention away.

"What a beautiful room!" Elbena smiled widely. A real

smile, even, not that manufactured expression she used on me.

"Thank you." Dara was all smugness. It showed in the set of her shoulders, the purse of her mouth, and the way she eyed the room as though evaluating a prized stallion. "I'm so pleased you like it."

It *was* an impressive space. She was right about that.

A hundred (easy to count because there were twenty groups of five) noorestones sat in mirrored sconces on the right side of the room, casting sharp illumination toward the left. And it could have been a trick of the light, or my eyes, but sometimes it appeared as though the shadows didn't quite match the people they were attached to.

Women and men danced everywhere, glittering in the brilliant light. Many wore pale-colored suits or gowns, contrasting with dark skin. It was a theme, I supposed. Shadows and light. The two things Bophans worshiped.

Most people did not have the tattoos I'd seen on Dara, Chenda, and Hurrok, though some had painted sparkly cosmetics across their faces and necks and shoulders and arms. Even fingers shone, and not just with jewelry, though there was a lot of that as well. Rings, bracelets, necklaces, headbands: most were copper set with various gemstones, though I spotted silver and gold as well.

I found myself swaying along with the music; I could hardly remember the last time I'd danced.

"Please," Dara said. "Let me introduce you to everyone. Or reintroduce you, as the case may be."

"We'd appreciate that." Elbena glanced at me and mouthed, "Remember what we talked about."

A warning. The same way Mother reminded me to stand up straight and pull back my shoulders and lift my chin. Like I could forget how to behave after a lifetime of her ungentle coaching.

Like I could forget to mind my tongue with enemies at my sides.

But I nodded just slightly. If I behaved, maybe she'd leave me alone with Hristo for a few minutes.

He, like the other guards, had taken a place along the wall. The mask hid his expression, but when our eyes met, I sensed a smile beneath the off-white linen. My heart thumped in response. He'd come for me. My protector. My friend.

I tore my gaze away before Elbena caught me, and I spent the next eternity moving from person to person. I smiled. I took hands in mine. I told strangers that I wished the best for them. I listened to subtle bragging. I gave vague answers to questions about what had happened with Lex at the docks, because Elbena was there and I wasn't certain what story she'd already spread beyond the basics.

At first, it was almost as though nothing had changed and this was still my life.

Then, dinner was announced, and everyone made space as nine round tables were brought in, followed by seven chairs per table. Before our eyes, the ballroom became a banquet hall as men and women covered the tables in silk and porcelain and glass. Small noorestone stands were placed in the center of each table, followed by nameplates in flowing script.

My place was toward the stage, with Elbena and Dara, plus two men and two other women—one the second councilor who'd come to Bopha. She sat across from me, which meant she was in the perfect position to observe my movements.

"Hello, Mira," said Councilor Bilyana. "It's so nice to see you again." Her look was all cool calculation. With the way they made me feel now, it was hard to believe I'd ever trusted the Luminary Council.

Dara sat to my left. A woman named Sothy to my right. She introduced herself as the owner of seventeen noorestone mines.

"Bopha has the largest mines in the Fallen Isles," she said. "It is a gift from our goddess, so that it's never truly dark. The Shadow Goddess has been good to me. I was able to provide all the stones you see here." She reached forward to touch the stand in the center of the table. It was shaped like a tree and had tiny noorestones hanging like leaves.

"They're beautiful," I said, trying not to think about the interrogation room. There was so much more to them than simple light. That moment Aaru's pain became unbearable and everything went black would haunt me forever. "I heard a rumor that some people can hear noorestones. Do you know anything about that?"

She shook her head. "Noorestones are part of the world. Occasionally, miners claim they can hear a very low, deep humming, but that seems like a rather fanciful notion. Still, often the places they point out do have large pockets. There are so many in Bopha, though, it could be luck." Her expression darkened, as though she'd just realized something.

"Go on," I urged.

"Well, there was a time we thought Harta's gift might extend to noorestones, so I hired twenty or so Hartans to work in one of my mines for a decan. My overseers there didn't notice a change right away, but we didn't expect to. Noorestones are not wheat, after all. But only a month ago, I was told that mine is depleted. No new noorestone deposits have been found in almost a year."

And she blamed Hartans. She didn't have to say it. The look was in her eye, and her head tilted like a cue for me to agree.

"I can't tell you how much those Hartans have cost me," she added. "I can't wait until they're gone."

Say something, my conscience urged. *Speak up*.

But Elbena caught my eye and lifted a brow, and her message was clear: she'd punish me for any perceived slight to Sothy.

Strength through silence. Even from far away, Aaru was

teaching me that. When to listen, when to speak, and how to measure: those were the lessons of Idris.

I turned away from both of them and watched the musicians play.

DINNER WAS UNBEARABLE.

Oh, the food was delicious. Exquisite. Over seven courses, I ate my fill and then some. But I spent the entire meal thinking about how many prisoners this could feed, and how many would think the plates were works of art, rather than food. Had Aaru ever eaten honeyed duck or drunk from a bottle of century-old wine? It seemed unlikely.

The meal took too long. And went too fast.

The musicians finished a minuet and Dara took the stage. She stood in focused noorestone light, her shadow jutting long and dark to one side. When she spoke, it was with a lifted chin and prideful smile. "Strong shadows, friends."

A low murmur of "Strong shadows" came from the diners.

"With the Hallowed Restoration behind us and the new year ahead, it's time for the Twilight Senate to reconvene to discuss ideas, problems, solutions, and the state of our home. I'm so glad everyone here could join us as we move forward. We're all so busy all the time. I hope the rest of you treasure tonight as much as I do." Dara held a beat while she waited for the polite applause to finish, and then went on to talk about the surviving Bophan spirit, the legacy today's leaders would leave, and the importance of cooperation.

I picked at the tiny chocolate cake (topped with three gold lala flowers carved out of pressed sugar) and listened to the speech, but those things held only half my attention. From the corner of one eye, I watched Hristo.

When the tables had been brought in and all the senators, diplomats, and important figures sat to eat, Hristo and the other guards had moved to keep a better watch on their charges. Which meant I'd been able to sneak glances at my friend throughout the meal, and now that everyone was focused on Dara, I could look a little more.

He appeared healthy. Strong, like always. He scratched his chin through the mask, careful not to move it. Elbena would probably recognize him, assuming she ever recognized servants outside her own house.

When our eyes met and he smiled, I wanted to stay like that forever. Hristo meant safety. Not just when I was seven and that man had tried to kidnap me, but more times than I knew about. Hristo was always protecting me. And, though we'd never hugged much growing up (he thought it was unprofessional and Mother thought it was inappropriate), right now, I wanted to run to him and wrap my arms around him. I wanted *his* arms around *me*, because he was the only person who could make me feel safe when I was surrounded by enemies.

And what did he think of this? Had he overheard my

conversation with Sothy earlier? Did he know what Elbena and Dara expected me to say? How did he feel about being Hartan on an island that hated him solely because he'd been born to the Daughter?

I couldn't imagine.

But he was looking at me with all the warmth in the world, and I knew it wouldn't be long before we were together again.

He made a slow, purposeful glance to his left.

I followed his gaze and my heart leaped into my throat.

Ilina.

My wingsister, my very best friend in the entire world, was clothed as one of the servers, collecting empty dessert plates from a neighboring table. Her hair was loose, and she kept her eyes downcast like the rest of the servants. But she must have felt my eyes on her, because she looked over and flashed a quick, secret grin.

The presence of the two people I loved most warmed me through to my bones. I felt like I could float, and maybe I would have, except at that moment, Dara's tone changed and I caught my name.

"Now, Mira Minkoba—the Hopebearer of the famous Mira Treaty—is here to speak with us." Dara motioned toward me. "My dear, if you please."

My mood plummeted and my heart pounded, but I rose to my feet and smoothed my gown. This, too, was a familiar feeling: the dread of so many eyes on me, all waiting to see if I would mess up; the surge of adrenaline through my veins, like my body urging me to run or fight; and the way my vision tunneled on the stage ahead, because my only option was to get through this.

It would be easier if I had my calming pills. Usually I did, just in case, but Elbena didn't know about them. Mother had made me keep that a tightly guarded secret.

A polite applause followed me as I took ten steps, went onto the stage, and turned to face all the most important people on Bopha. Senators, diplomats, generals, business-people. Sixty of them. One of me.

The musicians were motionless at my back. The audience waiting in front.

A hundred noorestones. Nine tables. Sixty people sitting. Fifty-five security members. Eight servers vanishing into the shadows.

Hristo watched me from his place by the wall. Ilina, too, as she edged toward him.

The words of Elbena's speech gathered on my tongue, ready. All I had to do was open my mouth and spill out the words she'd tried to fill me up with. Then I could go home. See my family again. Be with my friends and my dragon.

Tirta had told me to do everything they asked. Altan had said not to cause trouble or he'd hurt Aaru more.

If I just said what Elbena wanted, I'd be protecting Aaru. Hristo and Ilina, too, because Elbena would be *furious* if she discovered they were here.

I wished I'd had an opportunity to talk with them before. I wished I knew what they had planned.

But if I recited the speech like a good mouthpiece, then I wasn't fixing anything.

Unless I said the right thing.

But then I'd get in trouble.

I'd hate myself forever if I told these people what they wanted to hear, not what they needed to hear.

I'd made a mistake on the docks, costing Lex her freedom.

People were staring, waiting for me to say something. I'd been wearing a pleasantly neutral expression—after years of training, my face slipped into that by default—but I'd been standing here slightly too long without speaking.

I cleared my throat. "Thank you for inviting me here tonight."

Thank you for needing me so much that the Luminary Council was forced to pull me out of the Pit. Or maybe they only needed me because Chenda had refused them.

"One of the more interesting parts of having a treaty named after me is the expectations that arise. I often feel I should be an expert on all matters even tangentially related to the Mira Treaty because we share a name, but I've come to realize that isn't realistic. Not only is it impossible for one person to be an expert in all the things the Mira Treaty covers—dragons and conservationism, independence and equality, unity among the Fallen Isles, and more—it's far too much weight for a young girl to carry.

"Nevertheless, it was expected of me, and I've done my best to educate myself not only on the treaty itself, but on the ways our societies have upheld its decrees. And as someone raised in the light of the Lovers, I find myself considering all aspects through filters of love and compassion."

A few people offered patient smiles; many had heard Damina-based speeches from me before. But at my table, Bilyana frowned, and Elbena leaned forward, urging me to begin.

Give me peace. Give me grace. Give me enough love in my heart, I prayed. *Cela, cela.*

I glanced across the room, meeting enough people's eyes that it wasn't obvious when I found Ilina's and held. I hoped she could see my apology behind the mask of Public Mira. "Seventeen years ago," I started, "the Mira Treaty took a stance against discrimination, against occupation, and against the pillaging of our islands. The treaty states that to truly honor the Fallen Gods, all islands must be equal and independent. Anything less is immoral. Unethical.

"This truth is indisputable."

Elbena smiled and leaned back in her seat, triumphant. These were the words she'd meant for me to speak.

"Since then," I went on, "many strides have been taken toward making reparations, ensuring the success of Harta and her First Matriarch, and offering the freedom of choice for those who want to work and reside all across the Fallen Isles.

"But now we've reached another pivotal moment in

our history. We can be silent . . . or we can speak up."

Elbena's grin fell.

I spoke quickly, because this was my one chance to say something useful. If I wasted it, I'd never forgive myself. "Forcing Hartans to leave is *not* an act of love or equality." *Please, Darina. Please, Damyan.* "Love does no harm."

The room went absolutely quiet.

CHAPTER TWENTY-FIVE

THIS WASN'T TRUE SILENCE. I'D EXPERIENCED THAT before, so I knew the difference better than most. But in spite of the thumps of glasses returning to tables, the rattle of someone's breathing, and the hiss of cloth, the whole room was very quiet.

A silk-clad woman risked a giggle, as though I'd made a joke.

A man glared at her.

Hristo's eyes were wide, and I was sure that his mouth dropped open behind his mask.

Ilina pressed her palms to her chest and stifled a sob.

Elbena and Dara were both on their feet, striding toward me. I had to hurry. Say what I meant to say before I never saw the sky again.

"I hear complaints about losing money after investing in Hartans, but love is not consumed with its own gain. I hear attempts to minimize the pain of constant occupation, but love acknowledges the hurt and makes efforts to heal. I hear how everything is different now that the treaty has granted Harta independence, but love does not boast—it offers more. These are not only Daminan tenets, but commands from all our gods." I dragged a breath, but before I could say more, Elbena grabbed my arm hard enough to bruise.

"That's enough," she hissed as she dragged me off the stage. "I'll hear no more of this."

I went with her, but I kept my head high and my shoulders back. There was plenty more to say, but I would not leave this place raving like a madwoman. My words would not be dismissed so easily.

Even so, Dara took my place on the stage, her palms up in supplication. "Forgive her, friends." A note of fear edged her voice, buried under the practiced calm of someone used to speaking to the confused and frightened. "Mira hasn't been feeling well recently. She's been ill. And we're going to ensure she is taken care of."

"Poor girl," someone muttered.

That was it. Before I realized, Elbena had me at the top of the stairs above the great lobby. My back pressed against the banister and she left no room for me to move. All I could feel was the long drop waiting behind me, and the furious councilwoman looming before me.

Hristo hovered three paces away, unsure what he should do.

Nothing, I hoped. Nothing right now. He was still safe and I wanted him to stay that way.

Elbena's face was dark with rage, and her jaw set as though she wanted to bite.

"That was a mistake." She kept her voice low. From the ballroom, I could still hear Dara making excuses and promises, the rumble of gossip and rumors, and the musicians playing a light tune—as if that could repair the damage I'd done. "Most of the council was against pulling you out of the Pit for this, but I fought for you. I believed you wanted another chance, and I believed you would do anything for our forgiveness."

I pressed my lips tight together, trapping any words inside.

Hristo stared helplessly at me, hopelessly. If he broke his cover now, everything would be far worse.

"Do you even understand the severity of the mistake you made?"

Strength through silence. I met her eyes and gave her my most defiant stare.

"*Why* would you throw away the opportunity to go home?"

"I didn't throw away an opportunity," I said. "I took one. It was my chance to tell people what was right and I don't regret it."

Elbena seethed, but there was nothing she could do.

Not here, when someone might come out and see. And not later, because I was still Mira Minkoba. I was still the Hopebearer and the Dragonhearted and anything else they wanted to call me.

After a moment's hesitation, she seized my arm again and hauled me down the stairs. We crossed the lobby in twenty long steps, thundered through the wide double doors, and waited in angry silence while Hristo fetched the carriage.

The ride back was an ever-tightening knot of anxiety. Elbena didn't speak, just glared and made sure the curtains were closed so I couldn't see outside. Hristo sat next to me, but there was nothing he could do, no way he could offer support. I could feel it, though, in the way he kept looking at me, and the way his hands became fists where they rested on his knees.

In the inn, she dragged me to my room and shoved me inside.

"Give me your dagger," she said, turning to Hristo.

He froze, gaze darting from Elbena to me. Why did she want a weapon?

She wouldn't hurt me. Of that I was confident. And if Hristo refused, she would discover his identity and he would be in more trouble than I could imagine. His safety was at stake.

Still, my heart pounded as I gave the slightest nod. Hristo frowned, but unsheathed the dagger and handed it hilt-first to Elbena.

"Wait there," she ordered. Her voice was oddly calm as she came into my room and shut the door. The dagger hung from her hand, the flat thumping against her thigh. "It's only fair to tell you again how disappointed I am. I thought better of you."

"And I'm disappointed in the Luminary Council. I'd hoped for action when I approached you about the vanishing dragons, not a speedy relocation to the Pit." Suddenly, I couldn't stop the flow of words. "I'd hoped everyone meant what they said about equality throughout the islands, not this betrayal of the very *core* of the Mira Treaty."

Elbena slapped me so hard that even she looked surprised. The *smack* echoed in my head just one heartbeat before the pain flashed bright across my vision—and then my sight went dark.

Dizzy, I staggered back one step and grabbed for the footboard of my bed. My fingers slid over the smooth wood, but I glared and pulled myself upright. "You're afraid of me," I said. "You and the rest of the Luminary Council. You made me into a powerful voice, thinking I would always be *your* voice, but you were wrong. I am not a tool to be used at your convenience. I will not be wielded against the very foundations of the treaty named after me.

"I've spent my entire life hearing about the importance of the Mira Treaty. Don't be surprised that *I believe in it.* And don't be shocked that I will use my voice—the voice you gave me—to speak out about the gross injustices done by the very people who signed the treaty against such actions."

She exhaled. One long breath. "So instead of just saying a few simple words in order to go home, you'd rather defend a bunch of Daughter-children to a room of people who will never change their minds about the deportation decree?"

"Any day."

"I don't like this person you're becoming, Mira. I don't like this recklessness I see in you now. It won't benefit either of us." Her face was deadly calm as her fingers turned pale around Hristo's dagger.

I glanced down at the dagger just as it moved up.

Before I could think.

Before I could react.

Before I could realize.

Elbena cut me.

At first, it stung like needles, but as the blade dragged down my cheek, the sting bloomed into an inferno of anguish. Liquid fire fell from parted skin. Tears streamed from my eyes and burned in the opening wound. Blinding pain lit up the left side of my face.

I screamed and reeled backward, but the damage was done. She was too quick and I was too slow.

I'd believed she wouldn't hurt me.

How wrong I'd been.

I pressed my hand against the gaping cut, as though I could stop the flow of blood, but my touch was like hot coals. I convulsed under conflicting instincts: apply pressure, but *don't touch*. Also: *run away*. But where would I run?

The bedroom door flew open and Hristo rushed in, but Elbena held up a hand. "Stop."

He stopped.

I dropped to my knees, cupping my face, trying not to touch it. My hand trembled, sticky with my own blood. I wanted to scream. I wanted to be silent. My left eye squeezed shut and my mouth pulled painfully. A low, agonized groan filled the room; it was coming from me.

Elbena examined the red-smeared dagger. "I've never cut anyone before. I didn't think it would be so easy."

I wanted to say something snappy, but tendrils of fire spread around my whole head. My thoughts burned into ash.

"I'll send a doctor." Elbena handed Hristo back his blade and started for the door. She paused in the hall and turned back. "You'll be heading back to the Pit the day after tomorrow, once the *Chance Encounter* has finished securing cargo. So relax while you can, because the report I send to your keeper there will not be favorable."

Then she was gone, the door closed behind her.

My hands were like claws over my face, as though I could peel away the pain. It didn't help. Blackness swarmed up from the depths of my mind, and all the noorestones seemed to dim.

I collapsed the rest of the way to the floor.

Hristo rushed to me, but he was too late. My head cracked against the hardwood, and I knew only darkness.

CHAPTER TWENTY-SIX

A DOCTOR STITCHED MY FACE AND DRUGGED ME until everything was numb.

My face.

My thoughts.

My fingers.

Even my numbers.

I faded in and out of existence for a while. Every time I emerged and the pain was unbearable, someone pressed a cup to my lips and made me drink. Never before had I realized how much my cheeks were involved in swallowing, but the bitter liquid dropped the hazy sky of numbness over me again.

Finally, a voice broke through. "We have to leave immediately."

My heart stopped. Ilina.

"She's not well enough." That was Hristo.

"It's her face, not her legs. She can walk." Ilina paced through the room. "When the sedatives wear off, she'll wake up."

My mouth felt weirdly detached and slow, but I said, "I am awake."

"Mira!" Ilina rushed to my side.

I peeled my eyes open to find the room lit only by noorestones. The curtains, pulled closed, showed no light around the edges, and the inn had the stillness of everyone sleeping. Bandages had been packed against my cheek, and rubbed against the gash when I spoke. Everything hurt, but I needed to be here with my friends. Present. Awake. "How long have I been out?"

"One day." Ilina sat on the bed next to me and took my hand.

"I'm glad you're here." I tried to squeeze her hand, but I couldn't tell if my fingers were actually moving. Everything felt so fuzzy from the medicine. "What happened?"

"You left the dining hall in an uproar," Ilina said. "Everyone started talking after you left. Dara kept trying to explain that you were ill, but at least a couple of people wondered if you were right."

That wasn't what I'd meant, but I supposed it was good to hear that *someone* had listened. "Where are LaLa and Crystal? What happened to them?" That hadn't been my intended question, either. I kept losing track of my thoughts. But suddenly I desperately needed to know about my dragon.

Ilina spoke gently. *Too* gently. "Let's talk about it tomorrow when you feel better."

"I want to know now."

"Tell her," Hristo said. "No point in sparing her feelings when wondering is going to make her feel worse."

"Were they taken too?" I rasped. "Like the others? Tower and Astrid and Lex . . ." I needed to tell them about Lex, but Hristo already knew. He'd already seen— "Did they take my dragon?"

Ilina shook her head. "No. I mean, I don't think so. The morning we came to visit you, before you were sent to Khulan, Crystal and LaLa just flew away."

"They didn't come when we whistled," Hristo said. "Or called their names, or promised food. They *left*."

"Have they come back?" My voice was weak. Small.

"Mira . . ."

I wanted to sink into the bed and die. "LaLa thinks I abandoned her."

"No, I'm sure that's not it." But Ilina didn't say what else it might have been, and misery dug its claws deep into me. My friends knew why I'd vanished, but I couldn't explain the situation to a dragon. What kind of person befriended a baby dragon, spent nine years training her and growing close, and then did something stupid that resulted in prison? Leaving that baby dragon alone.

Of course LaLa and Crystal had flown away. They

knew all they had was each other.

"Don't look so sad," Ilina said. "We have a plan."

"For getting LaLa and Crystal back?"

Ilina made a face somewhere between a smirk and a grimace. "No. Your escape, obviously."

"Oh. Right." The medicine was making me slow.

"Escape can wait a few more minutes." Hristo stood at the foot of the bed, his hands behind his back and his head bowed. Though he wore the Luminary Guard uniform, the mask was gone and the jacket was unbuttoned. Both daggers were at his hips, even the one that had cut me. I wondered if it felt poisonous to him now. Traitorous.

But Hristo didn't think like that. He was sensible. Protective. I'd have said paranoid before, but after learning about Hurrok trying to kill me last year, I knew better. He was constantly on guard so that I didn't have to be.

"Mira," he said, "before anything else, I have to tell you that I'm sorry. I came to protect you and I failed."

"Hristo." I pushed myself up until I was sitting. Ilina helped support me where my arms trembled. The numbing medicine still rushed through me, making my movements uncertain. "This isn't your fault. This is Elbena's doing."

"It was my job to stop her," he insisted.

When I reached for him, he rounded the foot of the bed and took my hand. Ilina took my other, and there I was, connected to the two people I loved best. Their strength filled me, and for five long heartbeats, I just closed my eyes and breathed in this moment.

"You are both the most loyal, bravest people I know." I didn't deserve friends like them. "How did you get here?"

"It was your parents, actually," Hristo said.

"Did they send you?"

He shook his head. "They don't know we're here."

"Your parents worked day and night for your release," Ilina said. "When they heard about the Bophan Senate dinner, they suggested taking you out of the Pit for it. They said you'd learned your lesson about questioning the Luminary Council and you'd do whatever you were ordered."

My heart sank. When Mother heard about my performance last night, she would be furious. Even in prison, I was a disappointment to her.

"The Luminary Council fought about it for hours," Ilina said. "Your parents told my parents, who told me. I think they were just relieved that I was speaking to them, because they told me more than I should have known otherwise—about ship schedules, Luminary Guard selection, and when you would be here."

"No one let us come," Hristo said. "But we'd promised we'd help you."

"I was serious when I said I'd drain the seas if I must." Ilina squeezed my hand. "So when the council decided to give you a chance, we formed a plan to get you out, just in case they decided to try sending you back to the Pit."

Or in case I ruined my chances.

"It wasn't easy," Hristo said. "I stole a Luminary

Guard uniform, but I had to be careful about the times I was with you. I didn't want to insist I be near you and risk getting caught."

I nodded, but the movement made my head swim. "Even I didn't realize you were there until the other night."

Hristo smiled. "I wanted you to know someone was there for you, but I also didn't want you to know, because I was worried Elbena might figure out that I was your protector." Again, his eyes flicked to my cheek. His smile disappeared.

"You still are," I whispered, my fingers twisted tight with his. "No matter what, I know that you are always protecting me." I wouldn't tell him that I'd been imprisoned with someone who'd tried to murder me—not yet, anyway—but he needed to know I still trusted him. I trusted him more than ever.

His response was low and rumbling. "Thank you."

I turned to Ilina. "And you? How did you come to be a server at such an important state dinner on Bopha?"

She gave a weak laugh. "I'll tell you when we're out of here, but my story involves forgery, stowing away on a ship, and bribery."

They brushed all that effort aside, as though it had been nothing to learn where I'd be and come for a big rescue, but I knew it hadn't been easy.

Never had I anticipated them taking such actions, and my eyes stung with tears as I imagined the challenges they'd endured—for me. I didn't deserve such friends.

"As for the rest of our plan"—Ilina leaned forward—"the *Chance Encounter* leaves on the morning tide. Elbena won't be on the ship, and we know the captain. The crew will help us if we board tonight. No one will search it for you in the morning, and once they've made their stops, we can get off anywhere. Or we don't have to get on the *Chance Encounter* at all, if you don't want. We can leave the Shadowed City and go anywhere on Bopha. It will be more dangerous, though."

"Thank you." My voice broke, caught somewhere between love and fear. "You've done so much."

Ilina drew back, already sensing what I was about to do. "But?"

I dreaded saying the words. Their reactions. But if I didn't speak now, I might go along with their plan and feel terrible about myself for the rest of my days. "I have to return to the Pit."

"*No.*" Ilina squeezed my hand. "We won't let you. You're never going back there."

I was already shaking my head—carefully, because I didn't want them to think I was too weak for this. "I must. My allies—"

"Forget about them." Ilina surged to her feet. "Forget all about them. Everything that happened there."

"I can't. I left people there, and they don't deserve to be in the Pit any more than I did." Tears stung my eyes. "Altan hurts them to get to me. He's a Drakon Warrior."

Ilina's eyes grew wide. "*Really?* They still exist?"

"Not legally, I think." I bit my lip. "He wanted to know about the shipping order."

My friends exchanged uneasy glances. "What did you tell him?" Ilina asked.

"Where he could find the dragons, before they're shipped to the Algotti Empire for good. I thought better the dragons remain with the Fallen Isles than with our enemies."

"And did he send people to take back the dragons?" A glow of hope lit her face.

"I don't know." I swallowed hard. "He wasn't exactly forthcoming with information. But our goals aligned there. He wants the Heart's dragons, but I don't know whether he succeeded. If he did, his people should have reached them already." Oh, Damina. What if LaLa *had* been taken? And Altan "rescued" her?

I'd never be able to live with myself.

"If the dragons are rescued," Hristo said, "the Luminary Council will know the information came from you. It wouldn't be hard to figure out who told the Drakon Warriors where to find the dragons."

I slumped. I hadn't thought of that.

"The line of information points straight to you again. If you have to go back to the Pit and the council finds out you told Altan, you will never get out." Ilina moved to cover noorestones to keep anyone from investigating the light this late. "The other prisoners don't deserve you going back just for them."

Ilina was my wingsister, but I didn't know how to explain Aaru.

"What about Chenda M'rizz? The Lady of Eternal Dawn." I glanced between Hristo and Ilina. "She's politically useful to have on our side. Plus, her crime was the same as mine: she stood up against immoral actions and was betrayed by the people entrusted to protect her island."

"The deportation decree?" Ilina glanced at Hristo, her manner softening.

"She's the reason I knew about it ahead of time."

Hristo's voice was a soft rumble. "Is that why you didn't recite Elbena's speech?"

"I couldn't permit more suffering."

"You could have used the chance to tell everyone you'd been suffering too," Ilina said.

"I didn't even think about that." It was true. It hadn't occurred to me to announce my captivity. My fingertips grazed across the bandage on my cheek. "Imagine what Elbena would have done if I'd told everyone about *that*."

"They wouldn't have cared," Ilina said. "They accused Chenda of feeding information to a Hartan lover."

They were quiet a moment.

"Four extra people is a lot," Hristo said. "We'll have to obtain papers and supplies for them as well."

The burden I'd placed on them sat heavy on my chest. My decision wasn't about me alone. It wasn't just *my* time in the Pit, the danger *I* was in. Every extra person I decided to save was an extra weight on Ilina and Hristo.

"Mira, if you insist on doing this, how would it even be possible? Maybe Hristo can get in, but warriors don't wear masks down there, do they?"

"I—"

Just then, loud thudding sounded on the bedroom door. It was locked, but then I heard the jangle of keys.

"Mira!" Elbena's voice carried through the quiet inn.

Ilina glanced at Hristo, who drew his daggers.

"Go," I hissed. "Out the window."

But it was too late.

Elbena and her Luminary Guard burst into the room.

We scrambled for the window, but it was locked.

Three metal darts zinged through the room, catching noorestone light.

The first landed in Ilina's neck. Then Hristo's. Then mine.

One, two, three.

We dropped.

CHAPTER TWENTY-SEVEN

OUR PLAN HAD LASTED FIVE MINUTES. THAT WAS possibly a new low.

I awakened to find myself on a ship. The *Chance Encounter*, if I had to guess. The sway of the ship on water was unmistakable. Scents of the sea and sweat filled the small cabin, and all around I sensed the groaning of rigging, the thumps of footfalls, and crewmen singing on the decks above.

Four Luminary Guards stood around the perimeter. All had two daggers at their hips. I'd been shoved in the outer corner, among crates and boxes. One leg stung with blood rushing back into my toes. My face ached worse than before; it felt like the stitches had been ripped out.

Elbena stood in the midst of the guards, frowning. "I

can't say I'm surprised," she said. "Given your performance at dinner, this latest betrayal is far too easy to believe. But I am disappointed. I didn't think you'd recruit others to your cause and risk their punishment, too."

Chills swept through me. My wrists were bound and my mouth gagged, but otherwise I had freedom of movement. I could look around.

Hristo was slumped onto his knees to my right, but his head was cocked, listening. Ilina was on my left, unconscious on the floor. She groaned; she'd wake soon.

Guilt wormed through me. Somewhere in the back of my foolish mind, I'd thought maybe they had a chance of escape. I'd thought if I did the right thing, everything would be fine.

Instead, I'd taken them down with me. What kind of friend was I?

A dangerous friend, Gerel would say.

"It's a shame what has to happen now," Elbena said. "But I've discussed it with Councilor Bilyana and our Bophan friends. We have authority over disciplinary actions for your little adventure. I hope you know this gives me no pleasure."

She motioned at one of the guards, who removed my gag. Why had they used it in the first place if they were just going to take it away?

For effect, probably. Elbena liked effect.

And—apparently—shoving rags of dubious cleanliness into other people's mouths.

I resisted the urge to spit the taste of dirt. That would not make me appear strong and capable, and I wasn't sure I could do it, anyway, what with the gaping hole she'd left in my face. Instead, I pulled myself straight. "Let these two go. They have nothing to do with this." Out loud, the words didn't sound nearly as tough as they had in my head. But my throat was dry. My mouth was dry.

My cheek burned with the gash sliced through. And in the back of my head, all I could hear was Mother's voice: *What if it scars? What then? She's ruined. Useless. Hideous.*

I wanted to reach for my friends. Ilina would tell me we could hide it, and though I'd doubt hiding something that felt bigger than my entire head was possible, I'd pretend to believe her. Hristo would tell me it didn't matter because I was still Mira Minkoba, though he would always look at it and see his failure.

I was the worst friend in the world for worrying about my appearance at a time like this. Because the truth was worse. We were all on the *Chance Encounter.* The four Luminary Guards loomed over us. And Elbena had a sinister smile that quirked up one corner of her mouth.

"Your friends were here to rescue you, weren't they?" She phrased it as a question, but it wasn't one. "I'm almost sorry your plan failed so quickly. It might have been entertaining to watch you run."

I could imagine the scenario she envisioned: us fleeing the Shadowed City, her sending the Luminary Guards and local police after us, keeping us on the move until we were too exhausted to continue. I'd fall first, no doubt. Hristo and Ilina wouldn't leave me behind, though. No, they'd carry me if necessary.

It would always be my fault that they were caught.

"Let them go and I won't run. I won't protest." I hated begging, but if I didn't do *something*, my friends would surely die.

She prowled closer to me and knelt. Her face twisted into a mask of sincerity and compassion. "Mira. This is not a negotiation. We won't be making a deal. There's no hope for you—or your friends. By all the gods, you're so pathetic that I'm almost sorry to tell you the bad news."

Dread clutched at my chest, and my fingers twitched—lightning strikes signaling the coming storm of panic. I knew what the news would be. I'd known since the moment I'd realized we were on the ship.

"I'm having you all separated, of course." Elbena laced her fingers together and looked from Ilina to Hristo to me. "My dear. You're going back to the Pit as soon as the tide comes in."

"I know." My throat squeezed, pinching the words.

"And so are your friends."

PART FOUR

ARTICLES OF LIGHT

CHAPTER TWENTY-EIGHT

"I SAVED YOUR CELL FOR YOU," ALTAN SAID.

By the time I was paraded through the Heart of the Great Warrior, the Pit, and the first-level cellblock, I'd figured out that much.

We walked by Kason, who hated everyone. Varissa, who thought she was my mother. Kumas, who liked to sing. And Hurrok, who'd tried to kill me.

"What happened to your face?" My would-be murderer stared as I moved past. "You used to be so pretty." When he grinned, it was with jagged, broken teeth. I couldn't tell if he knew my identity.

If Aaru had told everyone my whole name.

If the alliances I'd made here were now over.

My heart slammed against my ribs, harder with every

step. It seemed impossible for this shameful walk to hurt more than the last, but it did. My whole body ached with humiliation and grief.

When I reached Aaru's cell, I caught only a glimpse of my silent neighbor. He sat on his bed, knees up to his chest, his back turned toward the door. Through his ragged shirt, I could see the ridges of his spine and ribs.

At my passing, he didn't look up. He didn't move as though he'd heard me or sensed my presence. He didn't want to see me after what I'd done.

I touched the healing gash on my cheek, fresh shame pouring in. Maybe I didn't want him to see me, either.

Altan shoved me into my cell and shut the door. The screech of metal on runners was achingly familiar. "See you in the morning, Fancy." His gaze darted to my cut, all scabbed over and angry. "Well. Maybe not so fancy anymore. I'll have to think of something else to call you."

A fractured whine caught in my throat. Even Altan thought I was hideous.

He laughed, reached through the bars, and patted my injured cheek. And no matter how I wanted to turn my head or back away or just *move*, I couldn't. He rooted me. Paralyzed me. And no matter how I told my legs to swing, or my feet to shuffle, I remained in one spot while his palm was near my skin.

My broken, scabbing skin.

I counted my own shallow breaths while I waited for

this to stop. Six, seven, eight . . .

"How the high Hopebearer has fallen."

Across the hall, Gerel's head jerked up and her eyes went wide with shock. When our gazes met and she read the truth on my face, her surprise shifted to anger.

"That's right." Altan lifted his voice. "The Hopebearer is just a normal piece of slime like the rest of you. Filth."

"I knew it!" From the end of the hall, Hurrok shrieked with joy. "I knew it was her!"

Altan had been so careful to keep my identity secret the first time. And now . . . Now he didn't care. Now he knew the Luminary Council wouldn't come back for me.

Now I was nothing.

Altan laughed as he walked away, keys jangling in his fingers. But at the cells next to mine, he slowed his steps just a fraction and glanced in. "You two, as well? We're going to have so much fun together."

Then he was gone.

His spell released.

I staggered backward and lifted my fingers to my cheek, like I might be able to wipe away the contamination of his hands. But I couldn't even touch my own skin; I didn't want to feel the rough line of Elbena's retribution.

A sob of misery choked out of me, but I wouldn't cry. Not now. Not when I needed my strength the most.

So I just whispered, "I'm back," and let my hands fall to my sides. My voice sounded strange, pulled sideways because of the cut; I couldn't open my mouth very wide without feeling like I might tear it open. "I'm back," I said again.

Back on Khulan. Back in the Pit. Back in my cell.

Back in my own filthy misery and memories that fizzled to the surface with every passing minute.

My cell was the same as before. Small. Dim. Disgusting. Three walls. One grated door. One bed that doubled as a bench, and one sewage hole. It was almost enough to make me wish the voyage to Khulan had been longer, but we'd made it back in eight days—same time as it took to get to Bopha.

All totaled, I'd been away from the Pit for eighteen days. And now Hristo was here, in the cell next to mine. Ilina was next to him.

I could tell who was where by the muffled grunts—Hristo was testing the bars of his door, but the metal gave only a weak rattle in response. After five more clatters, he kicked the grille. Heavy footsteps suggested he backed away, but I could imagine him glaring at the door, biding his time before he tried again.

I wished Ilina were the one closer to me. Maybe, if we tried hard enough, we could reach between the bars and touch fingertips.

Or maybe that would be dumb, since it was my fault we were all here to begin with. I should have let them take me out of the Shadowed City when they were ready.

But no. I'd protested. And now we were all three in the

Pit, and my face had been sliced open, ensuring Elbena and the Luminary Council would never have need of me again.

I wasn't exactly the smartest person in this cellblock, but I probably wasn't the stupidest, either. I knew what this meant.

We were never.

Ever.

Getting out.

Altan would see to that.

"Yes, yes," muttered Gerel. "You're back. *Hopebearer.*" She was sitting cross-legged in her cell, her glare like steel. "I knew you were dangerous."

My gaze dropped to the floor.

"I see you brought friends."

"Not on purpose." My voice shook.

"I should hope not, but I suppose I don't really know you, do I, Mira Minkoba?" She glanced toward Aaru's cell, and a vision of his back filled my mind. Turned away. Not looking at me.

Hating me, probably.

"I thought it was better if no one knew." I bundled my hands inside my dress. It wasn't the gold-and-white gown I'd worn to the ill-fated state dinner, but a simpler thing of pale blue cotton with nacre buttons down the front. The other was probably sitting in a trash heap now, covered in my blood.

"Better for you," Gerel said. "The rest of us? Well, what

did it matter if we got hurt because of our association with you?"

"I didn't want anyone to get hurt."

"Great job." Again, she glanced at Aaru's cell. "You know, he hasn't spoken since they dragged him out of here with you. He hasn't spoken one word."

The memory of Aaru's scream flooded me. Then the darkness, the silence, and the way he'd been unable to make sound come out of his mouth. I remembered him shaping my name on his lips—and nothing happening. His voice had been shredded into a useless memory, but he should have regained it by now.

Right?

"He hasn't even gone to work like you planned," Gerel went on. "He couldn't stand up for more than a decan because of the wounds on his feet."

My stomach dropped.

"This is your fault. Altan and the others might have been the ones to do the actual harm, but it never would have happened without you. They knew you liked him, so they tortured him to hurt you. It could have just as easily been me, you know? It probably should have been. I could have handled it better. But then, they knew that, too." With those venomous words still stinging through the air, Gerel climbed to her feet and turned her back on me.

A moment later, Ilina said, "You were right, Mira. These people were absolutely worth trying to rescue."

I hugged myself as a pale whine forced its way up my throat.

Diagonally from me, Chenda was standing at her door, leaning around to get a look at Ilina, Hristo, and finally me. Her cheeks were sunken and her eyes hidden in dark circles. Even the copper tattoos seemed dulled.

Once, she'd been radiant. Now, she was muted. A candle burned down and drowning in its own wax.

"I went to Bopha," I told her. "I saw Dara and the Shadow Spires and the High Tower."

"Why?" Chenda's voice was raw, and just as hollow as the rest of her. In spite of her previous rank, she'd been given no special treatment here. "Why did they want you?"

"They wanted me to say what you would not."

She blinked slowly, like even that much movement was a challenge. "Did you?"

"No." I held her gaze. "I would not."

"Mira refused." Pride filled Ilina's tone, and defensiveness. "Right in front of everyone at the dinner, she told them love does no harm. And then, when we tried to sneak her out of the inn where they were keeping her, she refused to come with us. Instead, she thought she had to rescue all of you too. But I can't imagine why. No one here seems to appreciate her."

"Tirta is nice," I offered. "But she's in a different cell-block."

"And that helps us not at all." Ilina's pacing sounded on

the floor—eight, nine, ten—and then she kicked the metal lid of her sewage hole, making it scrape the stone. "This place is disgusting."

Chenda turned back to me and nodded slowly, deeply. "Thank you, Mira."

"It didn't make a difference. They only listen when I say what they want to hear."

"That, too, I understand." Her mouth tugged up in one corner, not quite a real smile, but an attempt, perhaps. "That is the way of the world for us, isn't it? Valued, but in the way a painting is valued. Moved around. Shown to guests. Talked about and talked about, until one day a smudge is discovered. Then we are discarded."

"We are not paintings, Chenda. And from now on, I won't be treated like one."

This time, she did offer a smile. A real one. "Neither will I." But the way she said it was more like acceptance.

Because we were ruined, both of us. My cheek slashed open. Her whole body withered with some sort of illness.

And now that I looked at my neighbors, really looked, I could see that Gerel was skinnier than before. Aaru's spine, too, had stuck out in ridges of bones, protruding through his shirt. They'd all lost weight, because even the meager amount of food I'd sneaked for them had made a difference.

I faced the wall I shared with Aaru and waited seven thumping heartbeats, and then I tapped my palms on the sides of my thighs: short long, short long, short long short, short short long. **::Aaru?::**

The quiet code came slowly, awkwardly, since I hadn't practiced much while I was gone, but if there was one thing I could do, it was remember numbers.

No response. Maybe he hadn't just stopped talking out loud, but talking in quiet code, too.

My heart sank as I dropped to the floor and crawled under the bed. There was the hole in the wall. Our secret place. "Aaru?" My voice was soft.

Still nothing.

He didn't crawl under with me. He didn't reach through and take my hand. He didn't acknowledge my presence.

"Can you blame him?" Gerel asked, almost thoughtfully. "After he was punished for being your friend?"

"No," I said, even though Aaru had forgiven me for what Altan had done. It was my name that was the problem. My omission. "I don't blame him at all."

I SPENT THE night thinking.

Mother would have laughed, because I was never much of a thinker, she said, but that was what I did. I slept under my bed, caught in a weird sensation that I'd never actually left. Like the trip to Bopha had been nothing but an especially vivid dream. Still, I had the mark where Elbena had cut me. That was proof enough.

And all my thoughts came down to one fact: if I didn't do something *now*, I'd never leave.

We'd never leave, because I'd come back for Gerel,

Aaru, Tirta, and Chenda, hadn't I? And I'd inadvertently brought Hristo and Ilina with me.

Maybe . . . If I could get all my friends moved into the second level, with more food and better accommodations, they would be strong enough to escape with me. I just had to figure out how to make Altan agree to it.

I must have fallen asleep, at least briefly, because the noorestones were lit when I opened my eyes.

And I was alone under the bed. Aaru must have learned to sleep on his bed in my absence. I tried to ignore the sinking in my heart, but there it was. Disappointment.

Of all the people here—well, not counting Ilina and Hristo—he was the person who I most needed to apologize to. I wouldn't have called it a friendship, not like Gerel had said, but he'd been so kind to me. I *wanted* to count him as a friend. I wanted . . .

Before I could finish untangling those feelings, boots thumped through the hall. I scrambled out from under the bed and straightened my dress and hair as I pressed my spine to the rear of the cell. It was alarming how quickly it came back, in spite of eighteen days of absence. The thirty-three days in the Pit before that were too strong. Too real.

Altan stood at the door, a bag of breakfast hanging from one hand. That meant I hadn't been invited back to work. My stomach rolled at the thought of what waited in that sack. Rotten apples. Hard bread. Mold with a little bit of cheese left on it.

"Failure," Altan said, and the word spiraled through me, cutting. "Liar." He wore a deep frown that carved trenches in his forehead.

"Liar?" My voice carried down the hall. It had been quiet before, with only the taunts of the second guard and the exhausted yawns of prisoners. Now, it was a listening quiet.

His glare was all hot rage and hate. "I thought you cared about the dragons. I thought you'd been truthful with me."

I swallowed hard. "I *did* tell you the truth."

Slowly, he shook his head. His jaw clenched so hard I wondered if he might crush his own teeth. "If you thought your last visit was miserable, just wait. You haven't seen how unpleasant I can be when I'm really angry."

Fear coursed through me like fire. "I told you everything."

"No." He swung the bag of breakfast until it hit my door. One. Two. Three. The contents thumped on metal, bruising and destroying. "You tried to hold something back, which is why I took your silent friend. And now I know you lied about the dragons, too."

I couldn't speak.

"So you'll tell me everything," he said. "The truth this time. Or I will bury every one of your friends under hot noorestones while you watch."

Bile raced up my throat, and my chest squeezed with anguish.

He'd already tortured Aaru. Now he wanted the rest of them?

Echoes of Aaru's scream filled my head, and my fingers remembered the cold of his skin. My eyes recalled the sudden darkness, the desperate attempts to *see* through the nothing. And my ears knew the smothering, all-consuming silence cast across the room.

Altan would never move my friends to the second level. Never. I'd been a fool to even imagine it.

"What do you think?" Altan was still banging my breakfast on the bars of my cell. "I think it's a fair offer. Don't you?"

I couldn't let him hurt my friends. Not again.

"All right." The words were weak, shaky.

"What's that?" Altan lifted his voice; he wanted to be heard, wanted it known he was the victor. "I couldn't hear you."

I drew a fractured breath and spoke loud enough that he might be pleased. "Don't hurt my friends. I'll tell you everything."

"Very good." Altan tossed my breakfast bag inside the cell, a look of triumph shining in his eyes. "I'll see you in two hours."

When he and the other guard left, the cellblock was absolutely quiet, and my legs buckled and I dropped to the floor, knees striking stone with sharp bursts of pain.

What had I done?

CHAPTER TWENTY-NINE

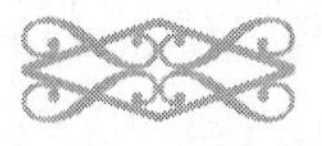

FOR A LONG TIME AFTER ALTAN LEFT, I SAT ON MY bed, counting panicky heartbeats. One hundred fifty-three, one hundred fifty-four, one hundred fifty-five . . .

TWO HUNDRED SEVENTY-THREE, two hundred seventy-four, two hundred seventy-five.

DEAR DAMYAN AND Darina, what was I supposed to do now?

I'D LONG AGO curled over until my forehead touched my knees. There was no farther for me to bend, not without crushing bones, but still I wanted to shrink down into nothing. Because I was nothing.

"Decide whether you'll tell Altan your secret," Gerel said, five hundred heartbeats later. "Lying isn't one of your options. You're clearly a terrible liar."

"Don't you think she knows that?" Ilina snapped. "Can't you see that she feels awful enough without you telling her how badly she messed up?"

Hristo cleared his throat. "I'm not sure that helps."

I tried a little harder to collapse into myself.

"Don't bother to defend her," Gerel said. "I told her decans ago that she needed to decide to tell Altan her secret or not. I told her to stick with whatever she decided, because Altan won't give up his quest to learn it. Planting your feet and fending off attacks is the only thing you can do against him."

Everything inside me shriveled.

How had my life come to this?

How could I *fix* this?

Maybe . . . Maybe just one person at a time.

I couldn't bring myself to move for another hundred heartbeats, but at last I crawled under the bed. ::**I'm sorry. There are so many things I should have told you from the start. Like who I am. Then you'd have known it's not safe to be nice to me.**::

It wasn't a surprise when the only answer on the other side of the hole was silence.

::**I want you to know that this was never my intention. Not that knowing helps you now. I was wrong. I should have been more careful, but I wanted to be your friend,** even though I knew it wasn't possible. Idris and Damina never got along.::

My chest expanded and dropped with a long sigh. I'd been so foolish. So naïve.

::Nothing can make up for what happened to you,:: I went on. ::Especially nothing I can do. I know that. But I also know that I owe you, and I won't forget it.::

I closed my eyes, but I saw him in the interrogation room again, strapped to the chair with noorestone heat pressing through him.

::You may not want my attempts at making amends,:: I said, ::and given what just happened, I wouldn't blame you. Or if you never want to speak to me again. But if you'll accept my efforts, I will help you however I can. Anything I can do. I want to start with getting you and the others out of the Pit.::

That hadn't gone well so far, though.

::That's all I've wanted since coming here—to get out.::

I closed my eyes. ::And I want to get you out. That's why I came back. For you.::

Two long taps. One short. ::Me?:: Or maybe there wasn't a question in that. Maybe it was simply a repeat: ::Me.::

Tension burned through my whole body, and my heart leaped up into my throat. "You." The word came out like a puff of smoke. I pressed my mouth into a line and went back to the quiet code; I wanted to use his language. ::I will find a way.::

::How?:: Somehow, he made the quiet code sound

doubtful. And of course he doubted me. I doubted me.

::I don't know anymore. Nothing I've tried has worked. I wanted to sneak food for you, but instead the Luminary Council took me away. I wanted to make sure you got a job, but the noorestones—:: Had shredded his feet. Were they better yet? Could he walk now?

Long notes of silence played between us.

::I haven't given up,:: I said. ::I have to get out, and I want you to come with me.::

With me.

I wanted him to come with me.

One. Two. Three. Seconds pounded by until finally, a shadow fell on the far side of the hole and Aaru peered back at me, his face silhouetted by the dim noorestone light. All I could see was the slope of his forehead and tip of his nose and gaunt cheeks until he turned and it was all lost.

He tapped on the floor. ::I want to escape. My family needs me.::

His family. Of course. ::I'll make sure you reach them.::

Though how I'd get a fugitive to the most isolated and protected island without getting us all arrested again, I had no idea.

One thing at a time.

First, I had to get us out of here.

I scrambled out from under my bed and went to my door. "Gerel." I kept my voice as low as possible.

She didn't look up from where she sat cross-legged in the center of her cell.

"Gerel," I repeated, just a little louder.

"I can hear you." Her relaxed hands became fists. "I was just ignoring you."

"Oh." I glanced downward. But then I remembered I was trying to help *her.* I steeled myself. "Tell me about Altan."

That got her attention. Gerel jerked straight up and met my eyes. Hers were hard and cold. "What? You think you can make peace with him? After lying to him?"

"I didn't lie to him," I said. "I told him what he wanted to know."

Gerel climbed to her feet, as lithe as a cat. "And what was that?"

"The reason I'm here." I could *feel* Ilina's and Hristo's attention from the neighboring cells. Chenda's and Aaru's, too. "I learned of treachery. In the Crescent Prominence sanctuary, dragons are being captured and sent to the Algotti Empire. But when I told the Luminary Council, they betrayed me. I thought they would put a stop to the exportation. Instead, they put me here."

Gerel was shaking her head. "Why would anyone send dragons away? Doesn't everyone know that without dragons to keep the gods here, our very *islands* will get up and leave us?"

"Everyone knows about the Great Abandonment," Ilina said. "But apparently there are people who are willing to risk that it's a myth." Bitterness edged her voice. "And some who will do anything for power—even deliver the children of the gods to our enemies."

Gerel pressed her face to the bars to look at Ilina. "And what do you have to do with any of this?"

"My parents work for the Luminary Department of Drakontos Examination in Crescent Prominence. I was the first to notice that dragons were missing."

"Hmm." Gerel turned to Hristo. "And you?"

"I am Mira's protector."

"Some protector." Gerel motioned at her cheek. "She has a terrible gash on her face, if you didn't notice. But you're Hartan. Maybe that's why you couldn't protect her. You're too soft for that sort of work."

Hair stood on my arms and my lips curled back with a snarl. "You will *not* talk to him like that. Hristo has saved my life more times than you could imagine."

Gerel's gaze whipped toward me. "The little dragon can spit fire after all."

"I would give my life for Mira." Hristo spoke low and even, like the shooting anger all around him wasn't even there. "As for your accusations, no one is more aware of my failure to protect her from the snakes on the Luminary Council than I. Nevertheless, my mission remains the same."

"It's my fault I got hurt. Not Hristo's." I dragged my fingertips over the cut on my cheek; it was hot with inflammation.

"If you say so." Gerel crossed her arms. "So what are you going to tell Altan? Insist that you were truthful before? Try to appeal to his better side?"

I shrugged helplessly.

"You'll gain nothing there. He doesn't have a better side." She almost sounded sad for me. "We were in the same trainee group and he constantly battled me for top position. He never won—not until I ended up in here."

"Then what do you suggest?" I asked.

"Nothing. He will expect you to tell him the truth this time—"

"I did—"

"And whatever you held back before. You'll have to give him what he wants."

That was all the encouragement my anxiety needed. As though my body wasn't connected to my mind at all, my fingers and hands spasmed. My mouth pulled into a grimace, tugging painfully at the gash. And my heart drummed in my ears loud enough to deafen me to every other sound. Even my eyes betrayed me, with my vision tunneling.

I couldn't *breathe*.

Then a door opened at the end of the cellblock, and the screech of keys and cells opening sang through the hall. One by one, someone opened every unoccupied cell.

Altan.

He strode in with his usual swagger, as though he owned the entire Pit. The map of thin scars across his face was a reminder of the battles he'd won, and that he was second only to Gerel. He stood before me, a sinister smile twisting over his mouth.

"What's happening?" I rasped. "What are you doing?"

"We're going to have a talk." He grazed a finger across the ring of keys on his belt. "But first, I need to ensure you're properly motivated to tell me everything. The *truth* this time."

Black fog shimmered around the edges of my eyes, made worse with every word he spoke. Even my vision dimmed, and sounds came muted and far away. My fingers and toes were numb, and every breath I took felt like glass through my throat. One breath. Two. Three.

Not now, I prayed. This was not the time for the panic to overtake me. But it was too late. Did I ever have a chance when the panic came? No. It was the part of my own mind that loved to betray me when I needed to be strong.

A key scraped my lock, and iron rang.

"Come out of there." Altan grabbed my arm and yanked me from the cell. I staggered out and stood in place while he shouted instructions to someone at the end of the hall. I could barely hear over the new surge of anxiety filling my head.

Movement fractured the tunnel of darkness.

Aaru.

His head dropped downward, and his stubble-covered face was ashy with grime and nearly two months in the dark. His clothes, which hadn't fit right to start with, were tattered and filthy. And his shoulders curled inward, his posture bent under the weight of the Pit.

But then he looked at me—met my eyes. His were still the black of extinguished noorestones, framed with ragged hair, and they pierced through the panic boiling inside me. My quick breathing slowed to something normal and the black fog around my vision retreated. A sense of cool relief whispered through me, and for an entire second, I forgot—

Then his gaze cut to my cheek, and I burned with shame. I couldn't turn my face fast enough to hide it, to prevent him from seeing what would surely become a spectacular scar. When I glanced back, he was gone.

Just a shadow in the cell.

What had he thought? I hadn't noticed any shift in his expression—his face was as silent as his voice—but surely he'd been repulsed. I was ruined now, and if he'd ever thought of me in a way that one might call fondly, that, too, was likely ruined as well.

"Embarrassed?" Amusement filled Altan's tone as he turned toward me again.

I'd been born with one gift: my face. There was no way Altan could understand what it was like to lose that.

"I have a surprise for you."

Most certainly I didn't want any surprise from Altan, but when a low whine—and a rattle of chains—came from down the hall, I couldn't stop myself from looking.

A dragon waited in the anteroom. *Drakontos ignitus.*

She was a juvenile, if the nubby facial horns and brown scales were anything to go by. In a few years, she'd look like a four-legged flame with fierce horns and a wingspan that rivaled even the larger species. But for now, she was a small creature—her shoulder would come up to my hip—and she crept low to the ground, shaking her head in small, determined motions.

Then I saw why.

She was muzzled and shackled, with heavy rings on each leg. Iron chains let four warriors hold her in place.

"What's happening?" I whispered. "What are you doing?"

"This is Kelsine." Altan jerked me toward the anteroom—and the dragon. "Her parents were taken with the others months ago. We managed to hide Kelsine and a few of the other juveniles, but they haven't been the same since."

We were twenty steps away, walking fast. I hadn't even had a chance to look inside Hristo's and Ilina's cells.

Altan kept talking. "The muzzle puts pressure on her spark gland, keeping her from breathing fire. This is the first time she's been out of the Hall of Drakon Warriors. She's probably frightened."

Ten steps.

The dragon lashed her head as we neared, but one of the guards gave his chain a sharp jerk, and she stilled, fixing her gold eyes on me. Accusing.

Five steps.

Altan guided me around the tethered dragon and

paused me in the anteroom.

"What's happening?" I asked again.

Altan only glanced at his fellow warriors and nodded.

Together, the four men prodded Kelsine forward, into the doorway. The two at the rear bent and unlocked the shackles, and Kelsine's talons scraped against the floor at the sudden freedom. A sharp grunt squeezed from her clenched jaws.

While the front two men bent to unlock those shackles, the two at the rear pulled copper rods the length of my forearm from their belts. Dragon reins. Kelsine didn't notice, though. Or care, because the front shackles were off, and the guards were working on the muzzle.

Her wings twitched as the iron fell away. Flame lurched from between her teeth as the guards nudged her through the door.

"Wait—"

My cry was too late.

The guards put Kelsine, the frightened young dragon, into the cellblock with my friends.

And shut the door.

CHAPTER THIRTY

KELSINE WAS GOING TO KILL MY FRIENDS.

But before I could take even a step toward the cell-block, Altan grabbed my collar and hauled me back. "Don't worry. She'll take her time. That's why I unlocked the other cells: to give her something to investigate before she reaches your friends. Imagine how frustrated she'll be when she can't open their doors."

My stomach turned over and anxiety swarmed back. I had some time, but not enough time.

Time to do what?

Escape. Save my friends.

I needed to count. Breathe. Make a list. Something. How could I even think about saving my friends if I couldn't save myself from my own traitorous mind?

My body betrayed me as well, trembling and stumbling. With my vision fading in and out, I lost track of where I was going. Suddenly, I was in the interrogation room. The same one as before.

One table stood in the very center of the room, holding nothing but a map, a stack of papers, and a pencil. Two chairs were pushed all the way in, both facing the side walls so that neither of us would have our back to the door. Twenty noorestones ringed the room.

We were completely alone.

"Have a seat." Altan motioned to one of the chairs. "We have a lot to talk about."

My hands shook as I pulled out the nearest chair and pressed myself against the cold wood. I scanned the room again. Still twenty noorestones. Still too heavy with memories of bloodstains and Aaru's screams and the unnatural silence.

No death chair.

No noorestones in basins.

No weapons, save the baton at Altan's hip.

"You're not allowed to kill prisoners," I whispered.

"I can't control what a young dragon does, Mira." He smirked. "Her flame only reaches so far. I suspect it will get rather hot in there, but they're probably not dead."

Altan was a liar, I knew that, but I told myself this had to be true. Young dragons did have a very short flame. So maybe . . .

"Let's start with something simple." My nemesis

moved near his chair, but he didn't sit. He remained on his feet in a display of dominance. To show that though there was a chair, *he* had a choice about whether he'd sit.

I glared at him, wishing he'd burst into flames and die.

He did not.

Instead, he pressed a fist to the table and leaned forward, his fury barely contained beneath his skin. "Now," he said, "tell me why the Luminary Council really sent you here."

"I told you the truth."

His mouth pulled back in a growl. "Warriors went to Crestshade and Thornfell. They scoured every port, ship, cargo hold, and warehouse. There was nothing. No trace of dragons."

Chills swept through me, numbing. If the dragons weren't there, then where were they? All this time, I'd consoled myself with the knowledge of their whereabouts. Part of me had imagined I might be the one to rescue them, but after Lex—

Well, I'd known then something must be different. That was why Lex and the other two had been at the Shadowed City docks, rather than Thornfell, where the shipping order had said they'd be.

"I'm waiting." Altan loomed too close.

"They changed the schedule." My voice was small and weak, but I lifted my eyes to Altan's and *willed* him to see that I was telling the truth. "When I came to the Luminary Council with the shipping order, they must have realized there was a possibility I'd tell someone—like you—so they changed the schedule to keep anyone from rescuing the dragons."

He seemed to grow larger, but he said, "You might be right."

A knot of tension in my chest eased a little. "I love dragons," I whispered. "I truly hoped you would find them. Better they return to the Fallen Isles with you than get sent to the Algotti Empire."

Tense moments passed between us. Three, four, five. Then Altan pulled back and crossed his arms. "All right. Say I believe you."

He did believe me. Everyone knew what kind of liar I was—a terrible one—so he did believe me. He was just trying to scare me.

I counted the noorestones. Twenty.

"What other route might your council use to send the dragons to the Algotti Empire?"

As if *I* would know that kind of thing. He was the one with the strategic mind. I was just some girl the Luminary Council had liked to parade around. "I don't know. I don't even know why they would do this. The Mira Treaty is supposed to protect dragons—"

"The Mira Treaty is a sham," he said.

I shook my head. People declared that from time to time, often at me, as though there was something I needed to do about it, personally. "It's no sham. Just . . . some people are ignoring it." Like the people who signed it.

Altan blew out a long breath, glaring at me like I was a fool. "You've caught the Luminary Council in enough lies, haven't you? You've seen enough to know that they aren't the benevolent government you once believed."

Well, that was true. But that didn't mean that the entire treaty was a lie. "The government is made of people. Humans are fallible creatures. But not the Mira Treaty. It is an ideal."

"Created by fallible humans." He stood taller. I forced myself not to shrink back; I couldn't show my fear. Not now. "The Mira Treaty holds all the appearance of being something good, but underneath, it is a sinister thing. A lie."

I didn't want to waste my time defending the treaty to Altan, but he wanted to talk about it. Needed to, maybe. I just couldn't decide whether allowing him to rant would put him at ease or make him more volatile. With Altan, it could go either way.

I forced my shaking hands into the folds of my dress. "What do you think they're hiding with it?"

He stared down at me, eyes hooded. "The Mira Treaty sold the islands to the Algotti Empire."

"That's preposterous." I bit my cheek. Like always, the wrong thing just fell out of my mouth, without guidance from my brain.

"Of course *you* think so. You were conditioned from birth to believe in the treaty."

If only I could make that preposterous comment

disappear. Now that I'd brought up a dissenting viewpoint, I had to continue this argument. I had to *let* myself be convinced of his rightness.

"All right," I said. "Tell me why you believe the empire owns us."

He shook his head and paced the length of the room; my brain uselessly counted his steps (three, four, five . . .). "I have a lot of reasons. I doubt you'd believe any of them."

"I am literally your captive audience. Tell me why you think my entire life was a lie." Too glib. That was far too glib. I clenched my fists in my skirts.

Anger laced Altan's tone. "We aren't in negotiations. You don't get to make demands." He pivoted and paced the other way. (Seventeen, eighteen, nineteen . . .) The anger ebbed, but didn't fade.

I had to be careful. He had my friends trapped in a small space with a scared dragon.

Altan kept pacing, and the echo of my question feathered into nothing. He had said we weren't negotiating, and I'd kept quiet, so he'd decided he'd won.

I waited. People loved to announce their opinions, whether they were asked for or not. He wouldn't be able to resist.

Thirty-six, thirty-seven, thirty-eight. His steps were even, precise, and clipped just so. "First of all, there's the language of the Mira Treaty."

I schooled the triumph from my face; this was only a minor victory. "I've read the Mira Treaty a hundred times."

A hundred and seventeen times, but who was counting? Still, I kept my tone even, maintaining the same invitation to prove me wrong. "Nowhere does it say that the document cedes ownership of the Fallen Isles to the Algotti Empire."

"No, but the preamble says the islands bow to the one true authority."

"The Fallen Gods."

"The empire," Altan explained. "The one true authority, according to the Mira Treaty, is the Algotti Empire."

"How do you know?" I stayed defensive, but added a carefully measured note of uncertainty. Just enough for him to pick up on. Mother would be proud.

He shook his head. "Only one place has the audacity to call themselves the 'light of Noore,' and it isn't us."

That struck a chord. I remembered asking about "the light of Noore" as a child, and being reassured the light was the seven gods, come down from the stars to bring us hope and peace. Why wasn't it *lights*, plural, then? Because the Mira Treaty united everything, even the gods and their light.

"No one used the phrase before the Mira Treaty," Altan said. "No one on the Fallen Isles, at any rate."

"Why would the Algotti Empire insist on Hartan independence, though? Or unite the islands? Or protect dragons? That seems like it would make it more difficult for them to conquer us."

"We've already been conquered. That's what I'm trying

to tell you." He growled with frustration, but the anger had dimmed for now. "All are equal in the Algotti Empire. Territories cannot own other territories; it all belongs to the empire and to the empress. As part of the Algotti Empire, the same must apply to the Fallen Isles." He pivoted again, still pacing. (Sixty-five, sixty-six, sixty-seven . . .) "We are a single body belonging to them. They see no difference between Khulani and Idrisi, or Anaheran and Hartan. For now, we're allowed to keep our individual cultures, but as time goes on, we'll become more and more acclimated to the new way of life that comes from belonging to the empire."

"What about the dragons?" I asked. "Why would they care about preserving dragons?"

"The Great Abandonment," he said, like it was obvious.

"To placate us?" Surely the Algotti Empress didn't believe the Great Abandonment was real.

He nodded. "The empress isn't stupid, Mira. She knows that territories she conquers value their cultures and traditions and myths. So she makes a show of respecting them, and over time, her new territories begin to meld with the old. It's not overnight, or fast, but she is patient. Eventually, she expects us to turn from our Fallen Gods and worship her."

People in the empire worshiped their empress? But she was . . . mortal. How could anyone worship anything mortal? I'd always believed they worshiped the Upper Gods—those who'd stayed in the stars when our gods fell to Noore.

"The other proof," Altan said, "is that we are shipping

our dragons to the empire. Proof *you've* seen." He stopped at the table and glared down at me. "Why else would we send the children of the gods to our enemies?"

I sank deeper into my chair. I believed in the goodness of the Mira Treaty. I did. But I hated how compelling that particular argument was.

Hadn't I been asking myself over and over why the Luminary Council would allow our dragons to be sent away? And our noorestones—ones we could use to protect ourselves? "You think the governments themselves are sending the dragons?"

"It's a payment," Altan went on. "We don't want them to attack us, so we've silently surrendered. Even with seven islands, we cannot defend against her. The Algotti Army is endless, growing with every country the empress devours. Her hunger is insatiable."

"We couldn't fight her off?" Wasn't that what the Khulani warriors were for? They'd taken oaths to defend the Fallen Isles, even when we fought one another. They were supposed to defend against outside invasions.

"Our advantage has always been the dragons. But with the population dwindling, we don't stand a chance."

"That's why the Mira Treaty specifies that even warriors cannot ride dragons anymore?"

He bowed his head. "To prevent us from taking up arms against the empire, because even a few Drakon Warriors could cause severe damage. We could cost the empire lives and money and time." He stopped pacing and frowned. "But it would be mitigative efforts. They would win, eventually. So we—the Fallen Isles—surrendered. We quietly gave ourselves to them, and now we pay them to keep out of our business. For a time, at least. As I said, assimilation is inevitable."

It sounded too wild to be true, but I couldn't think of a better reason why the Luminary Council would send dragons and noorestones to the mainland. "Who knows about this?"

Did Mother and Father know? Father was the architect of the Mira Treaty. Thinking he might have done something like this intentionally, knowingly betraying his own people . . .

"Your government. Mine. All of them." Altan frowned. "I'm not sure how many within each government, but certainly everyone who signed the Mira Treaty had to know what it was."

It seemed so farfetched. But the Luminary Council had betrayed me. The Twilight Council had betrayed Chenda. Why should I expect anything but underhanded awfulness from those entrusted with our safety?

"But why the secrecy? Why not just explain that the empire will destroy us if—"

"Can you imagine the riots? The revolts? We'd destroy ourselves. No, we have enough trouble growing accustomed to Hartans being equal with the rest of us."

Some people would contest that Hartans were truly *equal*.

"Think of the outcry if the truth about the Mira Treaty came out." He shook his head and sat down across from me once more. "No, the people of the Fallen Isles must not know."

Why? Maybe they deserved to be outraged.

He touched the crossed maces on his jacket. "I took holy vows to protect the Fallen Isles. I mean to uphold those vows, even if it destroys me." The danger crept back into his tone. "Now, I want to discuss what alternate routes your Luminary Council might have used for shipping the dragons."

This again. I'd hoped he'd forgotten. "I don't know. I really don't."

A look between disappointment and annoyance crossed his face. "Given your devotion to dragons, I thought you would be more willing."

Did he? After leaving me alone in the dark for days? After torturing Aaru? After endangering my friends as insurance for my cooperation?

He couldn't be more wrong.

"Mira." He leaned his elbows on the table. "Your friends don't have much time."

My heart lurched.

"You know I can be cruel," he said. "But I can be kind if you earn it. I can reward you."

My voice was trapped in my throat, useless.

"I'd like for you to take care of our dragons. The juveniles, and soon the adults, when they are retrieved. Doesn't that sound better than cleaning for Sarannai?"

I'd never wanted to be the face of the Luminary Council. For me, happiness had always been one dragon moment to another. It had been my time with LaLa, and my studies in the sanctuary.

"Let me make it easy," Altan said softly. "Tell me the alternate routes they'd use, or"—he glanced toward the back of the room—"tell me this secret about noorestones. The secret you almost let your friend die for."

The second shipment. The weapon that could level a city.

I didn't know the alternate routes, and I could not give him information he could use to hurt people. I'd always thought Drakon Warriors must be the most honorable and fierce of warriors. And maybe they had been. Once. But Altan was not the kind of man I'd envisioned being a Drakon Warrior. If he was the one they'd sent to get information from me, I knew I could not trust anyone who wore the claw badge.

"I know you love dragons," he said. "In that, we are the same."

"No." I lifted my chin and met his eyes. "You cannot buy me. I've spent my whole life being the Luminary Council's puppet. I will not be yours."

CHAPTER THIRTY-ONE

ALTAN SEEMED MORE TAKEN ABACK THAN ANGRY.

I pushed myself to my feet; the chair clattered to the floor behind me. "I will not help those who harm my friends, or seek to use me, or speak pretty words only when it suits them." My whole body tensed. These were statements I could never take back, and Altan would never forget. "Nor will I help those who harm others to further their cause. You call yourself a protector of the Fallen Isles. You call yourself a Drakon Warrior, but you are neither. You would tear apart the islands if you thought it was the only way to save everyone from the Algotti Empire, but you're wrong."

Altan hit me.

The baton whipped out of his belt and came flying at

me so fast I couldn't move out of the way.

Metal struck my shoulder and numbness rang through my arm.

I screamed and staggered back, clutching my shoulder. Hot pain surged up and blinded me. For a heartbeat, my whole body seemed out of my control, and when my vision cleared, I was on the floor. My knees ached where they'd hit the stone, and one of my ankles throbbed where it was twisted beneath me.

I'd fainted. It had just been a moment, but even that much was terrifying, especially since Altan loomed over me, his baton drawn back.

But he didn't bring it down. Not again.

Not yet.

"You will not speak to me that way." His voice was deadly cool, his eyes hard and narrowed. "Never forget that you are a prisoner here, and I control your fate."

Everyone thought they controlled me. My parents. The Luminary Council. The Twilight Senate. The warriors. But I was done being used. If my trip to Bopha had taught me anything, it was that *I* was in control of me. No matter how much others insisted, they did not direct my arms and legs. They did not determine what words came out of my mouth. The only reason they'd succeeded for so long was because I'd let them—because I'd never realized that I had the strength to stop them.

I knew better now.

"You're a worm," I said. "Utterly deplorable. You grab

for power because you have none of your own. Because you've let yours be taken from you."

The baton came down, aimed for my head, but I blocked it with my arm—the one with the hurt shoulder. My bones shuddered under the impact and I wanted to curl into a ball and hide. But this was the moment. I had to seize it now.

"You hurt others because *you* are hurt. Because even with all your training, you haven't gotten what you wanted, and you think you can just take it from others." My whole body shook with adrenaline, as if the memory of noorestone energy remained in this room and flooded into me.

"You don't know anything about me." Altan raised the baton to hit again, but I rolled out of the way and—miraculously—found my feet.

"I know you desperately want to be important." I gripped the table with my good hand, leaning hard against the smooth wood. With my aching knees and my twisted ankle, standing was much harder than it had been two minutes ago. "But you were second to Gerel as a trainee, and you are nothing now."

Even as the words tumbled out of my mouth, I knew I should at least *consider* watching my tongue. But all my life, I'd been speaking other people's words at their convenience, and not nearly enough of my own. These words—right or wrong, brave or foolish—were mine. I owned them.

Altan roared and ran at me with his baton lifted high.

I gathered my strength and stepped aside, struggling to keep my feet through the throbbing pain. "Are you going to club me to death?" I rasped. "Is that your great plan to win me to your side?"

His knuckles paled around the baton. "I don't need you on my side. The offer was courtesy only."

"Courtesy for a prisoner?" I scoffed, drawing on every time I'd needed to be haughty and aloof at a party. "No, you wouldn't have offered if you didn't still need me. If you didn't think there was something I could give to you."

One side of his mouth pulled up into a deadly smile. "I said the *offer* was courtesy. I didn't say you had a choice."

The darkness in his expression gave me pause.

My friends.

He still had them.

"You'll help me whether you want to or not," he said. "If I've discovered one thing about you, it's that you cannot stand to see people get hurt. And I have everyone you care about right here. Your best friend. Your protector. The girl who hates you. The girl who pretends to like you. The girl who ignores you. And that boy you admire so much. Do you think he admires you too?"

No.

"You should have seen your face when you realized he saw your cheek. You looked so upset. I almost felt bad." He advanced on me.

There was nowhere to go. He was between the door

and me, and he was not limping on two sore knees and a twisted ankle.

"But you should have been more worried about what I'd do to him than what he'd think about your face. I don't know how the noorestones exploded before, but I know that one of you must be behind it. If you think I've forgotten about you *murdering* three people, you're wrong."

"You brought the noorestones in," I said. "You called for more. You're the only one responsible for what happened."

Altan drew back the baton, but I wasn't done.

"You're the one who decided to torture Aaru. You're the one who brought him in here in the first place." I stopped myself before revealing too much—that it was Aaru who'd silenced the room, shattering the noorestones in the process. "There was no reason to bring him here. You only took him, too, because you're a terrible person who enjoys watching people get hurt."

"Just prisoners like you." The baton crashed into the chair I'd been occupying. One of the legs snapped off and clattered across the floor. "And like that boy. You both deserve the pain I inflict."

Common sense told me to retreat, but to where? He blocked the only exit, and there was nothing in here but one table, one broken chair, one whole chair, and twenty noorestones.

In vain, I wished for Aaru's power. I'd turn the room black and run out. But I couldn't. I was just me. Giftless Mira.

"You're responsible for those deaths." Dangerous words. Deadly words. "You brought Rosa and the trainees in here. You told them to fetch another noorestone. You are the reason they're dead."

Altan hurled the baton.

I managed to dodge, mostly; the blow aimed for my head clipped my hurt shoulder instead. Shocks of pain traveled through my arm and collarbone, but I gritted my teeth and dived for the weapon, pushing off with my sore foot.

My nemesis swore and ran for it, too, but I was closer. I threw myself onto the floor and grabbed the top of the baton, half feeling the memory of heat from its many impacts with me. I clutched the weapon, suddenly not sure what I thought I could do with it. Did I really think I could hurt him? Even if I was physically capable—

Altan was right behind me.

I took the handle, rolled onto my rear, and thrust the baton forward as though it were a long knife. It jabbed Altan in the chest, right on his breastbone, and slid up to his throat and caught him on the underside of his jaw.

He gagged and recoiled, one hand flying to his throat, the other grasping for the baton.

I gripped the baton with all my might, but I wasn't strong enough to keep it from him, so when he pulled with enough strength to rip it from my hands, I let go.

Altan tumbled backward, but kept his grip on the baton, even as he scrambled to his feet.

All the self-defense lessons I'd ever taken fluttered through my mind, but only one stood out for this moment: run, and let Hristo protect me.

But Hristo was locked in his cell. He wasn't going to rescue me.

I'd never been taught what to do if Hristo couldn't come for me, or how *I* should go about rescuing my protector.

"What are you doing, Failure?" Altan seemed amused, almost. "Are you trying to get hurt?"

On my feet again, I dashed for the broken chair and took up the leg, though it was no real defense against the metal of Altan's baton.

This was the stupidest thing I'd ever done. Still, I was committed. I'd inflicted enough damage to my relationship with Altan that it would never recover. My friends and I would never be safe after this.

Altan tapped the baton on his thigh. "Don't be foolish. I don't want to hurt you."

"All you do is hurt people. Remember Rosa? Those trainees?" It was mean to throw that in his face again, but I needed to keep him off-balance—if not physically, then emotionally. "Wasn't it just over there that they died?" I waved my broken chair leg toward the back of the room, where three people had lain dead on the floor.

When he followed my gesture, a fractured look crossing his face, I checked my position to the door. Finally, I was closer—but not for long. He came at me with his baton drawn back, ready to slam into my already sore left side.

I darted away and threw the chair leg with all my might; it thunked against Altan's chest, useless. Still, I had to try. I had to commit if I wanted to survive.

That meant I needed a weapon.

Any weapon.

I retreated to the nearest wall and snatched a noorestone from the sconce.

"What are you going to do with that?" A sinister grin touched Altan's mouth. "Burn me, like I burned your friend? I wonder what they're all doing now. Probably trying to calm the dragon while she spits fire into their cells."

Bile raced up my throat, because I could too easily imagine that.

But Altan was a warrior, trained to defend against the attacks his opponents threw at him. That meant every time I reminded him about Rosa, he'd hold my friends over my head.

"I'm going to stab you with it," I said. "Right through the eye."

"You'd never dare."

The glowing crystal was cool in my hand, cut into a long, dagger-like shape with six major facets, and six minor at each end where they tapered into sharp points. A thrum of power surged through the stone, echoing through my hand, and the glow dimmed.

Altan's gaze cut to the noorestone. "What did you do?"

Nothing. I'd touched noorestones hundreds of times before—just like anyone else—and this had never happened. This one was probably just old, nearly extinguished, but I didn't tell him that. Instead, I smiled, like I'd dimmed the crystal intentionally. "Get Kelsine away from my friends."

Another pulse rushed through my hand. Three, four, five. It matched my heartbeat, speeding ever faster, and I wasn't sure how to stop it. Not without dropping the crystal, and right now it was my only weapon. A mighty weapon, maybe. With every beat came this swell of energy, making me stronger in unnameable ways.

"What are you doing?" Altan hadn't exactly lowered his baton, but he watched me with more caution now. Girls who dimmed noorestones might be dangerous.

"Subdue the dragon," I said, advancing. It was an act—a show of courage where there was none. "Do it, and I'll let you live."

That was, perhaps, too much. Altan saw through my veil of bravery and rushed me with his baton.

I ducked to the side, and the metal struck the wall behind me with a loud *clang*. Then, without my instruction, my fist clutching the noorestone flew at him, and the knifelike crystal pierced his side.

Power sang through me, making light flare through my vision—so bright I had to blink. When my eyes cleared, all I saw was Altan's face, ruddy and twisted with pain. Sweat gushed down his body as he dropped to the floor.

The noorestone went dark.

Altan was breathing, bleeding heavily, but unconscious.

I stared down at the depleted noorestone. What had happened? How?

A gasp sounded from the doorway, and I looked up, heart pounding.

Tirta stood there, her eyes round with surprise. "What did you *do*?"

"I don't know." Flames rippled up my arm, red and blue and white coils. But they didn't hurt me. Burn me. Instead, it seemed like they were part of me. One by one, the flames vanished and my limbs were just my limbs again. My heartbeat slowed to a normal speed.

"Well." She glared hatefully at my nemesis on the floor. "Let's do something about that. You should kill him."

CHAPTER THIRTY-TWO

I COULDN'T KILL ALTAN.

No matter how much I despised him, I couldn't kill him.

"It's easy," Tirta said. "Just stab him somewhere vital. His throat or an eye ought to do, if you put enough muscle into it. I don't recommend the heart; too hard to get between the ribs."

My mouth dropped open. "Who *are* you?" Hartans didn't speak like that. Of course, I knew better than to assign stereotypes to people, what with the company I tended to keep, but tips on where to stab someone? That would be shocking from any of my friends, except maybe Gerel.

Tirta just smiled widely at me. "Are you going to do it? Or should I?"

"Are you an assassin?" I whispered. She'd always looked strong, but I'd never thought of her as *particularly* strong, and I'd definitely never thought she'd have been willing to kill someone, or teach someone else how to do it. Suddenly the sweet girl I'd known for two months was a stranger. A very scary one.

She'd been sentenced to the Pit for something, though. She'd never told me what.

Now, it seemed likely she was here for murder.

"I don't think the question is about what *I* am," she said, glancing at my hands. "The real question you should be asking is what are *you*? I saw what happened with that noorestone."

I pressed my palms together, smothering the remnants of fire. The noorestone still stuck in Altan's side was dark—dead—but the others glowed along the walls with their steady blue light. When I touched the nearest crystal, my whole body tense with anticipation, nothing happened.

The energy stayed where it was, trapped in crystal, released only as radiant light.

On shaking legs, I limped around the room (four steps, five, six . . .) and removed the noorestones from the sconces on the wall until all the light was gathered in my sore arm.

"What are you doing?" Tirta was still in the doorway, checking the hall.

"I'm leaving him in the dark, just like he left me." I placed the nineteen noorestones on the table, white-blue illumination shining at my fingertips. "Why did you come here?"

"To help you escape." She glanced at Altan. "To save you from him."

"*I* saved me from him." I hiked up my dress, stabbed it with one of the sharper stones, and tore it into a long strip to bundle the crystals together. The stones went into the widest part of the strip of cotton. With some weight in there, it'd make a decent, if shallow, bag.

Tirta checked the hall again, then stepped inside quickly, shutting the door behind her. "Someone's coming." Her voice dropped low as she crept toward Altan's motionless form.

I finished tying a knot at the ends of the cotton strip, easy enough to carry over my shoulder, and watched Tirta pull the baton from Altan's limp fingers. "Don't kill him."

Her expression was hard, deeply shadowed with all the light contained in my bag, as she glared down at my nemesis.

Maybe he was her nemesis, too.

It was hard to think of her as anything but the only person who'd *wanted* to befriend me here, who'd gossiped and reminded me to keep my humanity. But I couldn't erase the echoes of her words, or the implications that she'd stabbed men before.

Out in the hall, footfalls thumped on the stone floor, growing in volume and then fading. Whoever'd come by was gone now.

"Don't kill him," I said again.

Tirta released a long breath, and the tension that had gathered in her shoulders. She stepped back and tore her gaze from Altan, as though not killing him caused her actual pain. How little I knew about her.

"Are you really Hartan?" *Harta hates harm.*

"Are you really Daminan?" She wrinkled her nose. "What kind of question is that?"

Offensive, apparently.

"Sorry," I said. "So you came here to help me?"

"Yes, but as you already pointed out, you helped yourself." She headed toward the door again, Altan's baton in hand.

As for my nemesis, he remained on the floor, fingers twitching in his sleep. How much heat had I—or the noorestone—shoved into him? Enough to knock him out. Plus the stab wound. A pool of dark blood shimmered at his side, reddening as I approached with my bag of light.

I knelt to reach for the noorestone stuck in his side, but Tirta's voice stopped me.

"Leave it there if you really want him to live. It's plugging the flow of blood right now. If you remove it, he'll bleed out, and I get the feeling you don't want to be a murderer."

"That wasn't what I was doing." A lie. She probably

knew it. Instead, I removed the ring of keys from his belt, careful to avoid touching him. I wasn't proud—or even sure—of what I'd done, and I didn't want to risk doing it again. Not when he was already down.

I slipped the key ring into the bag of noorestones and retreated from Altan's unconscious form. How long would he stay out? Aaru hadn't been unconscious for too long, but he'd had a longer, sustained burn. Altan—that had been all at once.

It was a wonder he was still alive.

I padded toward the door, listening for clatters and clanks in the bag. Nothing. The nineteen noorestones and the keys were packed tightly enough they wouldn't move, as long as I kept the makeshift bag pinned against my ribs.

"How do you do it?" Tirta asked. "You hate him. Your life would be better if he were gone forever. But you won't take action to make it happen."

"I won't compromise my humanity for my comfort. I won't become him to be rid of him." I touched the doorknob, cool metal under my fingertips. "I thought you understood that."

Her eyes, once sweet and familiar, now held a secret darkness. "I understand survival. You should, too."

I didn't want to understand the world the way she did. Not anymore.

Tirta pushed past me and opened the door. "Come on." She slipped into the hall, grip tight on the baton.

I stepped out of the interrogation room and shut the door after me, leaving Altan alone. In the dark. Bleeding.

Still, he had no idea how lucky he was that I was not Tirta.

I stepped back from the door. One. Two.

"Are you coming?" Tirta tapped the baton on her thigh. "There aren't usually many guards in this area, but that doesn't mean we won't be spotted."

I was still staring at the door, wondering how this act measured up to all of his.

I'd *stabbed* him. I could still feel the resistance and pop and give of his skin.

"Don't look so upset." Tirta touched my good arm, almost the girl I knew again. Her tone was gentle and her expression soft, but now that I knew to look for it, I could see that this was just a mask. This wasn't the real Tirta. "He'd have done worse to you," she went on. "Anyway, don't you want to get out of here? Feeling bad for him isn't going to get you free."

She was right. As much of a stranger as she was now, she was right. Three, four, five. I moved away from the door. It got easier with every step, like a fraying tether.

Six. Seven. The tether snapped. "I have to save the others. They're still in the first level."

She shook her head, lengthening her stride. "I barely escaped as it was."

Now that she brought it up, how *did* she escape her guards? As a denizen of the third level, she had more freedoms than the rest of us, but she'd come charging into the interrogation room . . . to save me? "How did you know I was in there?"

"I heard warriors talking about how hard Altan was working to get information out of you. They were coming from the first level."

That seemed *really* lucky, but before I could question it, she turned her glare on me.

"You really won't leave without your friends?"

"I had a chance to escape while I was on Bopha," I said. "But I returned to the Pit for you."

Her frown softened. "All right. We'll get them."

"Take me to the Hall of Drakon Warriors first. We have to get something."

"What?" She slowed and checked down an intersecting hallway before we turned.

"Dragon reins." The copper rods the guards had used earlier were meant to direct dragons, like reins for a horse. The sanctuary staff used them to guide hurt or sick dragons.

"Why do you need dragon reins?"

"Because there's a *Drakontos ignitus* in the first level, and if the guards you heard were coming from the first level, they were probably the ones who brought Kelsine. Did they have reins with them?"

"I think so."

"What about a dragon?"

"Definitely not."

"Then the dragon is still in there and we need something to control her with. They might have calm-whistles, too, but it's hard to say if warriors ever want their dragons to actually be calm."

Her eyes widened. "There's something wrong with you, Mira. Normal people don't decide they can save their friends from a dragon."

"Maybe there's something *right* with me." Surely she could understand that. "After all, you came to save me. Why?"

She motioned me around another corner, keeping our pace quick. "Because it's my job to look after you."

A sense of unease struck deep inside me. "What do you mean?"

"I'm not a prisoner, Mira. At least, not in the same sense as the rest of the inmates." She walked faster and faster. "I did what I did to save my life, and I truly do care what happens to you. But I'm not like the others."

"I don't understand. If you're not a prisoner—"

"Hush." She grabbed my good arm and pulled me behind a column just as I caught the sounds of footsteps on stone.

In tense silence, we waited for three warriors to go by, and I cursed all the light coming from the noorestones I'd refused to leave behind. They were heavy, and they shone a brilliant glow up the column, where I pressed the sack and tried to smother the light with my body.

Tirta, too, leaned toward me, and as the warriors

strode by, she held her breath.

But then they were gone, and we both sagged in relief.

"You should get rid of those."

I shook my head.

She cast a deep frown. "That's not a Daminan gift, you know. The way you used it earlier."

Of course I knew. It wasn't an *anything* gift. But if I thought about the implications too much, I'd never be able to move forward. Right now, I couldn't let myself be distracted.

"If you're not a prisoner," I said again, "what are you doing here? How is it your job to look out for me?"

"Let's keep moving." She waved me onward. "And as for your questions, I haven't been in the Pit as long as I told you. I actually got here when you did." She held up a hand to silence interruptions. "Many of the guards—yes, even Altan—knew about me, but they weren't permitted to unmask me. They had to go along with everything and act as though I were a prisoner, too. There's a reason we met in the mess hall, and then were paired in the bathing room so often. There's a reason I was chosen to help you prepare the day the Luminary Council came for you."

Apparently our entire friendship was a giant lie. "And that reason is what?"

"To observe you. To learn you." She shifted her posture, lifting her chin and setting her shoulders just so. Shades of familiarity struck me: for a second, she reminded me of my sister. "I admire you, Mira. What you did on the docks in the Shadowed City—that was brave. What you said at dinner—that was incredible."

"How do you know about those things?" I whispered.

"If anything goes wrong," she went on, as though I hadn't spoken, "I'm supposed to get you out of the Pit."

"What went wrong?" Besides a dragon in the cellblock. Besides Altan attacking me. Besides *everything*.

"I found out the Drakon Warriors aren't disbanded like we'd believed." She looked at me askance. "I found out what kind of questions Altan was asking you."

"So you're going to help me escape?" I didn't understand. Who did she work for? Why did they care?

"It's not as though Altan or the Drakon Warriors will just give you up at this point. If we want to move you, we have to do it the hard way. We probably should have killed Altan."

"Who is *we*?"

Tirta stopped walking. "Here it is."

We'd come to a huge door, easily twenty paces wide and three times as tall. Khulan's crossed maces filled the mahogany planks. The silver inlay was polished to a shine, gleaming in the light of seven large noorestones that surrounded the door. But it was the second part of the image that arrested me.

Gold. Familiar. The very thing my dreams were made of.

A pair of serpentine dragons wound around the maces, their talons hooked on handles. Flame rushed from their mouths, crossing just above Khulan's beloved weapons.

The Hall of the Drakon Warriors.

The doors were open just wide enough for a small dragon to pass through. Plenty of room for Tirta and me.

We slipped through and into an immense chamber filled with noorestones and banners and stained-glass panels that showed Drakon Warriors of old. They flew through blue skies. Fire burned enemies. The children of the gods were respected and revered.

"We need to find the armory." I tore my gaze from the dragon; there was no time for admiring—not with my friends' lives in danger. I didn't want to imagine what Kelsine might be doing in the cellblock, but I knew it wasn't good. We needed those reins.

"This way." Tirta moved like she knew exactly which path to take.

The proper key was easy enough to determine: it was the biggest, and the brass matched the lock. Breathless, I gave the key a sharp turn, and Tirta and I stepped inside.

The room was much bigger than I'd expected, with seventeen noorestones illuminating the wood-paneled space. There were ceiling-high cabinets (twenty) and stands of weapons (one hundred). They held mostly maces, batons, and bows, but twenty racks held what might have been swords or long daggers; I couldn't tell the difference. All of them looked terrifyingly sharp, with a glittering edge that might have been cut from diamonds.

The cabinets held knives, knuckles, and items I had no hope of identifying, like wires strung between two brass handles, and something that almost looked like shears but had serrated blades and hooks on both ends. I couldn't tell exactly how one might use them to harm another person, but it was all terrifying and deadly to me.

Finally, I found the dragon reins, seized a pair for myself, and continued searching for calm-whistles, like the one Ilina always carried in the sanctuary. None. If there were calm-whistles in the Pit, the Drakon Warriors must have kept them on their persons. Still, I hesitated before leaving. There were fire-resistant jackets and burn kits. The last cabinet held leather backpacks.

"What are you doing?" Tirta checked the hall, bouncing nervously. "We have to go."

"Let's put the noorestones in here." My sore shoulder groaned in relief as I lowered the reins and my makeshift bag to the floor, and then took one of the packs from the cabinet. A small pouch on the front already held a small field medical kit. That was useful. I took two more all-purpose medical kits, two burn kits, and three jackets. "They might be hurt. We need to be prepared to treat wounds."

We worked quickly, wrapping crystals with the dress strip, two empty backpacks, and two of the jackets. There wasn't enough space for the third jacket, so I slipped it on over my tattered dress.

"Anything else?" she asked. "The longer we take, the more likely it is that Altan will wake up or someone will find him."

"Knives." I added seven—one for each of us—to the bag and pulled the drawstrings tight. The light of the stones squeezed through the seams and the cinched top, but this would do for now.

"Ready?" Tirta asked, sliding the dragon reins into her belt.

"Yes." I slung one bow and quiver over my good arm; Ilina had taken lessons when she was younger. Then I fitted two swords—one for Hristo and one for Gerel—into loops on the backpack. My hurt shoulder felt like it was on fire as I slipped on the backpack, and a low moan poured from my throat.

"Let me carry that." Tirta reached for the bag, but I backed away. I couldn't trust her. Not when she'd lied to me about who she was. She'd lied for months and knew things she shouldn't and . . .

"Who do you work for?"

Her expression darkened. "I don't want to talk about it. I want to help you—"

"Then tell me who you work for."

Her shoulders slumped in resignation. "The same people who sent you here. The Luminary Council."

CHAPTER THIRTY-THREE

PANIC FLOODED MY VEINS. I WANTED TO RUN. *NEEDED* to run.

But I was loaded down with the backpack and weapons, and Tirta was blocking the door. She stepped toward me, one hand outstretched. "Let me explain—"

"I don't want to hear it." The noorestones in my pack were impossible to reach, especially with my hurt shoulder, but I took one from a sconce on the wall and gripped it so tightly my knuckles paled. "You lied to me about who you were. About how long you've been here. You said you were here to look out for me, but all along you worked for *them*."

Her face hardened, and the sweet, friendly girl I'd known disappeared once more. "Don't do this, Mira."

I should have taken a weapon. A real one. Knives were fairly self-explanatory. And even though I'd done *something* with a noorestone in the interrogation room, I wasn't sure what. Or how. Or if I could again.

And I couldn't trade the noorestone for a knife now, or Tirta would realize I wasn't in control of this . . . power.

"I'm on your side, Mira." In spite of her insistence, her fingers curled on the baton she'd taken from Altan. "If you just listen to me, you'll understand that I'm trying to help. But we need to move quickly or the Luminary Guard will realize something's wrong. I've missed my check-in already."

"They're *here*?" My heart pounded as I shoved past her, but the hall was empty when I looked.

Tirta grabbed my arm. "Mira—"

Every single noorestone in the room dimmed.

Immediately, she backed off, retreating farther into the armory.

My face must have revealed my shock, but before Tirta could act, I stepped into the hall and pulled the door after me.

The keys were still in the lock, jangling as the latch clicked into place. A *thud* sounded on the other side of the door as Tirta rushed forward and grabbed the handle, but I twisted the key and the bolt slid home.

"Mira!" She banged on the door. "Let me out!"

"I'm sorry." I drew the keys from the lock and stowed the ring on the hilt of a sword. "I don't trust you anymore."

Just as I aimed myself toward the first level again, I realized my error: I hadn't taken the dragon reins. They were secured in Tirta's belt, where she'd put them right before admitting her association with the Luminary Council.

Indecision stalled me. I'd taken the long way to the first level solely to retrieve the reins. But if I went back for them, Tirta would be waiting on the other side of the door. And she had a room full of weapons.

Well, I had a room full of noorestones.

But I had no idea how to harness their power.

A low rumble filled my ears. Footfalls? Tirta? Luminary Guards? More angry baby dragons? It was impossible to tell, but that made the decision for me: I ran.

Although I'd secured everything as well as possible, the extra weight slowed me, made my heart thrum heavily and my breath scrape inside my chest. It *hurt*, but I forced myself onward, careening around corners and down a flight of stairs.

I was not built for running, even when I wasn't loaded down with noorestones and weapons.

But I kept going. Even when cramps gripped my sides, and when fire throbbed through my shoulder. Even when sweat poured down my body and soaked my skin, and when my breath came in short, shuddering gasps. Even when black spots swarmed around the edges of my vision—and then everything faded into faint shadows. I knew where to go. My work cleaning had burned into my mind the number of steps to and from different places, and I used that as a map.

At last, I found myself in the anteroom. Struggling to catch my breath, urging my sight to return to normal, I found the thin blankets always stored here, took six, and slipped them through the straps of my backpack. They dangled around my legs, but I'd take anything that looked useful now. I had no idea what we might face outside the prison.

If we got out.

Still wishing I'd taken the reins from Tirta, wishing warriors kept calm-whistles, I hauled open the cellblock door. It was time to face the dragon.

Heat gusted outward. I staggered back, but I forced myself to move deeper into the hall.

It was dim, as always, but eerily quiet considering there were nine prisoners and a dragon inside.

I lifted my noorestone to my side, to keep the shine out of my eyes, and that was when I saw her. Kelsine slinked out of one of the cells, no longer terrified and cowed by the Drakon Warriors, but with a confidence that revealed her understanding of her dominance. She might be a young dragon, but she was still a *dragon* in a cellblock full of delicate, flammable humans.

A small gasp escaped me, drawing her attention.

At once, Kelsine lunged down the hall, her brown scales shimmering in the faint light.

"Wait!" I shouted, as if she could understand me. As if she had any reason to trust me.

"Mira?" That was Ilina's voice.

Talons scraped the stone floor as Kelsine charged me, and deep, red flames dragged around her teeth. She was too young to ignite the air, and her fire was nearly extinguished now—probably from using so much—but that didn't change the danger I was in. She had teeth. And talons.

A cacophony of voices rose up, all screaming at me, at the dragon, at the bars on their cells.

I clutched my noorestone in one hand, wishing to all the Fallen Gods I'd managed to get the dragon reins. Or a calm-whistle. Anything that would help. Anything but this pathetic jacket that might be fire resistant but certainly wasn't crush proof.

I had two options:

1. *Duck into one of the cells on either side of me.*

2. *Retreat into the anteroom.*

They were both terrible solutions.

And then there was Kelsine herself. Though charging at me, she was exhausted, and the dying fire proved it. She was all fear and adrenaline, a dangerous combination for me *and* for her. This poor creature. Her parents taken.

Trapped in a strange hall. Humans screaming at her.

"Oh, Kelsine," I whispered. My heart broke. I could imagine the anguish of family ripped away, the terror of being surrounded by strangers, the wild need to *survive* against all odds—because I'd been there. I was still there.

At two dragon-lengths away, Kelsine stopped and lifted her eyes to mine.

My heart thrummed as her entire posture shifted from aggressive to . . . submissive? That couldn't be right. But her wings folded, her back lowered, and her face turned downward to the floor. A huge sigh rolled out of her.

"What happened?" Varissa's question hissed across the cellblock, and I quickly looked for Kelsine's response, but the dragon appeared sedated.

"Don't say anything," I warned them, doing my best to keep my voice level. Tone neutral. Kelsine made herself smaller.

I needed to move. To free my friends. This was our chance to get out of here, but the longer I took, the more likely it was that Altan awakened and came for us. And I couldn't imagine a world where Tirta didn't search this very cellblock when she escaped the armory.

So I took one step forward. Two. Three. The numbers steadied my thoughts as I strode toward the dragon, knelt, and caressed the ridge of hot scales over her eye. Her third lid slid into place, but she didn't back away. She didn't break her gaze.

"I know you're scared," I whispered. "So am I."

A deep shudder tore through her, but she was listening.

"I won't let them hurt you again, sweet dragon."

She blinked slowly as I stood up, then moved around her—toward Ilina's cell. Over the incredible pounding of my heart, I heard only a small scrape of talons on stone as she turned to watch.

I breathed. In long. Out long. Just like Doctor Chilikoba had taught me. I made every breath last five steps, and little by little, the worst of the anxiety cleared.

Finally, I reached Ilina.

"How did you do that?" she asked.

"She's a baby. I calmed her." I passed her the bow and quiver, then twisted so she could remove Altan's key ring from the sword hilt where I'd stowed it. "Fourth from the maces, I think." At least, that was the key for my cell. "If that's not it, we'll have to find a way to pick the locks."

"How encouraging," she said, but she was still searching me like she couldn't believe what I'd done.

While Ilina dealt with the keys, I went to Hristo's cell and passed him a sword. He nodded in thanks. Then I went to Gerel's.

"I'm trusting you," I said. "However unwise that may be, I'm trusting you, and I'm getting you out of here, too. Don't betray me."

"I have never lied to you." She narrowed her eyes. "Give me the sword."

"What about the dragon?" Ilina was just stepping out of her cell and moving toward Hristo's.

"The real question," said Altan, striding in from the anteroom with fourteen warriors at his back, "is what did you *do* to the dragon?"

In between us, Kelsine was slinking toward me, her wings still tucked against her sides. She was exhausted, and in no shape to defend herself, let alone fight on our behalf.

From the opposite end of the hall, another voice sounded.

"Mira Minkoba!" Tirta wore a hard scowl. In spite of her earlier claims of friendship, seven Luminary Guards flanked her.

My heart sank into the floor and through the depths of the island of Khulan. We were trapped on both sides. Twenty-three of them against six of us. And unless Aaru and Chenda were going to surprise me in the next few minutes, only two of us were trained for combat.

"With the authority granted to me," Tirta went on, "by the Luminary Council of Darina and Damyan, I place you under arrest."

"I'm already in *prison*," I muttered.

Gerel snorted and drew her sword. "Make your friend let me out of my cage next."

"Obviously." I swung my backpack off, blankets flying everywhere, and dug for one of the knives. Noorestones scraped my skin, but it wasn't a long search. I passed the knife through the bars as the sound of twenty-three pairs of boots grew louder. Closer.

"Why do you have all those noorestones?" Gerel asked.

I passed knives to Hristo, who'd just been freed from his cell, and then Chenda and Ilina.

"Stay in the middle," Hristo said. "I won't let anything happen to you. I swear it." He drew both his knife and sword, and positioned himself facing Tirta.

I believed him. Of course I did. But just in case, I made sure to get an extra knife for myself.

Ilina went to work on Gerel's door, and I found myself in front of Aaru's cell.

He was standing at the front already, watching me with those dark eyes. Wordlessly, I slipped a knife through the bars, and when he took the weapon, fingers brushing mine, it felt like my heart was scattering apart.

Metal screamed as Gerel exploded from her cell, and both she and Hristo clashed blades with our jailers.

And then the earth shook.

CHAPTER THIRTY-FOUR

THE FLOOR JERKED BENEATH OUR FEET.

Someone down the hall screamed in pain. Others cried out in alarm. Kelsine roared. I crashed against the bars of Aaru's cell, clutching the iron to stay upright. My noorestone skittered across the floor and the backpack spilled open. Blue light flared, creating eerie, jumping shadows across the walls and cells.

The whole earth seemed to roar below us, around us, and above us. Dust and debris rained from the ceiling, making the hall dim and difficult to see through. My breath scraped and my tongue went dry. Every sound muted except that of the earthquake, which remained a thunder and roar and overpowering vibration in my chest.

Tirta's voice pierced the din: "Arrest Mira!"

Altan, for his part, seemed to want me dead, though Gerel and the shifting ground made that difficult. I knew too much about him—about the Drakon Warriors—and he couldn't let me leave this place. Every instinct in me screamed to flee—to fly through the hall and up the stairs and fight my way to open air. This was the sound of Khulan raising his mace to punish us.

My fingers scraped against the dark iron of Aaru's cell as the ground swirled and buckled. I'd never had to fight so hard to stay upright, but the earth had never turned against me like this before. Was everyone in the world feeling this? Or was it limited to the cellblock? I'd already proven I could do something impossible with noorestones, and Aaru could plunge a whole room into darkness and silence. But this wasn't me. And it didn't look like Aaru's doing.

"Aaru!" I had to shout to be heard, but even so, his name shuddered from me in five pieces.

His knife had fallen, lost somewhere in the rubble. Alarm and fear warred on his face, and his hands were tight around the bars, barely touching mine. Though his mouth moved, no sound emerged.

"We'll be fine," I lied. "We're going to get out of this."

It seemed more likely we'd get buried alive. Or buried dead, if Altan had his way. How long could this earthquake continue? How much shaking and shuddering could the Heart of the Great Warrior take? It was two thousand years old. Surely it had been under this kind of stress before.

Aaru shook his head, acknowledging my lie without judgment.

"We have an advantage." My words came in short gasps and awkward clumps as the ground jerked. I couldn't find Altan in the chaos, but his voice soared over the cacophony, all volume and no clarity. "The hallway is narrow," I yelled to Aaru. Narrow enough to bottleneck the armies on both sides, preventing Hristo or Gerel from fighting more than two people at a time. It was still a lot, though, especially with the earthquake. How long could they keep it up? Especially against strong, well-fed opponents?

At last, Ilina staggered toward us, key in hand. I backed away as she fumbled for the lock; the key scraped around the hole as the ground rumbled beneath us.

Then, the bars slid open and Aaru was free.

The earthquake ended, leaving a sharp emptiness in the hall. A distant stillness.

The patter of dislodged stones, the clash of metal on metal, the sobbing of prisoners, the whine of a young dragon: it all seemed unnaturally loud. Hristo and Gerel still fought, grunting and heaving against the warriors and Luminary Guards. Chenda stood in the center of our group, knife in hand and looking unsure what to do, and wary of Kelsine, who'd retreated from Altan and his friends.

Ilina had the key ring, but now we were all free; her job was over.

We needed a plan beyond surviving this attack. We needed to get out of here.

"Come on." I motioned for Ilina and Aaru to move toward Chenda.

Aaru bent to retrieve his fallen knife, flinching when his knuckles brushed against a noorestone. I bit my lip against a tiny sob. Why did this mysterious power of mine have to be something so hurtful to him?

This was no time to feel sorry for myself.

"We don't have many options," I said when the four of us—plus dragon—were grouped up, squarely between Hristo and Gerel. Both were getting tired. We had to hurry. "There are three exits. One leads into the woods just outside the city. One leads into Warrior's Circle. And I'm not sure where the last one leads, but probably somewhere mostly uninhabited because they'd have needed to move dragons through there."

Ilina's eyebrows rose sharply. "Are there more dragons?"

"I don't know." Without thinking, I lowered my hand for Kelsine, who fitted the top of her head against my palm. Everyone stared, but I had no idea how to explain.

"Exits, you said?" Chenda glanced over her shoulder where Hristo was struggling against two Luminary Guards.

"Yes." I cleared my throat. "I'll give each of you directions to an exit, in case we get separated or one of you needs to lead. Gerel knows the Heart. That leaves Hristo to watch out for."

"He won't get left behind," Ilina said.

"I know." I organized the exits in my head, but the

clack and clash of metal was distracting; my brain wanted to count people and weapons and times people hit one another. I had to focus. "The exit into Warrior's Circle is probably the most dangerous. It should be the last resort."

Aaru gestured and, when he had my attention, tapped his fingers against the back of his hand. ::Me.::

I nodded. "Agreed. You get the Warrior's Circle exit."

Ilina opened her mouth—probably to ask about that exchange—but she closed it. "I'll take the dragon exit."

That left Chenda with the forest exit. Quickly, I gave them instructions—the number of hallways and turns—and made them repeat them back to me three times.

"We'll go at the first chance we get. We don't leave anyone behind."

"What about your other friend?" Ilina asked. "Tirta?"

My heart sank at the reminder, and my gaze drifted down the hall where she watched the fighting—and us—with her arms crossed over her chest. "She's with the Luminary Council. She was never my friend."

"Oh." Ilina eyed Aaru and Chenda suspiciously. "Are you sure these two aren't going to betray you, too?"

Chenda shot Ilina an annoyed look. "I am not someone who betrays."

Aaru didn't say anything.

"I trust them," I said. "And Gerel, too. They're taking just as much of a risk trusting us."

Ilina didn't even try to hide her skepticism.

"We should release the other prisoners," Chenda said.

"Their freedom if they'll fight for us. We need the numbers."

"You're right."

"Well, I'm not letting them out." Ilina grabbed the bow and adjusted the string. She drew a ragged breath and—after only a moment's hesitation—nocked and took aim. The arrow flew and connected with a Luminary Guard's thigh. He staggered back—away from Hristo.

It was horrible, this lining people up to kill them. And Gerel—Hristo, too—*would* kill her enemies. But it was us or them, and I would do anything to save my friends.

Even this.

::**I will free the others,**:: Aaru tapped.

On Altan's key ring, I found the cell key and handed the whole ring to him. "Let them out as we make headway."

He bowed his head and—knife in his left hand—strode to the cell next to his, just behind Hristo. My protector didn't even glance over his shoulder, just kicked up and caught his opponent in the chest. The Luminary Guard went stumbling backward, making room for Hristo to push forward.

Aaru released Kason, who lunged from his cell and into the fray.

I knelt to retrieve our supplies. The earthquake had shaken so many things loose—the blankets, the medical kits, jackets. Noorestones littered the ground like little jewels of light. I glanced up at Chenda. "Help with this."

Together, we shoved all the supplies into a backpack. When it was full, we put the noorestones into a second pack. "I didn't realize you liked noorestones so much," she said. "Can the dragon help?"

I glanced at Kelsine. Tension laced her posture as she pressed against my hip, but I couldn't tell if it was protective or wanting to be protected. "Maybe. She can't breathe fire again until she rests, but she still has talons."

Golden eyes met mine, and then she turned toward Hristo and the Luminary Guards with her teeth bared. If they were scared of the dragon, they didn't show it, and I wished she'd joined Gerel against the warriors. They wouldn't dare hurt her—but maybe she wouldn't hurt them, either.

I scanned the hall for Aaru. He'd released Kason and Varissa so far, and with their help, five of the seven Luminary Guards were down. Tirta hovered in the doorway, looking uncertain. In spite of our progress, Hristo dripped with blood, some of it his own. It soaked through his clothes in dirty red patches, but surely some of it belonged to others. His sword, too, was wet and gleamed red.

"Aaru?" I called, taking a noorestone from a wall sconce and lifting it high.

His face was stern as he shook his head. Carefully, he began making his way back to the center. Hurrok and Kumas were still in their cells, but they were on the other side of the Luminary Guards—unreachable for now.

"It's all right." But oh, if we could have darkened the whole hall, smothered it with soundlessness, and forced our enemies into disorientation, I might have been able to lead my friends to freedom.

"Kason, Varissa"—I motioned at them—"help over here."

"Of course." Varissa smiled proudly as she switched sides. "Anything for my favorite daughter."

Kason said nothing, but his motions were swift and strong. He was eager to fight the warriors—his oppressors for so long.

Gerel had already killed five of Altan's fourteen warriors, and injured seven others. That didn't stop their attacks, but she fended them off with the grace of a dancer. The sword was lightning in her hand, and the knife in the other was thunder. She whipped the blades, blocking and thrusting and slashing; it was impossible to keep up.

She'd kicked back seven batons, out of reach of her opponents. Kason and Varissa took them.

Altan was in there somewhere, but through the dust and mass of moving bodies, I couldn't see him. Surely he wasn't fighting, though. Not with a gaping hole in his side. But Altan was a Khulani warrior, capable of so many things. He might really be able to battle through that kind of injury.

In spite of Gerel and Hristo's considerable abilities, and the reinforcement of angry prisoners, we were still outnumbered, trapped, and exhausted.

If only I'd understood my noorestone ability. We had so many. Even the cellblock noorestones, which I'd thought were old and dim before, were merely dusty. When I wiped one against my dress, brilliant light shone through.

"If you like noorestones so much," Chenda said, eyeing the bag at my feet, and the large crystal clutched in my fist, "I have an idea. Hold that up."

I frowned, but obeyed, shining white-blue light across the cellblock.

Chenda bowed her head and pressed her hands to her heart. The knifepoint rested just under her chin. "Blessed Bopha," she whispered. "Grant me your gifts in my hour of need. Cela, cela." Then, she sucked in a sharp breath and her shadow behind her *grew.*

"More light." Her words came raspy. Desperate.

Quickly, I grabbed a second stone from my bag and lifted that as well.

Chenda's shadow deepened and shifted, independently of its owner. That was a Bophan trick, yes, but what good did that do us?

The Dawn Lady leaned heavily onto the nearest wall. "More."

My hands were already full and my sore shoulder throbbed, but more light did come. Aaru took four noorestones from my bag and lifted them skyward, touching the two already in my hands.

On the wall, Chenda's shadow was as black as the space between stars as it peeled off the stone and became a wholly separate object. With great solemnity, Chenda offered it her knife. Armed, it lurched toward the warriors.

I yelped, almost dropping a noorestone, but Aaru

caught me. He pressed his fists around mine, holding me steady. A breath tickled my ear, like he'd tried to say something. Silence, though. Only silence from him.

A warrior screamed behind Chenda's shadow, and when it moved aside, all I could see was the blood pouring from the man's throat. The knife dripped with red.

My stomach turned over at the sight. A shadow assassin. But hadn't that been what I'd asked for? Help removing the people trying to arrest or kill us?

I couldn't take my eyes off Chenda's shadow as it slipped away from the body, seeking another victim. The warriors turned on it, swinging their batons at its throat and head, but nothing touched the shadow. It thrust out with the knife, killing a second and third man, and that was half of Altan's warriors, with six others clutching shattered knees and bleeding heads.

That was wrong. There'd been fourteen, plus Altan. "One is missing!" I called. "One is gone!"

Just then, Gerel gasped and staggered back. The knife fell from her hand, and her sword dipped. Altan slammed his baton against her head, and she went down.

"This effort is futile." Altan looked up at me as reinforcements of twenty warriors came into the hallway, along with the one who'd been missing moments before. No matter how many we fought our way through, they would always have more. "You should have taken my offer."

Chenda called for her shadow, which surged toward the newcomers with its bloody knife. Hristo rushed past me, sword drawn back to swing in a wide arc.

The bowstring *thwapped* and an arrow pierced a warrior's eye.

Kelsine roared and positioned herself in front of me.

Aaru pressed all six noorestones into my hands, and though my shoulder throbbed with the strain of holding my arms up for so long, I pressed my hands together to keep the stones from slipping.

::Wait,:: he tapped, and found the keys again. When I glanced over, the sole remaining Luminary Guard was pulling Tirta from the cellblock. The way was clear to release the last of the prisoners. First Kumas, who took up a weapon and joined the fight without hesitation.

Then Hurrok.

Just as the bars rang open, tattooed hands reached out. Hurrok grabbed Aaru's arm, twisted it sharply, and stole the keys and knife.

"Aaru!"

His mouth dropped open and tendons stood out on his neck, but no sound emerged. His knees hit the ground as he grasped at his shoulder.

The screaming man stepped from his cell, over Aaru's crumpled form, and looked straight at me. "I've waited a year for this moment."

And killing me was more important than getting out of here?

Before I could say anything, Altan hurled his baton at Chenda. She collapsed to the floor in a heap of dirty copper silk. Her shadow vanished back into her, normal once more.

My heart raced at the chaos, at the flood of warriors, at the assassin come to end my life once again. We were going to lose. No matter how hard we fought, there was no way we could win. Our warrior was down. Ilina's quiver was empty. The shadow assassin was gone. Even my silent neighbor was hurt, trying in vain to put his shoulder back into place.

Kelsine roared and threw herself at one of the warriors, but he shoved her into a cell and threw the bars closed, trapping her.

Panic pinned me into place, rooting my feet to the ground. I couldn't lower the noorestones without dropping them—the pain in my own shoulder wouldn't allow that kind of movement. I couldn't fight. I couldn't help. I couldn't *breathe*. I couldn't *see*. Everything was fading, flickering, except this giant truth that boiled up from a chasm in my chest.

We were going to lose.

Still, Hurrok strode toward me.

Hristo had fought his way through to Altan, slamming him against the bars of a cell. Blood trickled from Altan's temple, but it was too late. One of the new warriors drew a sword, forcing Hristo to back away or be cut to ribbons.

There was no way.

Gerel and Chenda were unconscious. Ilina was weaponless. Hristo was fighting for his life. Kelsine was trapped. Aaru had pulled himself up and was running, but he would be too late.

There was only me, with Hurrok right there, with Altan raising his baton at me, and with twenty-six warriors thundering through the cellblock.

I hated my panic. I hated the way it captured my body and stole my thoughts. I was going to die because I couldn't make myself move.

But the thunder wasn't just coming from warriors. Slowly, I became aware of the ground shifting again.

Swirling.

An aftershock.

Not as violent as before, but it threw everyone off-balance.

Altan fell away.

The screaming man stumbled back.

I jerked free of panic's paralysis as the aftershock ended.

That's when I felt it: power pulsing into me, making my skin buzz with energy. The noorestones dimmed in my hands, and ripples of fire danced between the crystals.

A foreign-feeling smile pulled at me.

Hurrok swore and abruptly abandoned his quest to kill me. He turned and ran, knocking into Aaru on his way out of the cellblock. The keys clattered to the floor.

Altan dived for me, as though to pry the stones from my fists, but then *all* the noorestones in the hall dimmed, and the only light in the hall came from me. Altan moved back, eyes round. "What *are* you?"

Fire poured through my body, all heat and power bursting to escape. I adjusted my footing, hyperaware of warriors staring at me, my friends watching, and the earth beginning to tremble once more.

"Ilina." My voice sounded hollow as the whole cell-block went dark, save the nimbus of flame flickering over my skin. I was burning with the power of thirty-four noorestones, and it was too much. Too overwhelming. My chest pinched, making breath squeeze from my lungs in tiny gasps, until I felt as though I were collapsing, condensing into a singular point. And soon I would explode. "Get everyone out of here."

There was a scuffle. A cacophony of voices. The clatter of iron. And screeching.

I held on for five seconds.

Someone shouted that they would not leave me, but I couldn't tell who. The rumble and rush in my ears was overwhelming.

Ten seconds.

I was going to die like this. I was certain of it.

Twenty seconds.

If everyone didn't evacuate, they'd die, too.

Thirty.

Forty.

Forty-one.

Forty-two.

Please, Darina, I prayed. *Please, Damyan.*

Forty-three.

I had to hold on.

Forty-four.

Forty-five.

I held on as long as I could, but my vision blackened into the deepest night, and my ears became deaf to all but the roaring demand for release.

And then I burst into a thousand stars.

CHAPTER THIRTY-FIVE

IT WAS EXHILARATING, REALLY.

Exploding.

Being shred asunder.

Burning like a hundred thousand galaxies.

Fire rippled over my skin. When I screamed, strange muscles stretched and flexed until I reached every end of this prison, and finally I tore myself free.

Of the tight stone walls.

Of aching hunger.

Of desperate uncertainty.

I was bigger than all that now. Stronger. Brighter. I was *awake.*

My roar could shatter mountains, and my wings could black out the sun. Once I'd been a girl, but now I was more. The sparks ignited. Ashes swarmed around me. And this was only the beginning.

Fire blazed from my heart, rushing across my skin and pulling my eyes wide until I could see through the shuddering earth, up to the sky, and into the cores of the stars themselves. They were so very hot, and bright, and lonely. I wanted to pluck them out of the sky and wear them as jewels around my throat, but then I was larger and hotter, expanding into the farthest stretches of the night. A thousand trails of radiance burned in my wake, spanning centuries.

Nothing could contain me as I soared through the blackness between worlds and breathed in the devastating glory of darkdust.

I was immense. Immeasurable. Infinite.

I bridged the spaces between stars with my fingertips. I crossed galaxies within breaths. Aeons poured through me like thoughts, and my inferno heart beat with the tempo of the end of the world.

If this was what it felt like to die, it was almost a mercy.

BUT THEN.

My heart beat a new rhythm.

One. Two.

One— Two—

One. Two— Three.

One. Two—

M-I-R-A.

Mira.

Mira Minkoba.

AGAIN, I COLLAPSED.

I plummeted through the stars, falling to a world that glowed with crystalline light, with islands shaped like gods, and an ever-encroaching mainland. The waves reached up to greet me.

My fall left streaks of embers and ash drifting in the dark sky, and slowly I became aware: my wings were gone, my brilliant light had faded, and my sense of rapture evaporated.

I was a girl again.

Shivering.

In the dark.

In the soundless void.

Alone.

NOT ALONE.

CHAPTER THIRTY-SIX

I OPENED MY EYES TO PURE DARKNESS.

It was familiar now, this complete blackness. I knew it well enough to brace for the panic—

But the panic didn't come. It was all burned up.

Rubble bit into my knees where I knelt on the hard floor. When I groaned, there was no sound, not even a rumble inside my head. But air stirred, and my skin itched, and I knew I was alive.

I tried not to be disappointed.

::Mira.::

The tapping came on my shoulder.

"Aaru?" But the darkness swallowed up my voice. I lifted my hands until my knuckles brushed against tattered fabric, and then I found his shoulders. I let my fingers curl over his skin, feeling the ridges of bone. ::Aaru?::

::You're alive.::

I nodded—pointless, because he couldn't see it. But his hand cupped my cheek and everything inside me seized.

::Are you all right?:: he asked.

I felt tiny. Frail. My whole body trembled and a sense of loss folded around me like a silk cloak. But I was whole. The dark and silence were probably Aaru's doing; it would come back, and then I could take better stock of my injuries. ::Yes,:: I said. ::And you?::

::Unharmed.:: His fingertips breezed over my ear and down my jaw. How could such a simple touch make everything inside me feel so complicated?

::Where are the others?:: I asked.

::They ran. Your friend took them. The dragon, too.::

::But not you? ::

::I could not go. I fell at your feet and pretended to be dead.::

::Did they all escape?::

::I don't know.::

The spell of silence eased, and gradually, I became aware of the sound of my breath, the patter of rocks somewhere nearby, and the deep thrum of the world. A gentle glow rose up like mist.

Ruins.

The cellblock was in ruins. Noorestone dust floated through the air, lighting rubble and hollows and complete destruction. There was a small crater around Aaru and me, filled with black ash.

I'd done this.

I couldn't say how—I suddenly didn't remember anything after yelling for my friends to escape—but I knew I'd done this. A fact. Like numbers. Like objects falling. Like daylight fading.

Aaru watched me taking stock of the place that used to be our prison.

I dropped back and sat on my feet. "Why did you stay?"

He took my hand in his, both of us with a faint sheen of powdered noorestone making our bodies glow, and tapped his words into my palm. ::**You stayed with me after the chair.**::

"But it was my fault you were there to begin with."

His mouth pulled in a slight frown. ::**You came back for me when you could have escaped from Bopha.**::

"You risked your life." I swept my free hand around the room, stirring the motes of light. "How are you still alive?"

::**Silence.**:: He lowered his eyes to our joined hands. ::**You were covered in flame, like a creature made of raging wildfires and noorestone light.**::

"So you silenced everything?"

He bowed his head. ::**Like before.**::

All the noorestones in here. All thirty-four of them that had been flooding their energy into me. He'd smothered *all* of them? I couldn't imagine what kind of courage it took to stay here and help me.

::**You control noorestones.**::

A strangled laugh fell out of me. "I don't know what I do. I feel like it happens to me."

::**Practice might help.**:: He pressed his mouth into a line. ::**I need to practice too.**::

"I've never heard of anyone channeling noorestone fire." I lowered my eyes. "I don't know what it means, and I'm afraid of what will happen when people find out."

::**I will keep your secret.**::

As if he could tell anyone. He hadn't said a word in nineteen days. Maybe twenty; I wasn't sure how much time had passed since Altan dragged me into the interrogation room. Aaru hadn't spoken, though, and that was my fault. Like all this destruction, his silence was because of me. He couldn't tell anyone. Not unless he wrote it down, or someone else learned the quiet code, and—

Aaru bit his lower lip, not quite disguising a smile.

"Did you just make a joke?"

He lifted a shoulder, still with that smile. ::**Really, I will not tell a soul if you do not want.**::

"Thank you, Aaru."

His smile faded. A shame, because he had a nice smile. ::**Can you stand?**::

My legs trembled, but I got to my feet, again taking in the destruction of the first level. The noorestones themselves were all gone—there was only the dust floating through the air. It probably wasn't safe to breathe. "Let's go. I need to make sure the others escaped before I . . ."

Exploded. Or didn't explode, if Aaru had stopped it.

"Thank you," I said. "For staying with me. For helping."

He touched my shoulder—the one Altan had bashed earlier. It didn't hurt anymore, though, like the pain had been burned away in the noorestone blaze. ::**I didn't know if I could. I knew only that I had to try.**::

I wanted to ask why—was it for the sake of everyone, or for me?—but I couldn't make the words come. Not when I wanted him to say he'd stayed behind because he wouldn't leave *me*. I knew better than that.

But there was a moment. Two moments. He looked at me like he was waiting for something, too.

Maybe he was waiting for me.

I closed the space between us so we were toe-to-toe, and when he took my hand and pressed my palm to his chest, I counted racing heartbeats.

Cautiously, as though he wasn't sure whether he should, he brushed my hair off my forehead. Then nothing. Utter stillness. His fingertips lingered on my temple, and I looked up to read the confusion and concern on his face.

On Idris, being this close, our hands on faces and chests—it was too intimate for the unmarried. And on Damina, no one would think twice about two people—especially people who'd been through what we had—finding comfort in physical contact.

So we stood there as the noorestone dust began to settle, indecision holding us in place. Wanting. Hoping. Too afraid to move because what would the other think?

A glance shattered everything. Aaru's gaze darted to my cheek, and his expression turned thoughtful.

Because it had healed? My shoulder had, so why not my face?

Hope building in my chest, I pressed trembling fingers against my cheek.

The cut was healed, but the evidence was not gone.

In its place was a scar the length of four fingertips, slightly puckered in the center. It felt old, but Elbena had cut me only a decan ago.

Of course Aaru had noticed it. It was huge. It was hideous. He'd seen me before, not when I was pretty, but before I'd been damaged, and he knew the difference between the real Mira and this cut-up echo. I ducked my face and turned away from him.

::Mira?:: he tapped on my shoulder. ::Are—::

"Let's go." My voice broke only a little, but the knot of anxiety gathered in my chest again, a dim background pain I'd long ago learned to ignore.

Without another word, I led him from our cellblock.

To freedom.

THE HEART OF the Great Warrior was in terrible shape.

Once-high walls had crumbled. Fallen banners shrouded statues. Entire rooms had caved in. From the tremors? From me?

It was gone, though, and I had no idea how many warriors and servants had survived—if any had, or if I was responsible for innumerable deaths.

Aaru and I headed for the dragon exit. The giant doors hung open like a slack jaw, and inside we crossed a space that had once been resplendent, but was now a rubble-filled memory.

This far from the first level, a few noorestones had survived. I took a pair to light our way and hoped it would be enough. Aaru, for his part, did not touch the crystals. Didn't speak. Didn't tap. Seemed somewhat unwilling to look at me.

Of course. He couldn't unsee that scar.

We wandered the dragon area for a while, searching for the exit, before Aaru held up a hand for me to listen.

"No one's in there." That was Ilina's voice, cracked from weeping. "They're both dead."

"I have to look anyway." Hristo. I'd know the timbre of his rumble anywhere. "I have to see her with my own eyes before I believe it."

"You saw her start to burn up. Looking now will just hurt more. *If* there's anything of her left. For Damina's sake, do you want to see her charred corpse?" Her voice choked with tears, but I knew she wouldn't cry now, even in front of Hristo. Ilina always tried to save her tears for when the two of us were alone.

"Then we'll take her back home where she belongs. She shouldn't be left here."

It was so good to hear their voices that I almost didn't move, but after one moment's hesitation, I glanced back at Aaru and said, "Come on!" Then I took off running. "Ilina! Hristo!"

Ten strides. Twenty. I careened around the corner and crashed into them, but Hristo caught me in his arms and squeezed. Ilina threw herself in with us so that we were all hugging each other so tightly I couldn't breathe. But I didn't care. My friends were here. And even if Ilina—understandably—assumed I was dead, she'd come with Hristo to find me. They would never abandon me, not even in death.

"You're alive!" Ilina pulled back. "What happened? The last time we saw you—"

"I don't know." I didn't want to talk about exploding, or the way the noorestones reacted to me, or anything relating to our escape. I just wanted to get out of here. "I don't know what happened or how I came out of it. When I woke up, the noorestones had all exploded into powder—"

"That explains why you're glowing," Ilina said.

"—and it was just Aaru and me."

He'd hung back, quietly observing the three of us, and when everyone looked at him, he just nodded in greeting.

"I thought you were dead." Ilina reached for him, as though to draw him into all this hugging, but he jerked back like she might burn him. "Sorry," she said. "I don't know you, I guess. I suppose not everyone celebrates survival the same way."

"He's fine, too," I said, even though he was far from

fine. "But what Gerel said before is true—he doesn't talk anymore."

"Oh." Ilina frowned. "I talk enough for all of us."

Hristo grunted and glanced at Aaru. "She means it."

Aaru dropped his gaze to his feet.

Face burning with shame, I turned to Hristo. "Did Gerel and Chenda get out, too? And Kelsine?"

He nodded. "Gerel and Chenda are securing supplies. Kelsine is waiting outside. I've seen half a dozen warriors roaming around here already. We need to get out before they really start searching. Gerel said she knows a place we'll be safe for a while."

"That's good." It was a relief to know they were alive. I couldn't imagine what I'd have done if any of them had died because of me. "What about Tirta? Or Altan and his people? The other prisoners?"

Hristo shook his head. "I don't know about Tirta. Altan is alive. We saw him get out, along with at least twenty warriors. The prisoners we released are safe, I think, but I'm not sure. The others—no. I don't think anyone evacuated the other levels. Even if they'd wanted to, there wasn't time. We barely escaped before the blast wave hit."

The blast wave.

What had I *done*?

I glanced at Aaru, but he avoided my eyes.

What wouldn't he tell me?

A lot, apparently. I bent to pick up the noorestones I'd

dropped earlier. "Lead the way, Ilina. There's a lot we need to discuss when we get to Gerel's safe place."

True to the warnings, we had to duck out of sight three times because of warriors, but it wasn't long before we reached a huge, caved-in door where the dragons must have been let in and out before the Mira Treaty went into effect. And after, apparently. It was hard to believe that the Drakon Warriors had so brazenly defied the treaty.

Or maybe it wasn't. Altan had none of the qualities I'd always assigned the famed warriors in my mind.

Now, shattered noorestones glowed coolly in the rubble, bright reminders of what I'd done. Or the earthquake. I couldn't be sure that this was *all* my doing.

"How do we get out?" I looked around for a secondary door.

"Up there." Hristo pointed to a small space in the top where sunlight shone in, warm and gold, like honey. I couldn't wait to touch it.

It took some effort, but eventually the four of us climbed up the shifting stones and squeezed through the hole.

We emerged into a sun-drenched field, fragrant with wildflowers and honeysuckle. Green grass spread before us, with nothing to indicate a Pit entrance except the remnants of an immense door cut into the side of a mountain.

I knelt and ran my fingers through the blades of grass. Never had I been so relieved to see something so simple. We were out. Free.

A sharp, familiar cry sounded from above. And then another.

My heart jumped as I looked up to find two winged shapes diving toward us, one silver, and one gold. My arm lifted before my brain told it to, because my heart recognized her: LaLa. My little flower.

A golden streak landed with a thump. Talons dug into my hand as she balanced herself, but stopped short of breaking skin when she noticed I wasn't wearing a glove. "Hello, darling." I pulled her to my chest and laughed as she started to lick the noorestone dust from my skin.

Two steps away, Ilina was already holding Crystal, stroking the tiny dragon's head and spine.

"Have you been searching for us?" I murmured. "You must have looked everywhere."

LaLa head-bumped my chin and rubbed. The ridges of her scales scraped across my skin—not hard enough to hurt, but enough to feel like chastisement.

"I won't leave you again, little lizard." I kissed the top of her head and breathed in her scents of lightning and fire, of dust and sunlight.

Hristo watched us with a smile, but Aaru stood in the background wearing that same expression from before—when he'd noticed my scar. There was something curious about it, something a little scared as well. But when he caught my gaze, a flutter of surprise erased the fear, and then his face turned neutral.

He'd stayed with me through the noorestones, risking

his own life to save mine. So I trusted him. Of course I did. But he'd slipped just now. He was so used to being invisible, and maybe so exhausted, that he'd forgotten to guard his expression. Against me, it seemed.

I tilted my head so my hair fell across my cheek. "Do you want to meet LaLa?"

Aaru glanced at the dragon, nodded once, and took a cautious step forward.

"We should go first." Hristo spoke gently, but Aaru withdrew as though he'd been hit.

Hristo was right, though. We couldn't loiter; it was too close to the Pit. "How far to Gerel's safe spot?" I asked, shifting LaLa to my shoulder.

"She said the cabin is an hour's walk straight that way." Ilina pointed between two mountain peaks. "We'll have to go around the field. I don't want to get caught in the open when there are warriors around. Patrols are everywhere. Fortunately, they think you're dead."

And I'd let them think that. For now.

Because for fifty-two days, my goal had been simply to leave the Pit, but that wasn't enough anymore. It wasn't enough to escape for myself, or even for my friends. There was too much suffering in the world, and I could no longer ignore it.

I had knowledge. I had power. I had a voice.

And it was my duty to use them all.

ACKNOWLEDGMENTS

I HONESTLY THOUGHT this book would be easier to write. I don't know why. Needless to say, it was not easy, and I found myself leaning on my support group more than ever.

A good agent is like a lovable dragon, and Lauren MacLeod is no exception. Part fire-breather, part epic defender, part super adorable. I'd be a mess without you.

Speaking of dragons, the amazing Kelsey Horton edited this book. We survived a sudden deluge the day we first met. We survived this book (no simple task!). We can do anything.

And while losing an editor-dragon is a real blow, I was fortunate enough to have Maria Barbo swoop in and take on this book and the rest of the series.

Further gratitude to the entire team at Katherine

Tegen Books, including Bess Braswell, Sabrina Abballe, and Rosanne Romanello, for always being such champions of my books, to Joel Tippie for this beautiful cover, to production editor Emily Rader, and of course, to Katherine Tegen herself.

I definitely wouldn't have gotten far in writing this book without an incredible group of critique partners, sensitivity readers, brainstormers, and hug providers: Brodi Ashton, Martina Boone, Dhonielle Clayton, Valerie Cole, Cynthia Hand, Deborah Hawkins, Joy Hensley, Stacey Lee, Sarah Glenn Marsh, Myra McEntire, Christine Nguyen, Nicole Overton, Alexa Santiago, Stephanie Sinclair, Laurel Symonds, Angie Thomas, Sabaa Tahir, and Alana Whitman. You've all made this a better book.

A round of tall glasses of water to Emmy, Rachel, and Ely, who shared their experiences of dehydration with me. Drink up, friends.

Many thanks to Mary E. Pearson and C. J. Redwine: you are some of my favorite authors and I could not be more grateful for you saying such nice things about this book.

Thanks to my mom, who responded to texts like "Do you have time to talk about electrocution?" with enthusiasm to match mine. Clearly the apple doesn't fall far from the tree.

My sister. My best friend. My wingsister as well.

My husband, who puts up with an awful lot of talk about dragons. (It's cool, though. He likes dragons, too.)

God, whose love never fails.

And, as always, readers. From librarians to booksellers to reviewers to people who picked up this book because it has a pretty cover; from new readers to those who've followed all of my books; and especially my darlings in the OQ Support Group: without you, this book would be a collection of words moved from my head onto sheets of paper. But your imaginations bring it to life.